SOUTH OF

RESURRECTION

Also by Jonis Agee

PRETEND WE'VE NEVER MET

BEND THIS HEART

SWEET EYES

STRANGE ANGELS

SOUTH OF RESURRECTION

JONIS AGEE

Viking

age

VIKING
Published by the Penguin Group
Penguin Putnam Inc., 375 Hudson Street, New York, New York 10014, U.S.A.
Penguin Books Ltd, 27 Wrights Lane, London W8 5TZ, England
Penguin Books Australia Ltd, Ringwood, Victoria, Australia
Penguin Books Canada Ltd, 10 Alcorn Avenue, Toronto, Ontario, Canada M4V 3B2
Penguin Books (N.Z.) Ltd, 182–190 Wairau Road, Auckland 10, New Zealand

Penguin Books Ltd, Registered Offices:
Harmondsworth, Middlesex, England

First published in 1997 by Viking Penguin,
a member of Penguin Putnam Inc.

1   3   5   7   9   10   8   6   4   2

PUBLISHER'S NOTE
This is a work of fiction. Names, characters, places, and incidents either are the product of the author's imagination or are used fictitiously, and any resemblance to actual persons, living or dead, events, or locales is entirely coincidental.

The quotations at the beginning of chapters are from the following publications:
Gray Ghosts of the Confederacy by Richard S. Brownlee, Louisiana State University Press, 1958.
Missouri Wildflowers by Edgar Denison, Missouri Department of Conservation, 1989.
The Amphibians and Reptiles of Missouri by Tom R. Johnson, Missouri Department of Conservation, 1987.
The Common Rocks and Minerals of Missouri by W. D. Keller, University of Missouri Press, 1961.
Missouri by Paul C. Nagel, University of Kansas Press, 1977.
Ozark Magic and Folklore by Vance Randolph, Dover Publications, Inc., 1947.
Missouri Geology by A. G. Unklesbay and Jerry D. Vineyard, University of Missouri Press, 1992.

LIBRARY OF CONGRESS CATALOGING IN PUBLICATION DATA
Agee, Jonis.
South of resurrection / Jonis Agee.
p.   cm.
ISBN 0-670-85809-9
I. Title.
PS3551.G4S68   1997
813'.54—dc21   97-12896

This book is printed on acid-free paper.
∞

Printed in the United States of America
Set in Goudy Old Style
Designed by Pei Koay

For the children, Brenda, Laura, Blythe, Talbot, Tara, and Ashton.

For my friends, Betty, Sharon, Susan, Leslie, Jane, and Clare.

And always, for my sisters, Jackie and Cindy.

ACKNOWLEDGMENTS

I would like to thank Jane von Mehren, my editor, whose belief and tireless efforts have made it possible for me to arrive safely on the other side with this work. She is the best friend a writer could ever ask for.

Thanks to Ned Leavitt, my agent, who continues to believe in my writing after all these years.

A special thanks to Lon Otto, who is my finest critic and greatest supporter, with enough stamina to read each draft without complaining and still be my oldest friend.

Thanks to Jean Buscher and Kristin DeSmith, for their hard work on behalf of this work. Thanks to Greg Hewett, Tony Hainault, Chris Jones, Juanita Garciagodoy, George Rabasa, Rebecca Rand, Tom Binger, Gregory Page, Nicholas Delbanco, Charles Baxter, Tish O'Daud, and Andrea Beauchamp, for giving support and friendship.

Thanks to Thomas Dillon Redshaw for opening his house and his heart when I've most needed it.

And thanks to Joe Patrickus, who welcomes me every time I walk through the door of his shop, and who makes the most beautiful boots in the world at JP's Custom Boots in Camdenton, Missouri (where there is always plenty of sun, moon, and stars to go around).

CONTENTS

✳

Out of that stream there issued living sparks,
which settled on the flowers on all sides,
like rubies set in gold; and then, as if
intoxicated with the odors, they
again plunged into the amazing flood:
as one spark sank, another spark emerged.

— DANTE, PARADISO

SOUTH OF
RESURRECTION

1

IN THE SWEET BY AND BY

When one sees two snakes in a house at once, it means that there will be a wedding there before long. If two crows persistently circle over a cabin, it is a sign that a daughter of the house is about to marry. A girl who accidentally steps on a cat's tail will be married before the year is out. If a girl's skirt is always catching on briars, it is said that she will soon catch a husband.

—OZARK MAGIC AND FOLKLORE

IN A PERSON'S LIFE, there's always some place that possesses them, I figure, some place that owns a chunk of your soul, and a person cannot dispute it or escape it, not even in her sleep. It's the place where desire begins, the place longing brings you back to. For me, that was the little town of Resurrection, right on the edge of the foothills called the Ozark Mountains, smack dab in the middle of the state of Missouri. It was the sort of no-count, nowhere place even the Lake of the Ozarks, Bagnell Dam, and all sorts of Methodists could not revive to a bedraggled glory. It had never been upclined, so there was never an appreciable decline, despite the sign outside town announcing: RESURRECTION, GATEWAY TO THE OZARKS, POP. 1523. The "gateway" business was new, but the population was about the same. We were fond of saying that those Ozark hills just south of us were as tall as any Rocky Mountains, you just had to realize that most of them were underground. And so it was for Resurrection. It was as big a town as a person needed, once you'd been there long enough.

I'd driven twelve hours straight from Minneapolis to the middle of Missouri when I saw the red clay on the shoulders of the blacktop that told me I was home. And my heart did that little minnow jerk, and my hands got lighter on the wheel. Home. Not in twenty-three years. Took a Trailways out of here at sixteen and hadn't looked back but a few times a day since. That longing business. I rolled down my windows and let the hot baked asphalt and gravel smelling like nearly burnt toast push through the truck and lead me on through the intersection with Highway 11, which they'd widened to accommodate the traffic the new Wal-Mart, Hardee's, and strip mall were bringing in, and crossed the tracks into town.

The boards on the feed store and the old sawmill were blasted and warped gray, their roof shingles lifting like hands waving as I crawled by, ignoring the one or two impatient cars behind me. A vacant lot clogged with fresh spring weeds and wildflowers waited beside the line of two-story buildings whose peeling paint had faded to powdery pastels over their brick. The businesses seemed more meager than I remembered—thrift shops, tiny cafes, and bars on the verge of extinction where there used to be big, solid concerns. It was as if something terrible had happened in the center of town, and everyone was quietly retreating, but I knew we'd always been a little worse off than the rest of the world, so I figured it was just our response to the way things were being slicked up all around us.

Anyway, I didn't have any place else in the world to go, and what was left of my sister needed burying. I'd driven my few belongings, two hundred and fifty dollars in cash, and nearly new red Toyota 4-Runner the speed limit all the way, hoping to regulate my arrival and its effect. They were all gone, I reassured myself—my parents, Mister and Iberia; my sister, Paris; Grandmother Estes; Aunt Delphine; and a lot of the others too, I imagined. I'd hidden myself in a new name, a new life for over twenty years, and one day it'd dumped me out like old wash water. So be it, I'd said, and packed what little was left and come back to the only place I could ever really imagine and remember.

Fifteen- and twenty-year-old cars sprawled beside most of the houses on the little side streets, some with wheels braced on cement blocks, hood or trunk lids blown away, others ticking away in the late afternoon heat, kids crawling in and out of their torn seats, running toys along their sides as if they were large mechanical family pets. The first trailer I saw in between the shotgun cottages made me think it was only temporary housing until I noticed the neatly mowed grass growing right up to the pleated tin skirt around the base, and the honeysuckle bushes on either side of the cement porch nudging the green indoor-outdoor carpet as if they'd known each other for some time. Then there were more trailers replacing houses. Dreams hunkered down, refusing to be driven out. I wasn't so different, after all, I'd be lucky if my parents' little house was habitable. Nobody'd been in there in at least three years.

The four-story, Resurrection red brick DeWight County Courthouse, surrounded by a nice green skirt of grass wide enough to have the Methodist ice cream socials on, took up the whole square block in the center of town. I parked on the west side, outside the Royale Theater, so I could stay out of the way of traffic while I looked around. Although it was the supper hour, and the streets were mostly empty, cars and pickups were driving up and parking diagonally with their noses pointing at the courthouse. People jumped out and hurried past the only two statues the town owned. I had forgotten about those.

On the north side of the square stood a Union soldier paid for by Lumar Sell's family at the turn of the century, which for years had been the favorite resting place of a particularly quarrelsome group of sparrows, which fought the sparrows and starlings from the bank building across the way and the pigeons from the other statue—a Confederate soldier posted on the south side, paid for by the angry and exhausted citizens of Resurrection as soon as martial law was lifted and the occupying Union soldiers finally left, a good year after the War was over. High school seniors used to try to paint them garish colors on graduation night, but that looked like a lost tradition now. And it looked like nobody'd bothered with cleaning them in such a long time, they were pretty much alike now, white and gray streaks muddying what differences they used to have.

I remembered Grandmother Estes's old House of Fashion Dress Shop, and thought I'd go and see the models reaching out with that expression somewhere between a cry for help and the benediction Jesus used to offer to us kids in the basement of the Grace Memorial Methodist Church two streets over. But it was gone, and in its place stood the House of Pawn Shop, with the new letters blacked over the old white ones.

I was almost across the street when I saw him.

He should've been dead or long gone, but there he was: Dayrell Bell, dragging a moth-eaten green army blanket from the passenger side of an old black Dodge pickup and wrapping a shotgun in it before he laid it carefully on the floor of the cargo area behind the bench seat. He hadn't changed—same ratty clothes: thin, faded blue tee shirt with a hole under the right arm, shoulder blades poking out; torn-up Levi's and battered brown cowboy boots with the heels worn clear down to the scuffed leather on the outside. Looked like they might be the same boots as years ago, and the pure sadness of them made that pity thing stir around inside me like a mouse scratching through wallboard.

You'd think a person would get over most things that happen. I mean, not like nearly fatal bouts with cancer or losing a little one, but the other general wear and tear on a person's heart, the things that roughen your skin as they smooth your hopes and dreams until you're wind scalded on the outside and just about worn down to nothing but river tumbled rock inside. It's love I'm talking about. And Dayrell Bell was my first. The first person I ever said those words to, who ever said them to me, and that included my family. That ought to be worth something, I used to think, until the memory and I got tired of each other, so after a while Dayrell was only a twice-a-year kind of man, whose body and voice brought me crying awake in the dawn, and I had to reach over with my fingertips to press the warm shoulder of my then alive husband to bring me back into the rhythm of his sad little snore. Then Duncan, my husband, was gone too. My son moved away for years now. I couldn't think of a single thing to do but go home to Resurrection because that's what women in our town always did when life coughed them up again. It was where your name began, where you showed up to face the music, to show yourself as the world's sad example, because a woman, above all else, was supposed to keep things going, and if she couldn't—well, she better come on home until she learned better, or taught the youngsters that this kind of failure made you useless as a two-tailed cat in the rain.

Later I was to see that if I'd had any sense that afternoon, I'd of taken Duncan's gun off the seat of my truck and pointed its loaded barrel at one of us, settled it then and there. Instead I watched Dayrell Bell go to the tailgate, where two dogs tried to leap out of the back of that old black truck into his arms, succeeding only in standing with their paws on his shoulders like twin hairy girlfriends licking his face and nosing his hair off his neck while he laughed and patted their wavy black and brown sides in

4

big walloping whacks like they were horses. He rubbed their silly heads so hard their eyes squeezed shut with pleasure and their tails about thumped through the rusty bed of the truck, and then he said something and they dropped like he'd put a little round hole behind their ears.

The place he headed into had only a sign saying BUD in coral neon in the curtained window to announce itself, and the door was one of those cheap hollow cores with enough dents and scrapes to show the long years of night drinking. I didn't remember there being bars right on the main square of downtown before. Downtown used to be for decent people only; bars and dance joints were kept on the outskirts, tucked under the shadows of trees and hills where people could hide their pleasures and troubles. But things had changed, and I walked along the edge of the street, looking at what was left.

The bar was squeezed in next to Western Auto with its new aluminum front, which was next to a taller three-story white stone building, whose windows had been made smaller and smaller in a series of renovations that progressively downsized its view of the world. This building, which had been spared during the War Between the States, was made of the old brick the town was famous for before the factory closed, but it had been painted white for as long as I could remember. The Sears catalogue store used to be there. On the other side of the bar Dayrell'd gone into was a two-story brick with a tattered green striped awning and empty windows with the remnants of FINAL SALE in whitewash streaking down the glass as if the words were melting from the early summer heat. All along the four blocks that squared the courthouse grounds, there were empty storefronts and businesses that looked so temporary they hadn't bothered with more than cheap black and white signs tacked over old ones.

On the corner, fronting the street in a wedge, stood the Bonner Hotel, which now housed the Home Theater Video with its blue and white plastic sign. The windows on the second and third floors had been covered with sheet metal painted flat mauve, like the building was being punished for being gaudy when business needed to be done. In the side that faced the courthouse, rectangular patches had been cut in the two tall window spaces like gun ports, so they peered out at the far corner beyond the courthouse at the Rains Hotel, which my great-aunt Walker and uncle Able had always owned and maybe still did if they were still alive.

I was working pretty hard on feeling sorry for myself and missing what was already gone here in Resurrection. There was that thick in my throat, my chest felt hard like it'd been bricked up along with a lot of the windows around here, and that was when Dayrell Bell came through the door of the bar with a twelve-pack under his arm, half turned laughing to someone and spilling an old George Jones song, "It's Not God Who Made Honky Tonk Angels," in his wake. He pulled the bill of his dirty black gimme hat down on his forehead and opened the door of his truck, which got the dogs up pacing and groaning. If he'd kept going, just kept up the fluid motion he'd become, instead of reaching in to pull one of the beers loose from the twelve-pack on the seat, then held it away from himself to pop it open so the foam would ooze on the street, not him, if he hadn't taken that first sip, looking around to make sure the deputy sheriff wasn't waiting at any of the four corners, then he wouldn't have seen me.

I should've been halfway to Memphis or Shreveport. I should've pretended I didn't know him, but I've never been able to do that. I supposed that was why I smiled at him and smiled even harder when he nodded and looked away before he looked back again to stare. Dayrell, the voice in my head whispered in a low, sexy way, then louder, mocking me, Dayrell, Dayrell Bell. And that's when I said it: "Dayrell Bell."

He took another swig of beer and carefully set the can down. The dogs stopped pacing and murmuring, the traffic stopped, what there was of it, even the little breeze that had started to pick up my hair came to a clean and abrupt halt. He rubbed his hands on the front of his jeans, adjusted his hat, which had the logo of the Resurrection Lumber Yard on it, looked up the street as if someone was spying on him, and sauntered over to where I was standing.

Up close he looked more beat-up than I remembered, scars on his face that weren't there before, the general wear and tear of work in bruises and a mashed purple thumbnail, and little wrinkles where there hadn't been any before around the eyes, and grooving his cheeks and forehead. The nose was that same strong hawk-shape with the little crook from getting broken, the lips still wide and full, and those eyes that took my skin on that musical ride. He had eyes that started out amber and green and ended up brown and yellow or even gray and blue at times. They floated with the feeling and the light, so you never could figure out exactly what was at the bottom of them. Sometimes they went flat as paint and other times they were just like glass. Most of all, though, his eyes made me feel like looking

6

away, embarrassed. They were seeing too much of me, and I was seeing too much of them. There was no middle place to meet like there was with most folks.

"Hello, Dayrell." I folded my arms across my chest.

He searched my face with a cautious expression like maybe he'd done me wrong and I was there to even the score. He looked back at his truck and dogs and beer warming in the late afternoon sun.

"Moline Bedwell, remember me?" I stuck my hand out like we were meeting for the first time.

He looked at it, nodded slowly, "Moline, sure," and shook my hand but didn't let go when we were done. In fact, he put the other hand over mine so it was trapped. I couldn't tell if he remembered or not. He smiled and I remembered those teeth. He'd always had the whitest teeth of anyone around here, not a single cavity. In fact, Dr. Jenkoff, the dentist, used to say there was only one other man in the county had teeth like that, and it was Dayrell's daddy. That was how the town knew for a fact that his mother hadn't been pregnant before she took off and spent the summer at the Lake of the Ozarks while her husband, Hale Bell, and her baby son, McCall, had to fend for themselves and rely on the goodheartedness of the community until she came to her senses and got herself back home. Dayrell was always taller and leaner than the other Bells, who were short and stocky, and their teeth weren't likely candidates for any Crest ad, either. No one ever pried the name of the man with perfect teeth like Dayrell's out of Dr. Jenkoff before the dentist blew his brains out, but he did say he was not who we would ever imagine. Dayrell started life with a dirty mystery dragging along behind him, and he didn't do anything but increase it over the years. There hadn't been any question about me even bothering to ask Mister and Iberia if I could go out with one of the Bell boys, so I hadn't—asked, that was.

We stood there looking at each other and grinning like his two dogs panting in the truck behind him until a car honked and made us step back out of the street. "Stogger brothers," Dayrell said, letting go of my hand and nodding to the '65 Mercury, big as a yacht, slowly passing by. It was painted a pale shade of metallic green and trimmed in darker green, its squared body lines mashed and dented enough that the old shape seemed a ghost behind the current one. Big, sunflower-sized blooms of rust pocked the surface, and the trunk and hood were blistering and peeling as if they'd suffered chemical spills in the shape of Missouri. On the roof was welded a square, cross-hatched wire grate framed with double steel tubing a foot high. Inside dark, greasy motor parts and various other unidentifiable objects clung to the grating. The driver waved two fingers at us as he cruised by.

"That's parts for their car on the roof. Couple a years ago the car broke down on their way back from the Elkhart Lake races up in Wisconsin and they had to spend three days trying to get parts. Now they carry them around wherever they go. Haven't been stuck since." Dayrell waved a finger at the car as it glided on up the street trailing a faint odor of burnt cloth.

"What's that smell?"

"They did have a little fire inside the car a couple months ago. Eddie dropped a joint and the upholstery in the backseat got pretty charred before they put it out. Lucky the gas tank was on empty. Made a new rule that Eddie has to lean out the window to smoke." Dayrell laughed quietly, as if he'd seen a lot of such things over the years I'd been gone. "So what're you doing back here?"

"Family stuff." I expected to see my sister's urn come bobbing up in the back window, but it stayed put. If anyone could come back from the dead, it would be Paris. She had the kind of strength that didn't know any rules.

There was a burst of voices behind us, and Dayrell looked over my shoulder, lifted his cap, pushed his hand through his thick, dirty, brown hair, streaked with gray, then resettled the hat. "Hogs. That's all anybody talks about anymore. Damn ole pork."

I turned around and saw a grizzled-haired black farmer in clean overalls and stiffly ironed white shirt help his wife out of a battered gray pickup, then half lift her up the curb onto the sidewalk circling the courthouse. Her print dress hung a little big on her thin body, and as if her stick ankles were too frail to move the thick black shoes on her feet, she inched along in tiny steps, her black pocketbook clutched in front of her with both hands locked on the handle as if she were pushing it. On her white hair perched a small pillbox hat covered in dusty nylon flowers. But it was her small, determined chin that seemed to be leading both of them toward the commotion.

Most of the people gathering walked with tired, slumping bodies that came from working hard all day for many, many years. All of a sudden I felt stupid driving up in my fancy red 4-Runner, wearing red cowboy boots and jeans too tight to work in.

"What's going on?" I asked.

"Come on." He put his hand lightly on my back and I swear I could read the whorls of his fingertips through my shirt as we crossed to the courthouse and stopped well outside the gathering crowd.

"Just listen." He turned back and raised his arm and pointed a warning finger at his pickup, where the dogs had stood up with their paws on the tailgate, tails and ears stiff with worry. He wiggled his finger twice and the dogs sat, looking both happy and disappointed with the attention.

As we stepped closer to hear what was being said, a tall, white-haired old woman by the backdoor of the courthouse started handing around picket signs. When she turned in our direction, I recognized her. The angular body was stiffer than I remembered, as if one by one her cells were gelling, then turning solid rock. Great-aunt Walker. I started to call out, but she began shaking a sign at a younger, balding man with a round, red, sweating face, who was both shorter and fatter than she.

"That's Odell Meachum, my cousin," Dayrell said. "Silly son of a bitch started the whole thing, now he can't understand why everybody's so damned pissed at him." Dayrell pulled the thin silver chain from under the neck of his tee shirt and fiddled with the tiny plain cross at the end, turning it over and over between his big, dirty mashed thumb and the forefinger with the split nail. I made myself look back at the courthouse. I never knew he was religious.

Odell pushed away until he was standing with his back against the door, his arms held over his head like he was being robbed or captured. "Folks, here now, people!" Odell's voice squeaked in the higher range.

People told him to go away, it was their rally, but he tried again.

"No, listen, I mean it! Heart Hogs is a franchise, not agribusiness. They're not trying to push out the small farmers. They're not a factory farm—they're—"

"Not bringing in twenty thousand hogs in July?" Aunt Walker shook her sign so close to his face, the cardboard grazed his cheek, and he tried to jump back and shove at it with both hands while everyone laughed at him.

"Git him!" a couple of rowdy voices yelled.

He straightened again, filling his chest with air and hitching his trousers in back. "No, *I'm* doing that. The money stays here in Resurrection, in the local economy. You'll all see a piece of it, if you want. I've tried—"

"Yeah, to buy us out, tear down the houses and farms we spent our whole lives on, make us work for wages, *you'll* pay, on *our own* land left us by our granddaddies and their granddaddies. Some deal, Odell," a young white farmer said, then glanced over to a woman sitting on the grass near the sidewalk, holding a baby in her lap, while two other kids rolled in the grass beside her. She nodded slightly. Others nodded too.

"Odell, you know you're contracting for Heart Hog Corporation. This ain't no Dairy Queen or McDonald's franchise. Where would *you* come up with the kinda backing it'd take to buy all the land around you, put up those eight pole barns, and set up a computer operation so you could run fifty thousand hogs? Hell, I had to let you cheat off me to pass high school algebra, Odell. Unless ole Dayrell's slipping you his spare change—" The young farmer nodded at us and everyone looked over briefly, but Dayrell's face kept perfectly still. The young farmer's wife pushed her hair off her face with a thin, tired hand while she rocked the baby.

"Aw come on, Ferguson, you know it's not like that, exactly." Odell's chest deflated a little and he seemed to shrink with the whining.

"You want to build that waste basin smack where I live!" Aunt Walker yelled and shook her sign again and he ducked.

"Heart Hogs out now!" someone shouted, and others picked up the chant for a couple of beats, then let it die.

"We're offering you good money, Miz Rains," Odell yelled. "Cash for a farm you ain't worked proper in years. Don't even live in that house. Everybody knows it's falling down—"

Aunt Walker stepped toward him, letting the sign slide down so the stake rested on the walk. "How do you even know what I do or do not do at my own farm, Odell Meachum? Sneaking around, spying on your neighbors, you ought to be ashamed of yourself. Ashamed. Our families fought and died on this land, first the state floods it for that abomination called a damn and recreational lake, and now you want to cover what's left with pigs and their mess. What happens to troughs of pig manure the size of football fields, Odell? Does it melt away? Where do the fumes go? They'll be having our stink for breakfast in Jeff City. How're we going to stand it, twenty-four hours a day, three hundred and sixty-five days a year? This is our home and you want us to turn it into a pigsty for a few dollars!"

Then the old black man raised his hand and two younger black farmers shushed the people around them so they could listen, but whatever he said was in such a quiet voice I couldn't quite hear, although folks right near him murmured and nodded.

"It's not as bad as that." Odell shook his head firmly. "The whole operation is clean—farrowing pigs never move from their pens, feeders stay in theirs, everything stays inside, nothing outside." Odell's face got redder.

"Except the shit and stink!" someone yelled, and the crowd clapped loudly, even though the women frowned to show their disapproval of the cursing.

" 'Sides, factory farms kill us family farms off," someone called from the back. "They mass-produce and undercut the market so far, we can't compete. Happened north of here, and up in Iowa too, ask 'em—ask any of 'em. They're passing legislation as fast as they can to keep the land in local farmers' hands."

"You don't have the right, Odell, you shouldn't help drive us off the land. You weren't raised that way," Walker said, and raised her sign again, shaking it as if she were going to bring it down on his pink head.

"That's enough, Miz Walker." A deputy sheriff even taller and thinner than she was appeared at her side and gently took the sign. He glanced at it, suppressed a smile at the picture of the pig with a circle and slash drawn over it, and tossed it to the side. "Now you folks can stand here and talk all you want, but you cannot block the doorway. That's you, Odell," he beckoned.

Just as Odell paused, ducked his head, and started into the crowd, the glass door behind him opened and a blond woman, who had to be my cousin Pearl, stepped out. Although she was Delphine and Calvin's only child, she had Walker's angles, the same ones most of the LeFays and Wallers had, even Grandmother Estes before the thick Methodist flesh got laid over it. The Bedwell side ran runty and that was what I inherited from my daddy, Mister Bedwell, and my mother, Iberia, who picked up whatever leftover blood there was with all the tall Wallers and ended up producing my sister and me, who never topped five foot four, though Paris lied and said she was five-six whenever she got asked. Even when we stood back to back and came out the exact same size, she pretended she was taller. I always thought she was too, I guess. Paris had that effect on people. Even Pearl looked up to her, though she was a a good five-eight by eighth grade.

Pearl's straight blond hair was cut shoulder length and seemed to add to her height, another long thing on her long neck and long torso. Her hair was always too straight, mine too curly when we were growing up. She cried from smelly perms and I cried from combs stuck in knotted curls. Later we made each other cry, for some reason I would have to try to remember, and never spoke again.

Walker and Pearl ignored each other as she marched out through the crowd and down the sidewalk in the direction of the big white foursquare three blocks away that had been Grandmother Estes's house, with our tiny shotgun cottage squatting next door like an orphan dog with its tongue hanging out for the scraps that might land in the yard dividing us. I guessed Pearl still lived there, from when she moved in to take care of Estes in her final fifteen years. No one could ever kill off a LeFay or Waller woman. We lived forever and ever. It took generations to care for us, and we could outlive God if we put our minds to it.

"Seen enough?" Dayrell tucked the cross back in the neck of his shirt and lifted his hat again. There were black splotches and streaks on his jeans and tee shirt.

When he noticed me looking at his splotched clothes, he picked at a swath on his thigh with his fingernail. "Roofing tar. Fixed a flat place on my daddy's roof over the porch today. Least favorite job. Don't mind shingling, long's it not over a hundred, but tar is tar. That's why I stopped for the beer. Mama slipped me ten bucks, said she'd been after Hale to do that job for two years. But he's too busy. We're all too busy. Take care of your own house last, he taught us. Folks count on us. And they're the paying customers."

"Hey." A man who'd been watching the crowd from the other side swaggered over and punched Dayrell in the arm. "Got a cold one you can spare?" He leaned forward and winked, looking me over as if he were trying to remember me.

"In the truck."

His face was a little heavier with flesh, but the ice empty blue eyes and the light brown Conway Twitty pompadour were the same. McCall Bell, Dayrell's brother. Still wore his jeans low with the thin black belt buckle to the side, his keys attached to the loop and stuffed in his pocket. He still used his looks like a cruel instrument, I noticed as he walked to the truck, taking a detour to pat a woman on the behind.

"And leave the dogs alone," Dayrell turned and called after him, then cursed as his brother mock-barked at the dogs, setting them off so they jumped the tailgate and romped over, pulling up short at our feet and trying to find a piece of ground low enough to hide in. McCall sauntered after them, two beers stuck in his jean pockets, and carrying two more.

"Told you to leave them alone," Dayrell folded his arms, his knuckles white. The dogs eyed him and snuck away to sniff out the crowd.

McCall grabbed Dayrell in a bear hug and lifted him. "That's what I love about you, bro, so damn serious all the time." When he set him down, Dayrell shoved McCall, who just laughed. "S'pose you were over at the folks' place doing that roof." McCall eyed his brother's tar-splattered clothing, then turned to me. "He's the good one, ya see." Dayrell shoved him back a couple more steps, and McCall laughed and held both beers up. "Okay, okay. Here, thought you could use one—you too—" He pushed a beer at each of us and popped his own with a loud whoosh. When Dayrell didn't open his immediately, McCall flipped the tab and sprayed us both. I quickly opened mine.

"McCall—" Dayrell shook his head and took a drink.

"Got to have a beer with old friends, right, Moline?" McCall said, everything but his eyes smiling at me as he raised the beer and drained half of it. He'd recognized me then.

Drinking, I let my eyes wander over the crowd and found Pearl lingering at the far end of the block, watching us. I closed my eyes and took a second swallow.

"Uh-oh," McCall giggled. "Like old times, hey, Moline?"

"Damn it," Dayrell poured the remaining beer on the ground as the deputy made his way toward us. I followed suit, splattering my red boots with tiny dark spots.

"This one's done for, Monroe, but here's a whole one for you." McCall crushed the empty in his fist, thrust it in his back pocket, and tossed the fresh beer to the deputy.

"You know better'n this, Dayrell," the deputy said, his tall, thin figure leaning toward us. Dayrell shrugged and looked at the ground. "Folks are still keeping an eye on you, off paper or not. Don't try to prove 'em right, Dayrell." He didn't bother looking at McCall and just tipped his hat at me. I felt like a dumb teenager in the parking lot at a high school dance.

"Thanks, man," Dayrell muttered at his brother.

Off paper, no longer on parole. Dayrell had gone to prison for driving the car that night. I'd wondered and worried about it for years.

"Sorry." McCall scuffed his boot in the grass, digging a clot of turf out with the pointy toe. "Whyn't you let me buy you dinner out at the rib place—make up for it, okay?" He pulled the crushed can out of his pocket and tossed it over his shoulder, where it landed with a clank in the street. He looked satisfied and winked at me again. "Moline's never been there— new place out 11? Decent barbecue and cold beer." He nudged Dayrell with his shoulder. "We don't want her spending her first night in town alone, do we? Come on."

"I have to go home, see if I can sleep in the house, and unpack." I looked around at the sun settling into the trees and hills behind us, giving things that two-dimensional outline that makes them look insubstantial, flat but pretty.

"We could meet in an hour, hour and a half. Give me time to go home, clean up, feed the dogs?" Dayrell wasn't looking right at me, but his tanned face was flushed. "Moline?"

I looked at the clock over the bank, which still worked. "Okay, all right. What? At seven-thirty? South on 11?"

"And turn up that no-name little road by the old barbecue shack we all used to go to," McCall added. "New place is called the Rib Cabooze."

I looked around for Aunt Walker before I left, but the crowd was breaking apart and I couldn't find her. Tomorrow, I vowed. After all, I hadn't bothered talking to her for twenty-three years. Just disappeared. She probably had a lot less than nothing to say to me at this point.

2

FINE LINE BETWEEN
HEAVEN AND HELL

Any backwoods farmer will tell you that when a hog carries a piece of wood in its mouth there is bad weather a-comin'. . . . If a hog is seen looking up, when nothing is visible which would ordinarily attract his attention, some folk conclude that a terrific storm or tornado is imminent.

— OZARK MAGIC AND FOLKLORE

✳

I LET MY FINGERS SLIP UNDER THE CDs, empty pop cans, and candy wrappers on the seat beside me and touched the cool metal of the gun barrel. It was what made me different this time around. Nobody was going to mess with me now—not even McCall. That's what I promised as I watched those dogs staring mournfully back at me as I followed Dayrell around the square. There was a thin trail of blue smoke from his truck, and at the stop signs it rose up and sent the dogs snapping at it like they were catching flies.

The Dairy Daddy, where I ate my first soft ice cream, was shabbier, a cinderblock box with scabbed and scaled yellow paint. The lot was still potholed dirt and gravel baked hard as cement, and only a few stubborn weeds clinging to the walls gave any life at all.

On the same side of the street, past the corner, was the place the original Bedwell house had stood, right across from Horras Waller's house. Bedwells and Wallers were both descendants of Southerners, one slave-holder, one not, and had known each other for too long not to have figured out just what their differences were. The Wallers ran the Bedwells out of Camden County during the War, then got chased out themselves. Only some very queer fate would set them down across the street from each other here. Bedwells in a tiny one-story house with a half-basement dug in for an addition that was always waiting for someone to put the top on, which Mister's father and uncle started to do until they ran out of dollars and will and the kids came faster and faster.

Mister grew up running on the flat tarpaper roof over his brothers' and sisters' rooms. The flat basement roof must of sat like a black lid on a box of milk souring in the sun, as the white walls slowly took on the tarry tan streaks from the weathering roof. Across the street was Horras Waller's big foursquare, Methodist upright, white and rigorous. It was only a matter of time before a Bedwell made it across the street for good, and that was probably what Grandmother Estes Waller had feared all along when she forbade Iberia to play with Mister or any of his kin from third grade on. She might as well have hung a welcome sign around his neck. After all was said and done, Estes might have saved herself a lot of worry, because Iberia and Mister finally made their fame and fortune with the Swan Lake Trailer Park on scrap land that she left them.

Dayrell sped up and left me with a last wisp of smoke as I drove on to the corner and circled the block to come up the little one-lane road beside the house I was raised in. The irises had burst in the side yard, and the big old-fashioned yellow, purple, and rust heads were so full of woeful cheer, it was a wonder some kid hadn't come along and lopped them off.

Our house sat slightly behind and well away from the Waller house. While the bigger house had a fresh coat of paint, a mowed lawn, and the shingles torn off for a new roof, spirea, wisteria, and God knows what bushes had grown up around the much smaller house and were squeezing the porch along three sides. Day lilies had taken both sides of the front walk, leaving only a narrow path slick with wet and rotting brown that sent a humid, vegetable green smell up as I brushed between the ribbony leaves.

The porch roof sagged almost dead center and moss was growing like green velvet where the shingles were missing and the wood underneath was dark rotten brown and orange. I followed the sag to the main roof, which made the house seem bent in the middle like it'd been punched in the back. I needed to get the place ready to sell since it was my only hope of any money. There was just enough from my parents to fix it up if I was careful. There was a part of me that wanted to take Grandmother Bedwell's approach to her old house across the street and let the damn thing fall apart, then sell it for a trailer site, really piss cousin Dear Pearl off in the big house next door.

The porch floor was still solid by some miracle, and the big gray steel rural mailbox my father, Mister, had picked up at auction for fifty cents was still wired to the porch railing. The windows were solid too. Mister must have replaced those before they hit it big enough in cheap real estate to sell the trailer park and move to Tulsa.

"Nobody moves to Oklahoma on purpose, not unless you're in oil or cattle. The weather stinks," I'd warned Paris, who, in between her bouts of drinking, was somewhat in charge of them as they grew older. Lot of good it did them. They barely had time to go furniture shopping for their brand new home in the Southern Way development before the emergency room fiasco.

"You never heard of canned tomatoes in Tulsa? You should've asked them!" I'd yelled at the doctor long distance.

"They never heard of botulism?" he'd drawled. After I hung up on him, I wondered if they hated Missourians in Oklahoma because our guerrillas brought the War to the Indian Nations. These things go on forever.

Inside there was a powdery mildew smell from the house being closed up, even though the windows were now open. They'd left all the old furniture when they moved to greater glory in Tulsa. Mister's nubbly gray recliner still stood beside the old embossed metal floor lamp turning greenish gray. The brown brocade sofa with the stuffing fled to both ends sat behind the battered mahogany coffee table with the plate glass top where there used to be an etched mirror before the final battle between Paris and Mister. The red print wing-back chair Iberia recovered by stapling the material on so the staples kept migrating to jab the backs of calves and arms was across from the old black and white Philco TV on the scarred pine dresser with half the pulls missing. And assorted straight-back chairs we kids claimed because there was nowhere else to sit were lined up against the forest green walls that had turned darker with age. The braided rag rug Delphine made for every Waller even though she was only Calvin's wife was dark gray and brown from wear. Originally, there were other muted colors, but Iberia never made anyone take off their shoes because she had no use for Delphine.

I was beginning to feel like Goldilocks, peeking in to my parents' bedroom, then the bathroom and the closet beyond it, down the hallway past the room Paris and I shared, to the kitchen at the back of the house, and out the back door. Behind the house was a shed that must have held a horse originally but later became a chicken coop with the dog pen attached to the side. "Nice people don't keep poultry in town," Estes had sniffed the day Iberia brought home the baby chickens. Not a single egg changed hands after that. One day our crazy dog Spook dug under the fence and killed a couple of the hens but couldn't get through the feathers to eat them. Iberia didn't beat him. She tied one of the dead chickens around his neck and put him on a long chain so he could wander the yard. He tried everything to get rid of that chicken—shaking, running and turning fast, scraping against the house and trees. Nothing worked. He even dug holes and tried to bury it, but every time he backed away, the chicken came right out at him. Finally, he laid down by the back door whimpering until Iberia decided he was embarrassed enough to leave chickens alone for good. Iberia knew the nature of things, even if she wasn't much of a cook or canner.

The vegetable garden plot was a tangle of volunteer tomatoes and squash and weeds by the side of the house next to the dirt road where I'd parked my truck so it could be partly shaded by the catalpa, which had undergone some kind of disaster of its own. The main trunk had been amputated level with the roof of the house and three new trunks sprouted skyward as if trying to surrender. It had become the ugliest tree on the block when it used to be the prettiest. Life is about change, those idiots full of advice tell you. But not all change is for the better.

I took Paris's urn out of the truck because I carried it everywhere with me.

"You're happy," she'd accused me a week before she died.

"I'm not, really, I'm not," I'd pleaded, but she didn't believe me. It was too bad she hadn't lived to see the way this house had turned into exactly the sort of place Mister was always condemning our futures to. We'd both done better than this, even if it didn't last so terribly long.

• • •

There was a band starting up in the next room, and the beer was so cold I chugged the first one and ordered another before inspecting the Rib Cabooze's menu, hand-printed in white letters on a painted black jug. Dayrell and McCall were nowhere to be seen and I'd already waited half an hour. Fine with me if McCall never showed up, but I'd been looking forward to Dayrell. At least this once. What had happened before meant it couldn't happen again, of course.

There was a wait for the food, and I spent it getting lightheaded on beer, pretending not to mind that I was the only woman alone taking up space for four at a table, trying not to believe I was stood up. I didn't really mind the being alone part; it was that look of pity on other people's faces that got me. Especially women who scooted closer to their men and leaned over as if to say, See, I got what you don't. Ninety percent of the men looked like something I'd run over with my truck—roadkill, fat bellied, fat ass good ole boys. There were a couple of skinny ones, but they had that lean, teeth-picking look with greased-back hair that said, Honey, I'm a serial killer looking for a date. Next time I'd have to bring Paris and set her on the table for company. Since I was alone, I could afford to be awful choosy all of a sudden.

The pork sandwich was dripping with runny brown sauce full of hickory flavor and I was struggling to keep it from traveling down my chin onto my shirt by leaning over the plate like I was protecting my food when Copeland Harder Jr. sat down without asking.

"Hey, Moline," he drawled. Cope looked about the same as he had in high school—more filled out, though, with a fat blond-red mustache to match his eyebrows and matted, golden retriever hair. I'd talked to him on the phone a few times about my parents' estate, such as it was. The trailer park had been taken out by a tornado six months after they sold it, and the guy quit making the payments, like it was news to him that such a thing could happen. Their house in Tulsa was built over a landfill that kept shifting, and there were the bad investments some slick Tulsa broker had made for them. Rags to riches to rags in twenty years. In some ways, it was lucky they died before the dream failed on them. The little house on Jefferson was about all that was left now.

He held up a finger to the waitress, glanced at my nearly empty beer glass and put up another. I drained my glass to make room for the fresh one the waitress set down.

Cope held the beer up for a toast and took a long swallow. His small eyes squeezed into slits behind his rose-tinted aviator glasses, and he licked the rim of foam neatly off his lips and mustache.

"Quaint kind of place." He gestured toward all the railroad memorabilia. But I wanted to know why no one ever decorated down here without pieces of rusty metal and worm-chewed wood. I'd counted five moonshine jugs, four big clay sauerkraut jars, and twenty corn cobs, whatever they had to do with railroading—maybe wiping your ass at a rest stop.

"Not a lot of eating places yet, but we're working on it. Folks in Resurrection generally go home at night and eat their evening meal with family, then go out to liquor up. Have to change that now the tourists are coming back. They expect local color, a good time, and country cooking. This place is a gold mine so far." He looked around, his eyes narrowing at the sight of the waitress taking a drag from a cigarette in the corner by the coffee stand.

"You own it?" I wiped my hands and rummaged my mouth with my tongue for spare shreds of meat in my teeth.

He nodded and finished his beer. When he held up another finger, the beer appeared immediately. I noticed that his fingers had grown thick enough that his wedding band cinched the flesh like a sharp belt. The watchband on his wrist was pulled so tight the flesh looked like it was struggling to escape on either side of the black denting pressure. Maybe he pulled it that tight out of memory, not realizing how his body had grown. I had the urge to loosen the strap, to ease the ring off and stretch its gold thinner and put it back on so it rode comfortably, without a toll.

"You doing okay?" he asked.

I shrugged.

He reached a black plastic case out of his shirt pocket, opened it, and handed me a white business card with words on both sides. "Read it."

The front was printed with the usual stuff, but on the back were four lines:

> *If you meet me and forget me you've*
> *lost nothing*
> *If you meet Jesus Christ and forget*
> *Him you've lost everything*

There was no punctuation, and I wondered if that was supposed to be important. He looked expectantly at me, his mug of beer poised halfway to his mouth.

"Thanks," I said, which seemed to suit him because he smiled and drank as if we'd come to some sort of agreement.

"I have to order a new batch every three months. People like them so much, they ask for extras to give their friends and family. I'm happy to do it."

Picturing him as born again wasn't all that easy. He was too content, not pushing hard enough. Maybe it was a new sneak-up-on-'em-unawares style or something. Duncan and I hadn't ignored church during our marriage. Like a lot of people, we just hadn't gotten around to it. For me it was a relief after my grandmother's Methodism and my father's erratic attacks of holy roller Christianity. There were snake-dancing Bedwells out in the hills, and Bedwell cousins who practiced a weird mixture of witchcraft and Jesus worship that even my parents refused to talk about, but that Aunt Walker could be persuaded to discuss when she was in the mood.

"Now what's he up to?" Cope was staring at the doorway to the bar that branched off the main dining room, where Dayrell was hugging two of the waitresses, trying to lift the blonde who was waiting on us, his arm catching her black tee shirt and sliding it up her back until her bra showed. She looked younger and thinner than me by a lot, and I felt bad for myself and drank the rest of my beer too fast.

"You see his brother anywheres? I hate it when those two boys show up together. Bad enough alone." Cope raised his chin and searched the back bar crowd with his eyes. "Shoot, here he comes," he muttered, and hunched his head down as if Dayrell wouldn't notice us then.

He'd only fastened the bottom pearl button of the faded denim shirt, so the little silver cross blinked like a sequin when the light caught it on the bare skin of his chest. And as he walked toward us, the shirt gaped enough to show the long scar drilling right across his stomach like a mulberry stain. My eyes kept finding it as he wove between the tables, saying hi to people, touching a couple of men on the shoulders.

"Moline . . . Cope." He stuck his hand out to each of us in turn, as if he hadn't once put that hand in places I couldn't help thinking about again. Some date, shows up an hour late and shakes my hand. Okay, I was going to act like we just met too. Brushing his hair back behind his ear, he picked up the cheap pressed-glass salt shaker and began turning it from finger to finger like a coin, passing it across one hand to the other and back, spilling salt. I took a pinch and tossed it over my left shoulder like Iberia always did, and worried that maybe we were piling up an awful lot of bad luck here.

"Picked up Leonard's old shotgun at the pawn place today," Dayrell said as he put his hand around the waist of the waitress setting down a mug of beer and a shooter of whiskey. "Thanks, darlin'." He slipped a five into her pocket where Cope couldn't see, and she smiled and let her fingertips trail across his back as she left. I wanted to leave, but I wasn't ready to make a scene in case he wanted one, and in case he didn't, I didn't want to face that either.

"He sure won't be using that gun anymore," Cope said.

"Told me to go on over there and fetch it, he was through. Said it was his bad luck, getting the cancer at his age. Lived through everything else a man could, losing a wife and two of his kids, and still sound as a silver dollar till he got that cough in his lungs he couldn't get done with. Eighty-nine years and he smoked eighty of 'em, he says, no point quitting now."

"I better go see him then," Cope sighed.

"They got him at the VA over in Booneville, won't be long now. Says he's feeling about as poorly as he ever did. Said if he'd known dying hurt this much, he'd a put it off a while longer." Dayrell lifted a glass and held it up in silent toast to Leonard and his shotgun.

"Need to get him to sign off on that land then, otherwise could get tied up in all sorts of family tangles later. Family's better off with the money anyways, land's worth about a nickel over there and Heart Hogs is paying real good." Cope squinted into the distance of the room as if he could see the land and how it was going to increase in value.

"Thought Leonard wasn't interested in giving up that land. Been in his family since 1810, he told me. Those woods are still good hunting. Last good deer stands close to Resurrection." Dayrell's voice got quiet, but Cope didn't seem to notice. He was rubbing his hands on the front of his shirt as if the Heart Hog money he was earning felt like good loving.

"He'll sign now. Man's dying, kids gone. Nobody's hunting there anymore. He'll see the truth of it now."

22

"There's other people hunt there too. His black neighbors have always shared that land, Cope. Some of them rely on that meat for winter." Dayrell tossed back the shooter and quietly set the glass down.

"Well, they can go to the A&P like the rest of us, or they can sell their places too. They're being offered good money, Dayrell—not like anybody's stealing anything."

"Still . . . " Dayrell murmured as the blond waitress brought a pitcher, placing it carefully in the center of the table. He held up the shotglass and she took it without a word and came back immediately with a refill. She wasn't so pretty close up, just young, but that made an awful lot of difference. She didn't need makeup to shrink her pores, and there was still a sprinkling of endearing little pimples on her cheeks.

Cope's eyes lingered on her tee-shirt-bound breasts stretching the letters of RIB CABOOZE wide across her chest, and followed her back into the women's with the lady mule on the door in a dress and bonnet.

"Leonard who?" I asked Dayrell while Copeland Harder Jr. continued to stare at the door as if he could see through the wood to her mouth taking long hard drags off a cigarette ringed with red lipstick.

"Stans," he said, looking at the beer he held up to his mouth. "Place next door to your aunt and uncle's."

Someone punched up the sound on the jukebox in the bar area and Merle Haggard started singing "We Were the Wild Ones" in this throaty voice cored out by bad whiskey, cigarettes, and God knows what else. I drank some more, realizing that so far Dayrell hadn't looked directly at me, everywhere else but at me, in fact. I guess I was afraid to look at him too. After all, he was a grown man who'd been to prison.

"Your aunt and uncle's time to sell is coming too, Moline. You should be encouraging them," Cope said. "Might be something in it for you too, you help out here. These are generous people. They're going to help Resurrection stay afloat. So far, they've had two charity fundraisers, one for the elementary school, one for the library. They've promised to buy a new ambulance for the fire station. They're trying to be good citizens here—better than some I could name."

I followed his gaze, which had shifted over to the other side of the room, where McCall was holding forth among a crowd of people. From this distance his wide face was a series of rounded curves, as if the bones were soft or too far beneath the surface to define the fleshy planes, and it made him look like he was wearing a handsome mask with eyes peering out of the holes at you that gave nothing away as to what was really there. But I'd seen a glimpse of it a long time ago, I had a pretty good idea.

"Sweet Moline Bedwell," he said when he reached us, pulling me out of my chair and kissing my neck in one sweep. The musky cologne he was wearing had a sharp edge to it that ate through every other smell and settled over us. I pushed him away and sat down without saying anything. I pretended my neck wasn't cold where his wet lips had touched it, and waited until he looked away to rub it off.

"McCall." Dayrell tossed off the shooter and set the glass down a little harder this time.

McCall pulled an empty chair from the next table and sat down. "Dayrell's been keeping you happy?" He took Dayrell's beer mug, emptied it, and filled it again, ignoring the foam that spilled over onto the table and dripped down his shirt. He grabbed Dayrell's knee and squeezed it hard enough to produce a grimace.

"Cut it out, McCall." Dayrell glanced sideways at me as he looked toward the bar, but his eyes were so dark I couldn't tell what he was thinking or feeling. "I'll be right back." He quickly got up and walked through the crowd gathering under the TV set at the front of the bar and disappeared.

"He's a busy man. More women than a Mormon. What you up to, Cope? Still banging away at that secretary of yours?" McCall leaned across the table and punched Cope's upper arm.

Cope's face turned deep red as he sputtered his denial. It didn't take a genius to figure out he was doing it. McCall laughed with such clear delight, the people at the next table looked over and smiled too. I could've left then—I mean, I thought about it, getting up and leaving—but the food and alcohol were making me lazy, dulling most of my impulses to do anything but sit there in the middle of the crowd. I was in a position to watch the bar area, and every few minutes I'd see Dayrell's head close to a different woman's, laughing, talking. Once I saw him kissing someone, a skinny blonde, but I still couldn't get up. It was like I deserved this, as if the chorus of Widows that'd started appearing in my head after Duncan died a year ago had ordered this up on the pay-for-view. Waller and LeFay women had a long family tradition of outliving our men, and making the world pay for it, and now I was supposed to join them. Only this time I was doing the paying and they got to do the viewing.

Cope and McCall started talking about hogs then and I dazed out. If the town was going to the pigs, I was going to the dogs, I decided, and drank more.

After a while, Dayrell came back with a new swagger in his walk, and a glint in his eye that said he'd been drinking too. "Hey, baby." He sat down and scooted his chair closer to mine and put his arm around the back of it so his fingertips rested against my shoulder blade. I shrugged him off, but he ignored me and resettled his hand. I wasn't going to point out that he had lipstick smeared on his chin, but McCall did with a loud laugh.

Dayrell grinned and rubbed it off with the heel of his hand. "Your ex's," he said to his brother, and poured more beer in the glass he'd picked up along the way.

"Which one?" McCall rose halfway in his chair, scanning the crowd, then sat down again. "Sure it wasn't one of yours instead?"

Dayrell shook his head. "No, think it was yours. She was talking child support, so I figured it couldn't be mine. I paid up everything I owed back in January." He smiled and drank again. " 'Sides that, she kissed like your wife."

Both men laughed, and I reached for my purse on the floor beside me. "Where you going, darlin'?" Dayrell reached around and pulled the purse out of my hand and put it on the other side of his chair. "Night's young, we're just getting started. McCall's got to go sling some b.s., but we got all the time in the world." He pulled my chair over so our thighs were touching, and that felt too good to pass up. The Widows started cackling like a bunch of pissed-off chickens, but I shut the door on them as fast as I could.

McCall got up and wandered through the room, causing little ripples of disturbance everywhere he stopped. When the waitress came over with more beer, I ordered a tequila shooter and stopped looking at Copeland Harder Jr., who had that know-it-all expression on his face now that Dayrell was sitting so close and sticking his fingers in the brown curls at my neck, winding them around and around so they got tight at my scalp, then letting them go.

"Didn't realize you two knew each other," Cope said finally.

"I've known Moline since she was fifteen," Dayrell's eyes got soft yellow-green swirls in them like they'd had a lot of good washings and the sun had taken the dark out of them. His fingers dropped to the scar on his stomach and ran across it like the scales of an old piece of luck he didn't have to look at to remember. It about made my heart break, the way I remember wanting so bad for that luck to be me, but I hadn't been up to it, not at fifteen and sixteen.

"Day!" a beat-up-looking man in his sixties called from the doorway, and Dayrell looked in his direction and lifted his chin hello. There was that other scar. He caught me staring at it and I almost liked the shadow that knocked some of the cockiness out of his face.

"That's Booth from Versailles—has the Garlick Water Purification Company, plumbing and pumping." He couldn't keep his thumb from running the scar's path, the way a person will rub worry beads. Forcing my attention up past the cross, I saw a smooth oblong yellow stone hanging on a leather thong in the V of soft flesh where his neck met his collarbone. I hadn't noticed that earlier. Had he gotten it in the bar?

"Booth's that Tyrell girl's uncle, isn't he?" Cope asked.

"That's a fact." Dayrell looked down, picked up the glass, and drained it before meeting Cope's look. Something passed between them.

"Well, you paid for what you did. Water under the bridge, that's what I say." Cope was the first to look away.

All the while, I kept asking myself, Did he or didn't he? Was he really the one driving? Because if he wasn't, then . . .

"Roofing's hard work." I touched the blue-black fingernail and fresh cut stabbing down his finger and ignored the light little surge of feeling that went right to my chest. His hands were so chewed up, they looked like a map of Ozark back roads.

"Hard when you're hurrying the way we been lately. Next door to your place, your cousin—" He turned his hand over twice and examined it critically, and I had a wild moment where I thought he was going to reach out and take my hand for comparison. "Your cousin Pearl is a very, very tough woman," he said, and dropped his hands in his lap.

"Pearl should've gone on to school, criminal justice or law," Cope said, and leaned back to turn and talk to a couple at the next table, who looked like good church people. The man was dressed in a plaid, short-sleeved shirt and dark blue pants; his wife was wearing a plaid shirt matching her husband's and dark blue culottes that showed her trim little ankles and small feet thrust into gleaming white sneakers.

It scared me to see people in the same coats, the same hats, as if something was at stake that'd already been lost. I could never trade my whole personality in that way. When Duncan came downstairs to go out in the same colors I had on, I made him change. He'd get that little deflated look in his eyes and his shoulders would humph down a notch further the way the dog walks away when you say no to it, but I couldn't stop myself. I felt sorry for him, I truly did, but I did not want to be a salt-and-pepper set, a two-for-one deal. I liked the idea of mismatched sets, orphaned halves of wholes. After I moved to the extra room, I bought towels and sheets that I liked, without any attention at all to coordinating colors and patterns. It doesn't sound so radical now, but back then it was as wild as I could get. I used the monogrammed towels Duncan's family gave us only when they came over, and gave them away to the Mission Homeless Center for Men when he died. Sometimes in those first months I imagined him alive somewhere, living on the streets maybe, reaching for one of his old monogramed towels when he showered at the Mission on nights he might need to sleep indoors. I used to picture the puzzle on his face, the familiar ring in his head like a finger flicking a big bronze bell, when he felt the satin scroll of his own initials on his skin. I wondered if he'd want to come back then, come home, and if I'd hold him, and soothe the worries this time, let him know that it wasn't his fault, it really wasn't, none of it, not his son, Tyler, not me. Maybe this time I'd find it in myself to open my arms to him, to let him put his head on my chest and break apart the way he must have wanted to those three years when we stopped talking altogether. Maybe I'd reach under his skin with my smoothing hands and pull out the bird flutter of fear and turn it loose to fly out the windows I kept open for months after he died, in case he needed to come home again. Maybe, just maybe, I—

"Another glass?" Dayrell smiled, lopsided and sweet, reminding me of my son before his braces. Maybe we should've left Tyler alone, maybe we should've left him to his imperfectness, left him to learn something on his own without all the lessons. Maybe let him struggle harder, half drown in the lake, make more bad starts on his trumpet, miss the ball, fail a test. But failing wasn't possible in our life. Nobody had ever failed in Duncan's family, not until he married me. When we got married, we all worked hard to change me, so that the girl who first appeared disappeared so quickly, we all pretended she was just a figment of someone's imagination, a bad dream. I closed my eyes to stop the tears. No wonder Tyler moved on.

"You okay, Moline?" Copeland's big paw landed on my wrist like a pound of soft butter.

I opened my eyes to see Dayrell watching me closely. My face and neck flushed hot. I hated it that he'd seen me. I didn't let anyone see me anymore. I stopped undressing in front of my husband and the mirror years ago. "I'm all right." I drained my glass again and Dayrell quickly refilled it and ordered another pitcher. Maybe he was on commission, with his good looks and half-naked body and little boy mouth that made a woman feel like she was missing everything in her life. On the other hand, maybe I was getting drunk.

Flacco Jimenez was hitting an accordion solo while Dwight Yoakam mourned a world of heroin and poverty that'd broken him and the woman who'd gone back to Mexico. I'd been silent for a while, and the two men were on their way to becoming best friends. Somewhere between pitcher four and five they discovered a lot of old memories and stories. I was the audience as they tried to outdo each other and ended up making each other laugh instead. I'd get up and leave, but I was trying to sober up enough to stay out of the way of the other drunks on the windy road back to town.

" 'Member the time your family tried turkey raising? What happened to that idea? Seemed like a good one." Cope was sweating in blotches through his white knit golf shirt and the collar had acquired a tan smear from something. Maybe a waitress's makeup last time he went to the john.

Dayrell squinted through the smoke that had drifted into the dining room from the bar. "Too damn dumb to come in outta the rain. Had one of those wet summers. Every time a big storm hit, they'd pile up along the fence and drown unless we got there in time to force 'em in the sheds. Heat wave, they'd lay out in the yard until they died, swelled up and exploded. Chickens are a lot smarter. Pigs are smartest—stubborn but smart. Real smart. Smarter than cows and horses. Pigs are pig smart."

Copeland Harder Jr. lost another notch of respectability and slumped on the table, holding his chin up with his beefy forearm. "That's what I been trying to tell folks round here. Swine is fine, like the people say. Good opportunity, that Heart Hog deal. Nobody'll believe it, though, just like always. We're dying on the vine here in Missouri, dying on the vine. Haven't recovered since that damn war. Twelfth Confederate state my ass. What did Jefferson Davis ever do for us? Old fart condemned the only thing coulda saved us—wanted a gentleman's war. 'Bout did us in with that bullcrap. Wouldn't be anything left at all if Bloody Bill and Quantrill hadn't a stood up. Both sides ruined us, though. Nobody liked us. Still don't. We're such a damn contrary place, half the time *I* don't even like us. Truman was the last good thing."

His eyes gazed out across the room with a dreamy, young girl expression in them. "My granddaddy used to farm south of here. Kept cows, pigs— one old rickety horse lived till he was forty. Got a rooster he let sleep on his screen porch, called it God's alarm clock. Never electrified. Didn't believe in it. His daddy was a yarb doctor, and in those hills that meant a lot. He knew the name and use of everything that grew in those hills. That rooster, though, that was a tough old cuss. Used to chase us kids every time we got out of the car, until Granddad would hobble over, scoop him up, lock him in the henhouse. Terrible punishment for a rooster, huh? Granddaddy said he was witched, hens wouldn't have any-thing to do with him, but he was still a fine clock."

We had a new waitress for some reason, who plopped down three bowls with scoops of lime sherbet stranded in the middle of green puddles, and expertly dipped around Copeland's hand, which had dropped below the top of the table and reached for her butt. She was wearing an orangy-tan face makeup the shade of the stuff on his shirt. She'd probably poisoned the dessert.

"You ever hop on one of those pigs?" Dayrell grinned and pushed the sherbet away.

Half an hour later we were parked on the edge of a thicket of scrub brush, the headlights of my truck focused on a pen of brittle wire that broke off when we pressed it down to climb over. The two men were rousting a huge black and white sow in the corner, prodding her with a stick, while her babies murmured squeaky protests as they woke up and tried to get out of the way of the drunken feet. Waves of rich, sour pig smell rose up and spread out from the pen, capturing the sweet dark scent of the plum thicket and holding its thick breath against my face. I tried to cough it away.

"Come on, Mama, get up now," Cope nudged her hind end with the toe of his loafer.

"Naw, you gotta get their attention, buddy." Dayrell squatted in front of her, teetering off balance, in danger of sitting on one of the babies.

"Watch out," I called.

He felt around behind him and scooted the piglet out of the way before he collapsed giggling on his butt.

"She's weaning anyway, Moline—that's how come she's not bothering us." Cope raised his arms shoulder high and let them drop to his sides again.

"See, this is what you have to do." Dayrell grabbed a big floppy ear in each hand and pulled. The pig grunted and raised her hind end, walking under herself a little. He pulled again and she reared her head back, scrambling to her knees, then standing upright, the hard fat wobbling back and forth. Dayrell was on his knees, still hanging on to her ears, which looked white and fragile as petunia petals in his big hands. He put his face against her snout and made kissing noises. "Never met a pig I didn't like." He laughed and fell back on his butt again. Cope was bent at the waist laughing so hard he looked like he was about to topple too. The pig was standing patiently, nosing the babies away from her teats. The men straightened up and looked at her, then at me.

"No way." I backed up against the fence, but before I could scramble over its dilapidation, they were lifting me onto that pig. "Good thing you kept your girlish figure," Dayrell said as he pulled his hand out from under my thigh, where it hadn't needed to be. I was straddling the sow stiffly, my knees bent up like a jockey, trying to keep from digging my heels in because it might send her off. The coarse bristles of her hide poked my thighs and calves through my jeans. I tried to balance with my palms on her back and kept sending her pleasant thoughts, the way you did with a horse. The bristles stuck in my palms and stung them, but I ignored that. Okay, this wasn't so bad, no big deal, I was congratulating myself, fighting the dizziness from the beer.

"Let's get her going," Dayrell said, and slapped her behind. She grunted and took a step forward.

"Stop it—leave her alone!" I yelled.

"Here—" Cope cut across her hind legs with a switch he'd stripped from a plum tree. The sow stepped forward again and kept moving. When my heels jammed her sides to stop myself from sliding off into the mud, she broke into an awkward trot, her fat body churning. I kept trying to find something to do with my hands while I worked to stay with the motion. I considered leaning forward and grabbing her ears, but she'd got her head down, squealing as she circled the pen. I'd ridden enough young horses to almost stay with her, but I could feel myself starting to slide left into the fence.

"Help!" I yelled. "Help me!"—but the two men were laughing too hard to understand. The babies were scrambling in front of us trying to stay close while they stayed out of the way. I saw just ahead the mudhole she was aiming for glinting bronzy in the moonlight. "No, help—stop!" I hollered, and she kicked out and bucked, twisting enough to throw me off just before she scrambled into the muddy water.

"Here, what's going on down there?" a man's voice called from somewhere beyond the pen.

Cope and Dayrell were sitting down in the pen side by side, laughing, arms around each other's shoulders. Male goddamn bonding. My whole right side and front was smeared with dirt and what I had to believe was pig shit from the rotten smell. No way I was sticking around to fight it out with whoever owned this pig. I didn't even bother brushing myself off as I scrambled up and ran for the fence.

I was backing out before the two of them realized it and made a half-hearted attempt at waving and yelling. I kept going. I hated those two, and I wasn't very fond of myself as I ground the gears and thought about the stink I was putting on the leather seats.

Now why hadn't I just slid off that pig as soon as they put me on? That was the question I kept asking myself as I soaped the dirt and smell off me in the stained old tub with the rusty waterline two thirds of the way up. "You lie down with pigs, you wake up with them," I muttered at the bits of dried leaf and dirt floating by me. I had a cut on my knee that opened like a tiny pink mouth drinking the scummy water, and after a while I leaned closer to hear what it had to say.

3

THINGS BEING WHAT
THEY ARE

So varied has Missouri been that even the pronunciation of the state's name remains a cause of disagreement. As was true in so many matters, the division lay often between country folk and city people, as well as between one geographic section and another. Generally, citizens of longest standing and deepest regard for the state's spirit have said "Muh-zoo-rah." The less knowledgeable residents have settled for the simpler, newer "Muh-zoo-ree."

— MISSOURI: A HISTORY

*

"WE KNEW WE WERE FROM THE FUTURE before we knew we'd lived before." Great-aunt Walker took a pull on her ice tea dolloped with whiskey and fresh mint she clipped from the clump beside the back door when she first arrived an hour ago. "Poor man's mint julep," she called it, because we'd never been able to afford the sterling silver cups frosty from the freezer with ice hand-crushed by a servant and good barrel-aged whiskey you could sip at until the ice melted and another servant brought you a pitcher to freshen it up again. No, we were just the pig farmers on the front porch, according to Walker. She acted like she remembered all the way back to slavery and the War Between the States, but I didn't think she was quite that old. She was the historian, the genealogist without the dark, church-colored glasses her sister, my grandmother Estes, wore. I tried not to argue with her, never had. We got along.

"What do you mean, 'lived before'?" I asked, taking a slug off my ice tea minus the whiskey. Walker said a woman my age shouldn't be cultivating bad habits like morning drinking, not till I was at least seventy. I was dying of thirst from my hangover, and really just wanted the ice anyway.

She squinted, drummed her fingers on her bare, darkly tanned knee draped with withered skin, and picked up her drink again. "We were here before the Flood, and we'll probably be here after it, much as I can figure. No one's offered to let us off the hook so far . . . the good Lord my sister Estes spent so much of her energy on included."

"Walker, what are you talking about?" I scratched around the cut on my knee, which was weeping clear.

"Your parents died and came back as crows. Isn't that plain to see?" She gestured at the three that were gliding down the limbs of the elm, gradually riding and landing as if they were taking a department store escalator. It was what was sending a blue jay into a frenzy. Finally the crows settled on the grass of the side yard, their full black bodies glistening not quite blue against the white of Estes's big house.

"I suppose that third one there is Paris then."

"Never know, Moline, just never know."

I shook my head and let the ice tea cool my lips, then rinsed my mouth cold to the point where my teeth hurt before I swallowed. There was a dull ache above my ears, but I didn't feel too bad otherwise. I'd been asleep when Walker announced herself in the kitchen, although I'd been hearing the distant thud of pounding next door since sunup, when the damp cool woke me enough to grab some covers.

"No, I've had a lot of time to study the matter," Walker continued, keeping an eye on the crows. "We're just poor people's laundry. We keep getting put through the same wash over and over until we're too gray and wrung-out to amount to much anymore. That's when some of us become crows or maybe vegetables. Nice turnip or peas." Her hazel eyes looked tan and olive in the bright May sunlight as she laughed. She had the long face of that side of the family, as if someone took the heads at birth and pulled them down at the jaw and pushed the sides in a little. It gave them beautiful eyes when they were young, and good cheekbones, which Estes always said was a mark of good breeding—as if my round Bedwell face was a mistake in the overall farm plan. Paris had been a happy combination of both families.

When LeFay women reached a certain age, like Walker, they began to look like old men. The mouths thinned like table knives, and the eyes narrowed. The noses humped and lunged out of the faces. Walker's jaw jutted like the bone had got waylaid and shoved out of place, as if all that weird strength and determination had to have someplace to go. Walker had that thinness Estes loved too. Women could not be too thin to suit her, although Estes had herself became stout after her children were born. Every time my mother put on a pound, you could feel Estes's gaze clear across the yard, piercing the screen of the kitchen window when my poor mother took a tiny bite of cookie. These days Walker's arms were thin enough to slice bread, and her overtanned hide hung like a cheap motel curtain over the rod of bone.

"How's Uncle Able getting along?" I asked.

"Says people are riding his pigs at night. Aside from that he seems pretty sane. Same old man I married fifty-five years ago. Runs that hotel like a used car lot. Keeps after me to sell something, I don't know what. Cans of pop or postcards, I guess. Even I won't eat in the coffee shop, and the dining room's closed except for special occasions. I tell him nobody's going to eat those day-old rolls he gets for half price from the Dixie Donut Shop, not when they can eat them fresh a block and a half away. But you know Able. He just pretends he's deaf and does any damn thing he pleases. Sometimes I think I should have stayed with Carrie Prince when I had the chance. Especially after all the trouble Able's caused this family." Her voice trailed off and she nodded politely to the young black woman pushing her baby stroller past the house.

"At least Estes isn't around to have a fit about *that*." She tilted her head in the direction of the young woman's narrow back, covered discreetly with a yellow dress printed with a pattern of tiny bright flowers and dropping well below the knees. "She couldn't understand why a black person would have to use the walk in front of her house when there was a perfectly good one that ran straight uptown a block behind here. I told her all the races live together after they die anyway, and she said, not in her cemetery. I gave up trying to explain it to her." She squinted at the three little girls skipping down the walk, arms linked, pigtails flying, dark chocolate legs glistening with energy. "Oh hell, Moline, you think it's going to rain again up north?"

I shrugged. Without a paper, I wasn't keeping track. The TV didn't work, and I kept forgetting about the radio. I figured I must be on vacation or something.

"They've having floods along the Mississippi."

I pictured it lapping at downtown St. Paul like a big thirsty brown dog.

"Your cousin Dear Pearl been over lately?"

"I just got here." I didn't tell Walker the truth—that I'd be here a year and a half before my cousin visited my house.

"I see those Bell boys are still working on her roof. They're about worth the spit it'd take to lick a postage stamp. The two of them. Not a woman over twelve safe with them around. You know when those two show up, it's all hell in the henhouse. They're something I don't concern myself with, though." She looked sternly at me. "I hope you won't, either." She looked back at the table between us. "Pearl needs someone to keep an eye on her, though, and I'm getting tired. She has no friends to speak of, and at her age, she could make a worse fool of herself than any of you girls ever thought of doing."

"I haven't been close to anyone here since I left, Walker, you know that."

"Why did you run off and marry someone so different, Moline?"

"Short version? After I ran away I got a waitress job, passed my GED, and started taking extension courses at the University in Omaha. At the rate I was going, I would've finished about the time most people retired.

"But I didn't go off with Duncan Johns because he had more money than I did. I followed him back to Minnesota because he was nice to me, because he made me feel like there was hope again—like I could maybe count on someone else and make a life with them that someday wouldn't embarrass any of us. I wanted to be like other people. Just once, was that wrong?" I drank and set my glass down hard, as if to say, So there.

She nodded and drank. "You didn't even come back for your folks' funeral."

"It wasn't much of a choice, Duncan was dying and I hadn't seen *them* in twenty years."

"And that boy of yours?"

I had to swallow extra before my throat unglued enough to talk. "I hear from Tyler about once a year. He's fine. Living in Los Angeles, working in video-computer graphics or whatever it's called. Doing what he wants.

Used to send us a big basket of fruit every Christmas. He has his own life now." I felt the ache I kept put away in the bottom, bottom drawer. "It's what you raise them to do, I guess—make their own way. Just didn't expect it to happen so abruptly, so—"

"Sort of what you did, my friend," Walker snorted, and the huge diamond she was wearing clunked into her glass as she picked it up. "Damn thing's so big I could wear it on my toe, but I don't dare take it uptown to Schyler to get it cut down. Able swears he stole the good emerald out of his mother's ring that one time and put a cheap one in its place. It was the only thing his grandmother managed to save from the War—buried it before she and her mother and her sisters were dragged off to prison for being Confederate sympathizers."

She sipped her tea and touched the corner of her eye with her fingertip. "That's why Able went all the way to Jeff City for this thing. I never wanted anything this size. It's like wearing a big reminder of something stupid I did. But can't hurt his feelings, so I put it on, and it goes knocking into things like a blind pig." The ring rattled again as she set the glass down on the scarred wood table I'd carried out from its normal position beside Mister's recliner chair.

"What are you doing with this house, anyway? Cope Junior says you're selling the whole kit 'n caboodle and clearing out. I'm surprised at you— your family's here."

"I only came back to settle things here and bury Paris. After that, well, I don't know."

She nodded and drank, her lips almost erased as she rolled them in. "What's McCreavey have to say for himself?"

"He's looking for the right spot for her at the cemetery."

She rolled her lips some more, nodding in short jerks. "Things have changed since Estes ran the cemetery committee, Moline. They've gotten downright sloppy over there. I had to raise a stink last week to get them to hire more help so the mowing would be done on time for Memorial Day. Lee Pettimore wouldn't get off that riding mower and hand-clip anything to save his soul. It was a mess."

"How come you're not on the committee?"

"I try stay away from those who want to spend their time with the dead." Her expression said that I should take the same attitude.

"You could talk to them about Paris, couldn't you? See if they could find a spot near the family?" I could almost feel my sister looking over my shoulder and smelled a light puff of cigarette smoke on the breeze. As much as I'd missed it, this place was closing in on me again. And Dayrell wasn't going to stay away. Sooner or later it would have to be confronted, what I'd run from facing all those years ago. I was right back where I'd started from, but at least I knew how to waitress now.

Walker shrugged and drank. "I'll do what I can, Moline. But don't forget, Able and I are not Resurrection's favorite citizens. We get credit for bringing the civil rights movement to town, all on our own. It's not like we're from Kansas, I used to tell them, but I guess they don't see us as much better than those Jayhawkers burning and stealing during the War, before and after too."

"Just see what you can do, Walker—she's family too." I wasn't sure how she felt about me, since I hadn't so much as dropped her a postcard in all those years, but she wasn't mentioning it, so I wasn't, either.

There was a movement out of the corner of my eye and I turned to see a man come around the house next door with a paper-wrapped bundle of shingles balanced on his shoulder and his thick, scarred brown leather tool belt riding low on his hips. Dayrell Bell. He wasn't wearing a shirt, and his reddish brown chest and back glowed with sweat. His long gray-streaked hair hung in damp clumps, glistening like new motor oil. He looked over and nodded at us before disappearing around the front of the house.

Walker inspected the bottom of her glass as if some whiskey might be lurking there. Then she rattled the cubes. I took the hint and went for a refill.

Looking out the kitchen window, I could see Dayrell making another pass with a stack of shingles. This time he ignored the porch, where Walker was sitting alone. As mad as I was about last night, I liked his walk, unhurried, assured. It was a walk I wished Duncan hadn't given up when office work overtook his body, fattening his thighs and thickening his belly so he had to spread his legs more, making his gait look peggy. He gave away too much of himself to make his success and to lay it at my ungrateful feet. Now what did he have? What did any of us have?

Just before he rounded the corner of the house again, Dayrell paused, shifted the bundle on his shoulder, and looked back toward the kitchen as if he could see me watching him. With his free hand, he did that thing with his hair, pushing it delicately behind his ear, which was just about the most endearing thing imaginable. I yelled at myself and ran hot water over my wrists to raise the discomfort level. This was a man who made you ride a pig, I scolded. Yes, and this is a man who could take you to bed, if you weren't so scared of telling the truth and having it slap you down.

"It'll take him a week just to move those shingles, he keeps bringing them around this way," Walker said when I put the new drink in her hand. "You've never had the sense God gave a mosquito when it comes to boys, Moline." She drank and smacked her lips. "Wish I hadn't quit smoking, but I promised Able I'd take my last puff on my seventieth and I always try to keep my promises. Now I see that's got about as much virtue as a mare in heat, but it's too late to reform my character. Lord, he is pretty, though. Look at him, he's going to die roofing in this heat."

"McCall should be helping. Wonder what happened to him?"

She stared at the space he'd disappeared into. "Probably catting around. Dayrell always let that older brother do anything he pleases and picks up the slack after him. No matter who his daddy is, he's more like Hale Bell than McCall is. I heard Dayrell's starting to settle down some, but McCall hasn't changed a whit. Take a damn strong woman to set a Bell boy straight. Two of them keep marrying, spreading kids like Johnny Appleseed. Can't give it a rest. You'd think the darned things would fall off and give the females of this county a break." She set her glass down and peered at me.

"You should go over and see Tina at the Beauty Shop next door and get the gray dyed out of your hair. Just don't let Fonnie touch it. You always had such nice hair, with little highlights of red and gold in that brown. Like Lady LeFay when she was young. Tina could put that right back in there if you had a mind to. Being a widow doesn't mean you have to look worn out."

"You going to find me a new husband, Walker?" The Widows in my head sat frowning on the edges of their straight-back visiting chairs. The women in our family never remarried, of course. Lucky Iberia went at the same time Mister did.

She gave me a disgusted look, picked up a piece of my hair and turned it in the sunlight, then threw it back. "The dye might give it some body, so you'd get back more of those nice curls you had as a child. Drove Estes to distraction that Iberia couldn't get your hair combed. Able was the only one could do it, because he started at the bottom, like on a horse's tail. You two sure got along until everybody stopped speaking, and he sure missed having you kids out to the farm to ride horses and gather eggs. Missed the busyness. I think that's why he started spending so much time at the hotel. For years I was an accommodations widow, living out there for days on end without him. Finally, I gave up and moved in here too, for the most part. We neglected the farm, and now look what we've got to answer to. 'Swine are fine' my behind." She took a long drink, tapping her fingers on the chair arm impatiently. "I hope you know what's at stake here. There won't be a drop of water worth drinking in this county once that mass of pig manure starts seeping into the ground water. Pollutes the aquifer. High levels of nitrates. Causes miscarriages too. They're only building earth basins."

"They can think of a way to protect the water," I said, but Walker shook her head.

Dayrell brought the extension ladder and tried to set it up at the highest peak of the house, discovered it was too short, and had to go around back again where it fit. He didn't look any worse the wear for last night. Where'd he get the energy? I was just plain tired out and kept imagining I smelled pig on top of that. I hadn't dared look in my truck yet.

"Heart Hog Corporation," Walker announced, "is not going to get our farm. Can you imagine the smell of that many pigs? It's just plain unhealthy—those fumes will make anyone within fifty miles sick as a cabbage-eating mule. I hope Mr. Copeland Harder Jr. remembers who his people are before he goes too far with this company, or one of us is liable to remind him. Your cousin too."

"They putting on pressure to sell?" I didn't like getting her started on this subject, but I did sympathize with her. Nobody should have to take this on at the end of their lives.

"Drive us out is more like it. Whoever was out messing with those hogs last night should thank their lucky stars Able didn't shoot first, ask questions later. We've had a little too much trouble lately for it all to be accidental—the horses let out onto the highway, the chickens fed bad feed, a whole litter of baby pigs drowned in two inches of water. That kind of cruelty I will not stand for. We met with their lawyers and we told them no. No is what we mean to say. They'll have to kill us to move us off that land. No, that farm stays in the family. We've always said that. The hotel too. Those hog people come sniffing around there, I'm ready for them. Your great-grandfather made sure each of his girls could shoot as good as a man, and I'm not above using the shotgun I keep behind the desk at the hotel."

She paused, looked over at Pearl's yard, and frowned. "Able and I been taking turns sleeping at the farm, you know, but we can't keep up that schedule with his back hurting. He snuck out there last night after I went to bed or Lord knows what would've happened. I came today to see if you could help out until this business dies down. Wouldn't be for long. You could come uptown after lunch and I could show you the hotel routine. Sometimes maybe you could go on out and spell Able with the farm chores." She looked at me in a way that said I couldn't refuse. Her lips were pulled tight, and there was a slight tremor in her hand now as she lifted her glass.

"Okay, I guess I could help for a while." I sipped my tea, which had gone lukewarm, but I pretended it tasted good anyway. It was the kind of moment where a misunderstanding would set in if either of us moved.

Dayrell appeared on the roof in his sneakers, his hair flopping in his face as he started pounding and inspecting the boards underneath for rot. She swirled her drink, drained it, and stood up, handing me the glass. "I'll get Able to pay you for the time."

We both nodded. Although I hated taking it from these old people, I needed the money. Walker didn't hobble down the stairs like she was old, though. A gym teacher all her life, she still walked miles a day and burst into people's lives like a TV detective. On the sidewalk she stopped and turned back.

"You visited any of the local sights yet? You should go see what they've done with Calvin's Cave. Go on out there and tell them who you are, they'll let you in for free. You children used to love that place. Anyways, you need to get off that porch if you're going to cure that hangover. And you need to take a bath, Moline—you smell just like Able's old pigpen."

I was in the kitchen rinsing the glasses when Dayrell's form darkened the back door screen. "Could I trouble you for a drink of water, Moline?"

I shrugged and filled the glass I'd just rinsed. He pulled the rickety screen open and stepped inside uninvited, letting the door catch partway open against his shoulder. At least he'd bothered to pull on an old faded red tee shirt with the arms cut off.

40

"You're letting the flies in," I said, and he stepped into the room, sipping at the water, then draining it with his eyes closed, the yellow stone on the cord bobbing gently at his throat.

"More?"

He let me refill the glass three times. Then he went to the sink and splashed his face and stuck his head under the faucet. He shook his hair and rubbed his palms on his jeans, turning to look at me. "Moline . . ."

"I don't want to talk about it. I can't believe I let you drag me out there, and I hope you had to walk back."

He grinned and looked at the floor, shaking his head. "I am sorry, Moline, but even after your uncle Able showed up and we ran off into the woods, it took Cope and me a good long while to stop laughing. Does your aunt know it was us?"

"Yes, of course she does. Just so you know, I didn't come home to entertain the local boys, Dayrell, so why don't you just get yourself out of here and go back to hauling your roofing stuff around the house a few more times? You might as well have put up a billboard for my aunt Walker."

"I don't have anything to hide." He folded his arms across his chest and looked me right in the eye until I looked away at the old chipped gray Formica table with its rust-spotted metal legs.

"Just let it go, okay? I don't have time for this." I couldn't look at him again without wanting him to argue me out of this.

He kicked at the loose chips of linoleum under our feet, and his eyes did that thing, touching me. Don't, I wanted to say. He could read me, though. He could just stand there and the skin I'd callused over myself fell away and there I was, a dumb kid accepting a ride from a stranger like that first time in the parking lot outside the high school when I couldn't believe that Dayrell Bell would ask me of all people. Poor dumb Juliet the first time Romeo says boo to her. The room was still except for the hiss of the old fan from the front, wearing itself out trying to push the humidity back and forth. I could smell his skin again, musky with outdoor heat and beer sweat that was drifting off him in waves that circled and broke and pooled around me. There was a drop of water clinging to the bottom of a lock of hair, and I concentrated on the way it shivered there, glittering with possibility.

"Aren't you afraid?" It was a question I was asking in my head that came out loud before I could stop myself. "Roofing," I added lamely.

A thought passed across his face and the moment escaped. He looked away. "I've been afraid plenty of times, Moline—more than you'd ever guess."

"I don't know, Dayrell, it's been twenty—"

"Twenty-three years on Memorial Day—the old one, May thirtieth." He tossed the wet hair back, splattering the cabinets behind with tiny specks of water, as a look of understanding passing over his face made him glance at the table. "I have to get back to work, Moline. Your cousin wants that roof done yesterday."

He started to leave, then stopped and turned and stuck his hands in his pockets, scuffed his shoe on the floor, sighed, and looked me in the eye. "You can relax, okay? I'm not just trying to get in your pants."

The way he said it sounded ugly, dirty, too much like something in my head. "Don't you have work to do?" I pushed past him to open the back-door and he grabbed my shoulders and held me still until I'd look at him again. His hands hurt when I tried to twist away, and his face was flushed under the deep tan.

"Give it a break, will you?" He let go of me, and I stumbled back a step, and when he reached to stop me, I pushed his hand away. He looked at me for a moment, then left, closing the door softly behind him.

"Get in," he'd said that day in the high school parking lot, and I had, and everything he'd wanted after that I'd done too.

I hated the invasion of memory, felt colonized by the past you couldn't get free of down here. Even the stupid curtains Paris had hung on the windows of our bedroom, draping them artfully like she'd seen in a magazine until Mister came in and ripped them down—we'd left them there just as they were now, lopsided, dusty turquoise cotton curves that clashed with the rest of the room's plain homeliness. Everything here stayed alive and ruled me as if I were a third-world country considered too backward to be left on my own. I had my own history, damn it, twenty-three years without Dayrell or Bedwells, twenty-three years they didn't know anything about. But time was a noise here, a busy, exasperating sound I was always trying to run from.

I'd avoiding looking at the Rains Hotel on the far side of the square when I first drove into town, where Aunt Walker and Uncle Able might be parked on the front porch like museum displays. The rooms hadn't been redone since 1927 when I left in '73, and I didn't imagine much had been done since then. The sign on Highway 11 was so faded when I drove by on my way into town, I had to try and remember where the letters used to be, and the cheesy picture of the hotel had washed out to an orange slab stranded in the middle of a beige sky.

Pulling in front of the four-story hotel, I noticed that the paint had bucked and scaled on the window frames, porch columns, and floorboards. The screen door, which used to get new wire every spring, was washing a russet path across the doorsill, straight across the porch, and down the steps, as if something ancient were hemorrhaging to death. It squeaked and pulled lopsided as I entered. Besides the familiar dusk of the old hotel, there was now the faint underfuzz of mildew. Although the original dining room and back parlor had been turned into a museum for the Resurrection historical society, the front parlor remained the same, only now the furniture was more vividly stained and threadbare, with cotton stuffing peeking out of the chair arms and seats. A gray path had worn through the dark red oriental carpet from the front door to the high oak reception desk varnished in a thick dark shade that had turned black over the years.

I stood for a moment, wanting all the noises of the hotel to come trickling in on me, to bring that myriad life up full volume, the way it used to be, but there was only the loud ticking of the old railroad clock on the wall to the left of the counter, and the creak of the wooden stairs and floor above me in the warming day. Outside, cars drove by, and occasionally a person's voice would be carried in on the little breeze. I looked at the key board behind the counter. Only three keys gone. How were they keeping the doors open? Midweek slump, I reminded myself, but shook my head at the balls of dust collecting in the corners and along the baseboards. The big crystal chandelier I used to help Uncle Able lower for cleaning was draped in the dusty gray threads of spiderwebs, and when I flipped the switch, each bulb glowed a reluctant yellow cone of light. A foot-wide band of dark gray trailed the ivory and gold wallpaper opposite the banister leading upstairs. And halfway up, there were long curtains of brown stain streaming down from the floor above.

"You made it. Let's see . . ." Walker went behind the desk and pulled out a stack of registration forms and a frozen orange juice can of pens she banged down on the counter. "Don't use the book anymore—on display over there with the silver tea service, see?" She tilted her head in the direction of the display case next to the entrance to the old formal dining room. "The forms are self-evident. Supposed to check ID, but we never bother. Long as they pay cash or the credit card goes through. Do that. Able forgets and sometimes we end up eating the room. I always like cash best—can't change their minds later and cancel the payment because they're disappointed in the room. Okay, you'll take turns on the night shift. You used to help out on weekends in high school." She stopped and looked at me. "Have to think what's changed."

"Oh, I know." She came out from behind the counter and waved me to follow her down the hallway to the plainer part of the hotel that used to be the servants' quarters. "There's a little bed here for you to use, and the closets here have most of the linen now since we had the upstairs flood a couple of years ago. Able's till working on the roof over the closets, so I've moved everything down here. Anyone need more towels or sheets, get the dirty ones and trade them in on the clean ones. We're still using some of these real old towels with the hotel name, and people will get light fingered around them." She lifted a sloppily folded towel that was so thin it was flat as a pillowcase. Some of the black script letters of the Rains Hotel monogram were unraveling, and she absentmindedly picked at a long thread on the H and clipped it with her teeth before putting it back on the shelf. "Should pull these all out for rags, thin enough to read the Sunday paper through, just can't afford to replace them yet. Maybe next summer." She sighed and closed the double closet doors.

"Cafe's only open for breakfast now. At least the coffee's this side of brutal. Don't tell them that, of course." She laughed, but it ended in another sigh, and I looked up at her face, which had gotten old and sad all of a sudden. "Guess you can see there's not much business. There's rumors about a Comfort Inn going in on 11 a ways down from the Hardee's. I don't know what we'll do then. Maybe open a bingo parlor if they legalize gambling like they're threatening to do. Or a hog museum, more like it. Lord, I hope Able doesn't live to see this day that's coming. Not that I want him to pass away, mind you." She glanced at me and tried to smile, but I could see her heart wasn't in it.

Upstairs, we walked in and out of the rooms, which all shared that worn down, settled in look of old people's houses that had sealed up the years in smells and stains and dim light. She tried to point out the benefits and differences between some of the rooms on the second and third floors, the only ones in use now, but gave up when it became obvious that the best we could offer the tired traveler was clean sheets and warm water, the water warm only if they were early risers and the hotel was mostly empty. Some of the rooms had their own bathrooms; others had to share one in the hallway.

"The plumbing's getting up there," Walker said as we stared at the old toilet with the cracked wooden seat, the bowl inside rimmed orange with minerals. "Tried lye, acid, everything a body could think of to get that nasty stain out. Only seems to eat it deeper. Porcelain's shot. I try not to put people down here unless I have to." She reached over and brushed at a gray spider making its web across the big claw-footed bathtub. Capturing the spider, she held it carefully in her closed hand while I raised the window and then she flung it outside. "No point inviting bad luck," she said. We both knew killing spiders in the house to be the worst kind of thing to do. "Have to spray for centipedes again, with all the rain we've gotten this spring. Don't forget that—spraying can save us a lot of wear and tear, guest-wise. Especially after a room's been vacant. I try to do it once a week. You can help out by taking the third floor. My bones get tired of these stairs."

By the time we were done, I'd figured out that they had to be losing several hundred dollars a week. And that on top of the financial ruin, the hotel was on the verge of physical collapse. Even with the smoke detectors, many of which didn't seem to have their little green dots alive, it was a fire trap. The sprinkler system had been disconnected ten years ago when it started leaking, and Able hadn't gotten around to hooking it back up yet.

After our tour, I promised Walker I'd be back later that night to start my first shift and had my hand on the front screen door when it jerked away, pulling me off balance.

"Got that thingamajig," Uncle Able called as he stepped around me, waving a paper bag at his wife.

"Ball stopper for a toilet," Walker explained. "Able, turn around and say hello to Moline."

Aside from holding his wide shoulders crooked to match the stiffness of his back, Able seemed the same as he stuck out a large, callused hand. Since our family rarely hugged, a handshake was considered a real intimate greeting.

"Moline's going to start working here," Walker said.

" 'Bout time." Able winked at me.

4

JUST BEFORE THE RAIN

A youthful Missouri thus stood as a second Eden, as gateway and guardian for a wondrous new America and distant wealth. The prospect obviously appealed to the nation's greatest orator. Daniel Webster, who confessed his awe at Missouri's natural eminence. Speaking in St. Louis in 1837, Webster acknowledged that the nation had not yet full appreciated what he called an infant Hercules. According to the Massachusetts senator, Missouri had more mineral and agricultural wealth than any other area on earth.

— MISSOURI: A HISTORY

I'D WORKED FIVE NIGHTS AT THE HOTEL and was determined to get started putting my parents' house in shape early this morning by dragging outdoors the larger pieces of linoleum I could pry up from the floors of all the rooms and trying to pile them neatly in the side yard, but they were so brittle, pieces kept chipping off and leaving a trail. There were so many layers, I could feel the rooms get taller each level I took down. I'd found an old crusty pair of cloth work gloves in the chicken coop out back, and after hesitating for that brief moment when I imagined my father's cruel hands thrust into the fingers, I pulled them on.

I kept thinking I probably should've put a scarf over my mouth and nose as a musty smell oozed from between the layers of linoleum with the dirt that was invisible but quickly covered everything with a fine black film. It looked impenetrable, linoleum did, but it was as porous as old cotton after so many years of feet arguing it back and forth. The layers revealed faded green swirls and big cabbage roses and little checks in yellows and browns, paisleys and big blocks, dainty repeating flowers hopelessly getting nowhere. Each time we'd laid down new linoleum, there was a sense of starting over, of luck at hand, and we'd all pretend the floor was warm as carpet under our feet, and try not to scuff, but soon enough it took on the worn streaky patterns of our living, the gouges, scrapes, and dents of dropped and dragged objects. The linoleum never let us forget an accident, a moment of anger; the floor was a secret agent scribbling notes as fast as we lived, a library full of Bedwell time.

It had rained yesterday, and today was clear and hard and bright, the heat lifting the water off trees and flowers, making the yellow puddles on the gravel road beside the house look like hot sulfur springs. People passing the house walked or drove slowly so they could get a good look at what was going on. At first I waved or nodded; then I got tired of the spectacle and just kept working like I lived here. I'd found a leaf rake in the coop and tried raking the chips out of the house, then off the porch and sidewalk, but only succeeded in decapitating some of the lilies and wiping out entire generations of their long leaves.

After a while there was a pounding next door, and when I looked, there were two men bare to the waist on the roof—Dayrell and somebody. They were too busy to notice me, but they did notice the car of high school girls that drove by and honked. Some things never changed.

I had just finished dragging the last big piece I could tear loose down the front steps, and was pausing in front of the house to catch my breath so I could hold the sticky dirt at arm's length the rest of the way to the pile, when I saw this big black Ford Fairlane drive slowly by, heading out of town with a thick black man at the wheel. The car paused briefly in front of my house, and when the man pushed the sunglasses up on his forehead with a thick hand, I recognized him despite the extra weight. Titus M. Bedwell. We stared at each other for a moment, and when he finally nodded, I half waved and tried to smile. We hadn't seen each other since he put me on the bus to Omaha. He rolled forward then, and I noticed there was a white girl, a blonde on the seat next to him, straining around his bulk to look out his window at me. He nodded again as if he were the foreman on the job, and when the girl reached around him and pointed a skinny pale arm at Pearl's roof, he looked up and let the car slow even more as they rolled past. Once he was past our houses, he braked and the car sat there for a moment, idling quietly while the two of them argued. I couldn't hear anything, because they weren't loud enough over the hammering on the roof, but you could see they were having it out about something. Then the Sunoco gas truck came rumbling and hissing up behind them, braying impatiently on the horn, and they moved on down the road.

When I was thirteen Aunt Delphine had been involved with Jimmy Findum, who drove the Skelley gas truck then, and Pearl and I speculated about what it would be like to have him as a dad. Mostly we worried about the smell of gas that pooled off him every time he came over. We liked the smell of gas, but decided too much of a good thing could be bad. One night that August, I had taken Pearl window peeping after dark to see if we could catch anyone at anything. We saw a bunch of people getting kids ready for bed, but we thought it was pretty darn thrilling because we were peeking through the space where the shade hadn't been pulled down all the way, it being a hot night and all. Then we looked in our own windows.

Mister and Iberia were cuddled up on on the sofa watching TV, which wasn't any big deal, though Pearl liked it. At her house, the little one-story frame built in the fifties on the other side of Grandmother Estes's, almost all the lights were out except for the one in her mother's bedroom. Jimmy Findum was carefully folding his gray work pants and placing them on the chair whose back already held the shape of his gray shirt with his name embroidered in red thread over the pocket. As we watched, he pulled the white tee shirt over his head and shook it out before folding it too. His skin was pale with a hint of the gray paper turns when you erase your pencil marks. Or so it seemed in the weird half-light of Aunt Delphine's bedroom. I had the impression that she was in bed, but that wasn't important. Jimmy's underpants were. Neither of us had ever seen a naked man, this was as close as we'd ever come, and Pearl grabbed my arm and held on, half tugging me away, half keeping me there. Jimmy stepped closer to the window with his back blocking the room and pulled the little band around his leg out as if it cut, the way our new bras did at the end of the day. And then he touched the wide elastic waistband printed with little gray letters, his fingers tanner than the rest of him, as if he were gradually becoming the color of gasoline. Pearl and I spun and ran. Laughing loudly and galloping as hard as we could, we didn't stop until we were safe behind a big tree two blocks away. We could never look at Jimmy Findum without grinning knowingly after that, and were secretly relieved when Delphine decided not to marry him.

The Sunoco gas truck lumbered on out of sight, and I wondered what had happened to Jimmy, what had happened to a whole lot of people. Most of the people here now I didn't even recognize, including the man in the blue Chevy pickup who pulled over and parked illegally in front of Pearl's and went around to the truck bed and brought out a sign of some sort and pounded the stake into the ground in her front yard, then drove away without acknowledging me. I figured it was one of those signs carpenters and roofers put in people's yards when they're doing work, but went over to check it out anyway. Dayrell and the other man were working on the far side now.

The sign said HEART HOGS FOR A HAPPY FUTURE—VOTE YES in black letters on white board with a red heart printed in the background. Walker would have a fit. I tried to pull it out, but the stake was driven in too far, and my back gave that warning snap and crunch that said I was about to pull it out instead.

"Here, what're you doing? Stop that!" I looked up at the roof, where the man yelling stood on the highest peak glaring down at me. He had the sun behind him, so I couldn't see who it was.

"Screw you," I muttered, and walked quickly back to my own house and slammed the front door so hard, the glass rattled and I had to reopen it to make sure it wasn't about to fall out. Two white women in chunky white ladies' summer shoes and pastel rayon dresses with matching little belts, and hair nets over their fresh blue-white rinsed hair, had stopped in front of the sign and were looking up at the Waller house with disapproval on their tight little red lips. It was hard to say which was the real offense, a sign in the front yard or what the sign said. Either way, you could tell, standards were being breached. It was comforting to know that somebody out there maintained the rules, and I wondered as I went back inside to bathe if when my turn came at those shoes and dresses, I'd be any good at the job.

Pulling off the gloves, I found a big brown spider half crushed on the tip of my index finger, the torn-off legs falling away, the others jerking painfully. I stared and cursed, and flipped my hand hard to see if it would fly off. When I looked again, there was just this yellowish smear and a single leg like a bent hair.

Somebody tapped on the back door while I was getting out of the tub, and trying to hurry to answer it I caught my foot and almost killed myself banging around in a tangle of arms and legs, ending up with my chin touching the cold sweat where the toilet base sat on the floor. Naturally there was a line of thick black gunk and hair accumulated along the edge where the brown linoleum wasn't cut exactly even. Christ, get a grip, you're too young to be falling down in the bathroom, I warned as I got up.

I found a note from Dayrell stuck in the back door inviting me to lunch in Sunrise Beach at the Lake. I wasn't going to go, even when I looked around the half-destroyed kitchen with the mound of broken linoleum, glue and residue remover in big gallon cans already giving off toxic odors, and the fridge which I knew for a fact held only some beer. I'd worked up some appetite and was already sick of the lunch food uptown, what there was of it at the Dixie Donut and Dairy Daddy. There was only one other place—aside from the hotel cafe, which closed at three every afternoon— and that was Odell Meachum's sister's place, the Palmyra Dining Room, that served big Sunday-style dinners every night of the week and seemed not to notice how business was dropping off since the Hardee's and Subway opened out where 11 crossed 21, by the Wal-Mart.

Orpha Meachum Wegs had taken over running the Palmyra after her husband was killed when a semi loaded with cattle missed a curve and took him out in front of his own house early one morning when he was pulling the *Kansas City Star* from the holder next to his mailbox set at the edge of the road. He was still in his pajamas and slippers, Orpha told anyone who didn't know the story, newspaper clutched in his hand, when he was sent sailing across the long front yard into the hundred-year-old white pine. And the driver wasn't even from around here, as if that added insult, about what you'd expect from this country since the War. Meachums and Wegses had been early families in DeWight County, having moved down from Palmyra with their slaves just before the War, but they never forgot the little town on the river called "the handsomest city in north Missouri," site of both an early trial of abolitionists from Illinois and the Palmyra Massacre, when ten Confederate prisoners were shot by the Union.

But it wasn't historical differences that kept me out of the Palmyra Dining Room; it was Aunt Walker, who was boycotting the place because Orpha's brother, Odell Meachum, was the person responsible for opening the door to Heart Hogs. Odell had already contracted for the first twenty thousand hogs and was busy building and acquiring land and subcontractor farmers as quickly as he could to meet Heart Hogs' mid-July deadline despite the public debate and vote scheduled in a few weeks. The Rains farm stood smack in the middle of his plans, as did many of the smaller homesteads to the northwest of town, Walker had reminded me every day since I got here. To make matters worse, Meachums were Bell cousins. Dayrell and I hadn't talked about Heart Hogs or his cousin since that first day. In fact, we hadn't talked about much of anything, I realized as I reread the note scrawled in thick pencil on a scrap of newspaper. I imagined his fingers, tired and sore from hours of gripping the hammer and holding the roofing nails, trying to grasp the pencil and make it write steadily like an adult rather than the clumsy child sprawl of letters that resulted.

The rain began so softly a few minutes later I didn't notice it at first as I lay on the bed in the back bedroom staring at the brown tin box printed with tiny white horses, each with two legs held suspended in trot. This was the box I'd emptied my sister's ashes into yesterday to get rid of the cheap flocked urn that was always in danger of tipping over. It was the same box that had once held slightly stale chocolates from Germany, the box I couldn't bear to throw out since it was the last present Duncan had ever given me. It seemed natural to dump Paris into this cake-mix-sized square when I unpacked. Maybe someday I'd add water or vodka and see if she materialized. For now I simply kept a watch on her, trying to figure out how the heck I was going to pay for the plot. I could sprinkle her over the graves of our parents, some kind of justice there, but I couldn't tell anyone. And I couldn't confess that I didn't have enough money to take care of anything here. I was working just to feed myself these days. Even though the truck was paid for, I didn't dare sell it or I'd be stranded here again.

Then the soft hiss of rain grew to drops the size of fifty-cent pieces that splatted against the windows like they were going to break through and the thunder and lightning began to walk across the town, moving in waves like the big guns of an advancing army. Hail came in handfuls of marbles someone was throwing from just above the house. I was waiting for it to crack through the glass and pile in on top of me when Dayrell appeared, soaking wet, in the doorway.

He opened his mouth to speak, but the thunder shook the house as if the New Madrid fault had cracked open in the side yard and was about to dump the two opposing houses in on top of each other. He pulled at his red tee shirt, lifting the bottom to wipe uselessly at his face while water streaming down his jeans formed a puddle of dirty water at his bare feet. "Wet out there. Went to start my truck and go fetch my dogs up from the creek? Son-of-a-bitching tire's flat, no spare. I was wondering if you could give me a lift out to my place so I can move my dogs before the creek tops over and drowns them poor critters. I'd appreciate it." His eyes were dark gray like the sky outside as he watched me pull on my sneakers and grab an old red plaid flannel shirt of Duncan's.

As I drove, bits of green leaves slammed into the windshield and stuck, then flowed away again, like hands drowning in a dream. Despite the early afternoon hour, it was dark enough to need the headlights on. I couldn't see or hear much, and we were almost shouting. "Have to beat the creek rising, or they'll be swimming to China come dark," Dayrell urged me faster, and I kept thinking about those dogs swollen up like pigs, floating away in swirls and eddies of muddy water. "Turn here, road's not too bad."

It was a series of mudholes and ruts we slid in and out of, like riding a boat on a lake in rough wind, the way we rose up and down, up and down. What did he think a bad road was? The rain was coming straight down; hard as metal it hit the ground and spiked back up. Once in a while a big gust slammed into the truck like a cow tossed against us and we lurched and slid some more. Dayrell kept his hand locked in the grip beside the door and rode easily, as if this were just an unruly horse.

"Right here—" He grabbed the wheel and jerked, throwing the truck into a tilt before it straightened and plunged forward again.

"Don't do that!" I struck out at his hand and peered through the waves of water the wipers made, trying to stay on the path, which was only two ruts through shoulder-high underbrush, punctured by dark trees draped in wild grape and honeysuckle, the tops thrashing though the brush was mostly still, as if the wind were staying above us for some reason.

"Oh man, I hope my dogs are all right." Dayrell hiked himself up another inch in the seat and rubbed at the side window as if that would help clear some of the water off the outside. "Here, pull up right beside the house." He started to grab the wheel again but stopped himself and only pointed to a dark shape that turned out to be a small trailer splotched with faded, pale pink paint and a weathered wood shack slabbed onto the side. There was a pile of tires under a cedar tree a few yards away, surrounded by a sprawl of pans, sticks, and bones. "That's where I usually chain them," he said apologetically as he climbed out of the truck. "I'll go down and get them—make yourself at home, nothing's locked."

He disappeared into the gray water, leaving the door not quite shut. I turned the engine off and reached over to slam it, catching the wet dirt-and-sweat odor he'd left in the seat. On the gray leather handle grip was a set of dark smudges from his fingers, and I started to rub them off, then stopped. I wasn't sure what I'd do with that dirt then.

I waited until I saw the two dogs come surging toward me, followed by the tall figure striding but not running, as if that would be beneath his dignity in the face of these joyous animals. By the time I got out and ran to the flimsy screen door made out of crate fir with the staples lined up like dark fingernail parings, the dogs were sniffing my butt and whimpering. Stepping back to untangle my legs so I could pull the door open, I bumped into Dayrell reaching over my shoulder to pull the door out, brushing my cheek with his arm. My face felt as if it'd been too close to a hot light bulb, and I resisted the urge to touch it, to show that I knew how it was reddening, as we all lurched inside.

"Here, you two, settle down now. Win, Bob." He pointed and flattened his hand and both dogs dropped to their bellies.

There was an ancient refrigerator in a dark corner with a door so smudged and pocked, it'd turned brown, and kitty-corner from that was an ancient wood cook stove, sitting heavily on four squat legs, the big burners made of such thick iron they seemed fit for the pots of fairy tale giants. The walls of the lean-to shack turned kitchen were gray barn siding, but not the good kind you found in rich people's houses and rustic restaurants; this was the kind that looked like its origins, manure stained, abused, not a lick of charm, something a step below the packing crate fir door. There were newspaper and magazine articles and photos and a couple of old posters advertising stock car races and the Missouri State Fair tacked up in an attempt at decorating. I stepped closer and tried to make out some of the articles—about astronauts, planets, black holes, quasars, big bangs, and strings. Then I remembered how much he'd loved physics and astronomy.

"Beer?" he called softly across the dim room. I shook my head no, then shrugged. The dogs hummed in a quiet way from their places beside the door, heads between their outstretched paws, watching Dayrell with so much love, it was as if those eyes were tongues, licking the distance he moved in. "Hey, Win, Bob, want some beer?" Two tails thumped up and down, then stopped again, as if the code were worked out in advance between the three of them. Dayrell put two saucers down and split a can between them. He straightened, waited a minute, then moved his hand, and they sprang up and attacked the saucers, slurping loudly. He laughed and went back to the fridge for our cans of Bud. There was a table across the little room under a window with the frame askew, obviously salvaged with its chipping red paint and the light that showed on one side where the edges didn't quite fit the wall. He sat down there and slid the other beer across for me.

The chairs were made of bright orange molded plastic with metal inserts on the arms so they could be linked together, the kind you found in bus station and Department of Motor Vehicles waiting areas. Sitting down, we were both a little too low for the table, constructed from an old door slab on four thick pine legs. That was when I noticed the floor wasn't just dirty, it *was* dirt, packed down, brown river-bottom dirt that sent up a musty earthworm smell everytime something moved.

"Early stage of furniture building." He waved the can over the table. "I'm getting better." He was soaking wet with water beading on his arms and shoulders and face. Tiny drops glistened blackly from the ends of his hair that hung straight to his shoulders. Reaching down to the floor beside the wall, he brought out a bottle of George Dickel, which he uncapped. Lifting the beer in a semi-toast, he drank some off, then carefully poured in enough bourbon to top it off. He sipped and nodded to me. When I discovered it was just on the warm side of cool, I made a face. The whiskey would help, I decided, and overfilled the can so it sat in a little amber pond for a moment before the dry wood sucked up the excess. I took a bigger drink and felt the warmth spread into my blood like hot butter.

"Fridge doesn't work too good," he said, and shook his head so the drops splattered the surface between us and a few touched my face and arms.

"Hey . . ." I wiped them off and drank some more with him watching me, his eyes lighter now, but still unreadable. The dogs came wandering over and put their brown heads on his leg and rolled their eyes up at him. He smiled and rubbed their faces and pulled their lips back to expose their fangs. They groaned with pleasure and thumped their tails some more.

A new bout of thunder and lightning set up and rattled the shack and trailer so hard, I thought about how easy it was for tornadoes and big winds to lift these places up and away. The dogs inched closer to Dayrell's legs and seemed to curl their bodies up and around his arm. The glasses on the crude homemade shelf over the sink clinked together, and the room darkened with each strike. The dogs began to whimper in a thin stream of distress, and strings of saliva dropped from their black muzzles. We both took quick drinks.

"Damn it, Bob, Winifred—no throwing up in here. You're okay now, you're all right." Dayrell moved his chair back and squatted down to embrace the dogs, pulling their heads tightly against his. Their bodies shivered in his embrace, but they gulped and buried their faces under his arms. The muscles lifted along his biceps and forearms, which glistened like wet pennies in the room's twilight, and my stomach got tight so I had to pretend to look out the fogged dirty windows at the storm and drink some more to keep my mind off the way my body was feeling a little too loose and casual. I was sweating and took off the flannel shirt and let the oversized tee shirt beneath slip down one shoulder so my bra strap showed. It was a clean, almost new one with uplift wires that cut into me, but I liked how it made me feel to look down and see the cleavage when I pulled out the neck of the tee shirt, which I did just then. When I looked up, he was looking too, and I grabbed the beer and drank more, almost draining the can. He reached up for his beer and gestured for me to pour some more whiskey in, which I did and then added more to mine. We drank and grinned at each other. It seemed pretty simpleminded, really, but I was perfectly happy to be there at that moment while the rain pounded the trailer as if there were a bunch of enemies outside, trying to break into our hiding place. The dogs cowered smaller, trying to crawl into a single ball in his lap.

"They're good hunting dogs, really. They just have this thing about storms. Never saw dogs would throw up over a little bit of thunder. They were litter mates, that probably explains it. Like two little kids every time there's weather." He smiled and kissed the two brown heads with loud smacks.

I understood now that that was why we were here, and I liked him an awful lot for this. I wanted those long tan arms around me too, wanted to bury my head in his chest and let him take care of me until the bad weather passed. It'd been so long since I felt like that was even possible, it made me shiver and drink some more, which was easy now, the way the whiskey slipped down, and I remembered those early times before I'd run away when we'd kissed and done other things I'd never let any boy do and felt my body tingle like there was a lightning strike too close by.

When I met Duncan, I had thought my troubles were over, that when I let myself into his clean-white-shirt embrace, I'd find safety, but I'd been wrong. It wasn't too long before we worked it out. I was the strong, practical one and he was the flower that needed encouragement to unfold. It was like taking care of a litter of baby bunnies. I had to hold my breath not to make a big strong move while we probed and touched so gently it was hardly there. Afterwards, he fell asleep like a child, and it was so pure, I couldn't bring myself to act on all the pent-up feelings I was having. Marriage can do that, I decided; it can make you better than you are for a long time.

In a few minutes, the thunder walked out of hearing and Dayrell released the dogs, who were happy enough to get away, as if it had all been something they did for him rather than themselves. We watched them follow the edges of the room with their noses, pausing once in a while to sniff loud and fast at some spot or stopping to lick up some invisible crumbs in another.

"You're still into astronauts, space stuff?" I nodded at the clippings and pictures.

He looked around. "I like it okay."

"You got a lot here . . ."

"Yeah." He closed his eyes and tilted the can to drain the last drops. "Want to see the rest of the house?" A smile tugged the corners of his mouth up, and he was staring at me with one of those looks that meant a whole lot of things, and it was up to me to figure them out. I watched the tip of his tongue lick the foam caught in the corner of his lips.

"I don't know. . . ." My head felt fuzzy, sleepy, as if resisting him would take an awful lot of energy I didn't have now. And my arms and legs felt like they were melting into that same hot buttery whiskey that was slathered all inside me.

You wait a minute now, Miss Moline, Grandmother Estes's voice said, don't you—

"Sure, come on, you want to see it." He stood, picked up the bottle of Dickel, and told the dogs, "Stay here." Their faces wore a mixture of

57

understanding and grief as they watched him start up the old wooden door that served as a ramp into the trailer. He held his hand out behind him to pull me through the doorway and I had to follow him just to escape the nagging in my head.

"Look here." He touched my shoulder and I turned to see a whole wall and the ceiling covered with dark blue paint and stars, the way they did at those astronomy places. "Watch." He went to the little half-windows on the left and let the chipped plastic blinds down, dropping the room into darkness, until I noticed the sky pulsing with light from the stars arching in waves overhead.

"It's beautiful." I felt the room tilt into motion and I spread my hands to grab the air around me to balance on.

You turn yourself right around, Estes ordered. Don't forget what—

"Sweet, sweet Moline . . ." He wrapped his arms around me before I could protest the cheesy remark. Catching my face in one of his big rough hands, he lifted it and brought his lips to mine, holding my chin with his thumb at my throat. The kiss tasted grainy and sharp and lasted so long I ran out of breath because we'd found that odd angle that didn't let us breathe through our noses. I broke and turned my head to his chest which smelled of damp dog and sweat. He smoothed my hair, running his hands light and liquidy down my arms and back, over my butt, where he paused, stroking up and down, gradually pressing me into him. The voice in my head got real far away, like a fly trapped under a jelly glass, and when I lifted my face he was there again, this time his mouth more demanding, pushing mine wide open, his teeth catching my lips. I groaned, though I tried not to, and his breath quickened and he pulled me even harder against him.

"Come here," he said, and kissed me again, deeper, leading me in short stumbling steps. I knew where we were going, and didn't want to stop, his hands on my back pushing, on my shirt pulling, then down my jeans touching until I didn't stop his hands or mine.

We lay down on the mattress on the floor, shoving aside sheets and pillows, rolling and digging into each other as if we were taking the skin from the body, the flesh from the bone. He made me feel him before he pulled his jeans off, and I knew who it was—the one who teased my nipples hard, the one who spread my legs as far as they'd go, who opened me with his touch, who turned me over and kissed my neck, my shoulders, my back, who said remember, remember and made me ask please until he turned me over on my back and leaned above me waiting, say it, until I said it again, please, afraid to look in those yellow and green suns burning their way past my shame and fear, past my history, lifting me up, pushing myself up onto him as he met me bearing down and into me as slowly and carefully as that first time, watching me until it was please don't stop, yes there, please, there, yes, oh yes, because I'd never forgotten he was the first. I deserve this, I've earned this, I kept saying in my head to drown out the rest, letting the rhythm of our bodies whirl me down and around and around and around.

"You probably don't remember him," Dayrell said.

"I was pretty wrapped up in my own world then." I smoothed some tangled hairs off his face. "Besides, you were older than me."

"Still am, a little bit." When I tried to touch the scar on his throat, he caught my hand and kissed the palm. "Once you pass thirty-five, though, people start being the same age."

I took his hand and outlined the fingers with my tongue, down to the soft web where they met the callus-hardened palm, watching him close his eyes, suck his lower lip in, and groan. He raised a knee, then slowly relaxed it again. I liked doing this an awful lot, didn't feel shy, as if we'd stayed lovers all those years apart. There was enough familiar it wasn't quite the same awkwardness as doing it for the first time—it was more like the third or fourth, when you're starting to get good at some of it. And even though it was the middle of the day, we were taking pulls off the whiskey, which helped too.

"Your sister had him." His voice dropped and got dreamy, as if talking were the sound that went along with this moment. "He helped an awful lot of kids. Then the usual thing happened—somebody got nervous about all of us spending so much time at his house. Gossip started. McCall didn't help matters bringing beer one night and getting everyone high. School board ended up not renewing his contract. Didn't affect Paris or Mac MacDowed, they'd skipped three grades and were already on their way out of here, but some of the rest of us, well, it took the wind out of our sails, you might say. I needed another couple of years of tutoring before I could even apply for college, and there wasn't anyone left to help me, not really. My life hit a black hole and disappeared. Tried to study on my own, but it wasn't working out. McCall didn't like me being too busy to run around with him, gave me shit all the time. I don't know, I was young, trying to have it every which way, and then it all got settled, that one night with Marjean Tyrell, just like that. Everything fell into place." He rolled on his side facing me. "That's ancient history, though. Wheel of Misfortune." He spread his arms expansively, as if that made up for the pain in his eyes. "How do you like my palace? Glad you came?"

"We never got a chance to talk after . . ."

He shrugged and lifted my hand in his, measuring my short, stubby fingers against his longer, thick ones. "Didn't have much to say, Moline. Couldn't get you mixed up in it."

"So tell me, what really happened that night?" I closed my fingers around his wrist. He made a fist, twisted loose from my hold, and turned his hand this way and that, as if he were seeing something new and strange about it.

"We were drunk, Marjean Tyrell, McCall, and me. Hit a train—or it hit us. Car went over the embankment. Landed upside down in the ditch. It was full of rainwater. McCall pulled me out. Marjean . . . Marjean didn't make it. I did seven years because I was driving. Drunk. I killed her." He let his fist land softly on the mattress between us.

I wanted to say that wasn't right, he'd left something out. "You were hurt, though. . . ."

"Hairline skull fracture, cuts. Whole thing's fuzzy, most of it missing. But McCall was there, he remembers, even though he hit his head pretty good too. He told me what happened."

"What's the last thing you remember about that night?"

He shook his head. "Last thing I remember was sneaking ice out of Ma's freezer for the cooler while McCall stole the beer and whiskey from Hale's stash cause we were broke. Nothing after that. It's just gone. I woke up three days later in the hospital saying my name and address over and over in my head. Guess the jury never believed me." He picked up the little silver cross hanging off to one side of his neck and began rubbing it with his thumb.

I'd snuck out in my pajamas at eleven that night to meet Dayrell like we'd planned. He was driving at that point, and we'd gone to the cemetery to drink beer and neck by the creek on an old blanket he kept in the trunk. McCall left to pick up Marjean. Dayrell was getting too drunk and obnoxious, though, and when McCall came back, it took both of us to drag him into the backseat. Although it was midnight, I was so pissed, I took off walking. A few blocks later I ran into Titus. The crash wasn't but fifteen or so minutes later. You could hear the train blowing its warning whistle all over town, the screech of metal on metal, then nothing. I was in my pajamas or I would've gone with Titus to see what it was. I was climbing in my bedroom window when the rescue sirens started, and remembered the sense I had that something terrible was galloping toward me at that moment.

I wanted to go to the sheriff and try to convince him that maybe it was McCall driving after all. At least stand up for Dayrell at the trial. I tried to tell Mister that and got beat up for the answer. Tried to talk to McCall about it and almost got killed. That was when I ran and Dayrell went to prison.

Now how could I tell him that? I took a deep breath—should I tell him? What if his version was the true one? But what if it wasn't, and I could've done something to save him? Someone was going to lose either way. The jelly glass over Estes's voice lifted and I had to slam it back and kiss him fast and long enough that I got hot and wet again and didn't want him to stop, but he let go and turned on his side to watch me.

"We should talk about it, Moline." I looked away from those eyes backlit like citrine, a good cheap stone I was always attracted to on the shopping channels. "I got nothing to hide." He ran the cross up and down the silver chain.

He raised one of his scarred, tan arms and let his fingers trail along some path he found through the maze of light dots overhead. "That teacher died a year later. Drowned. They never recovered the body. I figure he's still out there someplace, floating in some dark hole they haven't named yet. Maybe Marjean Tyrell is there too. It must be like going into quicksand. It's not like you really die—you're taken. That's what I think. Maybe you're just out there waiting, hoping sometime someone will discover the hole, stick a hand in and pull you out. Who knows whether death really exists. With anti-matter and all that stuff, who knows what that is." He dropped his arm and sighed, rolling to his side and tucking me up into his body.

5

WHEN UNDER DARK SKIES

Of all the geologic features in Missouri, those of Karst origin are the most surrounded by mystery, awe, and superstition. Springs, caves, and sinkholes are often misunderstood by the uninformed. Even the early Greek writers of 300 to 500 B.C. were awed by the great volumes of water flowing continuously from the mouths of many caves. These writers believed that a vast body of water existed deep inside the earth from which the flow came and to which it returned by way of a connection from the floor of the ocean.

—MISSOURI GEOLOGY

I WAS SMOTHERED AGAINST HIS CHEST trapped in the smell of our lovemaking and the liquor on my breath, as if I'd never be able to escape that flesh and bone cave, and while his breathing began to slow and deepen, I inched away. His arms flattened against the sheet and I took a moment to look at the body I so quickly got naked to. Of course, I'd seen a lot of it with his running around half-naked the past few days to get my attention. There were other scars on his belly too, and a tattoo over his heart. I leaned closer, but couldn't make out the blurry letters inside the crudely drawn bleeding heart. I rolled carefully out of bed and crawled on the dirty orange and black shag to our clothes, which were still wet, moved over to the boxes erupting with clothes along the wall and pulled out a wrinkled tan work shirt, smelling it first. Aside from the musty odor, the shirt seemed fine. I put it on and grabbed a pair of ragged gray sweat pants from the top of the next box.

I looked up to see if Dayrell was stirring, but he wasn't, so I crept downstairs and out the door. It had stopped raining, and with the dogs at my legs I turned the corner and found the deck made out of salvaged lumber, some painted, some not, so the whole thing had a happy-go-lucky, circumstantial feeling, like a kid's fort in a tree. The air was dense and moist like the inside of a huge lung as I brushed the water standing on the orange plastic chair that matched those inside and sat down. I didn't see anything but mist lingering in the underbrush and trees along the creek, and the dogs pressed their slender brown bodies into my legs and whined.

The mist rose and edged up onto the rough deck planks. The dogs' noses found my hand and pushed into it, urging me to draw them closer. Their tails thumped the backs of my legs. I thought about my sister, Paris, in the black holes of space Dayrell had described, but it didn't fit. She was closer, more an immediate whisper, as thin and immaterial as the mist scarving the bottom land around me, climbing the walls of the trailer and shack, making me disappear with the dogs, only half-creatures now. I wondered if our feet and legs would be there when it receded.

"Paris?" I knew she was gone, but I had to try in case she felt like coming back like Bittman Bedwell, the family ghost, or the ghost dog at the hotel. Yesterday I'd gone to the cemetery for Memorial Day with Walker to decorate the last two hundred years' worth of graves on both sides of our family, and I still didn't know what the hell to do with her ashes. She should've told me what she wanted before she drank herself to death. I didn't understand my sister at all. Everything she ever did had been a surprise to me. "She was a hillbilly, what did you expect?" I had wanted to yell at her ex at the funeral, who mainly looked relieved not to be paying alimony anymore. "Look how she let the silver tarnish, stopped changing the sheets, started eating out of cans." I'd never understand her any better than that, and that was probably what hurt me the most.

The mist took the land and whitened it like a heavy snow, and Hungry Creek's swollen belly pushed at the banks in the distance, muffled by the fog so there was only this low suck and gurgle like a big stomach digesting. The dogs settled at my feet, disappearing and reappearing as the mist swirled and eddied around us. I liked the fine veil of moisture it drew over me, beading my lashes and lips, collecting on my hair, turning it curly again. The air smelled of wet green scissory stalks, fish heavy with muddy promise. When I wiped the railing, I was surprised to find that Dayrell had sanded it furniture-smooth. The water would raise the grain, though, and then he'd have to sand again. He should seal it with polyurethane. That's what I used to do, and it had seemed like I was making a statement, making the shine permanent so nothing could mark the fine yellow wood, blister or stain it, even though it couldn't breathe under the plastic. I'd wanted all the surfaces hard and bright and clean. I'd tried to raise our son that way, and it worked too well. Tyler's clean, empty face appeared the way it looked the last night he'd stood in the doorway of the family room staring at us as we watched TV. He'd gone to bed without a word. I had done it for Duncan. Now he was gone too. Heart stopped in the parking lot at Target over in St. Paul's Midway. What the hell was he doing all the way over there? I'd yelled at the emergency room nurse. We had plenty of stores out west of Minneapolis. This wouldn't have happened if he'd stayed put, shopped where things were clean and new. I'd panicked in the hallway of the Ramsey County Hospital as the prisoner in handcuffs and a broken arm eyed me without any expression at all. I never forgot that, nor the way Duncan's boy face had looked so disappointed and young lying on the gurney when they were through, as if he rose out of that fleshy cocoon after all those years to find himself gazing at an empty gray spring sky with only the parking lot cement as a pillow for his too-soft head and heart, and he meant to say, Is that it? Is that all there is?

But I had made that kind of life for us—for me—because I hadn't wanted to end up here, on the deck of some outlaw shack in the god-damned Ozarks. I hadn't wanted to be the woman with flat hopeless eyes on the bus going to see her boyfriend in jail, the woman dressed in a skrunken gray sweatshirt printed with the name of a fancy college she didn't recognize and a pair of jeans sitting alone in the prison waiting room with a paper bag of candy and cigarettes and magazines on her lap, the woman with the baby in her stomach and no ring on her finger who couldn't afford maternity clothes and added the pieces of a tablecloth to the sides of her skirt she tried to hide under the extra large wrinkled and yellowed man's dress shirt, the woman with the toddler in dirty diapers and another on the way while she was working ten-hour shifts at Wal-Mart, Kroger's, Dixie Donut until she couldn't keep her peeling vinyl handbag from slipping off her rounded shoulders, the woman with brown, broken teeth, the woman with gray skin, the woman with eyes that stopped crying after the last time she was slapped by her man, by her boss, by everyone around her. I'd grown up with those women seeping out of the hills down into the streets of Resurrection; I didn't need Mister accusing me of wanting to join them.

Fate. That morning when Mister told me Dayrell Bell had finally killed a thirteen-year-old girl and that's why he'd never wanted us around those Bell boys. They were bad, their families had always gone bad. But I wasn't listening by then, I was already feeling my heart being gathered up in the armload of dirty clothes that'd have to be forced clean again, scrubbed and wrung over and over until they were thready rags just to get all that hurt out. I knew then I had to leave my family as well as Dayrell, and for over twenty years I'd worked against that morning and everything that came before it. But it was like Dayrell'd been waiting back here for me all these years, waiting for me to come back and fill out the storyline to the bitter end.

At the cemetery yesterday, I'd suddenly felt how alone I was, with the breeze snapping the tops of last year's tall grasses along the edge of the creek and the murmuring of water that sounded like it carried the conversation of every single person who ever lived here, all talking at once. It wasn't a big, clattering kind of noise, it was a quiet kind of agreeable sound, like hundreds of stories being told one after another, one over another, with each one real and true, but not louder or more important that any other. I tried to listen, to separate the strands, but they stayed woven and pushed past me, dividing the two sections of the cemetery, the white one and the black one across the way up on the hill, toward the culvert under the blacktop and through that dark hollow, out the other side, on past the outskirts of town, into the fields and later the hills themselves, where the land erupted and obscured the little creek, pulling it deep underground into caves, then pushing it up and out again into rivers. Then dividing those and sucking them under again, and out again, leading and pushing and cajoling south, gathering for the final collection and sighing heave over Bagnell Dam, and on south again.

"Well, today's my birthday," I sighed out loud. Happy Birthday and So Be It, I thought as the last of the fog wisped back into the trees on the other side of the creek where the hills started. I stood, and the dogs stood too and stretched, their nails clicking dully on the dark wet wood. That's when I heard the noise of an engine whining and racing in the mud of the road up to the shack.

"Dayrell—Dayrell, wake up, someone's coming," I called, hoping he'd hear me.

"Grab the dogs," he hollered just as the mud-splattered Suburban slid to a stop. The stranger was too busy to notice me crouched down on the porch, hands locked in the dogs' collars. After a few tentative growls and yips, the dogs began to find their voices.

The man fighting the flimsy door was big and sloppy, his belly trembling as he kicked in the lower screen panel. "Where is she, Dayrell? Send her butt out here or I'm coming in!" You could tell he really didn't want to do this; there were big streaks of tears pouring down his face. "Leota Fay, I have to come in there, I'm gonna beat you to an inch of your life!" His lips kept getting caught in his teeth, as if he wanted to chew them down to nothing rather than face this thing.

Turning back to the open door of the truck, he pulled out a shotgun, but you could tell from the way he was handling it he hadn't done much shooting. The dogs set up a real roar, and the man succeeded in getting the screen door open. I let loose of their collars and stayed crouched there, afraid. The dogs poured like water through the busted screen and all hell broke loose inside, Dayrell yelling, "Win, Bob, down—now, Arch, put that down—Arch, don't—"

I couldn't stand it anymore and ran to the window beside the door. The two dogs were jumping all over the fat man, throwing him off balance, so he had to raise the shotgun over his head to keep it out of their way. It looked as if it could go off any minute. Dayrell was standing in jeans and bare feet, trying to give hand signals to the dogs, who had better sense than to listen to him. "Bite the shit out of that guy," I whispered. "Bite him." Dayrell stepped closer and Arch tried to lower the gun, but Dayrell locked his hand around the wrist closest to the trigger and squeezed while he quietly ordered the dogs down again and again until they dropped to the floor. Then he reached up and took the gun. Arch looked relieved despite how pissed off he was.

"Leota Fay is not here, Arch." Dayrell opened the gun and tried not to smile when he saw there were no shells in the chamber.

"Only wanted to scare you and her," Arch sulked, and ran his hands through what was left of his thin brown hair. His pink skull was so big and round and hard it looked like it belonged on a shelf, not a body. He looked down and saw his white shirt and gray dress trousers streaked with mud from the dog paws. "Christ almighty, Dayrell, look what your damn dogs done—"

Dayrell turned away so Arch couldn't see him laugh. "Want a beer?" He pulled open the fridge, which squeaked loudly on its rusted hinges.

"I guess." Arch looked around a little dazed and spotted the ramp going to the trailer. "She's up there!" he cried, and lunged, which set the dogs off again, tangling themselves in his legs until he stopped.

"Now I told you, Leota Fay is not here, Arch. Just take your beer and quit upsetting my dogs." He held the can out to Arch, who was clearly confused and torn between wanting her not to be here so he could have the beer and half believing she was. "Win, Bob, get out of here," Dayrell pointed to the busted screen and the two dogs slunk away, flopping down in front of the door, as if they'd misunderstood the command to go outside. Dayrell eyed them and took a long drink. The two dogs looked away sheepishly, giving a single thump of their tails.

Arch took the beer Dayrell was holding out, popped the top, and drank about half of it in one long gulp. He'd worked up quite a thirst with all these emotions. "Well, *someone's* here," he finally announced.

"And that's none of your business." Dayrell sipped at the can, catching sight of me hovering at the window. It was hard to tell what was in his eyes. "Told you it wasn't me seeing her to begin with, Arch."

"Gotta be McCall then. I know it's one of you Bell boys. She won't stay home—she's like some damn ole bitch in heat. I go traipsing all over the countryside looking for her—I got me a car-and-implement bidness to run too. You tell me, how am I gonna keep doing this and that too?" He sat down in one of the plastic chairs, which cracked loudly, with his butt and thighs spilling out like ten-pound bags of potatoes on either side.

"I told you last time we went through this to let her go. She doesn't want to be married anymore. Didn't you already divorce her once? Then you go and marry her again. It's your own damned fault. We've known each other since kindergarten, Arch, and you can be such a fool about a female. Go make yourself another pile of money at Rebel Motors and some new little girl will come along to help you spend it. Only this time you get Cope Harder to protect you first, not later in the divorce." Dayrell drained the beer and crushed the can before throwing it on the table. Arch finished his beer and belched miserably.

"I can't have you coming out here every time she disappears now,

Arch. Just 'cause your love life's in the toilet don't mean you have to keep putting mine in there too." Dayrell tugged his jeans up to his belly button, but they started inching down immediately.

Love life. How many of us were there? I pulled away from the window and pressed against the shack wall, letting the damp wood seep through the shirt and sink into my back like an unwanted arm around my shoulder. It's none of your business, I told myself. He's nothing you're going to tie up with anyway.

"Okay, you're right, I guess." Arch's voice came closer, and I had to scramble up the deck steps and slide around the corner quickly to keep from being seen. "Say, this here 4-Runner's from Minnesota. I shoulda seen that. Belongs to that Bedwell woman staying at her people's place on Jefferson, don't it?"

"I borrowed it, Arch." Dayrell's lie came easily.

"Yeah, I guess." The smugness in Arch's voice made it sound like a dirty joke. His engine started, and in a minute the Suburban was whining and spinning away.

"I gotta go. Throw the tire in if you're coming," I announced as I hurried through the door and up the stairs for my wet things.

When he didn't bring a tire along to change the flat on his truck at my house, I gave him a hard look and he shrugged. "How else was I supposed to get you out here? The dogs did need us, you saw that." He smiled and traced the side of my face with his finger, accidentally jabbing it in my ear when we hit a bad mudhole. I brushed him away.

I didn't mean to be so damned cranky, but the Leota Fay business got to me. It was my birthday, and so far the biggest present was getting laid after two and a half years without human touch. Well, I couldn't much complain about that, now could I? I was still wearing his clothes, and the crotch of the old sweats was wet from what we'd done. What we'd done. No condom. Shit.

Dayrell was doing his best to bring my mood back, smiling and calling me honey and trying to kiss my neck right below the ear where it met my shoulder. He didn't stop until I was giggling and slapping to keep him off like we were teenagers barreling down the muddy road with our hormones bouncing.

Back in town he kept his arm resting on the back of my seat, which made me a little proud and scared in case someone like Birdeene what's-her-name reported us to Walker. Green debris, small tree limbs, and trash blown up by the storm littered the streets and sidewalks, and by the dark sky more rain was on the way before nightfall. When we reached my place, Dayrell said, "Oh, shoot, look," and pointed to the bright-blue plastic sheet he'd covered the exposed section of Pearl's roof with, which had come loose and was flapping along the side of the house.

Sure enough, when we went around back, there was a sheet of white paper in a Ziploc bag held down by the wiper on his truck's windshield. It said, "You are Fired!"

"She's pissed." Dayrell glanced over at her house, where the lights glared from the upstairs windows, and we could see Pearl rushing back and forth. "Must've leaked. Daddy's gonna blow—I'd better get over there."

He started across the yard, came back, and hugged me. "Quickie?" he whispered.

"Get outta here—aren't you in enough trouble?" I swatted his back and he kissed me, catching my lower lip with his crooked eyetooth. It was a sweet pain, though, making me actually consider his proposition until he slowly pulled away.

"Gotta go. Don't suppose you'd consider coming over and helping? Must be a big mess with all the rain we got."

He was serious. Couldn't very well tell him I'd as soon harvest poison ivy. "I have to clean up and go to work at the hotel. I'm already late."

We held hands for a minute, looking at the muddy ground where I'd worn the grass away hauling out the linoleum.

"I'll—I can—do you mind if I stop by later? I could bring some supper." He had this crooked smile that made the right side of his mouth lift higher.

"That'd be nice."

"Okay, see you later." He sprinted across the yard and let himself in her back door, which was pretty darn familiar for the guy roofing your house. Then I had to ignore the chorus of Widows in my head on that subject and head inside to dress for work.

When I arrived late at the hotel, Walker handed me a birthday card that was so old the edges were brittle and yellow, but it held twenty-five dollars in well-creased fives and ones. Birdeene Cadmus had updated Walker on events at my house, but only mentioned Dayrell and me as innuendo. "I hope you know what you're doing, Moline," Walker said, as she began her long climb up the stairs to go and attend to Uncle Able, who was still in bed after hurting his back. Walker had been trying to shuttle back and forth between the hotel and their little farm, but it looked like it was starting to wear on her. So far she hadn't told me to go out there, although I'd offered. I kept wondering if maybe Walker and Able should go ahead and sell the farm to Heart Hogs, since they couldn't seem to keep up with either place, but I didn't dare mention it to them.

The David Solomon family (who had been staying at the hotel since the day after I'd started there) followed Cousin Pearl in the door. The Solomons waved hello to me and went on upstairs. Pearl walked quickly by each picture of our town's founding businesses on the walls of the lobby, ignoring the Solomons, but then I figured she would. Pearl wasn't against black people in particular; she was against most people in general. Although, for the life of me, I never could understand how she got from being the girl I played with to this woman with so damn much attitude.

"I need to talk to you." She came to rest against the doorframe to the parlor, her hands behind her, her body slumped tiredly. She looked more uncomfortable than me. Her white shorts and white cotton camp shirt were wrinkled and grimy, and she'd scraped her blond hair back from her face with a faded old blue kerchief.

"You look like you've had a hard day." I wanted to offer her a bath or a pop or something.

"Spent the last four hours cleaning up water from the roof. Barbecue at Copeland Harder's for Heart Hog investors got rained out or I would've lost the ceilings on both floors. It poured in. McCall was supposed to come over and help, but he never showed. Dayrell arrived just as I was finishing up. I'm batting a thousand with the Bells, I guess." She looked upset about more than the water damage.

"I'm sorry," I offered, but she waved it off. Looking at her, I realized we'd been estranged every since the night she saw me sneak out to Dayrell's car waiting down the block. I had looked up as I crawled along the outside of our house, and there she was in the upstairs window with a candle burning in her hand, showing her face in this eerie jack-o'-lantern glow. When I waved, she blew out the candle. Mister was waiting on the porch with his belt when I got home. It didn't stop me for more than a night or two, but I never spoke to her again. Now she looked like she'd felt a few fists herself lately, but it didn't give me the pleasure it once would've. It hurt to see it, as if we were both being beaten now.

"I've told Dayrell Bell to be on my roof first thing in the morning or I really will fire him. Dayrell is sweet, you know. He's just . . . well, he flies apart sometimes. He's not as put together as he seems. Prison changes a person. He's not the same as when you were sixteen. Things have happened. Just so you know. He's been with an awful lot of women, Moline." Pressing her lips together, she rolled them inward and glanced at the door. "A lot of the men here have changed—damaged from the war in Vietnam, the drinking, no work—they've had a hard time. Don't underestimate the kind of trouble they're in." She looked like she wanted to say more, but didn't.

Pearl moved up to the desk, wiping the dusty corner with her palm before she leaned an elbow on it to prop up her head. "It's nice of you to help Walker and Able, Moline. They're having a hard time keeping up these days." Tiny drops of sweat lined the white hairs along her upper lip.

I nodded and picked up a ballpoint pen and started scribbling on the old tan blotter.

"They can hardly afford the taxes anymore. One of them gets sick— really sick, I mean—they'll lose everything. Then what's going to happen to them?"

I had to agree again.

"Help me take care of them, Moline." She reached over and let her fingertips graze my arm before settling them on the figure of the horse I had been drawing. "Convince them to sell the farm to Heart Hogs. It'd give them less to worry about and provide a nest egg so they won't have to starve or be dependent in their final years. You know how that would be for them." Pearl brushed a strand of hair off her neck.

"Yeah." I had to agree with her here too.

"You'll help me then?"

"I'll think about it. They love that farm so much, Pearl. . . ."

"I know, but sometimes we can't have everything we want—we have to make trade-offs. They're adults, they'll come to understand that."

"I don't know, maybe. . . ."

"Well, I'm trusting you'll make the right decision." She smiled nicely, showing her small white teeth packed in neat little rows like buttons on a card. "Aside from all that, how've you been?"

"Okay."

"I better go." The earlier tiredness seemed to settle into her back and shoulders again.

"Okay. See you." What I wanted to say was that if she cared so much about Walker and Able, she should put in some hours at the hotel or the farm. But our conversation seemed to have exhausted her. She wasn't marching the way she had the first day I saw her; now she pulled herself along as if some new weight had been added to her frame that threw the whole balance and motion off.

I got restless waiting for Dayrell, and toured the hotel from the back kitchen to the coffee shop, public dining room, lobby, parlor and museum rooms and back. Once on my way past the front door, I was startled by the dark figure of someone standing just outside the screen, his face barely touching the metal. When I scrambled for the light switch, intending to flood the place, he stepped away. McCall. Then he was gone, fading into the dark of the empty building shadowing the walk on the other side of the hotel. I hugged my arms around myself, feeling suddenly cold and alone. Walker had said there was a shotgun, but where was it? What about my own gun? McCall had told me to stay away from his brother years ago. Did that still count? After today, I wondered. I thought about it for a while, then decided to wait and see what he was up to. Probably nothing.

When Dayrell showed up at ten-thirty, he'd bathed and put on clean clothes and brought a bag of barbecue in one hand and a fistful of fresh field flowers in the other, with a bottle of Cuervo Gold tucked under his arm. "Happy birthday," he said, and we kissed until the bottle of tequila started to slip. He still remembered after all those years.

At eleven, we locked the front door and went to the single bed in the back where the night person could lie down. All in all, it turned into the best birthday I'd had since I could remember, even having to hide the barbecue-stained sheets in the bottom of the laundry tub early the next morning. We didn't even smell the little fire someone set by the back door with paper and rain-drenched twigs, which must have smoldered for a while during the night before going out and leaving a black smudge on the rain-swollen wood for Dayrell to discover when he was sneaking out. When he came back and told me, we both laughed about the things kids did for fun, but it made me uneasy.

Something about it reminded me of the dream I'd had just at dawn about John Wesley Waller, the circuit-riding preacher people in the family only spoke about reluctantly, as if there were some shame or secret attached to his history. There was always a silence that appeared at the mention of his name, but it was a silence burdened with words waiting to be spoken, not yet said.

In the dream, John Wesley Waller is six-four, dressed in a black suit, with a black vest, yellowing white shirt, and collar buttoned to the top, no tie, too frivolous. In my dream I know these things about him, I am him. He's a circuit-riding preacher, and the seat of his suit pants is worn shiny and gray-brown from hours in the saddle.

John Wesley Weller has an old gelding with broken wind that roars like a train at the trot and gulps like a nearly dry kettle on a hot stove at the awkward canter which is more a scattering of legs too long and twiggy to do more than lurch and stumble down the road.

In the dream, a tiny silver cross blinks between the buttons of his vest, and I want to reach out and take it, but don't. I remember then how I used to have a little gold cross on a gold-plated chain, but Mister ripped it off the night he caught me sneaking back in the house in my muddy pajamas. I start crying with the blows of his belt across the backs of my legs and wake up. My eyes are dry, but my body is still weeping inside.

6

DISORGANIZED HEARTS

The five species of venomous snakes native to Missouri are pit vipers. They are represented by three genera: Agkistrodon (copperheads and the cottonmouth); Crotalus (rattlesnakes) and Sistrurus (pygmy and massasauga rattlesnakes). These venomous species are dangerous to man, and should be avoided. Even freshly killed specimens can inflict a dangerous bite due to reflex action.

—THE AMPHIBIANS AND REPTILES OF MISSOURI

※

THE NEXT MORNING Walker showed up in drag. That was the only way I could think of the pink and white swirled rayon old-lady's dress, which made her skin pale and sag as if the mere association with such a tired, shapeless piece of material took the style and shape out of her. The hem hung on one side where it'd come loose, and instead of her sneakers, Walker had put on some busted-up white old-lady shoes with eyelet toes. One of her bra straps kept slipping down on her arm, and she kept tucking it up like this habit had been with her for years. I checked the waistband to make sure she hadn't tucked a flowered handkerchief in the belt. The expression on her face was as tired and bewildered as the dress.

"Can't keep up this schedule, Moline. Tried to do something at the farm last night, but it's gotten out of hand. Lost control there a couple of years ago. Able dumps stuff wherever it lands, and I can't get enough help to keep both places going. Now his back's laid him up good and the animals have to be left to their own devices. Think you could go out there today and feed? Check around, make sure Odell Meachum and his crowd haven't been taking liberties with land that isn't theirs? Here's the list. Don't worry about the house." Her hand holding the paper trembled until she grabbed it with the other one. "Too much coffee again," she muttered as I took the list.

"You okay?" I asked.

"Don't worry about me, I'm fine. You'd better take yourself home and put on some barn clothes so you don't go tracking manure into my hotel tonight. You slept some, I trust. Nobody's bothered the night clerk's sleep in fifteen years. Anyway, you look rested. More than I can say for myself this morning. Go on now—scat." She waved me on and I left.

At home, the black residue from the linoleum was gummy under my boots, but it looked like the floors were going to have to wait. I was in my bedroom changing when Dayrell came in. "Didn't you hear me knocking?"

I shook my head and kept trying to pull back on my red boots.

"Cheap boots—you need something custom-made to really get a good fit."

"I'll need more than the job I got now to afford those."

He laughed. "You got plenty of money, Moline. What about that truck out front?"

I stood and stamped, feeling my heel land solid, then did a little jig and whirled around. He grabbed me and we hugged. I liked the sun-hot smell of his skin from the roofing. His hands felt warm and solid on my back, and there was this damp in the tee shirt he wore that smelled of the river bottom and the shack and the bedding in that strange room of his.

"What're you up to?" He pushed back, resting his forearms on my shoulders, tangling his fingers in my hair and pulling my head so I had to look up at him.

"No good. Wanna help?" I rested my elbows on his chest and leaned back so he was balancing me.

"Sure. Where we going?" He grinned and snatched his arms off me, then grabbed me before I fell. He'd always had these real quick hands.

The chicken waterers were full of mash, manure, and straw we had to scoop out, then lift the upside-down-bucket-shaped top to let new water whoosh into the circle tray. When I threw the handfuls of feed in the poultry yard, the two white Rock Islands fought the single Rhode Island

Red for position up and down the line until they came to the rooster with the green and black feather covered legs that looked like fur leggings. He darted his head at the quarreling hens and went back to claiming the last foot of grain in the sweep. The four Muscovy ducks ate by themselves, using their bills like paddles to scoop the food in. The three tan and gray Toulouse geese—from France, Dayrell explained—lunged toward me each time I spread more feed until I got to a place a few yards away where they would eat without bothering the others. It took them a minute to decide whether they wanted a piece of me or the grain. The tom turkey wobbled around and acted proud, ignoring me and the food until I walked back to the henhouse to fill the mash pans. Dayrell lounged around like a visitor at a petting zoo. "Walker sure has a variety here," he remarked with a smile on his face, as a goose tried to bite my leg when I walked too close to where they were feeding.

"I could use some help here, Dayrell," I yelled. "Get out of here, damn goose! Back—get back!" I made the mistake of standing my ground and it lunged for my hands holding the rest of the feed in a bag. When the bill pinched my fingers, I dropped the bag and shook the goose off hard enough to make it stumble to its chest. I wanted to kick it but made myself stop. "God, I hate those old things! They always bite me. Every single damn time." I looked at the red marks on my fingers and got madder, but the goose was oblivious to me now, rummaging in the gunny sack with its beak, pulling big mouthfuls out and gulping down as much as it could before the other poultry noticed.

Dayrell was laughing out loud. "Now we know why the Romans used them as guard geese."

"*You* come over here and try this!" I started to run at him, but my feet slipped in the liquidy bird shit and I almost went down. My cut knee jammed against my jeans with a sharp sting.

"Come here, Moline." He held his arms out and I slapped them away, but he grabbed me into a hug anyway, which felt fine. "You're so damn cute around animals," he whispered into my hair, but I could feel his shoulders twitching with laughter.

"Damn you, Dayrell." I laughed and pushed him away. "You have to slop the hogs for that."

"First one to the pen can call it." He took off.

"Wait! Which way?" I hadn't been there in so long, and the trees and brush had been allowed to grow up all around the barnyard and pastures close to the house. We'd come in the back way the other night, so all I could do was chase him. I wasn't very fast at sprinting to begin with, and now he was well ahead of me. My knee felt like the cut had rubbed open more and I was tempted to walk, but I didn't want him to think I was a poor sport or just being female.

"You're limping," he chided when I stopped beside him at the pigpen.

"Banged my knee the other night playing pig rodeo," I panted.

"You *are* a clumsy girl, aren't you? Might have to put you in training like they do football players to make them agile. Run you through tires and stuff. God, I haven't thought about football practice in years." His eyes went soft bronze and dark, and he looked back at the pig barn slouching several yards below the two-story cow barn. "Best be at it, Moline. I imagine the food's right inside there."

"You're not going to help?" I said over my shoulder on the way. The pig shed was a long, low, one-story unpainted wood building that was so old one end had collapsed and crumpled like it had had a bad wreck. The single pens for birthing were weedy and dry. The feed and water troughs were rusty and dry too. Cobwebs draped the rafters and beams with dusty designs. A few sparrows and swallows chirped and flitted in and out the glassless windows, but even they didn't seem to hold much hope for the future of this enterprise. I remembered the shed as a tight structure with an overwhelming, pungent smell that I had had to hold my breath against as a kid, racing in and out of there as fast as I could, even when I wanted to linger and play with the new piglets. The stink remained, but more as a steady, light perfume like a hay field in bloom.

The dirt floor bore the prints of chickens and ducks and geese as well as cats. I looked around at the stack of old bales of straw and hay stored in the end that had collapsed and thought I saw something white and motionless that had to be a cat. Ducking under a large cobweb with a big yellow and black spider that should've been out in the fields, I stopped a few feet from the white mound. It was a cat, a long-dead white cat, with legs and claws outstretched as if it could push itself away from what was hurting it. The head was tucked, though, almost to the chest, with the mouth open, the teeth exposed. The eye sockets were empty, but seemed to stare out at something that had made it furious, something the bared teeth were ready to bite.

"Poor thing," Dayrell whispered, resting his hands on my shoulders. "Looks like somebody poisoned it. I've seen the way they die from that." His hands tightened on me, and I let myself go back against him, the way I needed to. I'd seen it before too, and it was as if *he* were here, somewhere in the barn, hiding, the way he'd done the time our cat had died like this, or the time our dog had been tied to a tree and set on fire after Paris wouldn't go out with him any longer. McCall. Only Paris, McCall, and I knew the truth about the things he could do. Dayrell never seemed to see that side of his brother, always stood up for him, so I couldn't very well tell him what I knew then or now, and I wasn't *positive* it was him. Why would McCall hurt my aunt and uncle's cat?

"Maybe you should be careful about coming out here alone, Moline. Your aunt said things have been happening to the animals, now I'm worried too."

"We need to bury it," I reached out, but Dayrell put his hand on my arm.

"No, let me get a shovel. The decomposition . . ." The warmth left my back and I stood there, unable to take my eyes off the scene. I looked for signs of McCall or whoever did it, but of course this kind of death was always anonymous, cowardly, dirty only for the dying, not the killing. There was a hum somewhere, like bees murmuring in the dusk back here in the ruined part of the barn. It grew louder, more insistent, and I tried to follow the sound with my eyes, searching the bales of hay and straw darkened with rot.

"Here, move a little now." Dayrell led me to the side of the aisle, nearer the hum, swarming louder behind me as if the bees were gathering like clouds for a storm.

The shovel fit easily, lifted neatly, and with a small gray powdery sigh, the cat collapsed into the shallow plate, a flat mass of mottled fur and tiny bones.

"Oh . . ." I whispered, and felt as if we'd seen something we weren't allowed to—like a soul released and taken.

Dayrell stood there for a moment, as if he too were aware of what was happening; then he turned and the buzzing grew louder still. He stopped, having heard it for the first time, and followed the sound with his eyes until he was watching something behind me. "Moline," he said in a low voice "start moving slowly away from those bales. Don't jump—just slide your feet forward and go on ahead of me."

Then I knew what I'd heard, and my skin grew cold and hot both and my heart leapt against my chest like a dog at a door. I could barely hear it now for the blood flushing in my ears. My eyes got sleepy and wouldn't focus when I turned around and tried to see the big bronze and black diamonded body, thick as Dayrell's forearm, impossible number of curves, lying on the bales of straw next to me, with its head jutting up and out and the mouth—

"Moline, listen, do what I say now. You're not in any danger, just slide out—come on now, I'll take care of it." His voice was quiet and confident and I let it lead me where I wanted to go, toward the dim sunlight at the other end of the shed. But I didn't do it the way he said; I lunged and ran as hard as I could until I was way far outside, panting in the weeds and looking all around me for anything else that would attack.

He burst out of the dark holding the shovel and shaking his head. "You don't listen to anyone, do you?" He set the shovel down flat so the cat wasn't disturbed and walked to where I squatted, and stood over me with his hands on his hips. "What if that'd been a rattler? You didn't help me out there. Lucky it was only a big old bull snake, Moline, or I wouldn't be standing here." He was frowning and his lips were thin and angry looking. The blood vessel under his left eye jumped blue.

"You had the shovel," I offered, but knew he was right.

"Moline . . ."

"I couldn't stop myself. I'm sorry, Dayrell." I stood and put my hands on his wrists, liking how they didn't go all the way around. "Really, I'm sorry. I lost it."

He looked down at me with his eyes hooded and skeptical for a minute, then he relaxed and dropped his arms and I put my arms around his waist and kissed his chest through his faded tee shirt. He hugged me too hard, squeezing some of the breath out of me.

"Dayrell—" I gasped.

"You deserve worse," he laughed, and let go. "I'll take care of the cat and you feed the pigs, deal? That bull snake's hunting mice, he won't bother you. We'll toss the grain to the cattle together."

I glanced at the white form in the shovel that had seemed to dissolve even further in the past few minutes, so that it was barely recognizable anymore. "I don't want to go back in there."

"I'll pull the feed out for you."

While the brush and trees had grown up around the barns and sheds, the house remained relatively stark, with only two trees, a hickory in back and an old hundred-foot mossycup oak in the front to shade some of the grass, which was knee high and gone to seed. Walker's flower beds were tangled with weeds and dead stalks from last year, through which the roses and iris were managing to bloom. The front steps and porch were littered with dried leaves and half-dead weeds that had pried themselves through the cracks between the old limestone slabs. The wood of the two-story house was almost completely bare gray, and the chimneys at either end of the long roof were shedding bricks. The lower half of one of the tall narrow upstairs windows in the front had been covered with cardboard where a pane of glass was missing. Walking around the outside of the house, we found everything quiet and run-down. The back door was locked and I used the key Walker left hanging on a string beside the door, though the lock was so large and loose, I could've used a pencil to get in.

The mud room was waist high with pillars of old newspapers and magazines. Dried herbs and plants that seemed vaguely familiar hung in bunches from a brittle old clothesline strung overhead and dropped their slowly shattering leaves to the dirty orange linoleum below. The battered oak bureau against the wall to the house was lined with old jars of preserved vegetables and fruits, with dates going back ten years ago, waiting for God knew what.

The kitchen was worse. The stove, the refrigerator top, all the countertops, the maple table in the middle of the room, and the chairs around it were covered with dirty dishes, tins, jars, tools, canned goods, empty cartons, and plastic junk. Someone, probably Walker last night, had tried to clear the sink and wash some dishes, which they'd left soaking in a gray-scrummed water I didn't want to stick my hand in. The dish cabinets were almost bare of clean dishes, but I was tempted to throw out the dirty ones so dirty they were molding. Stuff had begun to accumulate along the floor, lining the walls and cabinets too, as if there were a kind of terrible, exotic organism at work here. And it smelled. Molding and rotting garbage laid the first, heavy putrid layer, followed by the higher, sharper scent of chemicals like paint remover and chlorine bleach and ammonia, and finally something light and sweet, like certain flowers just as they brown into ruin. The smell wrapped itself around us, licking skin, staining nose and tongue, and burning eyes like smoke. Then it reached all the way inside and blew into the stomach. That's when I rushed outdoors, followed by Dayrell.

We stood there coughing and glaring at the house. "What in the hell— how did this—what happened?" I choked.

Dayrell clapped my back lightly and cleared his throat. "Yech—can't get it out of my mouth."

"What the hell is it?"

"Garbage and stuff. They're old, Moline, they can't get around as good as they used to. The burn barrel's out there by the barn, and god knows how far they have to drag the rest of it to dump. They're probably not up to carrying it to the county dump site. Things get out of hand for people that age. And they're trying to manage two businesses. Look around."

"I didn't know. They seem so capable all the time. The hotel's not like this." It sounded lame, so I shut up. I hadn't worried about them before, I couldn't protest too loudly now. No wonder Walker hadn't sent me out here right away. "What do you think I should do?" I looked at the grass to my knees and used the toe of my boot to flatten a small circle.

"Need someone to haul the crap away. Maybe I could get someone to come out and clean if we got the garbage out and the windows open to air it for a couple of days." He stuck his hands in his jeans pockets and inspected the house like it had possibilities again.

I didn't have any money, but I couldn't admit that to Dayrell. "I'll have to clear it with Walker and Able. They're proud people."

Dayrell nodded. "I could see about getting it painted. At least there wouldn't be much scraping involved. When we go back inside, I can check the upstairs rooms for leaks and see if the roof's good. Slate. That's good for a long, long time, unless a piece slips or breaks. Real expensive to fix."

Then I remembered his cousin and Heart Hogs trying to force them out, and I could understand everyone else's point of view better now. The place was almost in ruins. A few more years and it'd be beyond hope. "Maybe Odell Meachum has the right idea. Maybe they should sell."

Dayrell searched my face, then sucked his full lower lip in and studied the house and yard some more. "What's over there?" He pointed to the pasture to the right of us with the square wrought-iron fence and half-tumbled stone fireplace shaded by two huge chestnut trees.

"Old cemetery. Early settlers whose house burned there started it. There's some other Rainses in there too. Ones nobody was supposed to know about in the war. I suppose when the drain basin gets built, it'll be under fifteen feet of pig shit."

"No, we can't let that happen." Dayrell took a step toward it, then looked at me. "Come on. Let's go back in the house and make sure things are okay, and then we'll go back to town and make some calls and get started cleaning this place. You up for it?" He smiled and pulled his red handkerchief from his back pocket and handed it to me to cover my nose and mouth. Then he pulled off his tee shirt and tied it around the lower part of his face. "Looks like we're ready to rob the place." Dayrell's words were muffled by the cloth.

"It's in the blood. Let's go." I waved and walked toward the back steps again.

We opened as many windows as we could, figuring water damage from rain wouldn't be any worse than what was going on now. The doors to the rooms upstairs were all shut, which had kept the stench down, and we left them that way, but with the windows open. Actually, the upstairs looked pretty neat and unlived-in. Able must have been having trouble climbing the stairs, so he'd taken to sleeping on the main floor, where there were two bedrooms and a half-bath. Probably bathing at the hotel. It made me sad and ashamed that I hadn't thought more about them before. They'd always been there, as perennial as the plants and the animals, so it didn't seem like they needed anything from anybody. I never expected them to do anything but what they'd been doing forever.

The dining room and living room were organized into discrete sections, with piles of clothes, birdcages, old tools and pieces of harness, rope, chain, stacks of mail and circulars, more magazines and newspapers, bags of folded paper bags, boxes of bottles for recycling, boxes of plastic containers, wrapping paper, Christmas presents wrapped, boxes of Christmas candy, pencils and pens in neat rubber-banded groups, pictures in frames, books, books, books. To sit down anywhere, you'd have to spend half an hour clearing. From what Walker had said, it was mostly Uncle Able out here by himself. No wonder the house was breeding the same disorder as the sheds and barns. He was such a putterer and saver, nothing ever got thrown away.

In the smaller of the two downstairs bedrooms, which it seemed Walker had been using, I found a big heap of dirty clothes spilling out of the closet across the floor. From the stains and ground-in dirt, they had obviously been worn many times without washing or cleaning. It made tears come to my eyes to remember her on the hotel porch in that old lady outfit she'd been reduced to wearing this morning.

I looked up at Dayrell, who was opening windows as fast as he could to escape the smell. "Can you check the washer in the basement?" He started to put me off but noticed my face and quickly left. I knew the answer, even if the machine was okay, neither of them was in much shape to go up and down those steep, narrow basement steps. Then it occurred to me that Walker and Able probably both used the old single-person elevator in the back of the hotel when I wasn't around.

"Not working. Looks like there was some kind of flooding and the washer was damaged. Besides that, those stairs are suicidal. One tilted and almost dumped me going down." He looked at the pile of clothes. "Want me to rustle up something to put those in?"

"Maybe sheets or pillowcases from the linen closet upstairs. And check the other bedroom down here. I think they're sleeping separate. He's probably got his own heap." I stood up. "Poor Walker and her pride," I murmured. Even if we had to have a fight about it, I was going to make her let me help. I'd tell her I needed to stay out here and protect things. I'd tell her we needed to fix things up so she could argue her case against the hog people better. I'd tell her anything so they wouldn't have to live like this or lose it as a result. They were old, but it didn't mean they deserved this. I wished Pearl could see this, then she might not push so hard on Walker. Then again, maybe she knew and felt that was the only way to save them, to keep them from going under someday. She probably had been here, smelled it, and thought that a manure basin was the best solution. I just couldn't though, I'd loved this place in my mind for too many years to let it stop being here.

We spent the rest of the day trying to clear the worst of the garbage out and do dishes. On the way back to town, with the windows open in my truck and the air conditioning blasting because the back end was full of clothes that had brought some of the smell with them, Dayrell and I planned the discussion with Walker and Able. We drove straight to Wray's One Way Laundry By The Pound and Dry Cleaners in the strip mall by the Wal-Mart and had to go around back to haul the clothes right to the big industrial-sized machines ourselves. Wray himself promised to get them done by noon the next day. He didn't even wrinkle his nose at the sight or smell, but he'd been in that chemical wonderland so long, I doubted he had much taste or smell left.

It was seven-thirty and the sun had slipped down while we were driving back to town, and there was this nice green and apricot early summer light lingering across the buildings and lawns and even the trailer homes, making things look soft and hopeful, not worn out and discouraged. I was driving and Dayrell had his hand resting on my leg like I used to do on his when we drove around as kids. It sent little lines like warm wires up and down my leg, and to other places too, and I wondered if that was what he'd felt all those years ago. If that was the kind of thing that had led him back to me, night after night, when I'd sneak out after everyone was asleep and drive around with him in my pajamas until he found a dark place to park and we'd move to the backseat of his '55 Chevy, and start with me across his lap sitting up, and soon be lying down, the cool Naugahyde rolls turning sticky and warm beneath our bodies. Or he'd take the wool army blanket that smelled like gasoline and hot dust from the trunk and spread it out so we could lie down in our clothes, the full length of our bodies pressed together. The first time we did that, it took me a while to move anything, it was such a breathless feeling, the parts fitting against each other the way they did in books, the way they should. I started with my toes, finding his, touching bare skin to bare skin, the most naked thing I'd done in my life.

After that he'd unbuttoned our tops, then unbuttoned his jeans, and took my hand and put it there. When I started trembling, I couldn't tell if it was excitement or fear at what was there, waiting for me. I stopped him when he tried to pull my pajama bottoms off. This was before the cave and I couldn't do it yet. Not yet, I'd told him, please, I'm afraid. And he'd kissed me and pulled me against him harder so I could feel it there, waiting, trying to wait and get in both. I touched it, letting his hand teach me, and when it got harder and harder, I knew what to do, and his whole body went rigid, and I made it happen, made him cry out with that lonely, sad cry that was always to be his in my memory. And it was that cry that finally made it all right for me to trust him, to take him to the cave because I couldn't do such a thing open in the world, and because we didn't have money for a motel and everyone knew us anyway, and because I wanted it to happen in a place that would always be there, forever, way past us. And I wanted it dark. As dark as being with Dayrell felt like.

"Ice cream," he said, moving his hand to the wheel. "Pull in here."

The Dairy Daddy lot held a few cars full of parents and kids having their after-supper treat, but it was too early for couples yet. "Just a cone," I told him when he climbed out. "Plain vanilla," in case they'd gotten fancy like a lot of those stands. It couldn't possibly be as good as it used to be, I cautioned myself; don't expect anything. In fact, that's why I'd held off on the ice cream before this.

The line was long, and I got tired of watching him standing in it, so I looked uptown at the big four-story Resurrection red brick county courthouse, which held all the other buildings in neat obedience around its square. As if it sat on a hill, the rest of town seemed to slope and tumble away, the houses and businesses becoming smaller and smaller, turning into sheds and trailers and shacks by the outskirts. To the north of town was the start of Little Dixie, with the remnants of huge, rambling plantation houses stranded at the ends of long gravel driveways fenced off by barbed wire and Keep Out signs while the cattle and hogs freely roamed what was left of the grass in the yard. On the eastern side of town was the black community in the hilliest, most wooded area, where the streets even now petered out into muddy ruts or dead ends. To the west was where all the new business was coming, malls and factories, as if that opening into opportunity naturally followed the old explorer and pioneer trails launched from here. The Rains farm was southwest of town, on the edge of the hills, along with the old Bedwell and Waller homesteads. And directly south were the hills, the start of the Ozark Mountains, the Lake of the Ozarks, and the kind of mysterious shadowy light that both invited and warned you to watch yourself.

"Moline." The man's face at the window startled me, and I jumped and leaned away from him.

"Titus—oh."

"Got a minute?" He stood up and came around to the passenger's side.

"Yeah, I guess." I said to his big body filling the seat beside me.

"How you been?" He looked me over.

"Okay. You?"

"I'm doing all right."

We sat there a moment staring out the windshield. I hadn't spoken to him since that dawn he'd put me on the bus to Omaha, my face and arms bruised from McCall. I left because of him and my father, even though it meant leaving Dayrell in jail. I'd found Titus's name in the Resurrection phone book when I first got back, but I'd been putting off seeing him. All those years without a card or a call, he probably wasn't missing me too much at this late date. I'd never sent him my address, just a note about getting married and moving to Minneapolis. It was important to be naked of the past in my new life. I'd almost made it.

"Smells funny in here." He wrinkled his nose and looked around the truck as if we were hauling garbage or something.

"We were just taking my aunt and uncle's laundry in."

He looked at me and raised an eyebrow. He still had the curliest lashes I'd ever seen, though he wore yellow-tinted glasses that gave his brown eyes this odd golden Technicolor glow. "You been out to the farm, then?"

I nodded. "Just got back."

"So you know what's going on out there? The trouble, I mean?" He began to crack his knuckles so slowly and painfully I wanted to grab his hands.

"I don't know about trouble. They say things have been happening, but I didn't see much except how run-down things are."

He looked out the windshield at Dayrell, who was fourth from the order window now. "They're pretty much alone except for their black neighbors. It's just the Rainses and the black farmers who aren't being offered enough for their land to be able to afford to settle anywhere else. That's because the corporation figures they can let those folks just go out of business and nobody'll care." He looked at me, bracing one hand on the dash and one on the back of my seat.

I tried to wait him out, but I couldn't. "Well, that's really . . . bad, huh?"

"Yeah." He started on his knuckles again, finishing with his short, thick thumbs, pulling each one and cracking it with a sound that made me wince. "Just thought you'd want to know since your cousin's involved too."

I looked up to check on Dayrell who was next in line. "I know. Pearl's even got a sign in her yard now."

"I'm talking about the Bedwells, Moline. There's two sides to your family, in case you forgot. Your second cousin Lukey won't have any place to live if they take her little strip of land along the creek. They don't need it for the pigs, but they've learned enough from other factory sites to be afraid of the runoff and drainage. Now they buy up the land adjacent to nearby creeks if they can. She only has fifteen acres, but they follow the creek. Some kind of cheap deal her husband made when he sold off the rest of the Bedwell land they got when they married. The land and cabin is all she has now for her two kids. They raise their food and live careful. But she's in real trouble. Her husband's trying to sign the papers and sell it without her. He'll blow the money as fast as he gets it, so she'll be out in the cold. No money for a lawyer, either. County Legal Aid is backed up to next year, and he's threatening to run her out if she doesn't sign."

I couldn't tell which side of the Bedwells it was, his or mine. "What can I do? I'm broke, if you're thinking—"

He looked around the fancy gray leather seats of my 4-Runner and nodded like I was lying. "You can talk to your boyfriend, though. It's—"

Dayrell appeared at my window and handed me a large cone with the ice cream already trickling down the sides.

"I'll catch you later, Moline." Titus stepped out of the truck as Dayrell came around to his side. The two men almost brushed arms, but ignored each other, and Dayrell settled in beside me, slamming the door a little hard.

"What'd he want?" Dayrell asked.

"Just to say hi, I guess." I stuck my hand out the window and held the cone there to drip until he handed me a napkin to wrap around the base.

"Yeah?" He watched Titus make his way through the crowded line and around the side of the building. "Lick it," he ordered, and I did. Vanilla, the real creamy vanilla that tasted like it smelled.

"It's exactly the same, Dayrell, how could that be? Thank you, thank you!" I licked as fast as I could to keep the ice cream from soaking my hand and shirt. He put his mouth around the top of his cone and sucked at it. "And that's the same way you used to eat it," I said.

Dayrell grinned and flicked at the ice cream mustache with the pink tip of his tongue. "Sometimes the good things are still the good things, Moline. Now hurry up and eat, I have to find my tools before it gets pitch dark out there and go work on your house."

Pulling out around the back of the Dairy Daddy, where the two picnic tables still sat under the dusty mulberry trees, I saw Titus with a large group of children, all eating ice cream with the concentrating look on their faces that I remembered from my childhood. I lifted my fingers in a half-wave. He gave his head a little shake and looked away like I'd already let him down.

Nothing in this damn town ever stayed simple or good. Dayrell was already getting me mixed up in a load of crap, and sooner or later if I kept seeing him, we were going to have to talk about the accident again. Titus would force me to if nothing else.

"Moline—hey!" We were already at the cemetery gates. I'd driven right past my house thinking about Titus and had to make a U-turn to head back. Parking, I was almost out of the door, but Dayrell just sat there, watching me without moving. "Something wrong?" he asked.

I shut the door again and looked out at the steadily failing light turning the streets rose and cinnamon, the houses mauve, the grass blue-black. "No."

He put his arm around my neck and pulled me across the gear shift and utility box between the seats, bumping my sore knee in the process, which sent a dull star of pain expanding in slow motion out from the cut. "Ow!" I stiffened and yanked away.

"What's the matter?" he said in a low voice.

"Nothing."

"Yeah, sure. One minute we've having a great time, next minute you're driving by your own house, acting like I don't even exist." He was looking out the side window at the two houses glowing weirdly blue-white, like a mama whale and her baby whale, side by side. "Am I really rushing things, or is it something else—stuff we haven't talked about?"

"No."

"Titus said something." He dropped his hands on his thighs, squared his jaw, and looked straight ahead like a man waiting to be sentenced.

"No. Come on—"

"I just don't understand. What is this? Some kind of game? 'Cause if that's it, I can do without it. I got work to do."

He was right. I had been pretending. I wasn't clear on anything except how I wanted him and knew it couldn't be any good between us. The feelings were still there from before, like those frog eggs laid in the mud waiting through a drought that dries the whole pond out, waiting until the cloudburst comes and they hatch, even years later. But I couldn't tell him the truth. I couldn't watch his face when he found out what I hadn't told about that night, the questions it would raise for him and his brother. My whole life had been locked up in that decision to run away from here instead. Everything I was as a person, good and bad, had issued forth from that one act—how could I set that straight now? I was too old to start over again. There wouldn't be any more Duncans after Dayrell this time. The Widows in my head lifted their eyebrows and tilted their heads like big curious birds.

"Moline?" His eyes were the color of sage in the odd evening light, which had turned his face bronze almost, except for the scars, which glowed white as tubers. He'd spent his life paying for what he had supposedly done. What right did I have to tell him it might not have been necessary? And what if it was? With justice like this, what chance did anybody have?

"Listen, thanks for helping out today." I glanced at his face, focusing on the black eyebrows, which seemed so odd with the silvery-gray-streaked hair. "I'm just tired, Dayrell—let's call it a night, okay?"

"Whatever." He jerked the door open, jumped out, and held it for a moment, looking at the side of the trunk and tires; then he took a deep breath and shut it carefully so it clicked into place without jarring my ears. He stuck his hands in his pockets, looked at me, shrugged, and tried to smile. Failing in that, he turned and walked with a tired drag toward the dull shine of tools and ladders in the dark grass next to Pearl's house.

I wanted to call him back, I really did, but there didn't seem to be anything I could do about the way things had turned out between us. Maybe if we'd been able to change something early on when we were kids, something not so pivotal or big, maybe put something in the place of that coming moment, that train on the track and the car racing toward it, something that would have kept the rest from flying away as it did. It was too late now, and that felt about as awful and sad as the ice cream slowly souring in my stomach.

7

STING OF DREAMS

In southeast Missouri old soldiers claimed that during the War between the States some men used to see the specter of a monstrous black hog just before a battle. This was recognized as a sign that the man who saw the thing would be killed in action. He told his comrades, made arrangements for letters and keepsakes to be sent home, and so on. It is said that a man who saw the black boar never lived more than seven days.

—OZARK MAGIC AND FOLKLORE

✳

IT WAS ELEVEN O'CLOCK, late enough that the streets outside the big front windows of the Rains Hotel were quiet except for an occasional squealing car or pickup of teenagers showing off for each other. Although it was only a few blocks away, I'd driven uptown, and the kids kept slowing down to envy my truck out front and spurting off again. It gave me a dumb satisfaction and kept me awake. I was sitting in one of the threadbare maroon satin wing backs by the front windows and nodding out over the pamphlet of town history when the screen door snapped shut. I opened my eyes and saw a man I didn't recognize at first, then I did.

"She here?" McCall slurred, his eyes squinting to focus in the yellow hotel light. His white shirt was streaked with dirt and sweat, and his skin glistened with a greasy, sick smell, though it'd cooled down considerably since dark.

"Where is she? Go get her." His eyes were bloodshot and confused. Although his boxy jaw was covered with reddish brown stubble, his strong features were so handsome you thought you liked him before you even knew him. That was your first mistake. McCall was a lot of people all at once, and he was different now than he'd been at the Rib Cabooze. Whatever this was, it made me shiver.

"McCall," I said, and cursed myself for leaving my purse with the gun in it behind the desk across the lobby.

"Who're you?" He wobbled slightly and reached out to steady himself on the back of the other chair, ignoring the greasy smear his fingers made. "Oh, Moline Bedwell. What're you doing here?" As drunk as he looked, there wasn't any booze smell coming off him, just a sick odor. His hands and arms were smeared with black grease and dirt, which he streaked through his hair and face each time he touched them.

"I work here, for my aunt and uncle. What're you doing here?" It took him a minute to register that, and I wondered if the years of hard living that showed on his face in lumpy pouches under his eyes and heavy creases from his nose to his mouth had taken part of his mind too. If so, he might be more dangerous than ever.

"Mo-line." He swung around and sprawled into the chair opposite me, his short, thick legs splayed out in front of him. The greasy cuff of his gray work pants touched my boot, and I pulled my feet back under the chair. He rubbed his dirty palms on the frayed upholstery of the chair arms. "What are you doing here?" His speech was still fuzzy, but clearer than before.

"Working, I told you." I'd never seen him like this, and it was scarier than his other sides. Who knew what this McCall might be capable of?

"They got you working here, huh? Staying this time?" He looked at me, his blue eyes having less trouble focusing than before.

"I don't know. Have to bury Paris's ashes and take care of some things here."

"Paris? She dead?"

"Died a couple of years ago."

"Sorry to hear that. Was it sudden—an accident? How was she doing?" He'd caused so much trouble for her when she stopped seeing him, I felt like saying it was none of his goddamn business, but I didn't want to risk pissing him off. So far he hadn't repeated his warning of years before, and I was hoping he'd forgotten about it. I never could.

"We didn't talk much until the end, and she'd only call late at night when she couldn't sleep. Then she died." I felt the familiar tug in my chest at those words, the ones she hadn't said, how she was busy drinking herself to death. The most important words always seemed like the missing ones when all is said and done.

The full Bell lips, which curved upwards in what was a sweet smile on Dayrell, turned cruel on McCall, when you noticed how his dead eyes calculated exactly what they could get out of you. That was what made him dangerous—the flat eyes that looked out of a dark place burrowed too deep in the skull for any human to understand. It was like staring into the eye of a snake sunning itself on a rock, just before the contracting skin ripples.

"Did ya talk about Resurrection, people you used to know?" he asked, his voice like poisoned honey. I shivered and wanted to back away, run upstairs or out the door. I didn't tell her anything, I wanted to say.

"I guess, some. I don't remember exactly."

"Talk about the Bell boys? Dayrell, pretty Dayrell? How about me? Your sister say anything about—"

"I—"

He held up his hand to stop me, and we both stared out the windows at the deserted street. I could hear a siren winding up a ways off, on the highway, then receding in the distance. I wished he would leave, but he just sat there, tapping his fingers on the wooden claw at the end of the chair arm.

Finally he spoke. "Sorry I busted in here. My truck broke. Had a friend haul it back here so we could fix it. Still waiting on a part." He leaned his head back, and his light brown hair streaked with silver and dirt shawled out around him. "Terrible headache. Took a handful of aspirin, need something stronger. Back at my place, need my damn wife to get it for me," he murmured with his eyes closed.

"That's who you're looking for?"

He nodded.

"Well, she's not here. I don't even know her."

"Ohh, goddamn pain." He bent at the middle and scrubbed his face and head with his hands. "Shit. Shit. Shit. Where is she?" He pulled his hands away, his face twisted. "You know her—her and that nigger Titus— you're all lying Bedwell trash. Where is she?" Before I could answer he reached across and grabbed the neck of my tee shirt, pulling me out of the chair.

I grabbed his wrist to stop him. "Get your hands off me, McCall, let go!"

He kept pulling me with the one hand while the other one held my right arm and squeezed so hard I thought he was breaking the bone. His eyes had lost their focus. He dragged me upright and shook me until my head snapped back and forth and I started to feel dizzy. Then, as suddenly as it started, it stopped.

"Here's your ole pills." The plastic bottle bounced against his shoulder, dropped to the floor, and rolled under the chair. McCall half-turned toward the voice of someone behind him I couldn't see because he was in the way.

"Come on now. The kids are asleep out in Dayrell's truck. I had to get a ride out and back to fetch the pills. You're sick, McCall, come on. Leave go of her." The woman's quiet voice soothed him into dropping his hands.

I scrambled back behind the chair I'd been sitting in to get out of his range. "You crazy bastard!" I yelled, just as Dayrell came through the screen behind the skinny blond woman, who looked vaguely familiar. I rubbed the back of my neck where the shirt had dug in. McCall glanced at me like I was someone he didn't recognize while the blonde picked up the pill bottle and pushed it into his hand. He quickly opened it and swallowed some.

"Come on, man. Go to bed and ride this thing out." Dayrell took his arm and tried to lead his brother out the door.

"Fuck you, Dayrell. Take your hands off me." McCall pushed his brother and staggered out the door with Dayrell and the woman behind. The woman climbed in the truck and looked like an eighth grader behind the wheel, her pale hair glowing whitely in the street lights. McCall stumbled down the street. A sheriff's car was inching past, ready to stop until Dayrell raised two fingers and the guy sped up.

Dayrell leaned in the driver's window and kissed the blonde's cheek, it looked like, but I wasn't sure. It bothered me a lot. I rubbed my upper arm where McCall had grabbed me too hard. Probably have bruises in the morning. Wouldn't be the first time. Son of a bitch was always putting his hands on me. "Goddamn him, next time he—"

"You okay?" Dayrell came in, catching the screen with his hand to keep it from shutting hard.

I didn't realize I was shaking until I tried to move and almost fell down and Dayrell was there and put his arms around me and pressed me up against his chest and held me there while I fought the trembling and weakness that made my knees sag. The tears came before I could stop them and it took a few minutes to get under control, but by the time I did, I'd left a wet splotch on the front of his dark blue shirt and the skin where the buttons were undone. I laid my cheek in the wet place on his chest where the little silver cross hung and kept my eyes closed, our skin hot and moist with my tears, the cross pressing its shape into my cheek. His hands smoothed my back like he was petting his dog, and when the smart aleck rose up in me and I leaned back to say something, his mouth was there on mine as I opened it. I pressed my hips against his and parted my lips more when our teeth clicked and let the tip of his tongue touch mine, then go deeper.

"You boys plan this?" I pushed away from him and his arms dropped to his sides. His face flushed as he looked at me with those eyes going from gold to gray-brown. Then it was as if he stepped back too, and I felt that tug of regret like I'd lost from trying to win.

"Sure. We got nothing better to do on a Thursday night. Tuesday's pig riding night and tonight's—well, you remember how it is." He rubbed his hands together, laced his fingers, and stretched his arms out, pushing on his hands so the knuckles cracked. He grinned meanly. "What about you? This your usual weeknight diversion when cable's lousy and the orchestra's off season?"

"You don't have a clue about my life, Dayrell." I felt my body cooling off and the tiredness hit again.

He folded his arms across his chest, covering the wet spot on his shirt. "You're right, Moline. Why don't you tell me about your life—tell me why you showed up after all these years and went to bed with me."

His eyes were curious now—not angry or mean, just questioning. There might or might not be sympathy in them. I let myself look at his mouth finally, the wide lips with the shape that knew how to find what it was I was trying to hide in my body. If we never said a word, if we simply lay down once again and I could feel that mouth on my skin, on my lips, again, I wouldn't stop, I wouldn't run, I wouldn't let him run. But I knew that was a lie as soon as I thought it.

"Let's sit down, Moline—you look tired." He moved to the chair McCall had turned in the scuffle.

"I'm not tired."

"Sit down." He moved our chairs closer and sat down, without taking his eyes off me until I sat opposite him. I didn't let myself relax, though. I'm as stubborn as any Bedwell when it comes right down to it.

"What happened to you, Moline? Was your marriage that bad? You used to have such a soft heart. That was one of your best qualities—you had compassion in you, you believed people were doing the best they could. Now, I don't know, every once in a while there's an attitude. Doesn't surprise me you got into it with McCall."

"You don't know anything about me."

"So you keep reminding me. But don't be so damn sure you know everything." His voice got cold.

"I'm just saying—"

"Look, you were a kid when we knew each other. In fact, I knew you were too young for me. I knew I shouldn't be doing what we doing, you were too young and too trusting. But I couldn't help it. I started caring before I could stop myself. At first it was—" He stopped and stared out the window at something.

"Why did you pick me up after school that day? You'd never paid me any attention before. I used to watch you all the time with McCall and—" I felt something click in the back of my head like a gun being cocked. "You didn't mean to pick me up, did you? You weren't there for me that day."

"No, Moline, I wasn't." His voice was muffled as if it came out of deep layers of wool.

But I didn't want the words, not out loud. "Don't say it—"

"I was meeting your sister, Paris. We'd seen each other a few times— well, more than a few—and I decided I was sick of sneaking around. She wouldn't get in the car, though. She never got in the car again. She was seeing McCall."

"You and my sister?"

"Not for long. She ran through men like she was sorting beans, Moline. She was looking for something none of us had. I wanted to save her. I got it in my head that Paris could be saved by a man who could love and understand her. She was so beautiful and so full of life, I wanted to . . . It didn't make any difference. I realized that later." His voice thickened up, and I noticed that the wet spot on his shirt was drying in a dark, irregular stain.

"So what was I? Revenge? Second best? Get even and screw the dumb little high school virgin?" I picked up the history of Resurrection I'd been reading earlier and left on the table between us and threw it across the room, stood up, and went to the desk for my purse.

"I don't know. I saw you there," his voice followed me. "I don't know what I was thinking. What the hell does it matter now? Or then, either." He stared out the window without bothering to check what I was doing, although maybe he could see my reflection in the glass. I kept my hands under the counter as I slid the .38 out of my purse. There was a roaring in my ears, the one that used to come when I knew I was going to do something crazy or wild. It made my body go underwater, distant. I hadn't felt it in years, but I knew it.

"In the end, I fell in love with you, Moline. I was afraid, and I tried to stop myself because of Paris. I knew she wouldn't understand. Or she'd tell you things, and I was afraid if McCall found out, he'd do something to blow it for me. He did a lot of that in those days, until the—"

I came around the counter and went back to the chair and sat down, leaving the gun on the desk. "The accident? How many other girls were you sleeping with while you were teaching me how to fuck, Dayrell?" I said it, but I didn't believe it. I was pissed about Paris was all.

"Moline . . ." He brushed his hair back behind his ear.

"Imagine what I felt like the morning my father told me about the wreck. Imagine wishing you'd been the girl who died next to that person you loved." I couldn't look at him. I was feeling so sorry and self-righteous, I didn't want to ruin it. Finally, I had a chance not to be in the wrong here.

There was a silence, then he sighed. "Moline, I—you can't wish that—it wasn't that way, I swear. God, don't you know the only thing, the only thing in the whole world that I was grateful for after the accident was that you weren't in the car with me. That you weren't the girl. It killed me that you didn't ever write or call or come to see me when I was in the hospital and jail. I figured you were mad, but I thought you'd come and at least yell at me. But nothing. Then I decided you were right. You were a kid with a future. You didn't need someone like me to drag around behind you. I was going to jail. What could I offer? Later, I figured you just didn't care. You were like Paris after all."

I could've gotten the gun and turned it on both of us at that point.

"Don't you remember *anything* about that night? How could you be driving?"

He turned toward me, a warning look on his face which made me stop. "I can't talk about it, Moline—just believe me. I paid for it with seven years in jail, in hell every minute, every hour. And now I get to look at my brother every day of my life, knowing that the pain in his head came from the accident, knowing I put it there. He hasn't been the same since."

I wanted to say that McCall was exactly the same as he'd always been—crazy and evil—but I didn't and we just sat there. I wanted to tell him I was there. I wanted to tell him I was there that night, and that it might have made a difference to the sheriff. God, how I wanted to confess, but I couldn't.

We were so quiet we could hear the big clock over the desk click each minute off and the distant *whoo-whoo* of a freight train on the tracks north of town.

"I'm sorry, Dayrell." I stared at the soft yellow stone on the thong around his neck. Wasn't the cross enough?

"We'd have broken up anyway. You were a kid. I was too far down the line." We were both quiet for a while. Every once in a while the old pop machine in the back would gurgle and moan.

"Will you do me a favor, darlin'?"

"Yeah."

"You're going to hear a lot of trash about me, mostly left over from when I got out of prison—crazy times, drinking, using, McCall and me. Figured we were tied together and there wasn't anything to do but stay with it. Had to make it up to him somehow. I think McCall and I were trying to see who could die first. It was almost me. This scar on my stomach"—he raised his shirt and ran his fingers down its ugly curve—"knife fight with some bikers in a rathole bar up in Booneville. Took forty stitches and almost lost my spleen. Did lose my wife and kid—they moved to California, won't speak to me. Can't blame them. Took the heart out of me, but it got me back to steady work soon as I could get on a ladder and lift a board. Just don't believe everything you hear, okay?"

"I won't." There was too much I didn't know, like about his marriage and kid. Too much had happened. Some things should remain dead and buried. You lived with them, adjusted to their being a certain way, a certain kind of truth; the pain to straighten them out was greater than the pain of letting them be, like rebreaking a bone to get it right after you'd grown used to its crookedness.

"Listen to me. We were going to talk about you tonight, Moline." He yawned.

I yawned and looked at the clock behind the desk. Eleven-thirty. I was just about to ask Dayrell if he wanted to come back to the little room for the night when the screen door popped open and his two dogs came slinking in, wagging their tails low and keeping their heads down, but with their eyes raised hopeful as all get out as they squirmed in around his chair. "Bob and Winifred, what the heck are you two doing here?" The dogs were wagging their bodies they were so happy to see him, and dying for him to pet them. Finally, he dropped his hands on their heads and they took turns licking and being petted for a few minutes, their eyes winking with happiness and shame. "I thought I had you two all locked up."

"Yeah, and they weren't about to ignore that fact. I set them loose, figured they'd find you or be damned. I followed to make sure they didn't take off." Although Pearl's hair was shiny and brushed neatly into an old-fashioned pageboy, her matching blue and white checkered shorts and shirt set was creased with big wrinkles as if she'd been sleeping in it.

"Uncle Able running an after-hours joint now?" She cocked one leg and folded her arms while she looked around as if she didn't pass the hotel every day coming and going to work at the courthouse.

"Lukey needed a ride back to town with McCall's pills. I gave her my truck so they could go home. Put the dogs in that kennel back of your house, Moline. Hope you don't mind." Dayrell stood up. "Guess they didn't like it. They're used to sleeping with me."

The dogs wanted to jump up and down but settled for lifting their paws like they were marching in place. Dayrell let his arms drop and the dogs went to work nuzzling and licking his fingers as if they were covered in bacon grease.

Pearl looked at me and smiled primly. "So where you spending the night, Dayrell?" There was something about Pearl that reminded me of the Widows in my head.

He squatted and the dogs attacked his face and hair with their tongues, heaving their bodies against him hard enough to almost tip him over.

"You could stay at my house, if you want. I have to spend the night here." I looked at the dogs. "Can they sleep on the floor for one night?"

"Sure. They never get on furniture in other people's houses. They know the rules, don't you, Bob and Win?"

"Believe that one," Pearl said. "You want a ride? I took the car in case they outran me too bad." She started out the door.

"No, I better walk them back so they can stretch their legs one more time." He stood up again.

"They stretched their damn legs getting here, Dayrell. But whatever, I'm going back to bed. See you on the roof with McCall at sunup." She let the door snap shut and padded away.

"That'll be the day," Dayrell muttered. Having exhausted their joy, the dogs started to wander around the lobby and find their way into the parlor. I watched them in case they got any outdoors ideas.

He moved toward me and I stood up with half an urge to turn away, but I didn't, and he took me in his arms again. This time we hugged long enough for me to feel the growing hardness that made me press myself more against him. Hell, I guess I'd always been a slut, even when I was pretending I wasn't.

He breathed a little quicker in my ear, and I kissed his shoulder through his shirt and then worked my way down to where I'd had my face before, when I cried, and found the opening to his skin and licked the one place the dogs hadn't gotten, where my tears had settled between us. The skin was salty and sweet and he made a sound deep inside his chest and pushed my chin up with his hand and our lips met again for a long time. Just because I hadn't completely decided I could carry this off with him didn't mean I couldn't work on it. My tongue found its way inside his mouth.

After Dayrell left, I was too keyed up and tired both to do more than settle back in the armchair and put my feet up on the opposite one and let the feeling of his body stay on mine like a ghost while I closed my eyes and felt its good weight. Later I would come to see this as the first mistake I made (not counting coming back to Resurrection to begin with): climbing down off pride's horse and thinking it was all fine now. Things were settling themselves. Everything that was owed had been repaid. That's what Uncle Able and I had always shared: optimism.

I fell asleep in that armchair, and some time later woke up to the sound of something moving up and down the hall upstairs. A tiny clicking noise, like a dog's nails pacing on the old boards. It had to be the big black dog

that'd died in the fire when the Kansas raiders burned the original structure. Uncle Able used to say it kept people in their rooms behaving to
have that dog haunting the halls, and refused all kinds of offers for exor-
cism over the years. He must have been right; I didn't even open my eyes
for fear of seeing something. He told me he felt sorry for the dog, and
didn't want to send it away to live with people who didn't understand.
"There's obligations to the dead as well as the living," he would say. "It's
not like he ever bites anybody."

I wondered if it was that same attitude that made him decide to let that
first black couple stay in the hotel, dividing the family and the town and
nearly ruining his business in one fatal night. It was the last straw of
insults and injuries between Grandmother Estes and her sister, Walker,
that finally welded together the houses of the three Waller women—Estes
in the middle, with Iberia, my mother, on one side of her and Delphine,
her daughter-in-law, on the other side—in a permanent frowning face,
disapproving of the world that would allow such things and shutting their
front doors forever to the prospect of change. These Waller women were
extremely courteous to anyone of color they met, of course. Still, there
was a thing that went on in their voices, a high-minded kind of ring, a
singsong that let everyone know how they felt. It was something they had
perfected in their polite, brutal way. Even Delphine, who married Calvin
to become a Waller, learned it; and Iberia, married to a Bedwell, continued to do it, because his family had once owned slaves. Of course,
Iberia, being the stubborn one of the family, also continued to let us children visit Walker and Able when she needed a break—which was often,
as it turned out.

The Waller women did not prevail with Able, however, and he never
explained to anyone why he let that black couple stay the night with their
small children. Helped them with the luggage down the stairs and into
the trunk of that dusty, dark-blue Buick from Illinois, and waved goodbye
to them while Fletta and Helbert Overfelt from the Methodist church
came to a dead stop in the street and stared until traffic backed up. Fletta
later blamed her stroke on that incident. The Reverend Gully Foye gave a
sermon about the tribes of Israel being separate for a reason that next
Sunday morning, and Walker and Able officially stopped being
Methodists that Sunday noon.

The Rains Hotel hung on despite the boycott, and over the years, growing shabbier, it had simply been the victim of its own failure to move ahead. There were no TVs in the rooms and only pay phones in the halls. Uncle Able believed a person needed a night's rest when they stopped, not entertainment. He had good hard beds, clean cotton sheets, and soft feather pillows. And the ghost dog, which kept its vigilance going long enough for me to wonder whether if I did open my eyes, I would catch a glimpse of it. Was that good or bad? Walker might know, but only Lady LeFay and my granny Bedwell in the hills could have been trusted to tell and tell it true. Why was it that people were always dead and gone by the time you realized you needed to talk to them?

The clicking reminded me of Bittman Bedwell, our ghost, the one Mister and Iberia pretended wasn't a relative. When the raiders burned the first Rains Hotel, they also took the school and the library, which was the only one in a hundred miles, even though people begged them not to. No one in Resurrection has ever forgiven a person from Kansas for that, either. These were men who claimed to be abolitionists come to free the slaves, or at least offer them a better deal working in Kansas when they left Resurrection with fifteen wagonloads of "freed goods" in addition to the black people they'd liberated with promises of wages, which turned out to be barely enough to stay alive on. At least they were free, Walker always reminded us, and that means everything; the rest doesn't matter as much.

The headless ghost of Bittman Bedwell, which people claimed to see around the Royale Theater that eventually got built on the library site, using some of the same bricks for foundation and walls, was said to have started the whole thing with the raiders. Bittman Bedwell had died in 1850 in what the newspaper referred to as a freak accident. A beheading always seemed like more than a freak accident, but no one in the family would ever admit that he was a witch. We've always had a tradition of calling things accidents when we don't like the truth. For some reason which was never explained, Bittman's ghost took up residence in the library, built from the very first batch of Resurrection brick. Although people tried to warn the raiders to stay away from the library, the raiders declared they had their own ways of dealing with Ozark witchcraft. When he started throwing books and chairs at their drunken revelry, they tried to burn him out, but the fire took five of their lives instead and burnt up every single book. Everyone in town knew Bittman wouldn't stand for noise in the library.

Letting go of the edges into sleep, I reminded myself to go to the theater and see Bittman Bedwell again. After all, he was a relative.

The next time I woke up it was because of a dream with that old-fashioned circuit-riding preacher in a black frock coat and stern flat-brimmed black hat trying to hand me something. Switching the Bible to the right, he held his left hand up. There was the picture of the tree bursting into flames, the clouds heavy as sin holding their bellies to the fire, willingly, the birds plunging against the fingers pushing the burning feathers into their bodies, and the smell of smoke which was so powerful I made myself wake up to get away.

But it didn't stop when I opened my eyes, although it was much fainter. At first my head wouldn't clear, my eyes wouldn't focus in the light. I waited until I could tell that the tick of moths and June bugs was on the outside of the windows, not the inside, and I could smell the smoke more distinctively, not as a dream aftermath. I looked at the screen door I hadn't locked. Maybe the fire was outside, but when I got up and looked, the night air was clean along the empty streets.

The smell disappeared once I left the lobby on the main floor and walked into the cafe, the old dining room, and the museum. That left only one place. I picked up the pistol from the desk and held it at my waist as I climbed the stairs and stood at the top. I'd shoot the dog or the fire, whichever showed up first.

It seemed as if the smoke was getting stronger, but I couldn't tell now, my nose was so full of the stuff, and I was breathing in shallow puffs I was so damned scared. I still had on my boots, and tiptoeing, which seemed essential, was impossible. The best I could do was try not to land on my heels as hard as I usually did. There were three rooms occupied on the second floor—a double suite with Dr. Solomon, the researcher, and his wife and child, plus two other families passing through. I didn't want to wake them unless there was a real good reason. Maybe someone was smoking, although it didn't smell right for that, too thick and musty.

The fifteen-watt bulbs in the wall sconces didn't do more than glow yellow-brown in the dark, but I could see that at the far end of the hallway, the tall windows with the red Exit sign above them were closed. I remembered leaving them open. In front of the window there were two low antique parlor chairs with shredded gray brocade upholstery and popped stuffing, no arms and high backs, the seats set extra low for ladies to perch on. In the dim light they seemed shrouded in fog.

But it wasn't fog. One of the seats glowed. "Oh my God, it's on fire." I ran down the length of the hall just in time to see flames starting to take hold in the center of the seat, which had been dug out to form a nest so the loose stuffing would burn faster. It was so old and packed, though, it hadn't done more than smolder for who knew how long. I looked around for something to put the fire out quickly and ended up yanking my shirt off and pushing it down into the hole, swearing "Jesus Christ, Jesus Christ." I could feel the heat pushing against my fists and rushing up my arms, but I didn't stop until I felt it give. As I pulled my scorched shirt out, the other chair sat in dumb witness to the black smudged back and charred seat. It was lucky the flames hadn't eaten down instead of up, or the wood floor would've taken the fire through the whole place. Goose bumps ran across my chest and down my arms when I thought of the people trapped in their rooms, choking on the clouds of smoke as the floor beneath them disappeared into a pit of fire. There's a small child here, I wanted to yell at whoever had done this, are you crazy? Tears from the stinging smoke ran down my face.

I was lucky I didn't run into anybody on my way down the stairs lugging the still-smoking chair well guarded with the gun stuck in the waistband of my jeans. I was even luckier I'd worn an undershirt instead of a bra. At least I had something on.

After I dumped some water on the chair and stuck it out the back door, which still bore the black marks of the first fire, I went through the lobby and turned on all the overhead fans and opened the windows. I knew I should go back upstairs and check around and open the hall windows again, but I was pretty scared. Maybe that's how he'd snuck in to begin with, whoever it was, and maybe he hadn't left, either. It never occurred to me to call the sheriff. No point in waking up the whole town, and I knew Walker and Able didn't want the volunteer fire department nosing around the hotel. Besides, nobody would stick around after a stunt like that, I decided. And I still didn't want to run into that ghost dog, even if he was trying to warn me. Lucky I had such a good nose. Hell, lucky I had that dream. And when I nodded out, John Wesley Waller was there again.

8

NOTHING BUT TIME

An old woman at Pineville, Missouri, told me that as a little girl she dreamed of a gigantic snake coiled around her father's log house. She says this was a sign of the Civil War which broke only a few months later, in which her father and two brothers were killed. In 1865 she dreamed that the big snake was dead, upon which she knew that the War would soon be ended.

— OZARK MAGIC AND FOLKLORE

"MAYBE SOMEBODY WITH HOT PANTS sat down." Uncle Able winked and settled the burned chair back on all fours.

"This is serious, Able. Look at the seat—God only knows what would've happened if I hadn't been awake." I picked up a black clot of stuffing and it crumbled into ashes between my fingers. "You should re-port it."

He stuck his hands in the open sides of his new denim overalls and rocked back and forth on his heels, his head thrust forward for balance as we studied the charred seat. It looked more pathetic than dangerous in daylight. "Not much of an arsonist. It's those dang Heart Hog people. They been sending me little warnings all spring. First time they set on my hotel, though." He pulled a hand out of his overalls and fingered a string of frayed upholstery hanging down the back of the chair.

I hadn't told him about the first fire, which seemed connected now. "If it's kids . . ."

"Not much chance of that. Wouldn't be kids coming inside to do this." Arthritis had humped the knuckles on his hands, but they were still strong looking, the hands of a person who'd earned his own way. His face showed the same history of work, with the weathered-in creases and wrinkles burned a permanent red so the silver stubble he hadn't shaved glistened. He had the wide thin mouth of the Rains people, with laugh marks like commas at the edges. When he looked up at me again, his light brown eyes were still bird-bright like Walker's, the only way they seemed alike except for the long faces. "Sure you didn't hear or see anything else?"

I shrugged and looked away across the alley at the backyards of houses and the cement apron of the old Skelley gas station that'd been torn out. Tall weeds waved at the passersby like young girls waiting to be stopped for. I wanted to say something about McCall.

"Moline?" His voice was weathered soft, too, but I'd heard how loud his silence could yell when something went wrong. He'd always been my favorite relative and I didn't want to let him down.

"Wasn't anything, really." He waited for me, pretending to look across the alley, but glancing sideways. I sighed. "Okay, I thought I heard that ghost dog clicking around up there before I smelled the smoke." I hugged my arms around myself despite the morning sun heating the tops of our heads. "Scared me—I didn't want to go up there, even when I smelled the smoke."

He chuckled and shook his head. "It's not the dog we have to worry about, Moline. He's never bothered a soul. It's the stray humans we have to look out for."

"Fine, but I think you have to tell the sheriff or somebody. This is serious, Uncle Able."

He tucked his hand back in the side of his overalls and rocked on his heels again. "They're trying to close us down, you see. Make us give up, mount the trouble so high we old people can't see over the top of it. I tell the sheriff, he'll tell the insurance folks. They'll raise the premiums. Had trouble enough getting insurance renewed last time—building's too old, needs too many repairs, they said. So you see how it is. We can weather it, we keep our heads and the shotgun ready. Big help having you here now, Moline. Your aunt isn't getting any younger, she needs you."

He put a hand on my shoulder and I felt the strength flow warmly down my back. I wanted to hug him, but it'd been so many years, I felt awkward, so I covered his hand with mine. It was the same argument Walker had used, only asking for help for Able.

"I'll do the best I can, Able."

"That'll be good enough then," he said. "Let's not tell her about the fire. I'll put this chair in the cellar and tell your aunt I broke it standing on it. She'll believe that."

It was my turn to look sideways at him, but he wasn't smiling.

"Thought I saw Dayrell Bell over at your house when I was up on the roof the other day. You can see an awful lot from that roof. Don't tell your aunt, but some days I go up there just to get some peace and quiet. See the whole town from our roof. Couple feet taller than the courthouse even. That's why the raiders burnt it that time in the war—it was such a good lookout point, the town was ready for them."

He looked across the alley as if he could see it happening as he told it, and I thought he'd forgotten about Dayrell.

"Bell boys. Watched them get in plenty of scrapes. Even as boys, coming in my cafe to steal candy. When Dayrell got caught, he'd stand and take his punishment, never lie. McCall was a different animal. Can't say it surprised me that Dayrell went to prison. Thing surprised me was McCall staying out." He stuck a hand in his side pocket and pulled out a tin of chew, opened it, and stuffed some in his mouth. "Now don't go telling Walker about this, I promised her I'd quit," he said around the wad. He worked on it for a few minutes, got it comfortable in the side of his mouth, spit a couple of times, and peered at me.

"Be careful, Moline. Prison's hard on a man, 'specially a man already wild for his freedom. Some horses aren't meant to be broke, got too much running in them."

What I liked about Able was his not condemning Dayrell for what happened, at the same time he was trying to protect me. I looked at his stiff new overalls and realized he'd probably bought those when the clean clothes stopped. He wouldn't for the world mention it to Walker or offend her by trying to do the laundry himself. In many ways, he was the most tactful, kindest man I'd ever known, and I regretted again the stupid decision I'd made at sixteen to erase my aunt and uncle along with the rest of my past when I fled Resurrection. Another reason why I couldn't let anyone hurt them now, not even for their own good, as Pearl was suggesting.

"I'm watching myself, Uncle Able," I said with a smile.

He eyed me and smiled too. "I'd say you're just as busy watching Dayrell, little sister. You always had an eye for that kind of colt, broke or not. Remember that time I took you to the auction in Sedalia to buy a horse? We agreed we'd get a safe old gelding you could take around the countryside. You'd saved yourself twenty-five dollars and I was going to put in the rest? Well, we looked at those safe old horses all right, but it was the two-year-old palomino stallion caught your eye. Sure enough, you convinced me, and a hundred and twenty-five dollars later we were loading him in the stock trailer in the middle of a pouring rain. Son of a buck didn't want to go in, remember? Finally whipped his butt with dry cornstalks they'd tied around the light poles for Halloween decoration. You got your way that time, and he turned into a real good horse. Had to hand it to you—trained him yourself by reading books. You were a good little rider too." He leaned over to the side of where we were standing and spit a brown stream.

"Only bad thing that happened was when he broke your back, Uncle Able."

He nodded and chewed. "Shoulda known better than try and get on that colt. Never had a man on his back before. No sooner got that foot in the stirrup than he took off bucking and running. Got real western."

"When you bounced twice, I didn't know whether to run after the horse and stop him before he rolled and broke my saddle, or stop and see if you could get up."

"Didn't blame you a bit. Your aunt was not happy that day, let me tell you. She was worse than the cracked bones in my back. Wouldn't look at that horse again until the day we gelded him. That made her feel sorry for him. 'Bout all it takes for your aunt to forgive." We laughed and shook our heads.

"You come on up to my roof sometime soon, Moline. We'll find out what's really going on in this town. Meanwhile, go home and get some sleep, you look worn out." He patted my back and spit again and shoved the toe of his work boot at the loose front leg of the chair.

· · ·

It was before seven when I walked quietly in my front door, but Dayrell and the dogs were gone. I'd half planned on surprising him. The house had that empty, just-been-left feeling to it, like all the air had been sucked away with the bodies that had disappeared. The only evidence that they'd been there was the one chipped and yellowed china bowl with the flower rim Iberia inherited from her grandmother Lady LeFay sitting in a puddle in the middle of the kitchen floor with an inch of water and some black dog hairs floating in it.

Looking over at Pearl's, I could see the kitchen light on and imagined them all in there having a big happy breakfast I couldn't join. No point in starting a poor-me party, I decided, and headed for my bed. I was so tired it took me a moment to realize what was different about my room. Jars of irises on the dresser and table and floor. And on the bed, big purple and yellow and white headed irises. I didn't even mind their sugary sap oozing green on the covers, they made the whole room smell that too-good sweet. I gathered up the ones on the bed, noticing how fresh they still were, and put them in the bathroom sink with the stems in water till I could get to them after I slept.

There was a yellowy-white one tinted with streaks of bronze that reminded me of Dayrell's eyes, and I held it as I lay down and rolled on my side. That was when I smelled him on my pillows. He'd slept here, leaving his scent behind mingled with the iris syrup, and I closed my eyes and let it take me to sleep.

"It's not the first fire, either, but he doesn't want to talk about it. Lucky Moline was awake from all the commotion earlier." Walker glanced at me out of the corner of her eye. After her call woke me up at noon, I came uptown to find her on the hotel porch with Titus who gave me a sour look and turned his attention to the traffic on the street, which consisted of a car or truck every once in a while.

"Didn't take me long to find the chair Able stashed in the basement. Smudge marks on the back door too. You should have told me, Moline," she said, her voice serious. "We got another call from Copeland Harder Jr. yesterday. That's how he announces himself, as if I didn't almost marry his grandfather, the old fool, and swatted his bottom more than once when he trampled my flowers in front of the house on Jefferson. Anyway, he upped the offer for the farm. Keeps insisting they need it for the earthen drain basin for the irrigated waste—guess that means the hog manure."

"Fifty thousand hogs." Titus tapped his fingers on the knees of his widespread legs. "Too close to the creek there—got two free-flowing springs right on the property. Cope knows. They all know, but they're pretending it's not going to pollute. Sure thing, I told him—that and spotted dogs don't lie in the road. Anybody not bought out will be driven off soon's we get the first flood. No more wildlife to speak of after that. Be one huge pig toilet for twenty miles in every direction. My parishioners got no place else to go. Looks like the man finally figured out a way to drive 'em out of DeWight County once and for all." Titus stared at me.

"This is all we have left, Moline." Walker swept an arm back at the shabby entrance to the Rains Hotel, whose faded red Resurrection brick exterior needed to be tuck-pointed and cleaned. The white paint on the wood trim had peeled and disappeared where rot had burst through, so the windowsills and eaves looked rodent-chewed. "We're not going to take the money and run to Florida. For heaven's sake, Florida's even hotter than Missouri—why would we move there?"

"I know, Walker."

"No, you don't know, Moline. You walked out on us. Not that I blamed you. I understood. But you never visited, never called or wrote. About broke your uncle's heart, not to mention mine. You were the only one we felt close to. Thought you cared about us. Then you disappeared. Iberia wasn't much on bringing news in those days, too busy making money ruining good land with trailers. White man's tepees. Titus was the only way we heard you were safe."

I looked over at Titus and felt the terrible shame I'd been trying to avoid all those years come bearing down on me like a huge hill of mud I could get buried under. He gazed out to the street, where an older black couple had parked their camper and were getting out and staring up at the hotel.

"You open?" the man called tentatively, and when Walker nodded, he glanced at the woman and shrugged. They came up the stairs and went inside. We all sat there for a moment until Walker excused herself and followed them inside.

Behind and above us, there came a rattling and clanging, and a pry bar dropped off the roof and bounced at our feet into the street. "Able?"

Walker yelled from just inside the screen door. "Get down off that roof this minute! I mean it." She smiled. "Old fool's up there patching the roof again." She looked at me. "Go stand across the street and see what he's doing up there while I check these folks in."

The front section, covered with sheets of tin, was slanted like a barn's, then became flat behind. The tin roof was mottled with rust and dull shine. Uncle Able still did his own repairs, pounding flattened tin cans over the holes and tarring the edges and joints and flat sections. I'd always wanted to follow in his footsteps and let the soles of my feet sink and slide in the melting black paste on the flat section, instead of watching him secretly from the top of the ladder. From the street I couldn't see anything except the two points of the old wooden ladder propped against the peak of the roof. Then banging commenced. As I looked around, it seemed as if everyone in this whole damn town was on their roofs. Must be more rain coming, or some holy roller got a message from God and they figured this time they'd be ready for the flood.

Back on the porch Walker was fanning herself with one of those paper palm leaves McCreavey's Mortuary printed up and passed out at church to remind you you'd better listen because there wasn't much time left. As I walked back across the street to the hotel, Walker patted her chest with an old yellowed man's handkerchief and tucked it in her bra again while Titus leaned closer and spoke quietly to her.

"He's just patching the roof, Walker. He's not on the ladder," I said, and came back to sit down, which made Titus lean back in his chair again. He cocked his head to one side and looked at me, his mouth working like he was about to say something, then changed his mind. He was wearing a plain black short-sleeved shirt and black trousers, socks, and shoes. His shirt strained at the buttons when he sighed and pushed his big chest out.

"You know what I'm afraid of, Moline?" Walker said.

"I can't imagine you afraid of anything," I said.

"Don't try to butter me up, Moline." She rapped my boot with the tip of her stick. "I'm afraid that if Able dies first—and he will, we LeFays are so cursed with long-livedness—that I won't be able to run the farm and hotel by myself, or that Pearl or one of those do-gooders at the church will see to it that I end up at Shadow House Nursing and Retirement Home. Home for Finishing Off Your Unloved Ones, they should call it.

McCreavey probably has controlling shares, the way people go in there and only get out to visit him."

"You're not old, Walker. You're just having a bad day. And you know I'll always take care of you."

She picked up the loose wrinkles of skin on her left wrist and rolled them between her fingertips. "I'm not sure history bears you out, Moline, but thanks."

She did look old today, dressed in that yellow and pink flowered house-dress that could've been anybody's except hers. Again, I reminded myself to pick up her laundry.

"Don't worry, Miz Walker, my mama made me promise to look after you when the time came," Titus said.

"I'm here to help out, Walker. Just tell me what to do. Only thing I have to do is fix up my parents' house for sale. Otherwise, might as well bulldoze the place."

She frowned. "Now that's an idea. I'm surprised nobody's thought of it before. You could sell the lot for a trailer site and—here comes your cousin Pearl." She smiled her old-lady smile like it could hide the humor and wit that was starting to spark her eyes again.

"Dear Pearl, pull up one of those rockers over there."

Pearl was tall and thin and pretty, as usual, and suddenly I felt chunky and overweight, stuffed into my jeans, with the potential for fat peeking out of my upper arms. When I crossed my legs, my thighs protested, and Pearl stared at my cowboy boots, which still had a bit of dried mud along the soles from my day out at the farm. She was wearing a silk skirt and blouse in a soft pink that looked like a blush against her blond hair, which was beginning to pick up the same silver strands as McCall's. Even with the sunglasses on, her face seemed frozen in time, as if it hadn't aged the way the rest of us had. Her skin was perfectly smooth and spotless today, with a light dusting of powder. Nothing could change the nose, which was definitely a Waller trait, overlarge and bumpy, but it gave her character with her strong chin and delicate jaw. An altogether interesting face— maybe one of the reasons she'd never married. It had too many angles to it, and she was too smart for most of the men here. All the Waller women had to marry beneath themselves, that's what Grandmother Estes said on several occasions.

"I can't stay, Walker. I'm due back to work five minutes ago." She glanced around as if we'd done a poor job of sweeping and pushed a dried leaf on the step with the point of her open-toed shoe in matching pink. She must be ordering out of catalogs, I decided; nobody in town carried clothes like that. She and Titus ignored each other.

"How're you, Pearl?" I asked, pretending we hadn't seen each other last night.

She looked down the street and lifted her sunglasses to rest on top of her head. Her eyes were the same: small, silver-gray, what-can-you-do-for-me eyes. When her mouth smiled, her eyes were calculating what you cost. "Actually, I'm not fine, Moline. As you know, I was up half the night because of the dog racket next door. I was wondering if you could keep it down after ten at night. I have to get up and go to work weekday mornings. We open the office at seven so we can get out early with the heat. So, if you don't mind . . ." She smiled and put the glasses back on.

"Pearl . . ."

She turned and started to walk away so quickly it was either chase her down the street in my cowboy boots or forget it. Then she turned around and came back, opening her purse and pulling a folded paper out in one smooth gesture. "I almost forgot, Titus—this is for you."

She held it out and he took it, then hesitated. "What is it?"

"An injunction against your interference with the Heart Hog Corporation." She smiled sweetly and glanced at Walker. "Yours is on the way if you continue to slander the company and its future employees. We need to save this town, Walker. You and this"—she waved an arm over us as if she were a wizard who could make us disappear with a bit of magic dust—"will be moving aside now to let progress through. You've stood in the way long enough. The town's on the cusp of its own demise or its own rise. Pigs weren't my first choice, either, but it's the only offer we have. You people can try to take this town down to nothing, but I won't stand by and watch it happen without a fight."

She glanced at me. "Stop over for some coffee sometime. We'll catch up. I'm the county assessor and registrar now, over at the courthouse. I'd be glad to show you around." This time she kept walking down the block and across the street to the courthouse.

"That was pleasant, as always." Walker drank some tea and sighed. "You'd think it would put her in a better frame of mind to have a man in her bed, even if it is McCall Bell, but not Pearl. She always seemed the only one of you with the right name. Pearl, an irritation with a gloss over it."

"She looks great. Made me feel about eighty." I looked sideways. "Sorry, Walker."

"At my age, you're not fooling anybody anymore. Don't worry about it." She touched my arm with her light, cool fingers. "She's nostril deep with those Hog people. See if you can get closer to her, find out something."

"It's not like she's going to talk to me, Walker. But I'll try."

"That's sort of what I was trying to tell you the other day, Moline, about the Bedwell cousin?" Titus let his glasses slide down his nose so he was looking over them while he leaned toward me.

"What?"

"Your Bedwell cousin who has the land her husband is trying to sell to Heart Hogs?" His tone sharpened, like he thought I was playing dumb, and when he lifted his arms to rest his hands on his thick hips, a sweet baby powder scent mixed with sweat from his underarms drifted across us. It was the smell I remembered him having as a boy.

"So?"

"So, she's married to McCall. Her name's Lukey."

"Small, skinny blond?"

"That's the one. Have you met her? No, I know you haven't. But you can help her, Moline." He leaned back, resting a thick-fingered hand on his thigh. Walker fanned herself harder and drank some tea. The smell of the whiskey was pretty strong now, but we all ignored it.

"I don't even know her."

"Well, we're going to fix that right now. She called a while ago and said she'd be down at Mary's Cafe in Raymond and would need a ride up here about now. Has her two kids with her. You go get her." Walker slapped the fan down on her knee.

"But I don't even know her. Why don't you go, Titus? She's the one I've seen you driving around town with—you could've gone and come back in the time we've been sitting here."

"I'm waiting for David Solomon to fetch his truck so we can do some research he's working on. Besides, you need to meet her, Moline, she's your cousin. And you're close to Dayrell now, you can talk to him and get him to talk to his brother. None of us has the money to play around in court. Look what Pearl's just done—she knows I'm stretched too tight to push this." He waved the injunction and tossed it at me as if it were my fault because I was related to all this trouble.

"Let me see that." Walker snatched it off my lap and opened it. "Says you're to stay two hundred feet away from anyone representing the Heart Hog Corporation . . . that you're not to take out newspaper, radio, or TV ads against Heart Hogs . . . that you're to avoid all rallys, conventions, conferences, meetings, etc. with Heart Hogs as the subject . . . that you're to refrain from mentioning Heart Hogs from your pulpit or in your weekly bulletin. In other words, you go to jail if you so much as say their name out loud." She refolded the document and let it fall to the floor. None of us tried to pick it up. "She needs a good spanking."

Titus tugged off his glasses and scrubbed his face with his hands. "Lord, I hate jail. Just hate it. Jos is going to have a fit when I tell her."

"Might not come to that," I said, and both of them looked at me.

"You don't think I'm going to shut up and let people down, do you?" He clenched his hands on his thighs and leaned toward me.

"No, I guess not."

"Mine's coming too," Walker said. "Okay, we'll have to step up the fight then, fill the jail with so many people it gets to be an embarrassment for them. They want to be seen as do-gooders for the community. Putting old ladies and preachers in jail isn't going to look too good, at least to some of the people in Resurrection. You can help too, Moline. You're with us, aren't you?"

I looked down at my boots and nodded. What else could I do? "I don't much want to go to jail, though."

Walker checked the pocket watch she wore on two yellow bootlaces tied together around her neck. "Who does? We all have to sacrifice here, Moline."

I started to say it wasn't my fight, but stopped myself in time. Whoever had started those fires had included me.

"So first I'm supposed to be careful of Dayrell, now I'm supposed to use him to stop McCall from hurting a Bedwell and helping Heart Hogs?"

"Don't be such a baby, Moline." Titus rubbed his hands together while he pinned me with his eyes. "It's your turn to help."

A man riding a Tennessee walking horse came up the street in that shambling gait they have where the legs move fast and the body stays still.

The fat rider looked comfortable with the reins in one hand, the other resting on his thigh, the brim of his old straw fedora flapping lightly in rhythm with the breeze they were creating.

"That's Sugar Stimson." Walker returned his nod. "Remember him? Went to school with Paris, I believe. His daddy was quite an inventor. First off, everything he tried was odd. He once tried to prove that mice have ESP, as if that would benefit anybody on God's green earth. Then he settled down and invented a new apple peeler, and finally a coupling device for railroad cars, and now they have more money than the pope. Sugar bought himself that place on Hungry Creek those Yankees built, before they discovered snakes and hot weather came with the property. Now he rides through town every day on one of those horses. Like he's punching a time clock. Goes one way at two o'clock and back at five. Those hooves going ratty-tat-tat come rain or shine. It's his wife, Mercy, he sees. She's moved back home. Even the rich have love troubles, I guess."

The older couple came out, nodded to us, and went down the stairs to their camper. "How far to the lake?" the man asked as he was climbing in.

"Not far. Take 11 out west of town there and go south. Can't miss it," Titus said. The man waved his thanks.

Titus picked up the injunction, smoothed it out on his thigh, and refolded it several times to fit in his shirt pocket. "Here they are," he sighed. He stood as the dark green Land Rover parked in front of us and David Solomon, his wife, and their small child climbed out. Both adults were dressed in tan linen shorts, striped polo shirts, and sandals. David's skin shone blue-black, and his hair was cropped so close, the nap sat tightly along his round skull. Although his body was thick and sturdy, his face was boyishly small and delicate, with bright blue eyes and very long lashes. The slender wife was much lighter, butterscotch smooth, the color of acorns when they first drop. Her black hair was straight and long, cut geometrically like a model's in a fancy clothes magazine. Her large brown eyes slanted up in a way that was so unusual, it made her oddly beautiful, the way those models were. Standing next to her husband, she was a good six inches taller, but didn't slump to hide the fact.

The little girl tugged at her hand to get loose, but the mother held firmly and spoke a word that settled her down. The chunky little girl had skin with a mahogany gloss and the same bright blue eyes as her father. She stuck her forefinger in her mouth and dug around watching Walker and me. She was wearing a red and white striped sundress.

"Care to register?" the thin, old man's voice called from the dusky light behind the screen door.

"It's the Solomons, Mr. Rains," David said loudly.

"Oh, sure—no problem," Able hollered back.

"Able, bring this child a sucker," Walker ordered.

The screen door opened and Uncle Able held out the cardboard cup of suckers the Kiwanis put on the counter to collect money for the crippled years ago. The little girl pulled out a dusty old sucker wrapped in brittle cellophane. The mother frowned and tightened her lips.

"Thank you, mister," the girl said in a clear little voice.

"You're welcome, missy." Uncle Able smiled, felt his false teeth slip, and clapped one hand over his mouth while he adjusted them with the other. The child laughed, pulled the crackling cellophane from the sucker, and handed it back to Able.

"My name's Kandera," she announced like we hadn't heard it ten times a day already, and popped the sucker back into her mouth.

Walker shook her head. "These people are growing cobwebs—let them go on with Titus, Able."

"Where're you going today?" I asked.

"Calvin's Cave," Titus said, looking away from me. We'd both had our share of experience there.

"You know I'm looking into the history of the slave trade here," David said, "and the caves in Missouri were perfect stopovers and hiding places for the underground railroad, as well as for the guerrillas in the War. Titus has offered to show me some, particularly those on lands owned by Bedwell or Waller people, two of the oldest families with descendants still living in the area. It's for a special kind of ethnographical history." His eyes got that true-believer shine and his wife looked away, bored with us.

"Well, you shake the skeletons in this town, you're liable to get hit by falling debris," Walker cautioned him. "Wear a hard hat and don't believe everything folks tell you—there just weren't that many colonels in the War Between the States. By and large, not that many people in Missouri could afford to own slaves, those that wanted to, that is. Bedwells and Wallers were always divided on that issue. Sixty percent of the men in this state enlisted on the Union side. And remember what I told you the first day—don't ever mention Kansas or they'll ride you out of here on a rail."

She turned to me. "Are you still here? Now git, go pick up your cousin Lukey."

Titus put the back of his hand against his mouth and looked away to keep from laughing out loud as I heaved up out of the chair and went down the stairs to my truck.

"I don't even know her!" I yelled out the windows as I backed into the street, nearly hitting a blue Honda pulling in with two college-age white girls, but Walker waved me on. The girls got out and went up the steps to the hotel, which took Walker's attention, but Titus watched me all the way to the corner, where I turned south toward Raymond.

9

MINISTRY OF THE LOST
AND FOUND

Sphalerite (locally called Jack, Rosin Jack, Black Jack, Ruby Jack, Zinc, Rosin Spar) is a tan-brown, resinous, brown or brownish black mineral having a very high luster on its broken (cleavage) surfaces. Much of it so strongly resembles lump rosin that the term "Rosin Jack" is truly descriptive. Less commonly, a ruby red variety occurs as crystals perched on other sphalerite or on waste rock.

—THE COMMON ROCKS AND MINERALS OF MISSOURI

✳

MARY'S CAFE WAS IN A SMALL TRAILER with a slabbed-on peeling white wood entrance. In the dusty sycamores towering behind it robins were singing, and a medium-sized brown dog with a black muzzle nosed the wire fence held to the side of the trailer with rusty nails leaking orange down the corrugated dull mint green siding. When I reached the wood steps, the dog gave a halfhearted bark and wagged his skinny tail tiredly. I wanted to reach over and pet him, but I just smiled and said "Hello," like we were at a PTA meeting. He looked at me with these watery bronze eyes, sighed, and walked away, as if that was about what he'd come to expect of the world. "Okay then," I said, and pulled on the shiny handle of the battered aluminum screen door with the dented kick plate in the bottom.

Inside there were only two empty tables—one by the little family parked right inside the door and another further back by a bunch of farmers taking their noon break. I went to the table next to the familiar blond woman and her two kids and sat down. "Lukey?" I asked, and she nodded. "I'm Moline—my aunt Walker and Titus sent me to pick you up. Mind if I grab a bite to eat first?" The skinny blonde nodded again and bit her lower lip. If I hadn't heard her speak last night, I'd have thought she was slow. As it was, I decided she must be shy.

The yellowish smoke-stained walls of the trailer were lined with hand-written notices held up with brittle old Scotch tape announcing bowling leagues, social events, rules, and jokes. There were no windows except the front ones, and the only air was from an old-fashioned black table fan mounted on a shelf in the back corner, whose blades were so weighted with greasy dust, it was no wonder it was moving in slow motion. Years of heavy, farm-booted men trudging down the middle of the dirty green linoleum floor had worn a gray trench.

The farmers in back were seated at three tables shoved together. Their gimme caps and straw hats were perched above the weathered creases of their red faces, and almost every one of them held a cigarette and squinted out at the world through the smoke. When someone occasionally said something, they laughed almost soundlessly with their shoulders shaking, except for the younger men, who sat uneasily, their chairs sticking out more to designate their new and temporary status. They laughed nervously, too loud and long, shifting constantly, stretching their long legs out in the aisle to get some relief for the jumpy muscles fired with life they were afraid of losing sitting there. Their hands were in constant motion, picking up silverware, jelly and cream packets, adjusting clothes and hats, rubbing faces and arms. They hadn't picked up the habit of smoking to stay still yet. They were still learning the ritual and hadn't been at it for enough years to know the comfort of those chrome and vinyl chairs under your bottom, a good cup of coffee, and some like-minded men.

When I scooted my table closer to hers, Lukey hastily pulled her stuff around her, grabbing the boy next to her by the arm and tugging him closer, as if she were embarrassed to be taking her legal allotment in the cafe. The lone waitress came up to her with a coffee pot in one hand that she didn't offer to pour from. "You done, honey?" she drawled, and looked down at the family, her expression saying she was sorry for them but she knew she wasn't getting a tip. She was middle-aged and showing the sag of flesh off her upper arms and the swollen legs that stretched the dark tan of her panty hose so you could see the start of a little white run at the knee when she turned around. Despite all that, her brown eyes snapped with humor and life. She was the kind of person I always wanted to talk to, which used to drive Duncan crazy. He liked ordering his food and getting good service, not making new friends, he used to point out when the waitresses and I got going. "Want anything else?" she asked Lukey again, cocking her hip tiredly.

I slid my forearm across the scarred porch-green-painted tabletop to brush away the last person's crumbs. Lukey gestured mutely toward her cup. The waitress hesitated, glancing toward the kitchen doorway a few feet away. The old woman cooking had her back turned to us, so the waitress shrugged and poured. The kids squirmed uncomfortably and started to whine until Lukey looked at them and put her finger to her lips. They looked down, pouting, but sat still. They were much better behaved than my son, Tyler, had ever been. His bored little face with the pale lifeless blue eyes was always turned away from us in restaurants.

The menu was scrawled on a blackboard in front, by the kitchen doorway behind the tiny counter where the old-fashioned black cash register sat. There were three specials and an all-day breakfast with potatoes, biscuits, gravy, and pork. I ordered the breakfast, ice tea, and a glass of water, which arrived in a Flintstones jelly jar, no ice, lukewarm.

With her stringy white-blond hair, my cousin looked like she'd been in the Ozark hills too long. The kind of person my parents used to joke about whose family tree doesn't fork, as if ours wasn't like Interstate 80; and here was just more evidence. She had thin blue eyes that looked about ready to disappear, they were so runny and faded, and there was a blue-white to her skin that looked like it last saw the sun some time in 1968, the year she was born. The two kids were another matter. They were healthy, towheaded, tan and dirty, with chubby faces and round, sausage-link arms and legs. They'd eaten everything on the single plate in the center of the table except the toast crusts, and that was what Lukey was nibbling on while she sipped coffee and looked out the cloudy front window wild-eyed and depressed.

"So, you got home okay last night?" I finally asked to break the silence.

Lukey looked quickly at my face, then down at her hands fiddling with the cup. "Lucky to have Dayrell."

"Yeah." I drank some ice tea and looked at the kids. "How old are your kids?"

She smiled shyly, pressing her lips together. "This here's Frances—

Fanny—after my mama's mama. She's coming eight in a few weeks. And the boy is Roy Hale, after his daddy's pa. He's just turned seven." The kids squirmed happily as her hand touched each of their heads briefly. "Say hi to Cousin Moline," she instructed, and they looked at me, grinned shyly, and ducked their heads. Fanny was missing her two front teeth, and Roy's teeth were determined little pegs separated by spaces.

"They're cute as all get out," I said, trying to ward off the pang of missing my son.

Lukey nodded and tapped each head again. When the food arrived, she moved over a couple more inches, as if my eating deserved more room.

The food tasted fine, though I couldn't eat much of it with the kids glancing sideways at the biscuits, big lovely rounds soaked in butter, which I loaded with pieces of side meat and dipped in the little bowl of gravy. They didn't know about things like this in Minnesota, I remembered as I chewed happily, trying to ignore the kids, but unable to. Finally I held out the plate of biscuits and asked, "Would you like these?" My cousin shook her head and looked away, her face taking on the first blush of color. "Sure? I'm really not gonna eat them." She looked at the kids' faces and took the plate.

The kids brightened and sat up straight as she carefully divided the biscuits and swathed each side with a pond of honey from the plastic bear and handed it to them. She had to work to keep her fingers from trembling. She got a whole one for herself, and I noticed the color remaining on her cheeks as she ate. I wanted to offer the rest of the pork, but didn't want to offend her. The kids were looking hungrily at my plate, but I knew there was a decorousness about hill people, a pride and dignity my parents alternately laughed at and honored. After all, our own relatives had come out of these hills, and some, like Lukey, still lived here.

"Hate to waste this." I waved my hand over the big plate. She hesitated, looked at her kids again, and murmured, "Thank you." I passed the plate to her, glancing up just in time to catch the blast of the old cook's gaze. She was white-haired, fat, and at least eighty from the way she was hobbling around her tiny kitchen, half bent at the waist as if she'd spent her life shoving small children into ovens. Had to be Mary, who owned the place. The waitress appeared and slapped my bill down, not offering any more ice tea, but not exactly criticizing me, either. She was just doing her job, earning her living like most people, trying to stay out of trouble at work so she could deal with the trouble at home. Half turning away in my chair, I avoided looking at Lukey and the kids and sipped at my water like I was drinking it.

The table of men stared without expression at our little group of women and children. It made me nervous. As they watched silently, Lukey tapped me on the arm and slid her bill to the edge where our tables met. "Please . . . McCall forgot to leave me the money. We met here to talk this morning, but then he got mad. I'll pay you back, I promise." The bill said $1.76. They'd hardly had enough food to dirty the dishes.

"No problem." I stood up and dropped a two-dollar tip on the table for the both of us. "Don't worry about it." I paid both bills, glowered at Mary's fat behind, and walked outside.

I paused on the front sidewalk, taking deep breaths of the fresh sweet woods air to clear the greasy smoke that'd soaked my clothes and skin. Across the street the lilacs and honeysuckle lining the snatch of grass in front of the gas station were in full bloom, swaying their blossoms at the road.

"Thank you, Moline." My cousin stopped next to me and rubbed her thin arms as if the scene inside had given her a rash. Her black tee shirt with a faded Budweiser logo across the front hung limply, like it recently belonged to a much bigger person.

She looked across the road to the motel, whose beds she couldn't afford even though the pull-along sign out front boasted: WORST BEDS IN TOWN! 15 DOLLARS!

"I thought McCall'd come back, but he didn't. That Mary's an old bat." She glanced back at the cafe. "She doesn't like us hanging around like we had to. Lucky I got ahold of Titus or we'd be walking."

She turned to watch the kids playing a game of tag on the steps of the cafe, happy to be let out of the prison inside; they reminded me again of Tyler at that age.

"Thanks for helping us." Her voice was so quiet I had to lean closer to catch it all. She was a few inches shorter than me, and in my cowboy boots I towered over her.

"Aunt Walker said to bring you back to town."

"Okay, I guess." When she lifted her arm to shade her eyes and look down the road for McCall, it released a faint sour smell. "Guess I waited long enough. Resurrection, that's where he went. Our place is in the woods other side of the creek, east of the Rains farm, but he wouldn't go there." I noticed her baggy cutoffs were held up by a man's thin black leather belt with so many extra holes punched in it she had enough to wrap the end around in a knot. She sounded so convinced that he was coming back, I wanted to shake her.

We rolled out of town and across the bridge, Lukey in front with me, and the kids in back playing with the electric window switches, making them go up and down, up and down, testing their nerve to see who could leave their fingers in the longest before the glass smashed up into the frame. I didn't want to say anything because they were clearly thrilled with the new toy. Lukey didn't know any better, either. Cars with extras like electric windows hardly ever showed up in front yards around here.

I hated how poverty was an embarrassment, how it made for scenes like the one in the cafe a few minutes ago. It was embarrassing to the people who were poor and to the rest of us, who kept looking away—we didn't want to embarrass them, and we didn't want to be embarrassed. When you were a kid and you stared at someone who was crippled or deformed, your parents said "Don't stare" and got real pissed off if you kept doing it. But how else were you supposed to find out about things? You learned to look out of the corner of your eye at everything, to settle for glimpses you could just throw out if they weren't nice. Poor people, anyone with dark skin, anyone who was different. Don't stare. Why didn't I raise my kid to stare, damn it? Why didn't I say "Look," why didn't I grab his jaw and force him to see things, to be interested, not to turn away? It might have worked. Tyler might have stayed then, he might have wanted to come with me. He might be in the truck, having this whole adventure together with me, instead of these strangers.

Lukey was pressed into the side of the door, hanging on to the handle above her head for dear life when I glanced over. Easing my foot on the accelerator, I asked, "Do you farm at your place?"

She looked startled and gave a brief shake of her head, then nodded slowly, releasing the overhead handle, so her hands could hold each other, twisting and kneading. "We ended up on this little ole strip of land my mama let us have, on the far edge of where her land and my brother's line up, about sixty acres. It's Bedwell land, but the creek's running smack through it, so some of it's underwater. Only got about fifteen left, I guess, but McCall was happy enough to get it when we needed that run-down cabin for the first youngster on the way. Now . . ." She looked out the window. "I guess you know he's trying to sell the land," she said so quietly I could barely hear her. "It's been in my family forever. Mama gave it for me and the kids. We don't have no other place to go," she whispered, and fell silent.

Lukey twisted in the seat to check on the kids, I could see in the rearview mirror. They were looking sleepily out the windows, their little eyelids shuttering that moment before they fell, their lips loose and full, with a glisten of spit in the corner.

"I tried to make it a good home, one that'd last all our years. I had McCall chop all the pawpaw and redbud from around the cabin first thing, just to make sure ghosts didn't have a comfortable place. I was putting stones on the family graves regular, but I guess that didn't work so good. When we moved into the cabin, I hung a wasp nest up in the rafters and nothing bothered us 'til now."

"What do you grow there?" It was rude to ask questions like this, but I figured what the hell, she was kin.

Her hands did a nervous dance, and she opened and shut her mouth twice before anything came out. "Vegetables." She looked with determination out the windshield when I glanced over.

Vegetables my ass. Moonshine or marijuana, knowing McCall. In these Ozark woods, anything and everything happened. After the War, there were lots of murders in these hills, all kinds of unreported violence. Plenty of ghosts. Beside the headless Bittman Bedwell and the ghost dog, there were horsemen and cars that vanished when you reached out to touch them, all kinds of misery that couldn't be put to rest—it came back in groans and cries and thumps and foxfire light. These woods always scared me, I'd never think of living right in the hills. Especially after they dammed the Osage and flooded towns and cemeteries and farms for the Lake of the Ozarks. Where did they think all those dead went but to higher ground?

"Titus said you lost your people up north. I'm real sorry," Lukey said. So I told her some about Duncan and our life up to the end.

" 'Nothing you did,' that's what they told him, but I didn't believe them. Duncan's heart couldn't just wear out, he'd been a big strong man all his life. We tried all kinds of things, cures, nothing worked. And then one day I was sitting there in Minneapolis in this empty house, Tyler gone, my husband buried, the money run out. I thought I better do something. They foreclosed on the house, took the equity for the bills that had piled up. Had to bring my sister home anyway. So here I am." I sighed. "What about you? How long you and McCall been together?"

"Ten years. Met him at the little ole store down at five corners, other side of Raymond? He followed me home, walked up the porch, and introduced himself to my ma. Pa's not with us anymore, he passed when I was a little girl. Snake bit at church. He said he'd been shallow in his faith and wouldn't let anyone take him to the doctor. Turned out it was such a young cottonmouth, venom was real deadly. Pa laid there and suffered it out with the preacher calling his salvation every step of the way to the end. I ain't seen anything like it since. He took religion deep into his heart before he died. Real deep. That's why Ma wanted McCall to go to church with us, see if he was the right kind of man." She squinted out the windshield.

"And?"

"It was a snake dancing service, and my brother stepped up and took his place with a big ole cottonmouth, singing and talking to the snake and looking at us. I didn't trust myself that night, not with McCall standing so close and putting his arm around me when my family wasn't looking. When the preacher called for someone else to praise the Lord and conquer the serpent, McCall stepped up and grabbed a good-sized rattler out of the box and started playing with it. I couldn't help thinking of Pa, and knew McCall hadn't taken the Lord into his life nearly enough for that snake."

"Did he get bit?"

She shook her head. "He twisted the rattles off and flung it down so hard it died. He didn't have no idea what he done. Well, people plopped those snakes back in the box and finished the service fast as possible and cleared out of there. Ma and the preacher and my brother tried to talk to me about it, but I knew I couldn't pass by him. He was the bravest man I ever seen. He was never going to let some ole snake give better than he got."

She paused and pulled her legs up and wrapped her arms around them. "We wanted to get married proper, by our preacher, but he wouldn't do it until McCall got saved. I—I tole my family and everyone we did it with another preacher down in Camden County, but that was a lie. At first I believed McCall when he said the Lord knew we were married even without the preacher. Now, I don't know. It's been bothering me real bad since McCall's started staying away more. Kids miss him too."

"That's hard." I knew she had to love McCall, she was that kind of woman.

She nodded. "I know he ain't perfect, but he's strong, and he's good to the kids, and good to me when he's in his right mind. And he needs me, Moline. I'm his chance in this life, his only one, he used to say."

I wanted to tell her the truth about McCall, that he was a rotten troll of a man, that he didn't deserve her fingernail clippings. But what did I have to offer her instead? He was fooling around with Pearl now, he'd be gone before Lukey knew it.

"What about your son? Where's he?"

She'd been so honest about herself, I had to try to do the same. "Truth is, Tyler didn't even come to his father's funeral. Too busy, I guess. They never got along very well. No fighting or anything, just nothing to say to each other. He acted like we were beside the point, his parents, and enlisted in the army to get special training, then went on with engineering out west. I think he's happy, no reason not to think that. He's doing what he wants, that's supposed to make a person happy. That's what they say on TV talk shows, isn't it?" I shook my head to get rid of the feelings that'd gotten raised up by this talking.

Lukey shrugged. "I don't know about TV, but it sounds like you miss him, Moline. He never writes or calls or comes back to visit?"

"Not hardly." My eyes squeezed full of tears and I looked away quickly to wipe them. "His job takes up all his time, he says. I know he works hard. Sent us a picture of a new sports car once, a black Corvette he'd bought. Californians love their cars, he says. Still, I wish . . . I don't know . . . I wish he felt more for me. I hardly know what I can do now, though."

"I'd hate for my kids to do me that way. It'd break my heart."

"It broke his father's heart. For all I know, I'll never see him again. I keep trying to forget, act like he died too. It's about the hardest thing I've ever had to get over, Lukey. Some days . . ."

"Must be terrible." Her voice was so soft I could barely hear it. "But it might turn to acceptance. I couldn't do it without my faith, I know that." She touched the little gold cross hanging around her neck, and I remembered baby Tyler sleeping in my arms as Duncan drove us north to Rainy

Lake for fishing that first year. The flush of heat in his pale cheeks that worried me so I put my own face against his, thinking how heartbreaking the little puffs of air from his tiny nose were.

Deep in Missouri's heart, the land around the road thickens with trees and underbrush. The farms seem to slash into the woods, keeping them at a small distance with their little buildings. As we headed northeast on a bigger blacktop road than I'd come down on, the land started to relax into smooth, flat river bottom and rolling pasture lands. Cattle and horses dotted the fields in the sun, and in every ditch and hillside, there were lilacs, irises and fat peonies escaped from houses long gone, clumps of rust, red, purple, white, and yellow extravagantly splashing the tall green, set loose but caught nonetheless by loops of bindweed, as if there were hope here, something growing, something you could hang on to that wouldn't die, wouldn't let go of you.

"It's so green here, everything's so full and lush. I'd forgotten about that," I said.

"We had a couple of real bad years with the drought. Crop didn't come to no good—no money except for what the government would give us. I hated taking relief stamps, but McCall didn't seem up to working. Said he got dizzy on those roofs—said his daddy let his brother do the easy jobs on the ground. We were just getting back on our feet when he—" She turned around to check on the kids, whose heads were lolling against the backseat as they slept.

When we were kids, Paris and I were put in the car and driven, we never had any clear idea where or why. There wasn't a lot of explaining, not like Duncan did with Tyler. My parents were wanderers. Especially Iberia. She'd have a fight with Mister and off we'd go. Visiting—relatives and cemeteries and battle sites, anything from point A to point B as long as it took a day or two and she could go as fast as she wanted.

Iberia used to tell us there were no speed laws in Missouri, the signs were only suggestions for what you might want to do. I believed her. Whenever she got stopped, she only got a warning ticket, so she must have known what she was talking about. We never listened to the radio on those trips, either; just listened to her remembering a kind of golden age before the Depression, when her daddy was alive and she was his beloved daughter. And her teaching in the hills those few months before she ran off and married Mister Bedwell. Then her memories came to an end, as if we would know the rest, because one of us was always there, even though we were babies.

We hated when she stopped. We wanted her voice, her details. They were like finding good, flat skipping stones, they served a purpose, staking out that time, that geography before us, making a bridge to us. Our history was Mama and Mister's way of letting us know we weren't just the white trash we were always in danger of sliding to. Grandmother Estes never saw Romeo and Juliet when she looked across the side yard at my parents' tumbledown house boiling over with wild kids. She saw white trash in training. I wondered if one person could do that—pull an entire family into the hole with her.

I took the road Lewis and Clark took because Mister said they were Bedwell relations, and I thought how if we stopped for a moment, everything might come back and we could all start over and do things right this time. The woods would thicken, and the road would crumble and disintegrate into dust, some original good dust, and we'd be working our way home right over the tracks, those deep-grooved wagon wheel trails we would see if we skinned the asphalt back and put our hands under there, into the earth; we'd feel the ridges of wheels and horse hooves, the heat still trapped from the sun that day, the dust ground fine as flour between our fingers, sifting, sifting, sifting.

Everywhere I looked there was a layer of time over time, iris over bones, always something growing, never really sealing the wounds, we all knew that underneath, just below the thin surface of soil here, was the rock heavy sediment of anger, loss, wrong. The scrub cedar and oak pushed up along the creeks whose waters were bloodstained forever by raids and battles, private and public vendettas, over a thousand skirmishes during the War in Missouri, some of the most personal, heartless killing. "Show me," we said here, because we knew we could recite our history. Our lives kept sifting down into the ground, but that didn't mean they were forgotten. We know who our people are, that's what counts, Mister used to say.

"You have nice things," Lukey said, stroking the gray leather seat with the palm of her hand.

Her voice jarred me and I sped up. "I got some money from my husband's insurance. It's all I have after the foreclosure on the house." I felt embarrassed, wanted to point out the flaws in the upholstery or the nicks in the paint.

"I want things nice for my kids," she said. We nodded in that universal language of mothers. If I could help her, I would. What would it take to stop the slow hemorrhage of her life? More than a couple hundred, more than I had, but then McCall would come back and it would all start again. Who knew what kind of dreams he was feeding? Hell, I couldn't even afford to fix a cavity in her teeth. Money helped, but it wasn't the answer, now was it?

Up ahead I noticed the big tin sign for Calvin's Cave, rust blooming darker against the faded red background, taking out part of the clumsy illustration I remembered from the old days. The words "Magical" and "UNusual" were peeling off the sign as if they were embarrassed. Calvin's Cave was named for my mother's no-good brother, who courted and married Delphine out of a gas station in Tipton to spite his mother. He finally drank himself to death or got stabbed and died on the railroad tracks, depending on who you believed. Grandfather Horras Waller got the cave in 1910. Nobody cared about little Missouri caves then, so the family used it as a place to take visitors and let the kids roam around in. He lost it when he lost the rest of his holdings in the Depression, but by then the name had stuck, so it'd always been Calvin's Cave.

I wanted to make the turn towards the cave because in some way it seemed like it all began there, when we were kids. It was the place Dayrell and I went to when he was teaching me how to make love. Then McCall that final time. Maybe when I got there, I'd spit on its darkness, its secrets. But the road to Resurrection continued on, climbed a hill, and wandered past a lot of dreams that were starting to fall apart. There was the dog grooming parlor greenhouse with the windows replaced by thin sheets of plastic that flopped around in the hot breeze. The sign out front promised: WE DON'T JUST GROOM YOUR DOG, WE SHOWER IT WITH LOVE.

There were the single-story concrete block houses as grim as a child's play set. Inside they'd trapped the damp moldy smell of the woods and the dark light that shaded the small lives being lived in there. It was the dark, damp green light you couldn't escape here; it lingered just beyond the old stained sheets and torn shirts flapping helplessly on the sagging clothes-line. The green strained the light and seemed to leave everything with a tinge on it, green, yellow, brown, as if the dirt itself were falling upwards and the sky had reversed to receive it. You expected it to rain in colors, tints that didn't let anything be pure and new here. You couldn't remember that there was ever anything new. That was the problem with the stuff that got shipped in—by the time it was unpacked, it had already taken on the damp texture of the woods, the dark light that left a smearing shadow.

Passing an old Bedwell homestead, I tried to keep my eyes on the road, but my foot came off the gas and I couldn't stop my head from turning at the last minute to glimpse the weed-eaten yard, and the old cabin hovering darkly behind a screen of ragged old cedars. "Bad luck started when they moved them cedars, folks tole them not to move them cedars over there," Mister used to say. I couldn't tell if anyone was living there or not. I wondered if these were Lukey's people. My parents stopped having much to do with the Bedwell kin once their Swan Lake Trailer Park started doing well.

But even when I was a child we were supposed to pretend we hadn't seen them when the Bedwells came down the streets, and only be the barest polite if we had to. It hurt me in a queer way to see those faces taking the insult as if they just knew they deserved it. We were nicer to the black Bedwells in town than to these cousins, because Mister said we used to own them, so we had obligations. We owned Titus Bedwell's ancestors. That made me feel bad in another way, and I remembered all the ways I had felt bad in Resurrection, even being in a twenty-mile radius, as if it were a nasty circle of friends you fell in with and had to fight your way clear of again.

Now the road was lined with sumac and sassafras and Queen Anne's lace, and I opened the window for the high, steady sound of katydids and tree frogs, and the sweet spice of the woods. The tent worms had chiffoned the dogwood to the right with gray and tan canopies, and off a ways there was a pond covered with huge water lilies, each with a tall white bloom, and the light was turning peculiar shafts and screws through the trees. I used to think it was God in those shafts of light. I used to think we'd drive into Him if He'd wait for us, and we'd all be blessed and saved and see His face, but I was wrong. The only thing in the light was light, and it just reminded you to drop your eyes until you were out of that perspective and back under some useful clouds. Travel used to be educational that way.

I looked over at Lukey, but her eyes were closed, her head rolling on the seat back with the uneven road. A damp strand of pale hair stuck to her cheek and I wanted to reach out and move it, the way I'd do with Tyler. As we passed a sign in front of a little farmhouse that said: JUST SAY NO TO HEART HOGS—DON'T SELL! just outside town, she opened her eyes. The same sign or a variation was planted at fairly regular intervals in front of every building all the way into town. The black letters were hand-painted in angry strokes: FIGHT BIG BUSINESS. NO $HEART $HOGS! DON'T LET HEART HOGS STEAL YOUR LAND. COLT .45 JUSTICE SOLD HERE! HEART HOGS STAY OFF! NO FACTORY FARMS! NO CRAP FARMS!

She shook her head. "It's just a shame. Mama told me, you never sell the land, it's all you got that's your place on earth where somebody can't just come and tell you to move along, get out. That's our gift from the Lord, the land, and we shouldn't never give it up, not till He's ready for us."

"Wise woman," I said. I liked Lukey, and I liked that she was my cousin, which made three relatives I liked in Resurrection so far. I even went so far as to wonder if I could talk to her about Dayrell sometime, since she knew him so well. Somehow I knew I could trust her if I told her the truth.

We pulled up in front of the hotel and her kids woke up and tumbled out, hugging each other until they sat down on the sidewalk giggling.

I laughed. "You have good kids."

She blushed, smiling. "Thanks for helping us out." She turned and surveyed the street as if McCall was about to pop up, then turned back. "You coming inside?"

I nodded. "For a minute, see if Walker needs anything else. If not, guess I'll go home and work on things there."

"Where you staying?"

"My family's old house on Jefferson. Come by—128."

A little worried expression shadowed her face; then she smiled. Duncan would never have let me invite these people home. Iberia and Mister had tried to put as much distance as possible between Lukey Bedwell's worn-out Wal-Mart canvas shoes and themselves. But I was in charge of the world now, and I figured travelers had to give each other shelter. Ancient rules of hospitality.

10

ON THAT BEAUTIFUL SHORE

Many mountain damsels carry love charms consisting of some pinkish, soaplike material. . . . The thing is usually enclosed in a carved peach stone or cherry pit and worn on a string round the neck, or attached to an elastic garter.

— OZARK MAGIC AND FOLKLORE

"FOOL, you know better'n that in this heat." Lukey slid off and scolded the roan as she rubbed his forehead hard with the flat of her palm, which came away foamy white. "Guess we should hose 'em down before we saddle." I nodded and slid off too, letting the muddy sweat draining in rivulets down the big brown's side smear the front of my shirt and arms. It was the hottest day so far, and Walker had sent us out to the farm to ride the horses and feed the stock while she watched the kids.

"You could use a dousing too," Lukey laughed at me. Somehow she'd remained completely clean except for the rind of pink-white hairs outlining the insides of her legs. We'd galloped the horses bareback from the pasture, but planned on using the saddles for the road.

"I'll walk them out while you set up the hose." I grabbed both ropes and pulled their attention toward me.

"Watch out—Harry cow-kicks," Lukey called as she disappeared into the square door of the cow barn.

Even though the pig barn was below and well on the other side of the cow barn, you could still smell it wafting along on an invisible breeze. I tried to imagine fifty thousand pigs and decided I wouldn't stay in Resurrection if Heart Hogs won. Maybe I'd suggest they buy the whole town in that case, because nobody in fifty miles would be able to stand the stench, let alone drink the water once pig shit fifteen feet deep by three hundred feet long by a hundred feet wide hit the aquifer.

The two horses pulled me off balance as they plunged their heads in the dark green grass along the little dirt road from the barn to the tractor shed. Tearing big mouthfuls, their sides still panting from the run, they ignored my tugs on the ropes. Maybe they did know best, shaking the flies off their ears, their skin wrinkling and shivering along their backs to discourage the settling stings, nudging aside the tall, thin stalks of Queen Anne's lace and grabbing at the fat yellow dandelion heads as if they were making a salad. Everything was quiet, except for the robin's musical call and the steady sawing of locusts and grasshoppers. I looked up in the oaks for the robin, trying to follow its sound, but there was only the dark green leaves as big as men's palms and the dark bark almost the color of David Solomon's arms and legs. The horses grazed forward, letting the grass lead them, eating some stalks and leaving others because they were particular. Cows and sheep and goats ate everything, but a horse pasture was always an uneven carpet of clumps.

The yellow cups of Missouri primrose turned upward on their green spikes almost underfoot, and I pulled the horses out of their way. Milkweed was blooming, flat fists of rose and cream on tall thick stalks, and everywhere there were butterflies, yellows and whites fluttering along the grass, around the heads of the horses, my legs, scattering like leaves as we walked slowly through them. A big grasshopper landed on the toe of my boot, spit some brown juice, and hopped off. They always seemed like they were made out of twigs or old hay, so brittle they could break apart. McCall and his friends used to sit in the parking lot outside high school with a coffee can of grasshoppers they'd caught. They'd tear the legs off one at a time to watch them try to escape and go in lopsided circles instead. Sometimes they'd attach firecrackers to the big ones and throw them, to see the bodies fly apart.

"Here." I pulled the roan's head up and brushed at the big bottle-green horsefly getting ready to bite hard enough to draw blood on its chest. The fly was so determined, I actually closed my hand around it before it let loose and threatened my fingers until I opened my hand again and it flew away.

The roan called Harry Truman pulled his head back and down, dropping his nose into the cool green. Aunt Walker named her horses for Southern presidents. Not George Bush, though; she said he was about as Texan as she was. Jimmy Carter, the brown horse, stopped and lifted his head, staring with his ears flicking back and forth, his eyes getting rounder and rolling so the white rimmed them. Snorting once, long and loud, he swung his head in panic at the roan, who had also stopped eating and watched alertly, though not with the same degree of worry. The brown groaned and started backing up quickly, dragging me and the roan with him as he tried to spin and bolt against the other horse. "Whoa, stop— easy, whoa!" I yelled as the ropes burned my palms and the horses tangled me up with their big bodies. I managed to avoid being crushed or kicked and was in front of them with the ends of the ropes held up, ready to snap their necks if they didn't stop. I gave each halter a hard yank and started letting them edge forward, trying to keep them from trampling me. Their bodies were quivering as they struggled to obey, a new hot worried smell seeping through their sweat.

I didn't know how I heard it, but I did, and swung the horses back around me in a small circle just in time to see the mound of grass we were about to walk on dissolve and unravel a foot-and-a-half-wide ball of brown and gold coppery scales. "Holy shit," I whispered, and turned faster than the horses and ran down the road, with their hard-trotting hooves pounding on either side of me. "Lukey! Lukey!" I yelled, pulling up beside the stock tank, where she was hooking the hose to the faucet. "Snakes!" I panted, yanking on the horses, who were settling down enough to push their noses in the green-scummed surface of the water tank and clear a space for drinking. "They were screwing or something, a ball of them, two huge snakes—honest to God—made me sick—go see—"

"I seen enough snakes, Moline. You just forgot about living down here, that's all. Snakes everwhere, can't let 'em upset you, spend all your time worrying." She turned the hose on the roan's legs first, getting him used to the cool water, then raised it slowly up his body, along his neck and back and hind end. I had to step out of the way when he kicked out each time he felt the water slide down his butt. The brown gave him some room and looked bored, like he was going to sleep again. He'd had his excitement for the day.

"Here, use this to pull the wet off, and spray them with their fly stuff while I round up the bridles." Lukey handed me the aluminum sweat scraper and I went over their bodies quickly, then sprayed the cloudy liquid on them, except where the saddles sat. I put some on my hands and rubbed their faces and ears, and the brown liked the rub so much he shoved his head under my arm when I stopped and tried to lift it again. I obliged, rubbing in slow circles, crooning to him so his eyes went soft and his lids dropped.

"You get along pretty good with Jimmy. He mostly ignores people, just turns into a big brown slug of a thing. Two times we've come out to ride he's made McCall so mad he kicked him in the belly to wake him up. Don't never try that with the roan, I told him. Get his own belly kicked." She smiled happily and started saddling Harry, the roan. Maybe she wanted to see that happen; maybe she wasn't quite as beaten down as she seemed at first.

This was a different Lukey, definitely. With the horses she seemed sure of herself, more like someone I would know in Minnesota, not a hill woman with youngsters to tend. I wondered if McCall knew as much as he thought he did about this woman.

The scar on her arm winked, squinching and unsquinching like an eye as she easily lifted the big western saddles, settling them on the horses, and fastened the girths. There was a red birthmark shaped like a drunken star on the back of her knee, which flicked in and out of sight as she bent and straightened. And no wedding ring. No jewelry at all. McCall, I chided silently. He was a bad boy; he'd always been a bad boy needing a good slap and a night without supper in bed while the rest of the kids played tag and freeze in the backyard. He needed to feel how lonely it could get with those joyful voices rising up to turn his room hollow and dark as he waited sweaty and thick-throated against his own nature. Or maybe he needed something worse yet—something like Dayrell had gotten.

"Come on, hurry up—we can make it to the Hungry Branch and take a quick swim." She mounted and turned Harry toward the road. "We'll take the shortcut."

A monarch butterfly stalled in front of us, then drifted away, and overhead the sun was just this soft yellow cream, putting a warm haze over everything, like the world was smoky, and it was impossible to see things as having sharp edges, and that was okay, it was really okay. My body had this sudden power, and I didn't care so much about anything, letting the steady creak of the leather and the huff of the hooves in the dust take me as far down the road as it wanted.

"Dayrell Bell's dogs keep the snakes away, that's why it's good swimming," Lukey explained as we lay side by side in the shallow water with the horses standing nearby without their saddles so they could cool off too while they cropped the grass and weeds along the bank. We'd left the halters on and tied the ropes to a snag caught in the larger rocks piled to pool the water a few yards away. She said they were smart enough not to get tangled, and smart enough to run home if they got a chance.

Dayrell's name jarred me, and I almost said that this didn't look like his place. "Where's he live?" I asked instead, studying the spots of blue and red and silver pulsing behind my closed lids.

"Yonder. Can't see it from here, it's around that bend up there. Surprised his dogs ain't raising a ruckus. They usually do. People complain, but this ain't any of our land. His mama's people owned both sides of the creek until the Depression, now it's down to 'bout the size of my place further on." She fluttered her fingers in the water, sending little ripples toward me when I opened my eyes. She'd taken her shirt off, and the blue polka-dot swimsuit top was faded a grayish white that grew darker and darker as it soaked up the creek water. "Crawpappies," she murmured sleepily, and closed her eyes. That was enough to make me keep my body alert. Although I'd taken off my jeans and boots, I hated feeling anything on me in the water. But in a couple of minutes the heat and the slow-motion rubbing of the current rocked me back to that place behind my eyes while my skin relaxed and loosened.

At first it felt like a minnow nibbling at my toes, working its way up my leg. I tried to shake it off, not wanting to open my eyes and move. After all, it wasn't pinching or biting. Then it got to my arm, my neck, and I opened my eyes. There was a dark figure blocking the sun so I couldn't see who it was. His hand went over my mouth as I was about to yell and he leaned down and whispered, "It's me, Dayrell—shhh." I glanced at Lukey a few yards away, but she seemed out of it, asleep. He replaced his hand with his lips and my mouth parted for his.

We kissed like that for a while, all lazy and fluid like the water, letting our bodies follow the current like underwater plants because we were anchored on the gravel bottom. He was still wearing his jeans, and his legs kept falling below mine, as if I could trust myself to rest on him. The creek water sloshed between our chests and up our chins, into our kissing, which got that summer taste of green. We didn't touch the other parts, holding out as if we could go backwards to go forwards again. Our hair flowed out and around us, mingling and sliding against our ears. Our tongues became new eyes in each other, touching so soft it hurt my teeth into sharp edges that wanted to bite hard and harder.

He had no trouble lifting me and climbing out. When I looked over his shoulder, Lukey was sleeping, her hair haloing her like a fine yellow fern. The horses were drowsing with their heads resting over each other's necks, eyes half-closed, tails sailing through the air to whisk flies in slow motion. It was the field he took us to, laying us down in the musty hot wet green smell of the bottomland corn, ribbony leaves creaking and rustling in the shadows overhead. His wet jeans were hard to pull off, and my underpants dropped a little mound of sand we flattened with our naked bodies. We rolled and let the dirt cake and cover us from the insects waiting under the corn. Our bodies grew wise, and we used our hands to stroke each other until we were panting and biting, and when he put it in I lunged upward to take the sting deeper inside. The creaking and rubbing got so loud it went away, and the hot smell came all the way through my blood, dissolving the last of my shame, I don't care, I don't care, a voice kept chanting, don't stop, just don't stop.

When he finally did, falling heavily on me and rolling us both to our sides, still inside, my eyes simply filled. I didn't have words for this, I kept thinking, I didn't speak of this, not this. He hugged me closer as the sobs started, and the wet pooled out between our legs. So much was not at stake here, so much time had been bought and sold to this moment, I couldn't say anything, and all he did was stroke my muddy hair and whisper "Shhh, it's all right" in my ear. After a while he started to thicken inside me, and this time we did it slow and with the tip touched me so high and far inside, it was like underwater exploring, did it feel here, and here and here until I couldn't get close enough, give myself fast and full enough and our skin dissolved into the low moaning of someone saying, "Moline, oh, sweet, sweet Moline."

Lukey looked like a dead person when I slipped back into the creek still buttoning my muddy shirt. Her arms were loose, floating at her sides, and her pale blue eyes were staring up at the sky as if they weren't seeing anything anymore. Her mouth hung open a little. I concentrated on her chest for breathing and for the first time noticed the finger-shaped bruises on her breasts where the halter top had floated away from her body. "Lukey?" I leaned my head back to rinse the mud out. Dayrell had gone back to his place, after promising to come see me tonight. The horses were busy eating again. "Lukey?"

"I was just practicing death," she said, and closed her eyes. "I keep thinking it'll be in water, and I want to know what it'll feel like when they find me. My soul's been washed in the blood of Jesus. I'm not afraid. I just want to know what I'll feel like and what the people who find me will feel when they see me. Do I look peaceful? I don't want to look scared, that wouldn't be right if you're saved."

This was definitely not a Minnesota conversation. Duncan's family always got superior around anyone who talked about God too much. "Well, you *look* dead."

She nodded, as if that was about what she expected. "Better scrub your skin good with sand, gets rid of the ticks from that field. Come here, I'll check your back." She sat up, the water streaming down her chest outlined the small breasts with sharp pointed nipples under her halter, and I felt more naked than I was before. "Undo your shirt so I can look for those deer ticks. They're the worst darn things, like looking for a freckle on a brown dog." She giggled.

"You told him we were coming, didn't you?"

"Uh-huh. Called him from the hotel. He tole me 'bout you long time ago, and the minute I saw you I knew you belonged together. Both suffered for love." Her small fingers traced a paisley pattern which was oddly soothing. She wasn't like any Christians I'd ever known. I bent my neck forward and shivered.

"Hold still." She fastened something around my neck. I picked it up and looked at the small, irregular reddish brown rock strung on a brown shoelace through a hole in the middle.

"I found this one day and been wearing it ever since—until I saw you. It's got a hole in the middle, means it's real lucky."

"Oh, thanks, Lukey. But what'll *you* do for luck then?" I turned and she knelt beside me so we could both examine the rock.

She smiled and opened those watery blue eyes wide and touched her little gold cross. "I got plenty of luck and I can always find more. You're alone, you need something extra. I used to think it was ruby, but McCall said they don't grow around here. I don't care, I like it no matter what you call it. I could of polished it, but it works better natural. When you put your eye up to it and look at the sky, there's a little hole there, all neat and clean, like a room you can visit, just yours."

I lifted it and peered through the hole at her. "Think it really works?"

"Brought Dayrell, didn't it?" She smiled and stood, water cascading down her body in bright silver streams. "We better go, horses are getting ready to start trouble."

The roan was tugging back, trying to dislodge the log or the rope, and the brown was trying to stay out of his way, pulling the other direction on the log. "Here you, Harry Truman, stop that!" Lukey called. She led the horses up the bank, saddled, and waited for me as I pulled on my jeans. I thought about the stone Dayrell was wearing around his neck too.

"You and Dayrell are close, aren't you?" I asked, and she looked down, picked at something on the saddle in front of her.

"He's a real good friend to have. Saved me more than once." She swung on and kicked Harry.

"Don't start in." Lukey held the door open for the kids and climbed in on the passenger's side. The kids were clamoring to ride in the back of the old maroon pickup, and she shrugged and got out, waiting while they hoisted themselves up the tailgate. She didn't look at me standing on the curb by the truck in front of my house.

McCall sat hunched over the steering wheel, pouting. "Thought you'd be back before suppertime at least. The kids are starving."

"You couldn't get 'em something?" She sounded tough, but glanced worriedly at the two kids squiggling around in the debris to make themselves a nest for the ride home.

"If it matters, I'm hungry too, you know." He shifted the truck into reverse with a vicious jerk on the knob that forced all kinds of grinding and lurching out of the transmission. Lukey had to hop in the last step and slam the door shut on the move. He braked hard.

"I wasn't gone that long." She pushed her thin hair back off her face and let her hand drop to her lap. It was like watching a dog being taught to heel. "Miz Walker asked—"

"I told you, I don't want my kids hanging around that crazy old woman, or her husband. Now you got kids to take care of. Remember that next time you get the urge to go gallivanting. I'm not going to keep picking up the pieces of this truck, either—so stay home where you belong."

"McCall—"

"Stay out of my family business, Moline. You got your hands full fixing your house. I don't see how you have time to play, either."

Lukey glanced quickly at me, a smile trying to stretch her mouth into matching her eyes. I grimaced and shrugged in an exaggerated way.

"Daddy Hale was here looking for Dayrell too, and I had to lie for him. Pearl says he took off the whole afternoon. Sun shines and the man takes off from his roofing. Some damn job. Lets his own daddy down."

It was impossible to read the layers of meaning there. McCall was wearing his highway patrol reflective sunglasses, which made him look like a petty criminal with his grimy white shirt and stained chinos. Suddenly I hoped he didn't hurt Lukey or the kids. Was the sour smell in the truck more than the horse sweat? Was he drunk or on drugs? Should I follow them to make sure nothing happened? I looked at his hands on the steering wheel. The nails were chewed painfully far below the fingertips, although I couldn't remember ever seeing them in his mouth.

"You could all come over and have supper with me," I offered.

"You can cook?" He stared for a minute out the truck window, his jaw flexing and relaxing so his whole body seemed to let go of something. He laughed and let his foot off the brake. "Gotta go. Watch that Dayrell, Moline—he's got a bedpost size of a redwood he's notched down to a toothpick. Lukey can tell you all about it." She punched his arm hard and he laughed some more. It made me wonder how Titus thought I could help her.

As they pulled a U-turn, the kids were scrounging for boards for a fort they were already building. Their small sun-browned bodies made me so lonely for my son, I had to drop my eyes. Not my son now, but the way he was at first, when it was all hope and pride that got taken down piece by piece, day by day.

"Too much," I said, "too much," clenching my teeth and grinding to that place of pain on the broken back molar the dentist said I'd done myself. Do you know you're grinding your teeth? he'd asked, and I wouldn't let him crown it. Seeing the way McCall treated Lukey had suddenly turned the day ugly on me.

The kitchen was so torn up, it was lucky they didn't accept my offer of supper. I'd been hungry during the ride into town, but now my stomach felt like I'd swallowed too much gravel and creek water. There were a couple of longnecks fighting the mold in the fridge, and the bottle of Irish whiskey I'd brought with me in the empty cupboard. Enough for a "pity party." That was what Paris called it those last few months she'd be on the phone with me, glass clinking against the receiver, the exhale of smoke almost coming through the line, it seemed so close and final. Well, maybe she had a point. At least a person shouldn't lie to herself while she's lying to everyone else. That was called having standards.

Our son, Tyler, was so loving at first, he loved everyone. I thought he was the Prince of Peace the way he would throw out his arms to strangers in the grocery store and say he loved them. I drained half a beer and took a long slug off the whiskey, straight from the bottle. What happened? Duncan and I asked each other, we didn't do anything. I remembered Duncan looking at me like I was a stranger, a mad scientist making a monster in my womb, lying to him the day Tyler left the note and disappeared into the military just before he was to start his senior year in high school. I didn't do anything, I whispered, because no one believed me. Tyler, my heart said, I want my son, my little boy, I want to believe in goodness again, just for a while. Let me smell your milky skin again.

"Stop it," I muttered, and hugged my arms around my sunburn and scratched to get back to where things were real again. I hated all this memory and feeling. I worked so hard over the past few years to push it away, to stop, just stop; I didn't want to go back to that old sorrow well and take another bucket. Duncan and I practiced on each other, making sure nobody felt anything. When other people bragged about their kids, Duncan and I avoided each other's eyes, nodded, and passed the plate of

lies around with the rest when it came our turn. At night we went to separate rooms to put our lies to sleep, because that was the only way we could
stand ourselves.

I was glad Dayrell hadn't shown up yet, I thought, as I finished the
second beer with a whiskey chaser, and decided to go out for barbecue. As
Paris would've said, Never die on an empty stomach. I put the box of her
ashes on the seat beside me for company. It seemed right; after all, I was
all alone except for Dayrell's visitations, and maybe I was starting to
depend too much on him. It could only end one way. I'd have to tell him
the truth about the night of the accident. And then he wouldn't want me,
now would he?

WHO'LL PRAY FOR ME?

*Over time and given the right conditions, each type of rock can be trans-
formed into one of the other types. . . . The Rock Cycle represents the
relationships among igneous, sedimentary, and metamorphic rocks.
Natural processes are constantly transforming the rock. Weathering and
transportation can be watched, but heating and compression take place
deep within the crust.*

— MISSOURI GEOLOGY

✳

BY THE TIME I HIT THE PARKING LOT at the Rib Cabooze I was
having all kinds of down thoughts, feeling a lot of sorrow that such a good
and fine thing had to come to such a sad end. Then I saw Dayrell's
"excuse truck" sitting lopsided right beside the front door. "Always some
excuse why it won't run," he'd said. The excuse truck.

I'd put on my cowboy boots and undone two more buttons on my shirt
and slapped a gimme cap over my creek-dirty hair. Come and get it, boys.
That's what I felt like hollering into the noisy crowd at the bar end of the
room. I was torn between another drink and some food when the hostess
came over and led me to a table at the food end of things. She must've
known better than me. I stuck with beer as an act of contrition. I did have
to drive home again. Fortunately, they brought some cornbread and bread
sticks so I'd have something to dilute the bottle I was emptying.

The room was banging with noise from the pickup combo stationed by
the door, with banjos and guitars and bass but without the drums they
needed, and the men in dirty baseball shirts and caps in the bar hooting at

a play on the TV game, plus the couples laughing and shouting across the room at each other. It'd been a long time since I'd come into a place like this looking for trouble. I wasn't worried, though; I had my gun in my purse. Go ahead, fuck with me, I dared any man who tried to stare. And there were a few, on a night like this when the noisy energy was wound tight and the full moon hung in the sky like a bag of trouble just waiting for a tap to break loose over our heads.

I didn't smoke, but I felt like I was inhaling a pack a minute, which only made me more thirsty, so I drained the beer and signaled for another. I was in the kind of mood no one wanted to cross, so the service was damn good. When two bottles appeared, it took me a moment to realize it wasn't *that* damned good.

"Man over there bought you one," the waitress flung over her shoulder as she hustled her shredded cutoff jeans back to the bar. I followed her with my eyes and tried to figure out who it was. My skin prickled when I saw McCall standing in the shadows at the far end of the bar, just below one of the big hanging TVs. When he motioned with his head for me to join him, I drank and tried to outstare him. He laughed, and when the crowd parted for a moment, my eyes followed the gesture he was making with his beer bottle toward something behind him. It wasn't hard to see, except for the tears that sprang up: Lukey laughing and touching Dayrell's leg.

I concentrated on Dayrell, who was putting his hand on her shoulder and talking earnestly at her. Well, no wonder he had to take half days off. He was busier than a beaver in a lumberyard. When he started to look around, I dropped my head and turned away. He hadn't bothered to clean up much from the creek; his dirty hair was pulled back in a rubber band, and his tee shirt was the same one he'd worn that afternoon. When I looked again, she was brushing something from his shoulder and playing with his ponytail. Then the crowd closed in again as if they were protecting the couple. I thought I saw the tired kids asleep with their heads on the table opposite before I turned to catch McCall grinning at me. Just one big happy family. I drained the third beer and held it up for a refill, fighting the bloody raw thing in my stomach.

The ribs were too pink inside and the sauce had a rough, just-made flavor that hadn't soaked into the meat yet. The french fries were pale and soggy. The only good thing was the basket of Moistettes on the table I could use to clean my hands after touching the food I couldn't eat. I gave them that too thorough going-over you do when you've had the right amount of alcohol to make the world precise again. There were these red bumps on my palms from earlier, sticker bushes in the corn maybe, something I'd put my hands on when I'd taken my turn on top, leaning over him, holding his hands above his head while he closed his eyes and bit his lip as I moved just slowly enough to keep him from coming. . . .

My knee gave a big throb, followed by a steady pulse of hot ache. The creek water and bottom dirt couldn't have helped the cut much. I tried to focus on the pain in my knee instead of waiting for the crowd to divide. McCall kept glancing over his shoulder and laughing when he looked up at the TV.

The pity party geared up again when I took one last look in their direction and saw Dayrell bow his head like he was praying and Lukey rubbing the back of his exposed neck. I shoved some money on the table and struggled to extricate myself until the chair crashed over. As I bent and picked it up, McCall started pushing through the crowd toward me, calling my name. "Fuck you," I muttered.

"Fuck you, fuck you, fuck you all," I chanted out the door and around the crowded parking lot, until I finally found my truck sitting in its own pool of glittering glass and gravel like Liberace slumming among the beat-up trucks and cars. I was just getting in when I heard loud voices behind me and turned to look. Titus, Lukey, and McCall were standing right by the door under the floodlights, arguing. As I watched, Titus swept Lukey behind him and shoved McCall with one of his big meaty hands. McCall came back and shoved Titus back hard enough to bump into Lukey, who went down on her hands and knees with a little cry. When Titus turned to check on her, McCall kicked out and caught him in the side, knocking him off balance into a sprawl over Lukey, who cried out again. McCall was just getting ready to kick him again when I yelled, "Stop it!"

McCall looked at them, across the lot at me, then shrugged and started toward me. While I was debating whether to jump in my truck and drive off or wait and give Lukey and Titus time to get away, Dayrell settled the matter by coming out the door carrying the two kids.

He put them down and helped Lukey up and made sure everyone was safely inside before he hollered at his brother. McCall stopped, took a deep breath, clenched his jaw, and half turned toward Dayrell. "What the hell you want?"

"I want you to leave her the hell alone—I told you already. And quit picking a fight with Titus. He's a preacher, for chrissakes." Dayrell reached out for McCall's arm, and McCall jerked away.

"And I told you to stay the fuck out of my business, Dayrell. He's a nigger, and a nigger's always a nigger, and she's my wife, no matter how many times you fucked her, I still got the say over her."

Dayrell's arm dropped. His face went cold and empty.

"This doesn't have anything to do with me," I whispered, climbing inside my truck and starting the engine. Concentrating on not hitting anything, I just missed the hulk of an old white camper lurking at the corner of the building like an aging spy on a lost-cause mission. "Get a life," I told it, and squealed hard onto the blacktop, leaving both men standing in the broken yellow pool of parking lot light. My knee throbbed harder against my jeans, but I figured that was good, just the kind of reminder I needed. The Widows bobbed their stupid white puff heads in time with the rhythm of the road, and their eyes were those red dots that glowed redder when I hit the brakes.

"Okay, people," I announced, slowing down for the tour of downtown Resurrection, which was closed tighter than a Sunday fist on a ten-dollar bill. Even the hotel looked abandoned, as if there'd been an air-raid drill while I was getting into trouble, and everyone had streamed out and headed for the underground shelters and forgot to come back up, they were having such a fine time. There was a big yellow dog sitting on the corner by the courthouse waiting for the light blinking orange in all directions. "That's useful," I called out the window as I swung by. The dog ignored me. So did the Dixie Donut Shop with the one dim light in the rear over the ovens . . . Hair Benders . . . even the Dairy Daddy, which I circled just to see if anyone was alive here. It was deserted despite the yellow bug lights calling all the bugs. "Okay," I said, swinging a U-turn in the middle of Jefferson and driving past my house, which looked just like everyplace else—lights on, nobody home.

I hated this town as I drove around and around the square until I was feeling dizzy and crazy both and stopped at the House of Pawn, in front of the yellow plastic covered windows that had held the same resin mannequins captive for as long as I could remember, dressed in the same demure plaid housedresses Estes put them in the day she had to go to work after the bank and Horras failed in one fatal stroke. I used to like how they held their arms out to the world as if to say, See, we have nothing to hide, our lives are open and free of secret sin. It was the way I wanted things to be, but they never were.

But who the hell bought those housedresses made in timeless style with buttons down the front and deep pockets on the side? Who chose the flat colors, the sad limp curls of flowers? Sometimes even Iberia would wear them because Estes brought them home for her when she got sick of seeing her daughter in blouses safety-pinned together, and skirts with long stains dripping down the front as if she had poured grease on herself on purpose. Iberia's clothes had such a short life span, I used to wonder if she hated them on principle, as if her nakedness on her mother's porch roof that hot July afternoon I saw her was the only form of truth that could be said for certain about her.

When Estes got too old, Delphine, then Pearl, took the shop. There was never any question that Iberia and Mister would get it. They got some cash and land, which Mister eventually turned into the Swan Lake Trailer Park, complete with large plastic swan decoys swimming on the pond that scummed up green and heavy with water lilies and bottle flies from June to October. No wonder the real swans died right off the bat. That was only the beginning of their fortunes, though, because after they built the trailer park on land that'd been in Estes's family for a hundred years, they were able to buy a small parcel nobody wanted out by the old sawmill on the edge of town, and that site turned out perfect for the pencil factory, and from then on for ten years of entrepreneurial bliss, Mister and Iberia were only a frog jump ahead of somebody else's desire, until the deeds for land in DeWight County looked like they had to be cleared through Bedwell hands just to be filed. It was an extraordinary string of luck, one that comes only once in most family lines, and the Bedwells hadn't seen its like since they first immigrated to this country on free land and managed to purchase three slaves to help with the work of farming. They lost even them to freedom, and always after that, white Bedwells agreed that no luck had come of that particular adventure, either.

The bank, the store, the sheriff's office, the trailer park, the land, all lost and gone. Shit. I punched the gas and skidded down the streets behind my house. Pulling up on the side road, I saw my house for what it was worth, a falling-down shack as torn up inside as it was outside. "Screw you, Moline, you are not going to feel sorry for yourself again," I muttered to myself as I climbed out of my truck.

"Moline." McCall stepped out of the shadow of the eucalyptus tree. "Thought you could use a cold one." He held up a six-pack of Pabst long-necks in each hand.

"McCall, get the hell out of here." I started for him with my fists ready and he backed off.

"We need to talk, Moline. 'Bout before—the accident and Dayrell." He held the beer in front of him.

"Like the cave that time?"

"You misunderstood . . . brought Titus. I wasn't trying to hurt you."

"Like hell."

"Long time ago, Moline. We need to talk about now." The bottles clinked against his chest. "He's both our problem now." Some warning in his voice made me nod and walk around him to the back door. I still had the gun in my purse.

I left the lights off except for the one by Mister's recliner because I didn't want to look at either one of us as we sat in the far corner on the sofa and drank some more beer. For a while he rambled on with a bunch of bullshit about how he was so sorry his marriages didn't work out, and how hard he tried, but how no woman understood him well enough, and how he was really a nice guy.

"What about those bruises on Lukey then?" I finally asked.

"Wasn't me." He was watching me out of the corner of his eye at the other end of the sofa. I'd been careful to draw my knees up and prop my feet on the edge of the cushion so I wasn't wide open, but he hadn't made a single move toward me. I remembered the time at the movies with Paris when I was still just a kid, and he'd come and sat down next to me and kept putting his hand on my leg, sliding it up my thigh into my crotch. All I could figure to do was keep pulling his hand away and scootching over toward Paris, who kept shoving me back because she was trying to watch the movie. Finally I got up and moved to the other side of her, and when I looked over at him, he was watching the movie with a smile on his face.

"You remember that time in the movies when I was thirteen and you started molesting me?"

He grinned and shook his head. There was something a little scary about his eyes in the shadows; they seemed to glitter like cut glass, harder than the bottles we were drinking from. "You were a little tease, Moline, always asking for it. I still don't believe it was Dayrell cracked your cherry. I never believed all that innocent stuff you were handing him. Tell the truth now."

"Go fuck yourself, McCall." I slugged the beer and leaned over to grab another sitting on the floor between us.

"Well, okay, say it's true. Why waste all that time anyway? What's the point? That's my attitude. People are always trying to make sex some big issue. My idea is we should just do it, get it over with. Feels good. We do other things that feel good—eat, drink, smoke, play. Why not sex? Early and often. Personally, I don't care who fucks my wife, except for some nigger or trash like that. And maybe that makes me prejudice, but I figure everyone hates somebody. Even Saint Dayrell who claims everybody's equal. He slept with my wife, we all know it. I didn't raise a stink. Said okay, have at it. He was drunk and stoned. Only thing I wondered afterwards was whether the girl is mine or his, but then what the hell, really, what the hell, we're brothers. Saint Dayrell gives her money, so it's worked out. Keeps him working double time to take care of all the women. Good for business, good for me. Lukey's simple, you know. She's about as simple as they come, with a room-temperature IQ. Not much there but what you see. I didn't mind once I got used to the idea. See Dayrell cannot keep his hands to himself. Once he starts drinking—"

I shoved my feet out and sat up straighter. "Will you shut up?" I drained the bottle I was holding and the room took a soft dance around the circle. I reached out to stop it from tilting and McCall leaned over and put his hand around my upper arm.

"You okay?" He moved close enough that I could smell his cologne through the smoke-and-beer residue of the bar.

"Leave me alone." I tried to shake him loose and he lifted his hand but put his arm behind me, letting it rest on the sofa back. "I'm not kidding, McCall."

"Nothing's going to happen, Moline. Settle down, now. I'm just trying to help—in case you feel sick or something."

I leaned forward, away from his arm, and reached for another bottle.

"Here, let me have that." He took it and managed to move closer at the same time, so that our thighs were almost touching and our arms brushed against each other. There was something powerful about him, something that made the muscles in my body drain, like in a dream where you keep trying to run away and you can't move. He twisted the cap off and handed the bottle back, but held the cap in his hand, running his thumbnail over the little serrated ridges, letting it catch and plink in a slow rhythm I couldn't stop listening to.

"You know we share something," he whispered. "Something nobody knows but us." He kissed the back of my neck, holding me steady with his arm. "We have a secret."

The kisses were small at first, nibbles, with the teeth catching the skin lightly and holding it long enough for the sharpness to sink through the alcohol numb. I couldn't tell whether I wanted to push away from or toward the feeling, it was so new and odd.

"I'd hate to tell Dayrell you were in the car that night. You wouldn't like that, would you? We need to make a pact, help each other out. We want the same thing, don't we?"

He wasn't breathing hard, but I was, as he murmured and hummed, coaxing me closer, his fingers undoing my shirt, the little pinches and nibbles working around to my face, until I pulled my mouth away. I didn't want him near my mouth, I knew that, and kept my teeth gritted, because somehow it wasn't happening if he didn't kiss me, I was only letting it go this far, see, to find out the truth; but then he had my bra unhooked and pushed up and was pulling my shirt back pinning my arms behind me somehow and I couldn't quite understand what was happening and I struggled and he laughed and said, "Yeah, that's it," and he began kissing down my neck toward my breasts, holding my hands tied with my shirt behind me, pushing me back while his hand and mouth nipped and pinched at my breasts, and this black balloon rose up my body and smothered my lungs and I couldn't catch my breath, and it was making my head dark and I yelled, "No, stop—no, please!" and he laughed and dug in harder and bit me for real.

"You like it rough, don't you? I knew that from before." He pushed his hand down inside my pants and pulled out his fingers and wiped them on my cheek. "You're wet—you're dripping wet." I tried to spit on him and he slapped me across the face and I knew what he was going to do. "You like being hit? That get you off? I can slap you." He slapped my breast so hard I screamed, and he slapped my face again and began to unzip his pants and pull himself out.

"Help me—oh, God, McCall, don't—" I cried, and he yanked my arms harder behind me so I arched out at him.

"Not too loud, Moline—don't want the neighbors to worry. I'll just have to gag you with this." He waved his swollen cock at me and pulled my head back by my hair and straddled me, pushing his heavy thighs against me so I couldn't move. "You been asking for this. Should've given it to you that time in the cave. You ran then—that was smart. You should do it again—leave, get away from here while you can, before something bad happens to you!"

He slapped me again, harder, so the dots of lights danced in back of my eyes, and I felt his fingers prying my mouth open, forcing their way down my throat, choking me, the other hand around my throat, squeezing the air off. He leaned next to my ear and whispered, "You're not going to tell him you were there that night, are you?" He pulled his fingers out and I couldn't breathe.

He whispered again. "He'll wonder why you didn't testify. But you really don't know for sure, do you? He was passed out in back, but maybe he woke up—maybe. Can't face the truth, can you? And he won't forgive you either way. So you do what I tell you now. Keep your mouth shut and stay out of things that don't concern you, or I'll fuck you to death and tell him the truth. That'll finish him and you both." I was choking, and the pinpricks of light blinked on and off as the pressure in my throat and lungs threatened to burst—And then it stopped. There was a thump and I opened my eyes.

A hazy figure was standing over something on the floor that rose up and started fighting. They smashed into the coffee table, which shattered, and the lamp by Mister's chair rocked back and fell against the wall, and chairs were knocked out of the way, and once they fell on top of me and I still hadn't worked my arms loose and it felt like the bones were breaking, and there was cursing and thudding and grunting, and then it was over. McCall was standing over the other man who was curled in a ball and was kicking him with his pointed boots.

This black and red came over me and I felt myself let go and one of my arms finally came loose, then the other, and I wanted my gun, where was my gun, and I heaved up and ran for my purse across the room and pulled the .38 out and shot without pointing, shot again and again, and the roaring in my head said Shoot, shoot him, and I tried to see this time, and was waving the gun to keep him pinned down so I could sight in and get him good this time. Don't miss, the voice said, don't miss, and that's when these arms came around me in a terrible hug and locked on my wrist, like it'd break if I didn't give up the gun, and I knew it was him and started fighting again and trying to swing the gun around, but he was too strong for me and took the gun as I was trying to squeeze the trigger, and turned me around and slapped me hard across the face, hard enough that I fell down, and couldn't see good for a minute, and I felt the hands raise me up and shake me hard and the noise from the gun kept the words away. And I was thinking, Why do men shake me so hard? my neck, my brain won't—and suddenly the vomit coming up my throat and I put my hand over my mouth and it stopped and I leaned over and puked on my living room floor and closed my eyes because what was going to happen was going to happen and I got dizzy and the room tilted and so did I, and the hands shoved me toward the heap on the floor which was Dayrell who rolled onto his back and groaned.

"You two deserve each other—fucking lame-ass shit!" McCall stumbled to the sofa and sagged down next to the overturned beer. Retrieving one, he twisted the cap off and threw it at us. "She was asking for it, Dayrell. Nothing to do with you, man."

"Fuck you, McCall." My throat was so sore from the choking and puking my voice was a hoarse croak.

"That's what you wanted." McCall grinned.

Dayrell tried to cover his eyes with his arm, but they were already swelling. His mouth and nose were bleeding too. I couldn't imagine how his stomach and ribs felt after the kicking.

"Liar!" I croaked.

"You almost shot us, you crazy bitch—what the fuck is the matter with you?" McCall and I both knew he was lying, but I couldn't get myself organized. Dayrell opened his eyes and stared at me.

"He—wouldn't—stop." My teeth were chattering so hard I could barely talk. Struggling upright, Dayrell pushed me away, then pulled me tight against him, squeezing me so hard I couldn't get my breath.

"She calming down?"

"You wait for me, I'm gonna put her to bed. She's drunk out of her mind. You wait, McCall, you hear?" Dayrell stood and dragged me to my feet with him and started toward the back of the house.

"Sure, no problem, bro. I'll have me another longneck while you do some 911."

He led me back to my bedroom, shoved me onto the bed, yanked off my boots, and closed the door after him. I sat there for a moment and thought how easy it would be to pass out, let it all go. But I couldn't. My gun was still out there, and so was McCall. Besides, it was my house.

All I had to do was stand in the doorway to the living room. They'd straightened up the light by the recliner, but they were too busy to notice me.

"You keep your goddamned hands off of her, I told you before, McCall." Dayrell was standing over his brother, who was sprawled on the sofa below the two new holes in the wall. A hole in the sofa sprouted stuffing between his legs.

"Okay, all right—you want me to wait till you're done, I'll wait till you're done. But I'm getting sick of second servings, bro." He lifted the beer bottle to his mouth and Dayrell smashed it away. McCall put his fingers to his lips and looked at the blood leaking out. "That's no way to behave, now is it, Saint Dayrell? Have to be Lone Ranger to the rescue all the time, don't you? Didn't learn a single thing in that jail. Keep your nose in your own business, maybe? Got cut good for not listening, didn't you? Probably nursemaiding some fag—some nigger—what was it?"

Dayrell stepped back and looked around as if he was hunting for the gun. McCall stood up, pulling the last bottle from the carton and holding it out. "Here, want to use this on me? Come on, hurt me, you want to, don't you—little chicken shit, little mama cunt boy! Come on, Dayrell, let's have it—"

Dayrell lunged at him, catching him on the jaw and knocking him backwards, but McCall caught him in the balls with the toe of his boot and Dayrell went down on the floor again, curling up. McCall stood over him, debating whether to kick him or not, it was in his face, decided not to, and sat down and picked up the bottle of beer.

"You ain't so tough after all, Dayrell. Didn't they teach you to fight in that jail? Tried to make a man of you my whole life, but you end up like some piece of pussy, crying and freaking out. What the fuck is all this shit, anyway? This goddamned bitch came on to me. There's so many out there, we barely have time to catch the good ones, why're you settling for a bad one? Come on now, get up and have a brew with your brother." McCall twisted off the cap and held it out.

Dayrell pushed his hand away and crawled to the opposite wall. His face was white and exhausted and terrible looking. "Listen," he whispered, "don't you ever fucking talk to me again about those seven years. Keep bringing it up. I don't talk about it, I don't ever want to talk about it. I want to forget it like the goddamned motherfucking shitload nightmare it was." He braced his back against the wall across from the sofa, his legs speared out in front of him as if his knees had lost the power to bend.

"Yeah, well, fuck you too, Dayrell." McCall slugged some beer, then threw the bottle across the room, spilling beer in a wide arc until it crashed into the wall.

"You done?" Dayrell asked in a cold-ass tone of voice that chilled my scalp.

"There it is," McCall said, and wiped his face on his sleeve again. "Dayrell the Good Saver of lost souls. Saved Lukey, didn't you—saved her for yourself. That was a good one. Saved Pearl, so I could have her and get her pregnant. Didn't know that, did you?" He smiled at Dayrell. "Now you're going to save Moline. She must be an especially bad case—needs saving twice. Or is it something else you're up to, brother? Trying for a cut of the Heart Hogs deal on that Rains land?"

"Fuck you, McCall—fuck you and get the fuck outta my life!" Dayrell yelled at the retreating figure of his brother.

"Tell her to go away, Dayrell. She's nothing to you, and she's trying to screw things up. Come between us, can't you see that? We worked it out about Lukey, but this ain't going to work with this bitch—dump her, Dayrell. She ran on you the minute trouble came into your life before. She's nothing, man, not a thing. She'll hurt you, Dayrell. Everyone can see it coming but you. Same as before, same thing, same as before."

After he'd gone, Dayrell sat there, staring at the bulletholes in the walls, while I stood staring at the same thing and wondering who the hell either of us could trust now.

12

LOVE IN THE COUNTRY
OF DESPERATION

Led by desperate men such as William C. Quantrill, Bill Anderson, George Todd, Joseph C. Porter, John Thrailkill, and Upton Hays the guerrillas. . . . plunged a fairly stable, congenial, and conservative society into intense partisan conflict that was felt by every man, woman and child. This was not a war of great armies and captains, this was a bloody local insurrection, a civil war in the precise definition of that term.

— GRAY GHOSTS OF THE CONFEDERACY

✳

"MOLINE?" He sounded so tired I wanted to put him to bed.

"I'm here." I came into the living room and knelt down in front of him, pulling his head to my chest and rubbing his back. "You okay?" I whispered into his hair, sticky with beer.

"Did he try to—"

"He wouldn't stop—I got scared." I shivered. McCall was right; we did share a secret. "Then he kept kicking you. God, I'm so glad I didn't shoot him."

"He never knows when to stop with women. He thinks you're all alike." He pressed his face against me, letting me rub his neck too. "I'm sorry—"

"Not your fault."

"Why were you drinking with him?"

"He just showed up. Guess I was drunk." He hadn't heard us, then. The relief made me giddy. "I blew a hole in the sofa. Some shot, huh?"

"Wouldn't exactly want you covering my back in a gunfight. . . . Moline?"

"Yeah?"

"Think we could go out to the farm to sleep? He keeps drinking, he'll come back for more, and I'm dead on my feet."

"Sure. Let me just call Walker and tell her we're heading out there."

The drive was quiet, neither of us doing anything but trying to let the moonlight running off the road into the ditches and pastures like skim milk smooth away the terrible scene with McCall. Dayrell was at the wheel, his body held stiffly against the bruises. My face felt swollen from the slaps. At one point, Dayrell reached over and touched the welts left by McCall's fingers, but I couldn't catch the expression on his face. We still had talking to do. Too much had happened tonight. I didn't know where to start sorting it out about McCall and Dayrell and me. McCall was right about one thing: I could never tell Dayrell the truth. I was sobering up fast enough to understand how much worse things were for me now.

"Look over there." Dayrell slowed and pointed to the pasture to the right of the road up to the farm, where three does and a fawn were eating, their backs sprinkled with drops of dew the moon made sparkly. The nearest one raised her head and looked at us as we edged past. This would all be gone with the pig business, the small farmers driven out by the competition. These pastures disappearing, the deer and wildlife going further away, always further away, until there'd be nowhere left for them.

The lane and the lawn around the house were mowed now, and someone had started weeding the flower gardens and trimming the bushes. A big pile of brush and weeds I hadn't noticed earlier today sat by the back gate of the fenced yard, waiting to be taken to one of the gulleys behind the barn.

When Dayrell turned off the engine, we sat for a moment, letting our heads fill with the night sounds of peepers. The old freezer, which had reappeared on the back porch after the papers and junk were hauled away, was like a dull square pupilless eye looking out at us, steady and unblinking. The gutter that had broken away from the second-floor eaves dangled like an arm caught in a machine, and the broken lightning rod pointed to the earth, not the heavens, as if all the trouble we could receive from now on was coming from that direction.

"I'll try and fix that gutter, probably just a loose bracket. Won't be getting on any ladder tomorrow, though." He leaned back and felt along his ribs, probing gently with his fingers as he took deep breaths ending in soft groans. "Nothing broken. Lucky. Guess I won't be talking to McCall any time soon. God, I hope—oh shit, never mind, they take his side, they take his side. He's their son too." He looked at the floor. "Ready?" He opened the door and it took a minute for him to climb carefully out. There wasn't anything to do but follow him inside, knowing I wouldn't sleep with the talk hanging over my head.

"You go on up and sleep," I said, and he limped on ahead and slowly climbed the stairs to the second floor.

I told myself I'd sit down in the kitchen and sober up, but I nodded out with my head twisted uncomfortably to one side, which was what woke me up a while later. After two tall glasses of water and some aspirin, I went upstairs to check on Dayrell. He'd simply lain down in his clothes and fallen asleep on the bed in the big back room looking out over the barnyard and pastures. I pulled his boots off and stood there watching the face I'd come to love so much again I hadn't even realized what it meant until a few hours ago when he took a beating to stop his brother. I'd fought those feelings all my life really, and now I could no more escape that fate of love than my parents had. What I feared most that long night of waiting his sleep out was that when he woke up, Dayrell would decide that I was too much trouble for him, or that I would somehow be forced to confess the truth about my knowledge of the accident and end up asking him if he was sure he'd been driving. But he'd said he couldn't remember anything. I was trapped between loving him and fearing the truth embedded in our past.

After coming back downstairs, I got hopeful again looking around the kitchen, thinking about Aunt Walker and Uncle Able and how I'd never counted them as part of the family curse on love, maybe because for all her complaining, Walker loved as thoroughly and completely as any person could, keeping Able's dreams alive as long as possible, despite their age, despite the community's and her family's opposition. Maybe Walker would be the person I believed in. Love hadn't killed her, or anyone else around her.

But before I'd sat much longer at the table, I had to admit another truth: It'd never work, never.

I felt helpless, scared, the way I had the night I had met McCall in what they called the Bridal Chamber at Calvin's Cave a few days after the accident. He had said he had an urgent message from Dayrell. Since that was the place Dayrell and I went to make love, I knew it had to be the truth.

It was raining that night, and Titus didn't want me to go alone. We could hardly see as we picked our way down the long road to the cave. Inside, there were floodlights, though, and Titus hung back in case we encountered him suddenly. The cave is pretty straightforward, not a lot of turnoffs, but it's very long, a mile at least, and full of twists and little cubbyholes and side rooms, and it's deep, deep underground, two hundred fifty feet. And when it rains, the rooms begin to fill with water, one after another, like dominoes caught in the six- and ten-foot floods. Every few years a person dies in the caves around Resurrection, lost, injured, drowned. But I wasn't thinking of the danger, only the message from Dayrell.

As we went deeper into the cave, the rooms got smaller and the walls and ceilings were dripping a lot faster, turning into streams, and sometimes we were sloughing through pools of water so black and cold all I could feel was the icy cuff like a sock on each ankle. The further we walked, the dimmer the lights and the more the water was beginning to rush down and cover the floors of entire rooms. By the time the pools were up to my knees, I was shaking with cold. My soggy pants dragged at my butt and legs as if they were trying to pull me down too. My fingers were starting to go numb, and I couldn't tell whether the rocks I grabbed for balance were sharp or not.

Suddenly as we faced the hole half a mile in that led to the Bridal Chamber, the lights went out for good.

"Titus?" I whispered, but he was somewhere behind me, hiding. "McCall?" It was so dark, when I held my hand in front of my face, there wasn't even a glimmer of flesh. Half a mile inside the earth, I was blind, and a flood was coming—I rubbed my eyes, but they only burned, didn't find any light. That's when I heard it: something falling into the water, something long and thick, like a snake maybe, a cottonmouth swimming toward me. I could almost feel it touch my legs, and I tried to look down, but there was nothing. I felt the water nudging its way up inch by inch past my waist.

"Titus? McCall?" I turned around, trying to remember which way the hole to the room was, but I couldn't. The cold wet put an arm around me like a deadly old friend, a lover who wanted me to lie down with him.

I didn't want to think about what was sharing the water with me—bats, rats, giant salamanders, snakes. The water caught at my shirt, billowing it out, climbing under it to my bare skin and riding up to my breasts, tugging at my bra. I fought it with my hands, trying to push it away in front of me, but there was a current from underneath, a rushing that wanted to sweep me along with it.

Something nudged my leg.

"Titus?"

Somebody grabbed my ankle and pulled me down into the water. My elbow scraped on the rock below as he squeezed my breath out and dropped me into the darkest bottom of the cave. I cried out and swallowed water. My chest filled up. The man lay on me, pinning me to the floor. The trapped air wanted to explode out of my lungs. I kept my mouth shut to stop the water from getting in. My ears roared and my nose stung, that's what I kept thinking: My nose stings, stop. I raised my knee and found a soft place and the man let go. He lifted my head by the hair and tried to bang it down on the stone, but the water softened the blows. The blackness covering me was darker than the dark water, the dark cave, the dark walls of my skull. Who was it? I began to feel the riot of air wanting out of my chest. "Now," McCall's familiar voice said in my ear like a watery lover, "Now," and I opened my mouth for it.

But he stopped. Everything lifted. I bobbed to the top, and there was a terrific thrashing even louder than the pounding in my head as I choked for air and vomited water through my mouth and nose. My eyes searched frantically for something light, but there was nothing except when something fell against me and knocked me back under. I was so weak I almost didn't make it up again. Finally there was a crack and the noises stopped. The water was up to my chin, and opened up from below to take me—a good bath, a good soaking, I thought, as my legs wobbled under me and I started to go under again.

"Moline?" Titus dragged me back up, slapping my back too hard. "Come on—we have to get out of here, the room's filling too fast, it's pulling the loose rock down."

I was so cold I couldn't feel anything. My arms and legs were thick with ice and wouldn't bend. "I can't. . . . " My teeth were chattering. I couldn't feel my clothes; was I naked? I tried to make my fingers tell me something, but nothing was working, as if my body had gone blind too.

"Where's McCall?" I gasped.

Titus started to pick me up, but I pulled back. "Doesn't matter—come on."

Afterwards, Titus snuck clean clothes from his house for me, and we sat up half the night holding hands until I had the courage to sneak home, pack, and let him drive me to the bus station in Tipton.

Why, I thought now, had I ever, ever trusted McCall again? Why had I drunk beer with him, allowed him to get close enough to lay a hand on me—wasn't nearly being drowned enough of a lesson? I thought about that for a while longer until I fell asleep, dreaming of the old despair that night had produced, the truth of being trapped in your life, of being so desperate to stay alive you're driven to flinging away the past, letting it sink and drown in a dark hole, believing it will stay missing forever. What was gone stayed gone, what was dead stayed dead. But I was wrong.

When I woke up, it was midmorning and I was upstairs in bed with Dayrell, who was on his side facing me, holding me next to him with his arm across my chest, watching me sleep. He smiled and I knew it was all right, and I'd never been so grateful in my life. He kissed me very softly on the lips and brushed my hair back and traced my forehead and nose with his finger. "Just a little bruise on this cheek here. . . . "

"Dayrell, I'm—"

He put his finger to my lips. "Shhh. Let me talk."

"No, let me—"

He stopped me again. His eyes were puffy from the fight, but not as bad as I'd expected. His chest was splotched with dark bruises, though. "I know you've heard a lot of things about me. They're true, but true in the past, not now. I love you, Moline—I don't want to spend nights apart anymore. I love you. I've always loved you. That was one of the worst things about the accident, losing you." He leaned down and kissed me again, but it was different than it'd been before. This had the weight of time, of those words, beautiful and fatal, I'd wanted so much to hear from him, which turned everything different, deeper and more fragile, as if now we'd have to act differently because it had been said out loud. Now our responsibilities began.

What it did was slow everything down between us. Our lovemaking took more time. It was as if earlier, when we'd torn at each other's flesh, shattering the clocks before they could stop us, it was to get at something else, something this calm and still—something beyond the slow march of the sun arcing across the sky, beyond the rotation of birds in song and flight, the noon coming of the summer flies, the late-day rustle of the cattle and horses returning to drink and eat in the barn shade, and the breeze rattling the leaves outside the window at dusk when we woke hungry and shy with love in our eyes.

As I filled the old white claw-footed tub with steaming water and dumped in some ancient bubble bath I had to dig out in clumps with my fingers, I did not let one thought about the night before take hold. Dayrell climbed in first, balancing himself on my shoulder to lift the leg with the biggest purple blue bruises. The sorest place was the long scar across his stomach, where the toe of McCall's boot had caught the seam and almost torn it open. After he slid down into the water, coating his hair and face with a film of bubbles, and popped back up, I climbed in and sat facing him between his legs, my back resting against the spigot. His penis floated just below the surface, and I couldn't resist putting my hand around it and holding on until I felt the first surge of blood. Dayrell shook his head and closed his eyes and groaned tiredly.

"Aren't you ever going to give me any peace, woman?"

"I figure you owe me about twenty-three years of this. You wouldn't want a debt like that piling up interest on you." I touched his groin and stomach, letting my fingers slide along the ridge of scar, worrying where the swollen bumps stopped me.

"You're the first person I ever let do that." He laid his hand over mine.

"How did it happen?"

He picked up our hands and looked at the scar through the clusters of big bubbles riding like ice floes in the bathwater. "That scar, well, that was a knife fight in Booneville, in a real rough bar, a biker place. McCall and I'd been drinking and smoking dope for a few days—that was when we had our Harleys. We were getting tired, though, and wanted to keep partying, so we went up there to cop some crystal—somebody always had some crank there. Only, McCall brought Lukey, that was the problem. Wrong move. Don't take women into a place like that, not unless they can handle it. Even Leota Fay would have trouble getting out in one piece, and she could keep King Kong on a short leash. So of course, there was trouble."

He pulled me toward him so I bent at the waist and laid my head half in the water on his chest, feeling the few little hairs tickle my ear like minnows. I tilted my head and asked, "What happened?"

"The asshole with the meth wanted to trade Lukey for the drugs, kept saying he didn't want money. I told McCall to leave her with the bikes, but he was more wrecked than I was and wouldn't listen. I was flying pretty good myself, so I let it go and there we were. Might as well have brought Bambi to an NRA convention. Crazy asshole pulls a toad sticker the size of a machete and wants to fight. I had my switchblade, but it wasn't much of a match. He outreached me a good two feet and sliced my belly open before I could do more than stick him once in the arm. Blood started pouring out and I went down hollering and Lukey was screaming for the cops—that broke up the party pretty quick and they ended up medivacking me to the University Hospital in Columbia. Parents made us sell the bikes to pay the bills. Asshole who sliced me got away clean. Lukey and I . . . "

My stomach tightened around that empty fist of feelings I didn't want. "What?"

"She felt sorry for me more than anything, I guess. McCall was being bad to her even then, leaving her alone too much, disappearing for a week or two at a time. She'd be out there at their place with no money, no transportation. She was just a kid. He knew what he was doing. Well, when I got out of the hospital, I couldn't go home—Hale had already told me he'd had enough and didn't want my dangerous ways destroying my mother and their marriage. Looking back, I can't blame him—after prison, this was pretty much over the top. So I went to recuperate at McCall and Lukey's place. That's when it happened."

"So he wasn't lying about the two of you?" I leaned back against the spigot again, wanting to see his eyes.

His face was soft, flushed. He shook his head. "Not my prettiest hour, but I did it. She's a fine woman and deserves better than both of us, whether she knows it or not. For a while I think we were both sleeping with her. Then she got pregnant, but I know it's not mine. I always used rubbers. I was real, real careful, not like McCall. He likes getting them pregnant. I was too scared of it after my wife and kid left."

"You can't be for sure, though."

He looked at his hands, front and back, shriveling in the water. "No, not for sure." He put them on my thighs and pulled me toward him so I was straddling him, and I pushed my feet out behind me and lay down on his length, my head on his shoulder, my lips at his ear.

"What else do you want to know, Moline?" When he spoke, I could feel the vibrations of his voice climb all the way up his chest.

"The other scar?"

"My throat? McCall was right about that too—not minding my own business."

I rubbed the hair on his arm, watching the tiny silver bubbles collected along the shafts percolate to the surface. "Is Heart Hogs your business?"

His body tensed, then relaxed. "You believe that about me—that I'd use you to steal your aunt and uncle's land? Maybe take Lukey's too?"

I felt the quick shame of his words and shook my head.

He turned his head and lifted my chin until our faces were so close I couldn't focus. "I'm not ripping you off, Moline. I wouldn't do anything to hurt you or your family—you ought to know that by now. I'd rather hurt myself than let anything happen to you."

I watched myself in the dark surface of his eyes, where I was a tiny speck of light. "What about McCall?"

He closed his eyes and shook his head slightly and let go of my chin. "I don't know. He's been acting weirder than usual lately, especially around you. What'd he say last night?"

"Not much."

"I don't know—he's got Pearl pregnant. Can't believe it. Poor Lukey. He's working with Pearl for Heart Hogs while he's trying to make a killing by selling Lukey's land to them. I've tried to convince her not to give him the land, but she loves him so damn much she can't stop herself." He picked up the ragged pink washcloth I'd thrown in the tub earlier and started scrubbing my arm and shoulder. "Can't figure out what he's got against you, though."

"Hey, I'm not a horse, you know." I yanked the washcloth out of his hand. I didn't want to think about McCall's warning right then and squeezed the washcloth over his face. And we started splashing each other, heaving water onto the yellow and green linoleum floor and soaking the towels we'd piled next to the tub.

"Wait," he finally gasped. "Hold still—let me look at that knee." I was leaning with my back against him, and he picked up my leg and touched the swollen red place that looked hot and tight, like a tomato about to split in the sun. He pushed on it and I jerked.

"Stop it!"

"That sore, huh? You should try to open it, let it drain. Get gangrene, your leg'll fall off and I might have to dump you for a good two-legged woman." He wrapped his arms around me so I couldn't hit him, and I scissored enough water with my legs to swamp us and slosh the floor again. After that I began telling him about my years away from Resurrection, trying to explain my son, Tyler, but couldn't reach to the bottom of the well for the Duncan story, not yet.

"Were you happy?" he asked.

I shrugged. "I was comfortable. Had a nice house and stuff. But I settled for so little it seems like—"

"No. You were right to try for something better."

I put my fingers to his lips, unable to listen. "I used to dream about you."

"I thought about you every day, Moline. Never put your picture on my cell wall, though. Didn't want those men in there seeing you with their dirty eyes."

"Dayrell, do you think we have a chance? I'm not very good at this. What if I end up telling you something you hate me for?"

"Shhh . . . " He tucked my head under his chin, but I pulled back and looked at him to see if he could read my expression. "Tell me then."

"Can't . . . not yet."

"It's okay, Moline. We have a long, long time to tell our stories." He kissed me and floated the worry off me and left me free of memory for a little while. I let out some of the tepid water then and ran some more hot in.

"Come here," he said, and I turned around and sat in his lap and we locked our legs behind each other. He took my face in his hands and said, "I love you, Moline," and he kissed me and kissed me until I agreed and I finally said it. "Yes," I said, "I love you, Dayrell, I do, I love you, I've always loved you, always. Always." And everything seemed so possible.

We scrambled a mixture of duck and chicken eggs, stale saltines and wild onion, and took the frying pan up to bed to eat. After the long soak and food, we only managed to keep our eyes open until dark when we fell asleep in each other's arms just as the night chirping started. At first, my dreams were vague and ordinary, but Dayrell groaned and pushed away from me in his sleep and I half woke myself, then dropped off again.

John Wesley Waller is here again, so I ask him, Why go in the river if it breaks your back? Why be rescued, why not drown if it's baptism, salvation?

Then I am actually going in the river, feeling it turn the horse aside, tip and toss it like a split tree, flesh tangled and churned, stripped, jagged. I feel the stirrup and my boot too tight already, the leg, twisting, swelling, waterlogged useless, holds me to the animal gulping water, kicking against the drag of my body, kicking the iron shoes. The iron shoes—banging, banging, banging—juggle me, my back snaps. I hear it in a silence I've found, a pocket of brown space, orange with water behind my skull. I look out the closed eyes and hear my bones go twig brittle and soft green under the grinding hooves—Am I swimming, or is the near-carcass of hopelessly constructed horse dragging me toward shore, or is it a rope around its neck pulling us up the spoiled banks, the two of us in this clumsy embrace? His hand's flames make the water red, orange, yellow, all around me there's smoking water, burning swirls sucking my lungs, drying them out. . . .

I woke up choking for breath, my throat so dry I couldn't swallow and had to grab for the glass of water on the night stand. I shivered and rolled over on my stomach so I could look out the window across the barnyard to the back pasture where the horses and cattle were grazing. Only they weren't. The moon was bright enough to outline the trees, rocks, and fences, but no cattle or horses. No, that couldn't be right, we'd watched the Tebow boy closing them in the top pasture before dark. Maybe they'd gone through the fence. No, wait, it was so quiet out there—where was all the night noise? I got out of bed and knelt at the windowsill, trying to peer through the darkness. There was something in the old hog barn, a flicker, a haze of light, then another, spreading, and a pop, and the far end of the hog barn broke into flames.

"Dayrell! Jesus Christ, wake up Dayrell—the hog barn's on fire!" I yanked on my clothes and almost fell down the stairs with my boots half on, but he grabbed my arm and raced ahead out the back door toward the fire, which was rising high above the trees now. By the time we reached it, the whole thing was a wall of flames sucking at our faces and arms.

"Oh no—the pigs!" I remembered the mama and her babies and tried to run around to the side pen butting the barn, but the heat was too intense and Dayrell pulled me back, shouting in my ear over the roar of the crashing timbers, "Call the fire department before it takes the other buildings—go on!"

Glancing over my shoulder as I ran back to the house, I saw him soaking his shirt in the water tank and wrapping it around his head.

By the time I got back, he'd pulled five of the piglets out of the pen and soaked them good in the tank. Even so, the air stank of burning hide, and when he didn't go back again, I realized the sow was gone with the rest of her babies. "God damn it to fucking hell," I swore, and bent to pick up the runtiest pig, panting in the dirt at my feet. His eyes were milky like they'd been scalded and his little heart was staggering out of rhythm. I tried to hug him, but he squeaked in pain, and I realized he'd been burned too. His panting slowly faded as I held him against me, whispering, "Come on now, come on," against the silence in his chest.

"Give it to me." Dayrell took the pig and disappeared, and I watched the fire roar impossibly, shrieking higher and higher as tall runners of flames grabbed pieces of darkness out of the sky. Then I realized the noise was really the fire engines, and by the time they'd hooked up the water, the fire was already starting to collapse. Then it was over.

"Old wood and hay, thing went up like paper," Dayrell was saying to one of the firemen.

"Spontaneous combustion," another man remarked as he laid the hose out to drain into the corral. "We try to educate the farmers about storing hay and straw—get a couple a these a summer. Lucky the other barn and house didn't go. Too bad about the pigs. Smells like cracklings, don't it?"

"Well, old man Rains won't be farming here much longer anyways," another firemen said as he went back to the truck to start winding the hoses.

They were gone as suddenly and completely as they had arrived, and Dayrell and I looked around at the soaked ashes and the four remaining piglets, who were sleeping piled against the far side of the water tank as if they understood that metal and water were their only safety. Their pink and black skin was singed in places, and they probably had smoke damage to their lungs. Maybe none of them would make it, I realized as we knelt there listening to the watery gurgle of their snores. It came to me then.

"He didn't have to do this." I stood and kicked at the mud. "They didn't do anything to him."

Dayrell stood up. "What're you talking about? You know who did this?"

"Pretty goddamn obvious, isn't it? Your brother."

"No way." Dayrell shook his head.

"Sure, he hates me."

"No he doesn't. He's just fucked up—he wouldn't burn a person's barn and pigs just to get at you—how would that work?" Dayrell kept looking at me with disbelief, and I couldn't tell him why this was a warning.

"Does anyone know where we are?"

"Your aunt and uncle. Tebow. And I called Lukey to go feed my dogs. But she wouldn't . . . "

"You think this barn burned itself? Come on, Dayrell!"

He looked at the smoldering ruins and shrugged. "From what I saw the other day in there, I'd say it's real possible."

"This isn't the first fire."

"You mean that business at the hotel with the back door? That was kids, Moline." His voice was getting a hurried edge to it.

"I mean the chair someone deliberately set fire to on the second floor a few days ago while I was sleeping downstairs."

He turned away, shivering without his shirt on in the damp night air, then turned back. "Why didn't you tell me?" He stared at me for a minute and turned away again, his shoulders letting down a notch. "You think my brother set that one too? Is that what the other night was about?"

"Makes the most sense."

He raised his shoulders and shook his head. "No, he'd never deliberately. I know you two don't get along, but he'd never . . . " He started back to the house. "I'll prove it to you, Moline—you're wrong," he called over his shoulder.

"What about the pigs here? Shouldn't we do something?" I called after him.

"Leave 'em—they'll all be dead by morning anyway."

"No!" I looked around for something to carry them in and finally settled on Uncle Able's shirt I was wearing. They protested with little squeaks and snorks, but I carried them up to the mud porch and put them in the corner on some old rags. Nestling in on top of each other like puppies, they fell asleep again with the same clogged breathing. At least they'd be warm and safe here.

I decided to wait for morning to call the hotel and tell them the bad news, but when I got inside, Dayrell was pulling on his dirty tee shirt. The soot from the fire had covered some of the bruises on his face, but it didn't hide the flat expression in his eyes or the set of his mouth. "I have to go."

"But I just brought the pigs up to the porch . . . "

"Fine, I'll walk." He was out the door before I could stop him, I stood there for a few minutes, listening to the snorkling pigs and the higher sawing of the insects and frogs outside like an old rusted-hinge gate blown back and forth in the wind. McCall, or whoever had done this, wasn't coming back tonight. They were already asleep, their work done.

His long, limping stride sent his shadow crashing across the shadowy bars of trees and fence posts on the road ahead. I pulled beside him and told him to get in and he did. He sniffed and looked behind at the cardboard box of pigs nestled on the backseat. I ignored his stare and decided to try and wait out his furious silence. When I stopped in front of my house, he got out and carried the pigs to the chicken shed without a word. I'd planned on keeping them in the kitchen in case they needed me, but he was probably right.

It was almost dawn, and when he got in his truck and drove off without another word, I felt such a familiar emptiness. It was as if I'd been allowed one peek over the top of the well of grief I'd been living in, and then my fingers had slipped and I was falling down again into that dark where I spent my hours constructing nothing but habits and gestures, grateful for the diversions of weather and sleep. And I could see how one act of cowardice leads to another and another until after a while you don't even recognize yourself in that cold metallic ring on your finger you traded your soul for.

"Please," I said to the gray morning light in the wreckage of the kitchen, "make him right, don't let it be McCall." I waited then, for some kind of answer, because really, there was nothing else a person could do, even if it had been years since I'd asked for anything. Praying hadn't worked before, I didn't die that morning after the wreck, and I guess I didn't really expect it to work now. After all, God and I hadn't been on speaking terms since I left Resurrection. No reason to think He was even listening anymore. It just seemed like one of the things you try when you hear the sounds of the well being capped above you.

13

HIGHER GROUND

Ten years after Missouri became a state, a band of settlers, believing Missouri was a holy land, appeared in Jackson County. With the arrival of this advance party of the Church of Jesus Christ of Latter-Day Saints, followers of Joseph Smith, Missouri began times of great torment. These Saints, often called Mormons, were eventually expelled following much brutality. Soon thereafter, bloody conflicts over the future of slavery broke out between Missouri and Kansas. Then came the appalling Civil War years in which Missouri's distress was beyond that of most other states in the Union or the Confederacy. After the North's victory, ten years of bitter controversy began over the character of a new Missouri. Finally, an era of lawlessness brought sections of Missouri into virtual anarchy. Order was restored in the 1880s, ending what had been fifty years of internal torment and leaving Missouri with terrible memories.

— MISSOURI: A HISTORY

✳

I SLEPT LATE INTO THE MORNING and woke up with the sense that bad things were happening on the edges of the world, just outside, where I couldn't see them yet. I'd always had this way of knowing, something from my ancestors in the hills—maybe a sense that developed naturally in people cut off by rock and trees and dirt. How else were you supposed to get ready for danger? The first time I knew I had it for sure was when I was a kid and woke up one spring morning with the feeling that something terrible had happened while I was asleep. I got up without waking Paris and tiptoed from room to room, standing beside my parents' bed to make sure everyone was breathing. Then I went through the kitchen and bathroom and finally to the living room and out on the porch. Everything was still and quiet, but something was wrong, I knew it, so I turned on the TV with the volume so low I had to stand right in front of it.

The dark-haired man was talking and smiling and shaking hands and then he was falling and another man was being wrestled to the floor. It was Robert Kennedy, and he'd been killed with the TV cameras on him.

They played the same scene over and over, as if they knew none of us could get past the awful fascination of seeing it happen right before our watching eyes. I knew then that things were going to be different in the world, that nothing was the same now. And I came to understand and fear that feeling for the first time.

It was the same feeling I had now walking back to the chicken coop, half hoping that it was the piglets that had died, that I'd be released by their sacrifice, but that wasn't it. Three of the pigs were up sniffing around the debris on the dirt floor, trying to find something to eat. The fourth was still in the nest of rags, panting in shallow puffs, its lungs gurgling. It was clear from the sooty, scorched hide and the glazed eyes, there wasn't much left to do except try to wrap it in the rags and hold it for a few minutes of comfort. Burrowing its snout under my arm, the piglet let out a short series of gasps and gradually stopped breathing. I held it there for a while, letting its small soul linger for as long as it needed to say goodbye. Once in a while the other pigs came over to where I sat in the dirt, nudged the bundle in my arms, then backed away.

It seemed unfair, the whole deal, and I thought about how nothing asked to be born but that didn't mean we weren't responsible for it. Finally, I wrapped the pig in rags and put it on the shoulder high roost mounded with thirty-year-old pyramids of chicken droppings. Over the years, people had thrown the extra junk in here too: the cracked plastic buckets, cracked lengths of hose, rakes and hoes and shovels, tarps, pieces of wire and rope and gunny sacks. The baby pigs picked their way through the clutter, mewling and sobbing at my feet. I had to figure out what to do with the one on the roost and what to feed the others.

When I called Walker, she'd already heard about the barn from five other people, including the deputy fire chief. She asked if Dayrell and I were all right, so I didn't have to break that news to her. "Nothing good ever came from those two, Moline," she commented, which meant I couldn't tell her my suspicions about McCall. We talked about the pigs and she said she'd call Tebow's boy to come and get them and take them to their place. "If they're going to burn us out, maybe we should move the cattle and horses too." I talked her out of that, saying I'd keep an eye on them.

"Besides," I told her, "everyone seems to think it was spontaneous combustion."

"That and a quarter will get you a carnival ride. I'm letting Able think I agree, though, so he doesn't get his underwear in a bundle and go storming out there. Maybe they'll be content with taking the old barn. Wasn't worth tearing down. Only regret my sow and those babies. At my age, they might be the last pigs I raise."

I thought about telling her no, but that sounded too phony, so I said I'd be uptown later. Without Dayrell, I didn't know who to turn to for help. It was noon and he still wasn't on the roof next door. But I couldn't make myself sit there any longer, I got so afraid all of a sudden, like maybe he was the one in danger and I'd never see him again. Maybe McCall meant to hurt both of us.

A door slammed at Pearl's house, and in a minute she appeared in her kitchen window. I wanted to go over there, talk to her about the fire, about the family and McCall, but I couldn't. I didn't know her anymore. Then the pigs in the coop set up a big racket, as if they really were at the end of their ropes after being burned in the fire, losing their mother, and now being locked in the dirty shed without food or water. Pearl disappeared, then reappeared crossing the yard to the coop. Opening the door a crack, she peeked in and slammed it shut, which set up even more of an uproar. In a single motion she knocked and pulled my screen door open.

"Moline, there's pigs in that shed!" Her cream-colored high heel caught in a little pile of linoleum pieces and her ankle twisted, but she only grimaced and shoved the pile aside.

"I know."

"Well, it's illegal! Get rid of them this minute! My God—" She stopped and looked around the wrecked kitchen and down the hall into the living room.

"Remodeling."

"Dayrell's not here today, is he? Didn't bother showing up for work again. Supposed to be major rainstorms moving in this afternoon, and he still hasn't finished the roof." She eyed me like I might be hiding him.

I shrugged. "You hear about the old barn burning last night at the farm?"

"Yes, and I've told those people for five years to tear that thing down. Now it burns and they're blaming Heart Hogs. If they weren't related, I'd march in there and slap their faces. Decent people are trying to do something decent for this town, and some of you are acting as if we're opening a multiplex pornography theater."

She toed aside some more linoleum scraps and looked disapprovingly at the empty beer bottles lying on the table. Her cream-colored skirt and top were a natural, nubbly fabric that looked good enough for a cruise to the tropics. All she needed was a broad-brimmed straw hat and dark glasses to come down the gangplank of a steamer in one of those catalogs with the clever narratives for each item. The tortoiseshell bracelets on her arm clanked dully when she raised her hand to sweep the blond wave off her forehead. Pearl, I wanted to say, you're wasted here—go, run, just as fast as you can, there's an incredible life waiting for you. Don't settle for McCall and Heart Hogs.

"I have to tell you the truth, Pearl. Someone did set that fire."

"You're crazy," she snapped, but her mouth wasn't as decisive as her eyes, which were filled with dislike for me. It was the same dislike her mother, Delphine, used to wear around me and my mother. She had absolutely no expression for my father; they knew too much about each other.

"Trust me, Pearl."

"Trust you, Moline? Why would I do that? I don't know a thing about you. For all I know you could be a serial killer. You come home after a hundred years and make the local ex-con your boyfriend—what makes you think any decent person in town believes a word you say?"

"You should talk, Pearl."

Her chin jerked an inch higher. "What?" She took a step closer.

"I mean, you don't have any room to talk about me. You slept with him, and now you're sleeping with another woman's husband."

I didn't have time to duck before she slapped me. It was a lot lighter than McCall's, but it made me a lot madder. I slapped her back as hard as I could, and she cried out, staggered, and went down on one knee, tearing her stockings. By the time she was up again, her face was red and she was fighting the tears brimming her eyes.

"I hope it *was* set," she said between gritted teeth. "And I hope every single piece of Bedwell trash gets burned out of DeWight County before this is done!" She turned and slammed out of the house. I watched her stumble run across the yard, her heels catching in the soft dirt and tilting her forward every few steps. From the chicken coop came the anguished cries of the pigs waiting to be taken away.

"Now you've done it," I addressed myself on behalf of the Widows, who were lined up in the front row of my mind, like Christians watching the Romans get their comeuppance from the lions.

"Walker send you?" Titus stood on the porch, arms folded across his barrel chest, leaning against the newel post. His sons and daughters stared suspiciously from the doorway with his wife, Jos, who was a much darker shade than Titus's rosy tan saddle leather, more like deep river bottom when it glinted chocolate black under the plow blade. The kids ranged from pine plank yellow and creamed coffee to stove black, as if they were making up a new kind of rainbow.

"No. But I want to talk to you about the fires. You heard about the one out at the farm?"

He nodded and turned to his kids. "Here, go on about your business now, but don't forget what I told you about strangers." He waved an arm and they crowded out the door and down the steps, giggling and running. We watched for a moment as they swept over the crest of the hill, crashing into the woods of the ravine, whooping and bucking with pleasure like ponies let loose in a field.

"All those aren't yours?" I'd counted twelve and couldn't help looking at Jos's slim body.

He snorted. "Not exactly. Since Jos and I have the Free African Baptist Church now, seemed natural with the extra room we have here to take some kids in when they need help. Some stay, some don't, depending on their relatives and all." We watched as three of the children stopped and stared at something, poking it with their shoes and sticks. "Two are ours."

"House looks the same." I remembered him sneaking me in when we were kids so we could hide from our families and talk. His family didn't want their son having anything to do with the white-trash side of the tracks, even though we shared the family name and more: the large brown eyes, the broad cheekbones and well-defined Bedwell nose.

"You come on and sit down while I get us something cool to drink." Jos gestured toward the porch swing and an array of old wood and metal lawn chairs shoulder to shoulder looking at me. "I don't know where our manners are today. Now you keep an eye on those children, Titus." She nodded toward the ravine and let the screen door brush shut against her.

"Walker called about the fire." He inspected me carefully. "You weren't hurt, were you?"

"No, but Dayrell got singed trying to save the baby pigs."

"Uh-huh. We better wait for Jos to get back. She'll want to hear this."

We sat in silence for a minute, then I asked him about becoming a preacher. "Last I heard you got drafted."

"Yup. Went to Nam. Got through without a scratch. Saw buddies of mine blown to pieces all around me. Strange. Decided God had something better to do with my life than spill it there. Went to Israel after Nam. Finagled a ride on a transport. Decided to see some of those places I read about in the Bible. Went looking for Him. He was there, too—He really was. He wasn't any Uncle Tom God, either. Just have to look at how hard the Jews have it over there to know that. He's tough. A kick-butt God, kind we need. Came home, went to seminary, that was it. Met Jos. Probably good she's not from around here, doesn't have the history. Easier. When I got the call from the parish here, told 'em we came together. I don't think they quite understood till it was too late. We share the preaching, you see."

A mockingbird in the locust out front started running up and down a tune like it was test-marketing the sound.

"Can't figure out what that is he's trying to sing, been at it for a week. Drives me crazy. Just want to tell the darn thing to figure it out or leave it alone." Titus pointed his finger like a gun toward the bird, almost completely hidden in the leaves. "Some days I feel like chopping down the whole tree just to shut him up."

"Very Christian of you, dear," Jos laughed, and set down a tray of glasses with a pitcher of yellowish tan liquid. "We mix lemonade and ice tea together for the children, and Titus and I have gotten so used to it, I forget to make separate batches. Would you like some?" She was being just that much too polite so I knew she wasn't sure she liked me being here, a white girl from her husband's past.

"Too bad we had to cancel Bible school this morning, children needed to finish their bean-growing project." Jos sat down on the other side of me so I was in the middle, and began unconsciously nodding her head as she counted the kids playing in the wooded ravine and hill. "Nine . . . where's ten? Oh, there, in that tree—good, there's the other two." She took a swallow of the concoction and sat back.

"Which are yours?" I asked.

She looked quickly at Titus, who was looking at the tree hard enough to make it fall down on its own recognizance. "The tallest boy and the girl there alone." She glanced at the children again. There was a moment of silence filled with mockingbird and kid sounds; then she said, "Do you have children?"

"A son. Grown up, on his own." It sounded so lame, I added, "My husband died." I was about to say "Spontaneous combustion," but I stopped myself in time.

"I'm sorry to hear that." She said it in an oddly comforting way, and I was torn between liking her and feeling jealous, not just of her being with Titus, but of the two of them, of their having each other.

"Moline says somebody set that fire at the Rainses' farm last night, Jos. Does seem awful coincidental. Three fires on Rains property."

"Don't forget the way the black farmers are being harassed too. Bank calling their loans after they were just renewed for ten more years." Jos leaned across me and touched his arm.

He nodded. "Two more people have reported trouble with their livestock."

"And Claude's had the health department out three times claiming his milking system's dirty." Jos shook her head. "Everyone who's resisting is having trouble. Lucky your cousin didn't think to include me in her injunction against Titus." She laughed without much humor.

"Who do you think's doing it?" Titus looked at me carefully, his intelligent eyes catching what I was leaving out.

"Oh, here comes Beanie. Freddie must need a break, poor thing. Titus, you find a job for him before he starts rebuilding the house around us." Jos stood and waved, smiling broadly at the figure walking quickly up the street toward us.

Titus got up and went to the small, skinny black man, who could still pass as an adolescent from a distance. At the fence, Beanie gripped the top board as if he were going to lift it off, and rocked on his heels as Titus talked and gestured. Then Titus gently pried his fingers loose and led him up the walk.

Beanie's expression alternated between confusion and wonder as he

176

looked around until his eyes landed on the woodpile on the crest above the ravine. He made a noise and pulled away from the hand at his elbow. We watched as he walked purposefully to the woodpile and began to dismantle it piece by piece into a loose heap.

Coming back to the porch, Titus said, "It's all right. He'll put it back. That's his way. Everything has to be in a certain place. Watch." Sure enough, Beanie began laying the foundation for the pile three feet over to the left. He was doing a better job of stacking than the previous person, too.

"He likes things to be orderly. Likes to do it himself. The woodpile won't take him long, though. I'll have to come up with some other jobs to keep him happy. Maybe the kids are ready for a tree house." Titus stuck his hands in his front pants pockets and stared off down the hill.

"Let him climb a tree?" Jos frowned.

"You remember Freddie Eden?" Titus sat down and picked up his glass. "Beanie's her son."

I nodded. "She's been cleaning Walker's house, but I haven't seen her yet."

Freddie was the same age as me, and when we were in school was always getting in trouble because of white boys. They bothered each other, the boys and Freddie, and that bothered all kinds of other people. Mostly, she just wanted to do what she wanted, which included cutting school, marching with civil rights people, drinking, and driving wild around the dark roads as soon as she figured out how to sneak out of the house when her mama was asleep. Titus introduced us. Part of my secret life, being with Freddie and Titus and sometimes his sister Cecelia and whoever Freddie was with at the moment. If it was a white boy, we eyed each other in class the next day, newly suspicious. But Freddie was fun, the kind of girl who'd snap her fingers in front of your eyes and laugh at your troubles until you got over your self-pity and felt like doing the craziest thing anyone could think of. She had skin so dark it shone like bitter chocolate on a hot day, and she had let her hair go natural, one of the first, into a fine bush of wires and knots that surrounded her head like a black halo. Old women of both races would watch her walk down the street, shaking their heads, pinching their lips, and clutching the handles of their pocketbooks tight enough to wring the color out. It was a wonder she stayed around here. I'd thought she'd be in a big city. Lot I knew.

"I think Beanie lost his job at the Sheltered Workshop again," Jos said. "Heard they sent him home a week ago. Kept trying to do everyone else's work after he finished his own so quickly. Not enough of a job anyway, making those cedar boxes for tourists, with 'Souvenir of the Ozarks' burned in the lid. Beanie's much higher functioning—can't hear or talk, but he can do a lot more things than they believe. He helps Titus when they kick him out of the workshop, which they do periodically to get a break, I think."

"He's fine here for a while," Titus said. "But you have a theory about those fires, Moline?" He caught me off guard, so I nodded before I could think, and his eyes said they knew too.

"What's going on?" Jos asked softly.

Titus ran a finger up the sweaty glass of tea and flung the collected water over the porch rail.

"Moline?" he asked, looking at me. I just shook my head.

"Is it the Klan?" Jos leaned out of her chair and studied the ravine where the kids were playing.

"No, nothing like that, honey. Is it, Moline?" As he talked, his expression grew more open and more sympathetic toward me, as if the friendship we'd shared hadn't really disappeared after all. I felt a little lifting in my chest and back.

But McCall had warned me about talking. My jaw got so tight, my tongue was too big for the space my clamping teeth left. Tears started in my eyes, and Jos and Titus both put their hands on my shoulders.

"What's happened?" Titus said in a low voice. I couldn't look at him, and Jos patted my shoulder and stroked my head.

"What is it?" Jos asked.

"Just trust me, I know that fire was set."

"You know who set it?" Jos asked.

I couldn't look at Titus when I nodded, then shrugged.

"You'd better tell us then." Titus quickly cracked his knuckles.

Jos looked at me. "You have to do something."

"I can't."

Jos stood up. "I'm calling the sheriff."

I grabbed her hand to stop her. "You can't."

She shook her head, but let me pull her back into her chair.

"Moline's right," Titus said with a curious glint in his eye. "You have any proof?"

I shook my head.

"Then how . . . ?" Jos asked. I looked at Titus. He knew.

"There has to be some way to bring them to justice." Jos gripped the metal arms of her chair hard. "You can tell the sheriff and he'll take care of it. I'm sure he doesn't want an arsonist here in Resurrection." She tried to smile optimistically.

"No," I whispered.

We sat there silently watching Beanie calibrate the last stick of firewood. Titus got up and took him around back for another chore.

"Feels so helpless knowing someone has this much power, and even Titus can't lift a finger to stop him," Jos said.

I wanted to tell on McCall, I'd come here to do that, but now I was afraid he'd get worse if I did. "I'm scared they'll hurt my aunt and uncle."

Titus came back and settled in his chair.

"Moline's afraid for Walker and Able," Jos said.

Titus rubbed his jaw, using his thumb to follow the deep cleft in the middle. "If it's who I think it is, he might be setting the fires to warn you, since scaring you worked before. Or, he could be doing it for Heart Hogs. Either way, somebody's doing something could end up bad. Real bad."

"But what can she do, Titus?"

"Stay out of his way, and in the meantime maybe we can get proof. Damn it!" He hit the arm of his chair with his fist. "They better not come near me."

"What?" Jos asked.

He scrubbed his scalp with his hands and dug his fingers into the back of his knotted hair. "It's this damn hog business. I don't care how many jobs it brings. Damn Pearl Waller and her injunction. Damn them all!" His lips twisted with anger as he stood up. The cries and laughter of the children seemed to both mock and chorus his words: Save us, there's nothing to save us.

"You're forgetting something, dear." As tall as he was, Jos put her hand on the back of his neck and looked him in the eye. "We ask the Lord to help. That's what we do now." She tried to embrace him, but he was stiff and unyielding.

He pulled away and laughed bitterly. "What's the point? You tell me."

"Titus—" I began.

Jos sent me a warning look. "Titus, I want you to please stop now. You're scaring our guest." She put her hands over his and brought them down so they rested together between them.

Titus's head jerked up as the cries of the children grew louder, more intense, like the frenzy of crows at a carcass. Beanie had gone down into their midst and was giving them rides on his back, galloping in an awkward stumbling gait over the uneven ground through the swirling bodies, some of whom tried to keep pace with his steps while others plunged ahead as if they could lead their pretend horse to triumph. There was a steady darkening of the sky from the clouds bellying up against the hills, and as we watched the hollow went dim and smoky as if it there were a fire just beneath the shattered pine needles and last year's leaves underfoot.

"It's going to pour again, we better call them in." Jos stood and stepped toward the edge of the porch.

"Let them play while they can." Titus smoothed his black hair, gleaming dull as new iron in the odd light. "We're fighting for our lives here, Moline. Your aunt and uncle . . . Lukey. All the black farmers in this community. Maybe you should stay out of it, though."

"I have to help Walker and Able. And you asked me to try to stop McCall from stealing Lukey's land."

"But maybe your help is making things worse. Maybe those boys are using you as bad as they used Lukey—handing her back and forth like an old towel. She doesn't even know who the father of her first child is."

"That's not true! Dayrell helps her and he wouldn't hurt me."

"Maybe," Titus said, but he didn't sound convinced.

"No. It's not Dayrell, believe me." I stood and pushed back my chair, but I still couldn't confirm Titus's suspicions and go to the sheriff.

"You're stuck then. We're all stuck then." Titus turned and yanked the screen door half off its hinges and went inside.

Jos glanced at me quickly, then away. "Have to keep a closer watch on everyone now. Satan's walking. Never satisfied, never enough bad to make him happy for long."

14

PILGRIMAGE OF
THE DARK HEART

After 1870, in some parts of the state sheet-clad Klansmen demonstrated their determination that Missouri must be kept safe through white supremacy while lynchings of blacks took place even as late as the 1930s. Segregation quickly became the way of life, marked especially by the establishment in 1875 of separate schools for blacks and whites, a practice which the next constitution of 1945 reaffirmed and which was not repealed until 1976.

— MISSOURI: A HISTORY

SOON AS THE RAIN LET UP AND THE SUN CAME OUT, I decided to walk uptown to the hotel and see if Walker needed anything. Tebow's son took the pigs, but Dayrell still hadn't appeared. I didn't feel like going back to the farm, and my talk with Titus only made me feel worse. I hadn't lost that sense of danger from the morning, but I had put it aside.

My knee didn't want to bend all the way and kept tripping me up, so I kept my eyes on the sidewalk, charting the geography of cracks and holes. That was why I didn't see Lukey waiting around the corner from the hotel, tucked in the shadows of the State Farm Agency doorway, out of Pearl's patrol of the street from the courthouse windows.

"Moline?" she called in that soft, wistful voice of hers that had this white to it like the laurel in the woods just when everything is starting to green up, clouds caught on the wet black branches.

"You look okay, didn't get hurt in that fire?" she asked, and touched my arm with the tips of her fingers, giving me a little warming of pleasure. She was my friend. Then I looked closer and saw how one side of her face was battered to that yellow and brownish purple stage, like a bruised egg-plant, although her eyes were a clear direct blue, such a light shade you'd think the sun was shining in their sky. Her hair was clean and pulled back from her face, which made her look like she was in high school, especially with the simple faded denim jumper and tee shirt she was wearing.

"What happened? Did McCall do this?" I pointed to her face and leaned back against the building, letting the shadow of the awning take some of the heat off the top of my head from the sun that kept trying to skirt around the clouds.

She brushed a loose strand of her white-blond hair behind her ear and smiled shyly. "I'm fine. The kids—don't tell anybody?" She held both hands up to stop the time she could see coming toward her in that instant.

"Okay, of course, whatever you want, Lukey."

"The kids and I are staying with my brother and his family. Mama's just a bit aways and I can see her every day. I haven't felt this good in a long time. The preacher's going to come over every day to help me get back to the Lord, and the kids are starting to listen too. I couldn't be happier, honest." There was a little hollow in the back of her voice where the words didn't quite fill up right.

I smiled and said, "You missed your family, didn't you?"

She nodded her head and looked down at her hands twisting a piece of the jumper, wringing it out like a wet scrub cloth. "Kids did too," she mumbled so low I had to lean closer to catch it.

"Well, why don't you stay with them?"

She shrugged and looked down the block toward the empty lot of the Dairy Daddy. "I came to find you." She took a deep breath but had trouble letting it out all the way. "McCall was with me that night." She touched the bruise on the side of her face. "He didn't burn the Rainses' barn, like Dayrell says you think." She couldn't look at me. "When the fire was s'posed to be set? We were fighting." She touched her cheek. "I didn't get home till almost light."

I nodded. I'd believe that the day after the resurrection. That must have been where Dayrell'd gone, then, to find out about his brother, so he could prove I was wrong.

"I went back to the cabin after the kids were asleep to fetch some more stuff and he was there. We argued, and that's when—" Her voice dropped again, and she twisted her hands some more. "I'm going to sign the deed over, Moline. Give him the land to sell. I just hope Reverend Titus and your aunt understand. They've been so good to me, but I couldn't keep saying no. He said he'd leave me alone if I signed. It's my only chance. I have to think of my kids."

"You're really going to?"

She straightened and dropped her hands. "Dayrell's right. I can't go back to McCall the way things are. No more drugs. No more living out there like outlaws and heathens. I have to make things right again." She stopped, catching her lower lip under her front teeth, looking at the cement at our feet, shaking her head. "I was so scared the whole time living with him, I didn't even realize it until I left and slept under a righteous roof again. I wake up in the morning, I can breathe, I can let out this part that was always afraid to take a deep breath."

"Lukey—"

"No, I'm okay." She folded her arms and shook her head, looking at me with eyes that had gone some distance away. "I thought about it and I can do it if the Lord Jesus Christ takes me back. I have to believe, don't you see, Moline? I have to put myself back in His hands, there's nothing else safe enough. I can't be like you, and I'm not like McCall. I'm my own self and I need to feel His love, I need to feel that I'm doing the right things, that He approves. I tried to live like the rest of you. I tried to let my kids make up their own minds, the way McCall wanted. But you know what? It didn't work. None of us was happy living in that much wrong. We just wasn't, and our misery grew and grew until finally it overtook me and punished me for what he was doing wrong, for not getting married with the Lord's blessing. But He sent the sign. And McCall might repent someday. Then we'd be reunited in His eyes." She laid her tiny hand on her bruised face. "I'm praying for it."

She stopped, her eyes and face with a new look of calm. "He called me, from your cousin Pearl's for some reason. He's drinking, says he needs me to sign the deed right now. Then I'm free, he'll leave me be. He's going to sell the land and divide the money, so both of us gets fresh starts, and he won't never bother me again." Again her voice dropped to a whisper I had to lean closer to hear. "It's for the kids, Moline." She walked a few steps away, then turned back and came closer.

"Can you go with me, Moline? To sign the paper? I'm afraid. I wouldn't ask, but I can't face him alone . . . please?" She was shaking her head, looking at the toe of her tennis shoe pushing the body of a dead bumble-bee back and forth.

"Couldn't this wait? What's the hurry? We should see a lawyer. Find Dayrell. What if McCall's lying and he starts—"

She looked at me, the light fading from those sad pale eyes. "He won't back out. We made a deal."

"I'm not against you, Lukey, I just don't trust him. You do. Just please, please be careful." I kept my voice low and quiet to make it convincing. She was trading the lie and the land for her freedom and safety, but the sense of danger rode the nerves up my arms to rest like a pair of dark wings at the back of my neck.

She shrugged. "God is taking care of me now. It's in His hands. He forgives the sinner who repents. There's always mercy, remember?"

"He loves the sinner, it's the sin He hates. That's right, Lukey." I touched her small hand.

She sucked her lower lip in again and rubbed her forehead hard enough to leave a red streak across it. "Can't you come with me? I have my brother's truck." She gestured toward the oldest truck on the street, with mismatched door and hood and a missing fender on the driver's side. The tailgate had been replaced by an ancient wood pasture gate held in place with bailing wire, and the tires were bald enough to show gray spots. We'd be lucky to make it down the street alive.

"Lukey? There's something else."

She put her little finger in her mouth.

"The other night, the night I saw you at the rib place?"

She nodded and chewed the nail clean and short.

"McCall came over to my house. . . ."

Her eyes got sad and wary and she looked longingly at the old truck. "I know."

"No, that's not—"

"It's okay, Moline—really."

"No—"

"I don't—I can't—you see?" The little fingernail was outlined with blood, and she pushed on it until the tip filled.

"Okay, never mind." I didn't know whether I wanted her to tell me if Dayrell could have overheard McCall's and my entire conversation or if I should tell her what he'd done to me. But it was clear that Lukey knew what I knew when I left Resurrection: how love can make you an outlaw, how love is a fast car down a dirt road, turning your life to dust behind you.

He looked like hell, and there were dark smears on his dirty white shirt. He reached down and brushed at himself in that absentminded way drunks have, but he looked like he might have been sleeping it off.

"I was bleeding," he remarked, and looked around the room as if it might be a jail cell since he couldn't remember too much. He reached behind him and stumbled back to sit on the bed, keeping his bloodshot eyes on me. All his menace gone, he was just a small-town boy in a body that was being used up too fast.

I leaned back against the wall while Lukey stood half in, half out of the doorway.

He looked at my leg propped stiffly out in front of me. "Did I do that?" His voice was marbled with phlegm and he had to cough and clear to get it right again.

I shook my head.

He looked at Lukey's face. "I never meant to hurt you. . . ." He was starting to sweat out the booze, that greasy wet on his face, and his shirt sticking to his skin in gray patches. He was sick smelling even with the window wide open.

"The kids, how're my kids?" His shoulders convulsed and his face scrunched up as if he were on the verge of tears. But that only lasted a moment before he switched his focus back to me.

"Wasn't me burned the barn. Lukey and I—most of the night . . ." He put his head in his hands so I couldn't tell if he was lying or not. Damn convenient, his hitting her and leaving a mark so there was proof. Between jail and Lukey, though, I guess it wasn't much of a choice.

"You were with her all night?"

"Ask her." He looked up, his expression so perfectly neutral, bordering on sincere, I honestly couldn't read it. We stared at each other while the menace regained his body and eased out across the floor toward me. I felt the numb panic of the frog when it sees inside the dark of the snake's open jaws.

When I glanced over at her, Lukey's eyes were filled with tears, but she nodded. She was the one I didn't believe. God only knew what it cost her to lie.

He pulled the deed and a pen out of his shirt pocket and she signed it and looked at me. "I'll be right down, wait for me," she whispered, and I left them, glad to get away from him.

The house still smelled like Estes, that inside of the dry old trunk in the attic smell mixed with that clinging sweet lavender powder she put in the linen drawers. Dear Pearl had never dared throw all the windows open and air the place out. She'd never gotten rid of the rigid overstuffed sofa and chairs in the parlor, all corseted in dark tapestry, that were never allowed to soften and collapse the way furniture usually did. There'd never been a dog or cat, hell, even a gerbil or parakeet, to bring in the grainy, meaty odors of animal life.

The only fresh flowers allowed were the ones sent for deaths of relatives, then promptly thrown out. I knew this because I used to rescue them from the burn barrel out back by the garage and bring the good ones home to stick in a Mason jar in the room Paris and I shared. Carnations were my favorite, but Paris said they were cheap, ordinary, and always made me search for roses for her side of the bed. There weren't so many of those, and maybe that was what she preferred, the unpredictable, the rare, maybe that was what she held out for, and when it didn't come after those years of searching and waiting, she gave up. She couldn't stand ordinary things, ordinary life. It all had to be a special order, fancier than anyone else got, and meant just for her, her alone. One of a kind.

I couldn't imagine Paris as a mother. She wouldn't want to share the stage with anyone who didn't reflect her perfectly, wasn't quite her equal. No wonder she killed that terrible imperfection called her life. Paris wasn't acting. She meant it. Even her death wasn't quite the way people saw it. It was a big fat message, saying I concede the game, but I won't lose it. I understood. She'd understood me, too. She knew that I wasn't going to be able to resist anything. After all, I loved those carnations because they were always there, that way you didn't have to wait for the rare ones to come along and maybe miss out for weeks and months and years.

I looked around the vestibule and parlor, took one last lungful of that old Estes air, and clumped out the door and waited for Lukey on the big stone steps. I didn't believe either Lukey or McCall, but Lukey was a grown woman and she had God on her side. Maybe she'd do better than I expected.

"Well, if McCall didn't burn the barn down, who did?" Walker asked when I explained his alibi.

"I'm not saying I believe him, but he does have Lukey convinced to lie for him, and she's always struck me as pretty darn honest." I recounted the whole scene with her, and really wanted to tell Walker what had happened a few nights earlier in my house, but I couldn't. Maybe I'd never have to, I reasoned.

"That girl always did have more goodness than sense in her. Same as her mama. Your father tried to get that land out of his cousins long before McCall Bell managed it. Reason they stopped speaking. And Lukey's mama prayed up a storm to heal Mister's 'contrariness' as she called it. Hate to say it, Moline, but Lukey's prayers for McCall are going to be about as useful. McCall Bell reborn? We'll see the Lord parading in a bathing suit around the courthouse on that day." She took a sip of ice tea and bourbon and set the glass carefully on the warped boards of the hotel front porch.

I was relieved she'd dropped Dayrell from the family equation. "I am sorry about the barn, and the pigs especially, Walker. What'd Tebow say about the three he's got at his place?"

"Eatin' like pigs," she laughed, then turned to me, more serious. "Moline, I admit I might have to change my view of Dayrell now. But you can see how at my age that's a lot of trouble in and of itself. By the time you've become one of the oldest people on the street, you'd think you earned the right to your opinions, no matter how wrongheaded or stupid they happen to be." She drank some more and watched a young Mennonite family walk past the pawn shop and Runyan's old hardware, now stocked with junk called antiques. The women wore their little caps and long dresses and cheap tennis shoes, from the oldest to the baby.

"I'm glad about the pigs. It could've been worse—if we hadn't been there."

"True. And the sheriff and I have had several discussions of late about sending a patrol car past there every once in a while. This fire should motivate him. Louis Sly tried to hint that someone close to the family might have started the fire—God only knows what he's drinking in his spare time. Seems to think we'd go to any length to defeat Heart Hogs, including destroying our own property and animals. Man's an ignoramus."

"Walker, they don't think Dayrell and I burned it, do they?"

"Look, they think anything complicated enough to be downright ridiculous. More complicated the better. And to tell you the truth, I don't know who burned it, and I don't want Able concerning himself, either. So this talk is between us. Let him think it's spontaneous combustion or the tooth fairy for all I care."

I heard a rustle behind us and turned to see Able in the doorway, grinning at his wife's diatribe. He made a drinking gesture and pointed toward her and I nodded. He nodded back and disappeared into the dark behind him.

"I never blamed Dayrell as much as some folks, though. You know that, Moline."

"I guess."

"Titus and I both hold one thing against him, though."

"What's that?"

"He didn't dissociate himself from McCall when he got out of prison. Not then and not later when he'd settled down some. He should've. Would've raised him in people's eyes."

"They're family, Walker. Doesn't that speak for him in a good way, that he doesn't reject his kin the way some people have?"

"Some things are stronger than blood, Moline."

"But isn't that always the biggest problem too? Kinship means you don't get a choice. Dayrell loves his brother, won't give up on him." I wanted to say, even when his brother tries to rape someone he says he loves, blood comes first. What can a person do about that?

"Well, he might live to see the light. I doubt McCall's going to. Now, let's move on to another piece of business."

I glanced over at her serious face. The glass in her hand was empty, but she didn't look like she wanted more. "What business is that?"

"Titus has called for a solidarity meeting on the courthouse lawn at four tomorrow. He's got his people calling all the area farmers opposed to the corporation, and a group of ladies going door to door here in town. I want you to help. You can call everyone on the list by the phone at the desk. I'll pay you for your hours."

"That's not necessary." I was sounding halfhearted because I hated calling strangers more than about anything except getting shots and visiting the dentist.

"Just go do what I asked. I wrote down what you're supposed to say. The town meeting's in two days to discuss the issue, and we have to be ready. I'm waiting for Titus or I'd do it myself." She waved me inside.

Uncle Able was sitting on the high stool behind the desk leafing through a cruise brochure for the Caribbean from the travel agency in Laurel. "Some people in 213 left this behind. Thought I'd drop it on Walker's pillow tonight to get her roused out of this mood. She'll hit the roof." He grinned and ran his tongue over the brown stains on his front teeth.

I smiled. "She's in a mood today. Has me calling half the town for the rally tomorrow."

"Ought to be worth a few chuckles on its own. Maybe I could take a spell at it too."

I looked at his face trying to make itself serious and shook my head. "I don't think that's a good idea, Uncle Able."

He unfolded himself from the stool, putting his big hand on the small of his back as he straightened. Leaning to one side until there was a crack, and then to the other, he nodded and walked around the desk. "Guess I'll be going to my office upstairs—the air-conditioned one. That's what I told the boys at Dixie Donut this morning. They all looked at me, then I told 'em it was the roof and they got a big kick outta that. Yessir, air-conditioning." He grinned and shook his head. "Haven't seen old Dayrell around much lately. He win the lottery, or has his prospects so improved he doesn't have to work anymore now that he's got a woman with a steady job?"

I grimaced and rolled my eyes at him and he went off laughing. Actually, I was worried about Dayrell. I needed to explain, to say something to make him understand—but what? That his brother—what? Maybe I was just being paranoid. I tried that idea in between phone calls, but it didn't stick. No matter what Lukey and Dayrell thought, McCall was doing something bad.

Then people started checking in, because it was the end of the day and they'd driven so far they didn't care where they stayed, as long as they had a roof over their heads. There were light bulbs burned out in three of the rooms, and the shower in one room I rented wouldn't produce more than a rusty cough and dribble. Whenever someone asked for a wake-up call, I pointed to the row of old-fashioned windup alarm clocks, the kind with the extra-loud clanging bell, and told them to help themselves. Walker's latest innovation.

It was almost ten o'clock when I left the hotel. Walker was still in a mood and said she'd probably be up all night anyway so one of us might as well get some sleep. I'd talked to almost a hundred people, and my throat was tight and raw as I said goodnight.

All the lights were on in my house. "Hello?" I hefted the .38 half out of my purse and tiptoed toward the kitchen, as if anyone could hear me over the racket of country music.

There was a bare clean band stretching across the room between the stove and the sink where the pine planks finally peeked out from the black tarry residue left by years of linoleum. A gallon can of solvent sat next to it. The room smelled like a cross between a spill at the dry cleaner's and gasoline, even with the back door and window open. Dayrell stood up and grinned like a kid with some goofy science project. "You still trying to shoot somebody, Moline?"

"What're you doing?" I hugged him.

"Too happy and keyed up to sit out there with Bob and Win. That storm really cleaned things out, charged up the air again. Decided to do some work on this floor. How's it look?" He pointed at the clean place with the burn scar in the middle of it, and I nodded, but I was really looking at the sad tarry shit around it.

Nothing went away just because you couldn't see it. Not that skillet-round burn in front of the stove from when we were little kids and Iberia and Mister had a fight about her being naked on Estes's roof and Mama dropped the skillet full of frying pork and apples and let the grease splatter all over her legs and mine. Left it there until Mister could see the smoke oozing around the edges and grabbed it without a hotpad and was too stubborn to let go until he'd thrown it on the stove top and started a grease fire when more of it bounced into the open flame. He was yelling when Iberia calmly poured the baking soda she kept beside the stove over the flames. That burn mark stayed on the floor all summer until Mister's hand, which blistered and swelled and infected, had finally healed. My legs carried little red dots, like measles, that itched and stung for a week but didn't disappear until the following spring.

After that, Iberia made it a point not to go to her mother's roof when I was around. I knew she thought I'd told, but in fact I had not. I don't think she ever forgot, but I couldn't bring myself to mention it after the first linoleum was installed. In a day or two I'd have to decide whether to have Dayrell replace the scarred boards or leave them as an emblem of our being here. What else was there, I wondered, what else would ever tell anyone that the Bedwells were here, lived and died here? Pretty soon we'd all disappear, our stuff get carted away and sold, new people move in, then what?

I hated to think of the way significance was ruined, wiped out, scarred and burned over, tarred, scrubbed, and covered. What was my mother doing naked on that roof? Why had that image of her, so much in fla-grance against the family, her mother, the town, the church, and God even, stayed with me? Her long brown nipples like accusing fingers pointed at the sun, that image so relentless in my memory of her.

"I never said that—Pearl—Pearl!" The angry voice from outside the window startled us. There was the sound of three loud slaps.

"Turn out the light," Dayrell whispered. I ducked and flicked the switch and we edged closer to the window to see.

"Is he hitting her?" I whispered loudly.

"Shhh." He put his arm around me and pulled me tight against his bare bruised chest scented with chemical adhesive remover, but when the taller figure raised an arm to the smaller one in the side yard, I didn't want to be there.

"You need a good beating," the man threatened.

"You don't know anything about me," the woman said, and calmly stepped into the sweep of his arm and slapped his face as hard as she could. When his arm came down at her, she laughed and took the blow he pulled the power from at the last minute.

"It's Pearl, in her nightgown or something. What's she doing?" I felt torn between wanting to run out there and stop them and wanting to see how far she'd push it.

"That's McCall," Dayrell said, and loosened the hold he had on me.

"You touch me again and I'll kill you," Pearl taunted, slapping at

McCall's arms and chest as he tried to hug her. "I mean it." She hit him on the side of the head and he wrestled her to the ground.

"We should go out and stop him before he hurts her." I turned for the door.

"No, wait—look."

McCall was lying on Pearl now, holding her arms at her sides while he talked to her in a voice so quiet I couldn't make out what he was saying. As much as I hated McCall, I felt a twinge of something watching them. You had to really care about a person to fight them like that.

"There, that's what she wanted." Dayrell let out a long breath and put his hand on my neck as if to hold it there to face the truth, as if it would prove to me that McCall wasn't who I thought he was. McCall leaned down and kissed Pearl, their flesh disappearing in the moonlight and grass, her gown glowing neon white like shards of broken china beneath his darkness.

15

IN THE GARDEN

Rough Green Snake: It remains motionless among the leaves and branches and relies on its coloration to remain undetected. If a slight wind moves the branches, the green snake will bend and wave in unison.

—AMPHIBIANS AND REPTILES OF MISSOURI

※

WHEN I WAS PULLING UP THE DRIVE to meet Able at the farm at nine o'clock the next morning, the sun was already shining extra hot as if it had to grind every living wet thing into sand. His call had been vague, but I knew he wouldn't waste time on the house, although somebody had been doing something from the way the yard was beginning to get crowded with stacks of lumber and mysterious-looking boxes. He was busy arguing with the two horses by the water tank when I pushed open the corral gate and said hello. Harry Truman, the roan, looked at me, laid his ears even flatter, and rolled his blue eyes, but Jimmy Carter sauntered over and stuck his big brown nose under my arm and lifted up hard, as if I could fix what was troubling the two of them.

"Dang pump went out on me," Able gestured toward the water tank, which had been drunk to the last scummy couple of feet. "These two idgits can't get it through their thick skulls that there's a whole blame crick down the hill with fresh water just waiting for 'em." He waved his arms at Harry. "Now git—git outta here!" The roan flung his head up but braced his front legs and refused to move. "Dang buncha Democrats!"

"Here, let me lead Jimmy Carter down and put him on the other side of the fence, then Harry Truman will want to follow. They'll figure it out." I put a hand through the brown's halter and had to tug a couple of times to get him to move; but finally, with a big sigh that ended in a snort, he trudged beside me down the little hill to where the corral opened into the big back pasture. I was careful not to look over to my right where the charred barn sat in a black heap, leaving an odd empty space in the air. The sun was already taking advantage of the new angle, making the ground drier and firmer than it should have been for the recent rain.

The Black Angus steers looked up at us and blinked curiously, then began to crowd in our direction, bringing a cloud of black flies and gnats. I waved my arm and hollered before opening the gate, and Jimmy tugged back. "Come on—I'm talking to the cows, not you," I soothed, and he nuzzled the side of my face and began licking my arm for the salt, which tickled so I laughed. He blew in my ear and nuzzled my hair, and I patted him. "You're all right, Jimmy. Now you go on down to the creek for some water until we get the tank fixed, and I'll bring you some carrots next time I come." It was easy promising things to horses; their memories weren't as precise as ours, and they were way more forgiving.

Jimmy trotted down the hill, scattering the cattle, who acted as if they'd never seen a horse before. He stretched out his neck and snapped the air with his teeth in their direction to remind them of the pasture hierarchy in case they'd forgotten.

"Watch out, Moline, here comes Harry!" Able yelled.

I swung the gate open again, and the roan galloped on through and drove straight into the nearest group of steers, kicking out sideways to scare them into trotting off in all directions. I closed the gate and stood there for a minute, letting the sun settle like a warm hand on my arms and back. Over in the woods, the trees were giving off a hot green hickory smell and birds were calling back and forth, their bodies flitting in quick brown motions. As the cattle moved back together to eat, the nutty tall grass smell mingled with fresh splashed manure and drifted across the pasture, picking up the sweet acrid smell of damp wood ashes on its way. Above us to the south and west, there were high thin clouds advancing like the first soldiers for the army of large white clouds resting on the horizon.

I turned and walked back to where Able was trying to bail the rest of the water from the tank. Each time he lifted the half-full bucket draped in slimy green strands and black clumps of decayed matter, he grimaced and had to massage his back with his free hand before he let the bucket spill out and run thickly down the hill.

"Here, let me do that, Uncle Able. Don't you have to work on the pump?" I picked up the bucket and leaned over the tank and almost fell in with the weight of the water rushing in.

"Well, I already made a disaster out of that motor—thought I'd try my hand at this here tank. Hasn't been cleaned since I don't know when." He took off his seed cap and smoothed his narrow skull and resettled the hat. I hadn't seen his head in so long, the baldness surprised me. "S'pose a person would do better taking a hose and siphoning that water off."

I stopped work and looked at him. My jeans and sneakers were splattered with mud and green scum.

"Then we could tip her up and get at it real good," he grinned, and spit some tobacco.

"What about the motor to the pump? How we gonna clean it without water?"

"Oh, I got the younger Garlick Pump fella coming any minute. By the time you get that bottom scraped clear, we can get him to help tip her and he'll have the water pumping in no time flat. Been meaning to do this for years."

I wanted to believe that this was a necessary job, because it was about the dirtiest work I'd ever done. God knew what lived in the bottom of that tank, but it put out the rankest stink in the barnyard. I sighed and shaded my eyes with my smelly hand to see if he was laughing at me. "Where's the hose I can use?"

"Take the shortest piece right inside the cow barn there. I'll help you hook 'er up." He took a step toward the barn and stopped and headed toward the corral gate instead. "Oh, here's that young Garlick fella now. You get yourself that hose, Moline, and put one end in the tank and suck as hard as you can on the other end, until you taste the water, then you let it drain out."

I figured there had to be an easier method than putting my mouth anywhere near that hose and that tank bottom, but no matter what I tried, nothing worked.

Finally, Able left the repairman in peace to check on me. "You never siphoned gas?" He shook his head in disbelief and stuck his hands in the sides of his overalls, an old, shredded, patched pair from the laundry we'd done. Despite the heat he was wearing one of his washed thin flannel shirts and a long underwear top. Probably had on the bottoms too.

He shamed me into it, but at the first touch of moisture on my tongue I threw the hose down and spit and spit, convinced some aquatic critter had tangled in my teeth or already slithered down my throat. Able was grinning happily by the time I straightened up and wiped my mouth on my shirt. "You going swimming in those clothes?"

I looked at him suspiciously. "What swimming would that be?"

He shrugged. "You're gonna get a little wet when you climb in there to clean. Might be an old bathing suit up at the house you could use. Why'n't you go check while I keep an eye on this operation." He shifted his focus to the hose and the lowering level in the tank. "Don't know but what this bottom gunk will stop the hose right up."

"Well, I'm sure you have a plan for that too," I muttered, and went off toward the house. I didn't know why I listened to him, I was already filthy, but maybe I could rinse my clothes and let them dry in the sun while I cleaned the tank. Then I'd have something semidecent to put on for the ride home.

I heard pounding on the far side of the house, but when I went around to check on it, I didn't see anybody. There were long rows of stacked bricks, five feet high, lined up where they couldn't be seen from the road or drive, and six huge rolls of black plastic sheeting had appeared beside the back door to the mud porch. Everything was pretty much the same inside, except for some new clutter from Uncle Able's overnight visit. A quail egg and a big copper, black, and brown barred feather sat on the counter by the sink. Must be wild turkeys in the woods by the creek. I went to the sink to wash my hands before I remembered the water was off. On the windowsill stood a row of spent shell casings and odd metal and wood fragments from the Civil War among the arrowheads I'd found as a child. For years, Able had been walking his land and the neighboring fields, finding bits of the past he brought home for Walker. I wondered what would become of his little collection if the house were reduced to a crap pit. They couldn't take all this stuff with them to a small house in town or the hotel; it wouldn't make sense. Here, in this place, it had a logic, a rationale; it signified something about this particular piece of land and all the people who walked across it.

I remembered going to the Art Institute in Minneapolis and seeing these little shards of this and that and having absolutely no idea what they meant, how people felt or moved with them in their lives. Objects needed us to give them significance, and a little bit of that died when we did, and ever after that they were just bits of sentiment, nostalgia, becoming more and more silent through time until they were discarded, lost, and us with them, gone forever.

Digging around in the bottom drawer of Walker's dresser, I found an old two-piece faded black cotton suit from the forties. The trunks fit, but the top was big enough that I worried I'd slip out the bottom of the cups. I ended up tying a knot in the back before fastening it, and all the way to the corral it felt like somebody had a knuckle stuck in the middle of my spine.

"What's all the brick for, Uncle Able?"

He stopped the hand bailing to clear the last of the thickest gunk, straightened, and shaded his eyes as he looked toward the house. "Have me a plan, Moline. They think they can burn us out—well, nothing easy about burning a brick house with a slate tile roof. I always wanted a brick house. Like as not this is the time to do it, before a person gets too old to enjoy it."

"You're bricking the entire house?"

"Going to have me a brick fence too, and a wrought-iron gate with the original name of this old place in an arch overhead: Rains Lane. Pretty fine, isn't it? Your aunt will sure be surprised."

I couldn't begin to imagine the cost, but I knew she'd half kill him for spending that kind of money on something with every likelihood of being demolished. "When are you going to tell her?" I wanted to be sure to be missing for that scene.

He took off his cap, turned it around in his big hands, and resettled it. "Not till it's done, that's for certain. Besides, we lose the fight with those hog people? They'll have to pay us a sight more money for a brand new brick home than a run-down frame house full of dry rot and termites."

"Right." I couldn't think of any way to argue with this idea, aside from the basic absurdity of it. "So, we about ready to tip this thing?"

He looked at me in the bathing suit and chuckled. "Your aunt should see that suit now. You keep emptying the last of this bottom stuff while I fetch the Garlick fella so we can tip it. Have to unstop that hose later."

The Garlick Water Purification and Pumping man turned out to be Noble Nash, a kid in his early twenties I'd met at the rib place that first night before the pig riding fiasco. He grinned shyly when he saw the old swimsuit and kept glancing sideways at me while we sat on the lip of the tank and tried to tip it out of its ancient muddy bed. When that didn't work, we took scrap two-by-fours and tried to pry underneath. And when that failed, Able got the John Deere tractor, attached a thick chain around the back of the tank, and dragged and tilted it enough for us to tip it on end and brace it with wood behind.

The watery part of the sediment oozed out, leaving a wet crust several inches thick with the consistency of rotting black pudding. Able fetched a scrub brush, a broom, and a shovel, which he handed over without a word, and disappeared with Noble Nash to discuss motors and water. Thread-thin white worms wove quickly through the remaining muck, and I prayed they weren't climbing into my tennis shoes as I stood in the shadow of the tank, leaning in to scrape and scrub. There were bones from a couple of small birds that had drowned and rotted away, and a whole lot of congealed forms which might have started as pieces of tree branches or mouthfuls of hay. The dull yellow blink of unchewed corn lay like raw jewels in the muck I shoveled and threw into the corral beyond me. Then I threw a bunch where my eye caught on something glinting brighter than the corn and I stopped and went to see. It was a plain gold wedding band, encrusted with green and black, big enough to fit my thumb, the only safe place to keep it at the moment.

Some of the gunk overhead unstuck itself and started falling around me and finally on me as I fought it off with the broom. When a piece landed on my forehead and slimed down my face before I could stop it, I started cursing and yelling for Able.

"Lord, girl, I thought the tank had fallen on you!" he laughed.

"I need water, right now, or—" I didn't know what I'd do. Couldn't climb into my truck this way, covered from head to foot in the primordial ooze of all times, and the sun was starting to bake the muck onto my skin so it looked like old rhino hide. "Water—quick!" I was choking on the fumes and couldn't lick my lips or open my mouth much for fear of what was crawling on me. Able tried to talk, but he was laughing too hard now.

It was Noble Nash who lifted the pump handle and turned the spigot, which after a few coughs of orange started spewing the most beautiful clear, clean water I ever saw in my life. I almost cried, splashing myself and sticking my whole head under the stream. When I finished, I remembered the ring, which was still stuck on my thumb.

"Look what I found." I held it out to Able, who squinted and reached for it.

He turned it over and over, rubbed it on his overalls, and put it on his ring finger, where it fit perfectly. "You know, I didn't dare tell your aunt it was gone. Tole her it was in my other pants. Been keeping that lie running for ten years, 'bout wore me out. You've saved our marriage and my life, Moline. Your aunt was finally beginning to doubt my word. Thank you kindly—remind me to save *your* life someday."

I laughed. "Lucky for you I didn't decide to keep it as payment for this job, Uncle Able. Can I have a hose now?"

Noble Nash had hooked up the hose and turned it on, but stood a ways off to hand it to me as if he was afraid the slime might ooze on him next. Piss-poor attitude for a man who spent his days cleaning out septic systems.

"I'da paid a person to do this, nobody but you's ever volunteered before. And don't worry none about getting every single bit of that black scale off the sides, animals don't mind a little dirt." Both men laughed some more and left the corral to me while they walked up to the house.

"Volunteer?" I muttered.

Hosing the inside of the tank and scrubbing with the hard bristle brush brought the galvanized shine back to the sides and bottom. There was some pitting in the metal, but no holes or leaking seams as far as I could tell. Despite the green stain on my hands and splotches on my arms and legs, I felt a whole lot cleaner now that I was spraying the ice-cold spring water in the tank. The only problem was the water was making the ground slippery and I was having trouble maneuvering in and around the tank. When I finally went down, it was my infected knee that banged the metal lip and sent me to all fours with such a wave of pain I about threw up.

"You praying or panning for gold?" Dayrell stood leaning on the top board on the other side of the fence. His cap was pulled down too low to see more than the dark aviator sunglasses and his wide mouth from my angle. Something about his cocky attitude reminded me of his brother.

"What's it to you?" I stood, trying not to grimace at the throbbing pain as I put my weight on the leg.

"If I looked like you right now . . ." He grinned.

"What're you doing out here?"

"Delivering a load of sand for the mortar. Your uncle wants it done right, so we're mixing Portland cement and lime the old-fashioned style. No brick veneer or premix mortars on this job. Combination flashings of copper, polyethylene, and modified asphalts. He's going to have the best made brick house in DeWight County by the time we're through." Dayrell nodded as if he were agreeing with a whole group of men.

"You're doing the job?" I picked up the hose, tempted to squirt him, but went back to scrubbing the inside of the tank, which made a lot of noise so I couldn't quite hear him. "Have to talk louder, can't hear you," I yelled.

"I said my dad's the contractor—he's subbing some of it out, but overseeing the whole deal."

"I thought you had to finish Pearl's roof." I threw the hose down behind me and gestured for him to shut off the pump.

"I can split my time." His tone packed more of that McCall attitude, and I thought about how blind Dayrell was when it came to his brother.

"Like today? Standing around talking while the rest of us are working?" I pushed at a strand of wet hair that had fallen in a spiral on my forehead. I knew I looked like the she-devil from hell, but I didn't care. That damn McCall was probably sneaking around here too.

He pulled at the bill of his cap. "Sounding more like Pearl every day, Moline." He let that sink in for a minute before opening the gate and coming through it. "Your uncle sent me down here to help you tip the tank back and start filling it. Not enough water pressure at the house for the mortar work with the hose on down here. Now get out of the way." He brushed against me and I had to fight the urge to shove him as he went around to the back of the tank and started removing the support boards.

"Take one of the boards and push the middle toward me when I holler. Not before, though, you hear?" His voice sounded hollow behind the metal.

"I'm not stupid, you know," I muttered.

"Moline, shut up and grab a board and push, will you?"

When I stepped to the side to pull out one of the boards, he was holding the tank in balance on his back, like that picture you always see of Atlas with the world. Somehow it suited him.

"Ready?" I called, and pushed.

"At the top of the tank, dummy," he yelled.

"You said the middle, stupid." I jammed the board into the upper seam as hard as I could, and the tank swayed, tilted, and fell with a whoosh as Dayrell darted out of the way. He stopped and looked at me without saying a word.

"I did what you said!"

He shook his head. "Go around to the other side and see if we can shove it back into its old spot."

When that was done, we put the hose in and turned on the water to refill the tank. I collected the tools and set them in the grass on the other side of the fence and flopped down beside them with my arm over my eyes to rest for a minute, ignoring Dayrell, who stood over me with his arms folded across his chest.

"I wouldn't get too comfortable if I were you," he said.

"Why's that?"

"Your uncle told me to help you mix the lime and water for the whitewash."

"Whitewash? What the hell do I need whitewash for?"

"The inside walls of the cow barn and the chicken coop. That broom's rinsed pretty good—use that. Makes the job go a lot faster than a paint brush."

"My God, what is he? Tom Fucking Sawyer? I'm too old for this—tell him I can't, Dayrell—whitewash the barn and the chicken coop? I won't be done till dark," I groaned.

"Better get to it then, time's a-wastin'." He grabbed my hand and yanked me to my feet but quickly let go. "I've got the buckets and lime over by the barn. I'll mix enough to get you started, and you can fix what you need after that."

The ten old stanchions inside the cow barn were rusted in place from disuse, and the thick oak planks of the floor stood under an ancient layer of manure as brittle as old linoleum. The wooden walls and stall partitions had had their last coat of whitewash sometime before I was born, as far as I could tell.

"First things first," I announced, and began sweeping the walls clear of their heavy coating of dust and cobwebs. When I was sneezing and coughing so hard I could barely see and the broom was black, I went outside to rinse it with the hose. The tank was full to overflowing, so I turned that off and dragged in the first bucket of whitewash.

It was lucky I was wearing the bathing suit, but I began to worry about my skin peeling off after mixing the second round for the low ceiling and last three walls. I'd done all the stalls and inside partitions already and was slathered with white. Careful to keep my eyes closed, I tried to rinse myself with the hose. Wouldn't need a facial for another ten years after today's chemical peel.

Without stopping to eat the sandwich Dayrell brought down on a paper napkin, I moved to the next job and finished the coop by the middle of the afternoon. Everywhere I looked except for the shit-covered perches, the chicken coop glistened fresh white. If I'd had my wits about me, I'd have scraped the perches and replaced the smelly old straw on the floor before I whitewashed. But now that I was in the mood, I went out and started on the fence posts holding the chicken wire around the back-yard to keep the poultry out of the kitchen garden. Dayrell and Uncle Able were nowhere in sight, but occasionally I heard pounding and men's voices from the front of the house. Mostly I'd spent my day paying attention to the way the whitewash streamed down the walls if I made it too thin, or clumped on the broom if too thick. It felt good to get away from all the drama in town and make myself tired from hard physical work.

I guess I was smiling when Able came trotting down the walk toward me. "Like this job, huh? Well, I hate to see a good worker interrupted, but your aunt Walker just called wondering where in the Sam Hill you are. The rally she's organizing starts in half an hour and she wants you there. I told her I'd try to find you and send you along."

"Oh no, look at me!" I dropped the broom and showed him my coated hands and arms.

"You come on in here and get yourself showered in the basement, where Walker always makes me take a rinse before I can come upstairs after chores. I'll look around for something you can put on. Where's the clothes you came in? Oh, I guess they're not real clean, either." He waved toward the house and I ran.

202

"Call her back and tell her I'm coming—I'll be a few minutes late. I don't know why I have to be there anyways."

"She's counting on you," he called after me.

The little group on the courthouse lawn was making up for the lack of size with noise. Someone had brought a portable megaphone that cut off parts of every fifth or sixth word, but you could grasp the meaning anyway. Odell Meachum and his family came in for plenty of abuse, as did Copeland Harder Jr., and anyone associated with Heart Hogs. Gully Foye Jr., who had not followed his father into the Methodist ministry but had gone off on his own to a Pentacostal, holy roller sort of group instead, preached a mini-sermon about idolatry and raising the pig above its lowly status with this new industry. They were fine for eating but not to be relied on, seemed to be the gist of it.

I was nodding out on my feet when Walker leaned over and said loudly in my ear, "That old fool must've broken your back today, Moline. You look terrible. What's this white stuff in your ear? Whitewash? He didn't—" She chuckled and looked behind her for the chewed-up dark wooden folding chair she'd commandeered from inside the courthouse as her right as the oldest person at the rally. It bore a brass plate on the back that said: PROPERTY OF DEWIGHT COUNTY.

"Sit down before you fall on your face." She pointed to the grass beside her.

My knees buckled easily, even the sore one, which was going numb and tingly with new swelling. There was something that'd been bothering me all day, so I motioned for Walker to lean down and I asked her, "What was the name of your farm, before the war, in the early days?"

She looked baffled and shook her head.

Rains Lane my ass. Uncle Able having his little joke. Probably the whole day was his idea of good humor. I was fighting to stay awake in the late afternoon heat and the drone of voices when the group broke into a series of chants like the signs posted in people's front yards. I stood up and looked around. Our numbers had swollen to fifty, plus the people lounging around on the sidewalk watching, as the sheriff and his deputies got out of their cars. Big drive from their office—one block.

Monroe Sharpe went over to where Titus was standing, and the sheriff stopped in front of Walker and knelt down to eye level. "Now, Miz Rains, you know you don't have a permit for this sort of thing. You said it was a church meeting. I got a complaint call on you and you have to break it up, or else." A medium-sized man, Holbert Holkum had had the Dixie Fire and Life, an independent agency, until he ran for office. Nobody could remember a thing against him, so they voted him in, though according to Walker, nobody could remember a thing *for* him, either. He barely existed, and therefore looked perfectly natural in the khaki uniform.

"We *are* a church group, we're Reverend Titus Bedwell's parishioners and fellow Christians, and we're grouping to discuss theological issues. Reverend Gully Foye Jr. gave a stirring sermon, you just missed it."

"Well, Reverend Titus Bedwell is walking an awful thin line here. He's about to get hisself arrested I hear another word about Heart Hogs," the sheriff said.

The chanting against Heart Hogs turned into a dirge of "Let My People Go" that was growing loud enough to drown out arguments. Monroe Sharpe, the deputy, had his hat in his hand and was trying to talk to Titus, who turned away and began conducting the music with his hands as if the crowd were his church choir. Probably the first time in Resurrection history that a bunch of Baptists, Methodists, and Holy Rollers sang a spiritual together led by a black preacher. The sheriff was doing more to solve the spiritual crisis in America than a month of Sundays.

I looked at the courthouse to see how they were reacting to the ruckus and saw Pearl at one of the first-floor windows. I waved, but she ignored me. She had that all too familiar Grandmother Estes scowl on her face, the sort of expression that had come marching home from the House of Fashion the day Paris and Pearl and I had stood on the front porch of her house and shouted and danced and waved at our parents in a Bedwell funeral procession inching by at five miles per hour. It wasn't the first procession we'd ever seen, and to this day I could not explain what took hold of us. Estes's explanation was devilment. Well, Pearl's explanation for this afternoon was probably about the same.

The sheriff stood and glanced in her direction and she nodded. He shrugged and was about to say something with great authority when the singing swelled and Titus led the group out onto the sidewalk toward the middle of the intersection. Ignoring the blinking red light and the traffic, the group stopped in the middle of the four-way and sang one more verse and scattered. No one even honked a horn, so startled were they by the sudden event.

"You tell the Reverend that's about enough of that, Miz Walker," the sheriff said, before he left the two of us sitting there in the late afternoon sun. The trampled grass gave off a good green smell, and some crows came flapping down to look for any leftover food.

"Those crows act like we're the renters, the way they walk around," Walker said in a tired voice. I shaded my eyes and looked at her. She'd fooled me again into thinking she was twenty years younger and it didn't take a toll for her to be doing all this on little or no sleep. Her skin looked looser around her chin and throat, as if she'd recently lost weight. Was she sick? She was the one needed looking after, not these men we paid so much attention to. After fifty years or so of marriage, Able was too close to her to notice the little things. It was up to me, and I wasn't doing much of a job.

I reached up and rubbed her arm. "Feel like some supper, Aunt Walker? I could take us out for a change, or cook something for you. You could sit and put your feet up and take it easy."

She patted my hand to still it. "Moline, I'm just fine. After the day your uncle's put you through, I should be the one cooking. Promised Able his favorite meal tonight. I think what we all need is some good old-fashioned home remedy. My blood's feeling low, and you look like yours is too. We're needing all the strength we can get these days, so let's take ourselves back to the hotel and I'll whip us up some fried liver. Help me out of this crucifying chair, will you? Your Dear Pearl found the worst one she could for me. Always a pleasure, that girl. Such a disposition, she makes the Ayatollah look like Mr. Billy Graham." She waved at Pearl, who was still fixed to the window, watching us to make sure we didn't pull something else to embarrass her in front of the whole town. "Bye, Pearl, say bye to your cousin, Moline."

I wanted to tell Walker that Pearl was pregnant by McCall, but I didn't. It wasn't my news. It belonged more to Birdeene Cadmus and her brother, who'd have to gather it from the doctor's receptionist or the clerk at the Wal-Mart pharmacy when Pearl started buying her prenatal vitamins. So I waved at my cousin, too, and slipped my arm through my aunt's, and we walked down the sidewalk side by side as if we were two grand ladies on a stroll.

16

THAT SWEET LIGHT

*The red milk snake is often mistaken for a coral snake, a venomous snake
that does not occur in Missouri. At one time this snake and various sub-
species were thought to have the ability to suck milk from cows.*

— AMPHIBIANS AND REPTILES OF MISSOURI

*

THE TOWN WAS WILTING FASTER than lettuce in hot bacon grease,
my feet were twin baked potatoes in my tennis shoes, and I had trouble
pulling my underpants up after I peed. It put me in no mood to be taking
care of the hotel desk while Aunt Walker was back in that kitchen fixing
a big hot dinner I knew I couldn't eat. So I pushed my hot hair off my
neck and fantasized about being naked, flopping around in the water of
the wading pool out back of our house when our son was little. Duncan
and I sneaked out there late one night and made love in the grass after our
dip in the pool. That was a good time, when we'd had enough beer to
leave our split-level safety and not worry that someone might see us. I
never told Duncan about my trailer-trash relatives who peed off their
front steps when they drank beer. I usually made sure we were buttoned
up tight and proper to keep that image from becoming my own. But that
night was one of those times when you make love and don't even care
who it's with or where, it feels so thoroughly good to yourself. I worried
about times like those, that maybe I was betraying Duncan in a small,

mean way, and vowed not to let him become anonymous, though it sometimes failed. I never knew if that made me a bad person or not.

A couple came in with their sobbing baby, and the three of them
looked as tired and sweaty as I felt. I gave them a corner room on the third
floor, which got enough cross-ventilation to make up for the lack of air-
conditioning. Their faces fell a little when I broke the fact to them, but
they were too beat to argue. That should be our new motto, I decided:
Stay Here When There's Nowhere Else to Go. The baby wailed all the
way up the stairs.

A plump young woman in a brand-new Dodge pickup checked in with
only her purse. She was either a bank robber or a woman on the run from
her husband, I decided, and gave her a room with her own bath. She
wouldn't be in the mood to go down the hall. And I put her on the opposite end from the crying baby. Maybe I should've put them all together,
though, since the woman's streaked face looked like she'd done her share
of crying in this heat too.

It was a wait between guests, and I had time to notice something drawn
on the big brown desk blotter. I turned it around and looked at it from the
other angle—some kind of map or diagram. The word "Hell" stood out,
because it was very organized and had the most words under it, like
"Loneliness" and "Wal-Mart" and "Birdeene Cadmus" with little wings
flying her name. "Heaven" was an afterthought word scrawled in pencil to
the left side. When I looked more closely, it looked like DeWight County
was an island in the middle. There were landmarks shaped like potato
hills for the farm, Calvin's Cave, the Lake of the Ozarks, Bagnell Dam,
Tipton, Stover, Cole Camp, Versailles, Raymond, and some places I'd
never heard of that must have had some personal significance. "Potato
Hell," someone had written at the top. In the middle was a lightly shaded
area like a football field threatening to descend over everything like a
storm bad enough to spawn tornados with "Heart Hogs" penciled along
the edge. Aunt Walker's cosmology, no doubt. Heaven looked like a flaky
idea compared to the nitty-gritty of real life below.

Back in Minnesota, I was very careful about everything. And so clean,
I lied about my past to keep my heart from smudging the floors with feelings. I lied to keep the bed from bumping holes in the walls. Lied to keep
the appliances in place, our kid in Reeboks, our cars in the garage
promptly each night. I might as well have said I had peach-colored aliens

living in the attic as to mention Dayrell. Our house didn't even have an attic, though. It was from the generation of ranches and split-levels, developers' dreams of how to be close, how not to get separated, until something scorched your skin so bad that when it peeled away, you weren't the same person anymore. I'd watched my whole family burn and die that way.

"Memories." I wrote that word down and drew a cloud around it. I hoped Walker wouldn't mind that I was adding to her map.

I found a place for "Paris," then drew dark swirls under it like a tornado coming down to touch the earth. The Wallers were mostly there, with "Pearl" over a black dot for some reason. I gave the Bedwells a little subdivision of their own, about where the Swan Lake Trailer Park was on the edge of Resurrection, but changed my mind and put us in the hills that were a continuous scroll of soft script *m*'s to the south of town. I listed every Bedwell, black and white, I could think of, mixing the races freely. I wondered if you got to eat in Hell, if it was the same fast food every day or something like the familiar greasy smell of burning liver and onions drifting in from the cafe. I penciled in the new Hardee's by the Wal-Mart just in case before I got up to check on dinner.

I stopped and moved some papers on top of the blotter. This was between Walker and me. We were the righteous. *Self*-righteous, the Widows pronounced. How quickly we become judge and jury, they said, and pulled their mouths tight as little purse strings. You should know, I thought, but it was easy to see what needed doing, tell right from wrong, coming back to Resurrection like I had.

There was a chirping I followed to the corner behind the desk, but I knew better than to kill a cricket.

Something flashed in the front windows and I looked up in time to see Sugar Stimson on a mahogany bay walking horse with flaxen mane and tail in that too-good-to-be-true color your hair turns when you put peroxide on it at home. The set look on his face was as deep in thought of his past and present sins as mine. He was late, it was way past five. The horse's chest was flecked with white dots of foam from the bit, and he reined in for a car backing out of a parking space. The cricket changed tempo suddenly and I wondered if rain was coming.

The fried liver could wait, I decided, and went to the front windows to check the sky to the west, but there was nothing except the slow-motion end of the day. The stores were closed or closing. Up the block on the other side of the street, the Jesus Barber Shop's red pole spun slowly lop-sided where the paint had chipped. Inside the shop, the head of Jesus with long curls and smiling beard glowed white and brown from its plastic backlit circle, just like it did when I was a kid, except now the plastic was yellowing. Jesus looked like He was waiting in line for a perm. I remem-bered those Friday after-school sessions in there when Iberia would take us for hair croppings once every two months. We'd get a good dose of Christ and cutting, coming out feeling ashamed of the white line like a halo around our scalps and our ears ringing red as if they'd been boxed, not preached at.

I thought about running over and putting a note under the door to point out that long hair was a sign of humility, but I doubted Jack Ashley would get it. Jack's hair had been white his whole life since he was thir-teen when the Lord touched his family with lightning, killing his sister and their best hunting dog, Eugene, as they all stood under a big sugar maple in the field of their farm fifteen miles out of town. The dog lived a few minutes longer than the sister, and Jack swore the Lord Jesus Christ spoke to him in that brief time, in the dying groans of his beloved dog, Eugene, promising to take the family to Paradise if Jack would devote himself to cutting hair and spreading the Word.

No one could remember Jack being interested in hair before that time, and there weren't any holy rollers in his family tree that people could remember, but as Able said, "People in the Ozarks tend not to question the authority of true vision, especially when it's meant to further the good-sidedness of the general population, and there's only been that one time . . ."

The only time anyone remembered Jack faltering on his path was when the bald-headed hippie girl came through town and settled upstairs in this hotel for a few months. It was the tattoo of the bleeding heart of Christ that confused Jack. It was right on her chest, and although he knew it was the work of the pagan-worshiping Catholics, he was still struck dumb every time he went to shave her head and caught sight of its red pain-filled expression under the thin gauzy shirts she wore.

I was in fifth grade and it was a big topic of conversation at supper, especially when it became clear that as soon as Jack closed up the Jesus Barber Shop for the day, he went to eat at the hotel cafe, which was still serving supper then, and was observed on more than one occasion climbing the back stairs of the hotel to the second floor, where the hippie girl, Bathsheba, she called herself, had taken up residence in a splendor of candles, incense, and cheap scarves she bought at the five-and-dime.

The visits lasted right up to the eve of the Sunday sermon Gully Foye Sr., the Methodist minister, was going to preach on the problems of Temptation and Falling by the Wayside, but ended up teaching the Good Samaritan again, for the fiftieth time by my count. That Saturday evening Bathsheba was seen leaving town on the back of a motorcycle, clinging to a man in black leather and a World War I German helmet, which wasn't all that disturbing since there were still an awful lot of Germans around here and they had never really formally declared their allegiance one way or the other, preferring to keep their mouths shut and their pride and friendships intact.

Her scarves had all been tied together and streamed out behind Bathsheba like a wonderful rainbow rope that somehow Jack had failed to hang on to, that's what I realized later as I watched him grow old and nastily Christian before my eyes. Love had failed, and with it most of the New Testament. Jack switched churches to a holy roller group that made its members spend Saturday nights on their knees being beaten with fresh willow whips while they hollered out their sins and ate handfuls of bitter leaves. Once in a while someone died from eating poisonous ones, but Jack survived and only grew a little more green and bitter himself each year.

Two doors down was Copeland Harder Jr.'s law office, and two doors beyond that was the storefront office of his younger brother, Cecil, needing more than the hand-lettered drippy black paint on the window to assure people he was a real lawyer too. The story of Cecil, Cope, and their father, who chose one brother over the other and sealed the family fate for generations, was just another piece of pain the town held in the palm of its hand and kept for years like any good family member. In Resurrection, it seemed, nothing was forgotten or forgiven: the Harder men laying siege to Main Street and the litigious hearts of men and women; Uncle Able Rains and his hotel, despite being burnt down by Jayhawkers, remaining a symbol of all that was wrong with trying to push black and white folks to live together as one when most of the town thought God meant the races to be separate; the ruined awning of the abandoned bank Grandfather Horras once owned that broke him and nearly the whole town, pitting Wallers and Bedwells against each other for all time; and Grandma Estes's House of Fashion turned House of Pawn. I wondered why Dear Pearl hadn't kept that going, and felt the urge to call her up, ask her.

I could hear the Methodist minister trying to scare us with Hell, his voice rising up as the caverns hung with bodies writhing in agony from the pain of their sins came to life in the white wood church, staining it with the dark gore of souls unable to lose their flesh fast enough to avoid punishment. I would feel my own body grow hot and prickly with the furnaces of Satan so close to my feet. Aunt Delphine used to say my hair curled because I was tempting the devil all the time, and I always wanted to ask her what in the world she got a permanent for then.

Maybe Walker was right, maybe I'd always been somewhere in the landscape of Hell and just didn't know it. Duncan was Catholic and had had this very elaborate system of talking about good and evil: limbo, purgatory, hell, deepest hell, venial and mortal sins. It was so complicated I could understand how a person could just run out of time and energy and simply quit caring. At his family's church everyone was so nice and understanding, it didn't seem like they cared at all. Not the way Gully Foye had when I was growing up. He cared plenty and actually listened to people like Aunt Delphine and Estes when they had something bad to say about a person's soul. He called me on the phone more than once, and I wasn't the only one—Paris got calls almost every day before she left town, that was until she told him to fuck off and hung up so hard she shattered the mouthpiece of a perfectly good phone. Mister was plenty mad about that. She told him to fuck off too and ran out of the house, and didn't come back until the next day. By the time she showed up again, everyone had calmed down. Until she left for good, that was.

I wondered if you ever died in Hell, if you ever wore out your darkness, if it got thinner and thinner, like the finish wearing off a cheap black leather belt: first gray-white appeared in spots, then gradually the whole thing changed.

Outside the hot still air was falling evenly against the town, as if we really were living in some Hell. I thought I'd escaped it, only to find myself back in the center of it twenty some years later. What had changed, really, since we first came here, since 1826, since the War

Between the States, since all the wars, I had to ask, aside from a few more dead and a few more born. They'd flooded part of the Ozarks for the lake, but you could still hear the bodies separating under the water, those dark, dark waters filled with cottonmouths, serpents that come spawning out of caves whose passages stretched from Missouri across the world, inter-linked. There were two worlds here: one above ground and one below. There were many entrances but few exits. Too many went down and never returned.

Even Iberia and Mister and Paris, who tried to get away. Once you were in Hell, you didn't just elect for another vacation plan. There were no visas, no urban renewal, you were a permanent citizen. No Duncan could help out. Sure, I got away to Minnesota, but that had evaporated so completely, it was like a dream. My son didn't talk to me, I might never have been a mother, not really. The only thing I knew for sure was that I was standing in front of a hotel that had existed since the beginning of time here in Resurrection, a hotel that even the special viciousness of raiders and occupying armies could not put an end to, that even the dying-out Rains family would not allow to expire, a hotel that housed not only the racial history of this town, but also the history of everyone and everything in its museum. If there were anything permanent at all, it was the Rains hotel.

"Now where does that darn Clarice keep the salt?" Aunt Walker was searching the shelves beside the big black commerical stove in the cafe kitchen. She'd burned the first batch of liver and was starting all over. She sluiced some salt over the thick black frying pan, then dropped a wad of lard onto its hot surface. "Knew this stove was cockeyed," she said as we watched the lard skate to the left edge and squat into a clear puddle of melting fat. Walker spit lightly into the grease, nodded at the sputtering, and dropped the pink floured slabs of liver into the smoking fat.

"Grease's too hot. Going to burn it again," I said.

"That was because I didn't have my salt. Salt keeps it from burning. First time I burned my liver in fifty-five years. Estes, she never liked to use the flour, dropped that meat right in the fat, couldn't understand why it dried up on her." Drops of blood bubbled through the flour and spilled down the sides. She watched with satisfaction and poked a fork in each piece as if to make sure it was dead. "Fresh, full of blood. That old cow may have had meat like shoe leather, but she sure had a nice big liver."

She prodded the liver again, nodding at the slow hemorrhage that spilled crackling into the hot grease. It made me dizzy to look at, and I didn't have the heart to tell her she shouldn't eat organ meats anymore. "Just salt and pepper, none of that fancy business, salt and pepper and a handful of onions. Mashed potatoes and green beans simmered all day with fat back and mustard greens cooked down dark so they just melt in your mouth. My best dinner. Have to admit it's harder to get the timing on this big gas stove. Not like my old wood-burning stove at home. Everything done to a T there." She nudged the bottom of the stove with the toe of her shoe as if to get it to move along.

"Got a rhubarb pie in there's taking forever to brown. Wanted to make lemon meringue, but it's too damn humid. You're staying, aren't you?" She wiped her hands on the flowered bib apron that was so big it would wrap around her twice, and squinted at me like she was reading my mind.

"I have to see if Cope's still around." I drank some ice tea I found in the fridge. It was good, the way I remembered it. No lemon, just a tinge of sugar. Today's little work binge had made me so hot and thirsty, I felt like I was drying from the inside out.

"If you see Dear Pearl, find out if she's going to have Titus thrown in jail. Wouldn't put it past her. Remind her this is a democracy, will you? We still have the Bill of Rights which guarantees free speech." The grease popped and Walker rubbed her wrist where it'd caught her, the fork held dangerously close to the liver like she wanted to punish it.

Running my finger through the sweat on the glass, I felt so tired what I really wanted was to go upstairs and sleep for a year. The last thing I wanted was another round of arguing voices. Walker stabbed each piece and flipped it to a new chorus of splatters and hisses.

"She is family. I try to remember that. Never had the opportunities you others had. Never got out from under her mother and grandmother. A little kindness wouldn't hurt now and then, I suppose."

"Never thought of you as her defender, Walker. 'Specially now."

She grimaced when another pop of grease jumped up and caught her arm. "Look at her life. Pearl's never had the chance to be bad enough to have to leave. She's spent her whole life running for the cover of my

213

sister's narrow-mindedness and her mother's downright stupidity, and now she's alone. Even though getting married is only a temporary solution to a woman's problems, she's never had the chance to make that particular evil her own. Nobody's asked her. Now she's mixed up with a married man. Not the first, either. Just the worst, even if he is Dayrell Bell's half-brother." She smiled too sweetly, her lips pressed together and her eyes laughing at me as she turned. "Hand me that plate of onions."

"What would I say to her? She hardly ever says a word to me." I stared at the tea; now would be the time to tell her about Pearl being pregnant, but again, I couldn't. I glanced out the dusty windows behind us. Nothing was happening out there. Too hot. Then Sugar came by on another one of his walking horses, this one shoe polish black. Apparently, he'd thrown his whole schedule to the wind. Every few strides, Sugar touched a whip to the horse's hind quarters to make it pick up its feet more.

"Have some sympathy, Moline. The girl's never been any further than St. Louis, didn't even dare cross the river into Illinois." She reached over the pan of liver and onions to drag the big pot of boiling potatoes off the burner. "You come along, drive around in your fancy red truck, grab off the best stock, do what you please. Think how it looks to her."

Now Dayrell was the best stock? "She stopped speaking to me before I left, Walker."

"She was jealous, Moline, jealous of Paris and you with those boys. She was echoing those two women."

A fly tried to walk up my arm, and when I brushed it away it went over to the window and started ticking away at the glass as if any second it would split and let the damn thing out. Now that was faith, or stupidity. Hard to say. Because the sound was so tiny, almost nonexistent, it was loud enough to drive me crazy. I went over, cupped my hand over the fly, and threw it out the back screen door. The air was just as hot outside as inside.

"You know, if we're going to stop your cousin from selling us down the river to Heart Hogs, you need to talk to her more. Lord knows, I can't."

"It's not just about Heart Hogs anymore," I mumbled.

"What do you mean?" Walker stopped and looked at me.

"Nothing." I didn't even try to look at her.

"You got something on your mind, you better tell me, Moline."

I shook my head.

She added a dollop of blackstrap molasses and three dashes of Tabasco to the liver, "for digestion and character." She tasted the brown gravy on the edge of the spoon and smacked her lips. Her face was like a used-up axe blade, all angles and nicks and rusty spots and the memory of strength and power in the old metal. I'd always wished I were her child, even on days like this. Or sister maybe. Or friend. More than a niece, much more than that kind of relationship that could come and go like a piece of string unattached to anything very meaningful.

"You go along and see Cope now. Supper's in an hour, give the place a chance to cool down and let me have time to haul Able out of whatever devilment he's up to at the farm." She waved her long thin hands at me like I was ten again and underfoot, which was fine because the food smells and heat were now making me very queasy.

Walking to Cope's office in the six o'clock heat was like wading through used bathwater. The red letters on the white plastic sign in the Jesus Barber Shop said: SINNERS CAN REPENT, STUPIDITY IS FOREVER. There was a new place just past the Jesus Barber Shop and before you got to the House of Pawn shop. Show Me Tattoos announced itself in soft, modern letters that looked like they'd been inflated with a tire pump. Each fat letter was shaded in red, white, and blue as if to suggest that getting a tattoo was really the last word in patriotism. Had I always wanted one? I tried to remember, but my head felt full and fuzzy as I slowed down to peer in the window, which wore a yellow plastic coat to cut the glare. A couple of redneck kids were watching a man leaning over someone in a chair that looked like it was stolen from a dentist's office. Well, maybe this *had* been a dentist's office, I decided.

When I looked inside again, the man was fiddling with a table of bottles and tools, and I realized it was McCall in the chair, with his shirt open, and his belly like a small hard melon sitting on top of his body. There was a thin line of light brown hair making a cross on his chest, and on the left pectoral there was something drawn in black and red. Maybe instructions on opening and closing his heart. Dayrell had one there too, but I still hadn't made out the word. When he noticed me watching, McCall started to get up, and I hurried off with the image of the needle poking in and out of skin making me shiver despite the heat.

Suddenly the street was so still, it made a noise that wasn't there.

"Take me, oh Lord, into the contagion of light," I used to sing when I was little and stumbling into the world, waiting for Jesus Christ my Savior to come through the shine of sun like a good rubbed piece of glass, blinding me like now. I squinted. Did the buildings have a holy glow, or was that just wishful thinking? For years everything had had a dark aura around it I'd gotten used to. But right now, the world was scrubbed so clean of dark even the shadows looked bleached. "Are You here?" I murmured. "Will I finally get to see You?"

Before the answer came, Copeland Harder Jr. appeared in his doorway kitty-korner from me. He stared out across the street too, mopping his forehead and face with a wrinkled handkerchief, his white short-sleeve shirt sticking wetly to the undershirt beneath. There was a tiredness about his gestures, a giving in to it all, that made me sad. I wanted to take his little boy fat face and calm the red out of it with a cool damp washcloth. I wanted to feed him ice cream and tell him a story that would take the worry lines off his face and bring the smile back. I wanted him to like being alive again, to like the way things shone and grew. I wanted his fears to ease into restful sleep beside his wife and the goodness she har-bored in her heart for this man who was only a small effort the size of a child's fist, but who was something nonetheless, doing the best he could, I saw suddenly. Pigs or no pigs. How could we not love each other, how not, I didn't know, but I did. I hadn't wanted love, had run from it, and now I was outside the world that could bring me some peace of expiation, some purgatory to work out my crimes. Now Copeland Harder Jr., who drank a little too much, kept too tight a rein on his employees and cheated them for their pennies, and probably wanted to bed down with the waitress at the Rib Cabooze after all those years of marriage and kids, now even he seemed closer to God and His mercy than I was.

My stomach spun lightly and my neck suddenly felt too frail for the weight of my head as I watched Cope take the handkerchef he'd wiped his face with, blow his nose into it, and spread it to examine the contents before he folded it neatly and put it back in his pants pocket. He ran both his hands through his hair, scratched the center of his head, then looked at his nails. I wanted to be as casual as him at that moment, to be a person in a place they were easy with, to be a person with a past, present, and future they understood, predicted, weren't ashamed of, didn't have to hide.

He looked around again and saw me and waved, his mouth opening for words that got lost in the travel across the space between us, eaten by the light, by this watery light. The street lurched and rocked and I reached out for something to hold on to, and missed, and fell, long and slow.

"Moline? Honey, are you all right?"

"What's wrong with her?"

"I don't know—she just fell over like a chopped-down tree. Just fell." One voice was Cope's, the other was familiar, but I didn't open my eyes, not yet. It had been so sweet there for a moment, when the world had shifted and moved on its axis and I felt myself unable to resist. Now I just felt like throwing up.

"She's awful hot. Must have heat stroke. Tell one of those boys to fetch a glass of water or a cold Coke. We'll move her out of the sun here."

"Bring her down to my place. I got a couch." A new voice.

When I felt more hands on me, getting ready to lift, I opened my eyes. "I'm okay, I can walk. Let me walk," I protested as they lifted me in a fireman's carry. McCall's chest hairs sticking through my thin tee shirt on one side, and Cope's sweat wetting me on the other, we staggered to Show Me Tattoos.

Inside it was air-conditioned and the couch was a sticky, cracked dark red Naugahyde that crackled like old cellophane when they put me down. Then they stood and stared at me while one of the redneck kids handed me a battered bottle of Coke. I took a mouthful, swallowed, and promptly felt it coming back up. My hand clamped over my mouth, the stranger led me to a small, surprisingly clean bathroom in back, where I threw up. There was a chemical smell around the toilet that reminded me of my house, Walker's kitchen, and then the frying red blob of liver, and I threw up again and again, caught in the retching that became automatic as each thought and image passed. When it finally stopped, I felt hands under my arms, and McCall dragged me upright and brushed my hair back out of my face while he wiped my mouth with a wet paper towel.

"I hate you," I said, trying to push his hands away, but the dizziness came in another way this time, just a slow roll that would have put me horizontal except he was there to hold me when I started to go with it.

"Taking you to the hotel," he said.

"Home . . . wanna go home, please." I thought I heard him agree before

I let myself go under again and he picked me up and carried me so my face was next to the new tattoo. God is mad, that was what I should've told him. God won't like the tattoo of a broken heart held by the snake with Pearl's name riding its body. "God doesn't like things, McCall . . . better watch it," I whispered as he carried me through the store with Cope in tow.

"Only person I'm worried about is my soon-to-be ex, Moline, and she can barely read," he laughed, and put me down in the cab of his new yellow pickup. "Giving you a ride in the truck Pearl's buying me."

I gagged on the color and the new-car smell, and he rolled the window down while the air-conditioning pumped. There was nothing left in me to come up except some sweet and sour spit, and I felt like a dog trying to walk away from its own vomit when he said, "See, I'm not such a bad man."

Dr. Bradford showed up some time near dark and I sent him away. He told me to drink Gatorade and stay out of the sun. He looked old enough to have been the same one passing out all the bad advice during the flu and measles epidemics: Bake your fruits. I wanted to pursue it with him, but the image of hot sloshy bananas stirred my stomach up again. I rolled over and noticed my knee was even more hot and swollen and tender. If he weren't such an old quack, I'd of had Bradford look at it. Might as well ask Walker what to do, I decided, she'd been doctoring Able and her pigs for years.

Then Dayrell showed up to check on me in between depleting the ozone layer with more of his floor-cleaning chemicals. When he touched my face, I gagged from the smell on his hands. "Just dig the goddamn floor down to the dirt," I told him, and he shut the door to try to keep the smell out. Fat chance. The fan hummed in an uneven rhythm that was busier than productive, with the watery little breeze landing on me like someone else's wet, dirty Kleenex. Finally, I pulled the flannel blanket over me to get away. Better to bake than have all that disease laying on you. Enough to have it in you, I thought as I drifted off, my swollen knee pulsing in agreement.

John Wesley Waller's knees are not worn gray. He has not been praying on the floor. He has a large black growth in the middle of his back that expels too-sweet creamy fluid. He feels it growing in between times his wife, Henrietta, pinches it open. Like a bush it sends roots up and down his spine, looping his ribs, his liver, securing his intestines, like a hand, a finger, it pushes him forward. What does it say?

It says, Go into the watery flames. You will meet a wagon full of devils on the road, looking for the neck that fits the silver collar on the silver chain so soft you dent it with your fingernail. Around each of our necks it jingles like bells on sleigh horses, and we prance in the wagon, a ship-sized tub on wheels, eight to a side, in a row like centipede legs curled round. It rolls forth—don't get in—don't go there. I am sad and sick with worry and think we shouldn't know the devils who might turn out to be friends.

17

TESTIMONY

. . . *The meeting place of the Missouri and Mississippi rivers was one of the earth's most momentous sites. For Missouri it meant strength and pride until technology overcame the ancient primacy of water civilization. Missouri never was the same after the river gods were deposed.*

— MISSOURI: A HISTORY

✳

I DIDN'T GET UP until six forty-five the next evening and had to rush to make the Heart Hogs town meeting. Walker was waiting on the front porch of the hotel, tapping her fingers on the banister, impatient I had taken so long. "It's *this* year," she said, coming down the steps and taking my arm on her own initiative for the first time in memory. I realized that I was watching her age, these past weeks since I came home, and it made me feel both sad and desperate. What would I do without Walker to give me the backbone, the orders I seemed to need, like a sharp stick in the behind?

"That bout of heat stroke took it all out of me. Can't believe I slept so long."

"Can't work day and night and not expect to suffer some, Moline. Dayrell Bell can keep that kind of schedule because it's in his blood." She stumbled on the curb and clutched my arm tighter. I raised it as if that would somehow make her lighter on her feet.

"Well, we got plenty to worry about with our blood, Walker." An old red pickup squeaked to a stop and the farmer touched his hat at us. I dipped my head in return. Walker kept going.

"Don't pay any mind to Rowan there. He's been in town all day trying to convince folks it's all right to sell their land and go to work for those damn hog people. Company's not going to buy most of the land, they'll just drive the farmers out of business, that's what they'll do."

We circled the big brick courthouse and followed the others through the back aluminum storm door, down the short, narrow hallway leading directly to the biggest room, which served as an auditorium, named for Missourian Stand Watie, the last Confederate general to surrender at the end of the War. The front rows were still empty, as if nobody really wanted to stick their neck out. I settled us on the aisle seats to the left and turned around to see who all was here.

I looked for Dayrell, but could only find McCall standing along the wall to our right, laughing with two men dressed in fatigues and polished black combat boots and three others who looked more like him, with long hair, gimme caps, tee shirts, and jeans over sneakers or cowboy boots. Then I saw Birdeene Cadmus waving at us, but pretended I didn't see her. The Tebow men were there, Levon, the father, looking tired and hot, Claren, his son, glancing over his shoulder for any girls he could spot.

Tul Vestal, the trash hauler, hadn't bothering changing from his patched overalls and shirt so old and faded the flannel had been worn into a dull gray and pink. Even his hat was a series of patches, as if the feed mill didn't give them away free every spring. Lee Pettimore stood in the back, waiting to make sure there were enough chairs and helping the oldest people find their places, like Uncle Taber Harder, Cope's great-uncle, who had to be a hundred and spent his days at the Dixie Donut, trying to entice people to play cards with him, which no one would because he cheated so bad.

Wray from the laundry was sitting with his wife, a clean, small woman with a black growth the size of a dime on her eyebrow. She wouldn't have it removed for fear it was cancer. A blonde I took to be Leota Fay walked in on Arch's arm, spied McCall, and went right over and started joking and tossing her hair. She deserved McCall Bell, but then, she'd probably already had him, thrown him back, and moved on. She was like one of those big old lazy trout that last for years, tasting bait and spitting it out in your face.

Titus arrived with Freddie Eden, Beanie's mom, and a group of black men and women large enough to take up the rest of our row and the one across the aisle from us too. Titus looked at Walker and me and nodded formally.

"Sheriff made a deal with Heart Hogs so he could come tonight. Has to leave if there's a ruckus," Walker said.

As more and more people crowded in and lined the walls, the air grew hotter and damper. Walker took a man's big white handkerchief out of her purse, blotted her forehead, chin, and neck, and waved it in front of her face for the small hot breeze it created. "You'd think in this heat, they'd have the courtesy and brains to start on time," she announced loud enough that several people around us muttered agreement.

Walker introduced me to the black ladies in our row she knew: Miriam Dee Ware, Etta Weant, and Rose Shew. "Gardeners supreme," she said, and the ladies smiled and nodded like they might be humoring her. "Seriously, Moline, you go on over there tomorrow, to Dealia Street, and look at their yards, one right after the other full of flowers. I've accused them of being in competition, but they won't admit to it."

"You were a fine gardener when you had the time, Walker—you know it too," Miriam Dee said, and before Walker could answer, the talking quieted from the back and the hush swept forward as people began filing onto the raised platform in front. In the late fifties the room had received a face lift in the form of blond oak half paneling, white walls, refinished oak plank floors, lowered ceiling of white flyspeck acoustic tiles, and fluorescent lights that had hummed and blinked for so long it'd be too jarring to have them stop now.

Copeland Harder Jr. led the parade, smiling and waving at people he knew like he was running for office, then Pearl in a red silk dress and matching shoes and a man we knew wasn't from around here because while his clothes were the same general sort as those of the farmers in the crowd, his were too new and well fitted. Following him was a man in a white shirt, khaki slacks, and a linen navy sports coat who had a haircut that would put President Clinton to shame. Then came Odell Meachum, looking thrilled to be the center of attention, dressed in his black wool Sunday suit, and someone in a collar who was either a Methodist or Baptist preacher, as if they needed God to ride herd on the politics of pig in

222

Resurrection. Pearl looked comfortable being the only woman, and I caught McCall smiling at her like a proud parent.

"That girl should be spanked," Walker whispered loud enough for half the people in the room to hear. When the laughter died down, the preacher stood up and said a prayer for God's blessing on the community in the throes of turmoil. "Another reason not to go back to those Methodists," Walker said, quieter this time. I had to agree; besides, I had never believed God hung around at these little community meetings just so he could tell us whether it was better to rename a street or have hogs in our backyard.

There were two floor fans batting the heavy air back and forth across the front of the room, which only seemed to pull the various smells off people and stick them onto me. Cope was giving a booster speech, and my stomach was slowly turning over and over in rhythm with the fans. By the time he sat down to a few people's applause, my jeans and shirt were soaked with sweat.

An argument broke out behind us and the crowd was shouting so loudly the man in the sports coat and haircut, who was trying to say something in the microphone, gave up and sat down. Looking at his wristwatch, he leaned over and said something to Odell Meachum, who stood and yelled loud enough to stop the noise.

"You tell 'em, Odell," McCall yelled while the men around him laughed.

"He's always been a loudmouth," Walker was saying clear enough to be heard by Pearl, who turned her furious eyes on us.

"Look, this community needs this business for the jobs." Odell held his hands up to quiet the growing noise. "Hear me out—please. For the jobs, for the business it'll bring, and for the future of our kids, so they won't keep leaving fast as they can." He paused. "Look around you—where are the seventeen-, eighteen-, twenty-three-year-olds tonight?"

"Out getting drunk, like we should be!" one of the men by McCall said, and everyone laughed.

Odell smiled and shook his head. "That's another thing. The Lord is giving us this opportunity to make something better of our lives here, so we won't be getting drunk and hurting ourselves and other people." Everyone knew who was being referred to here—not only the Bells, there'd been others before and since. "Men who have jobs, regular jobs and regular lives, don't need to get drunk every night. Keep that in mind." People clapped. "Now Mr. Spenser wants to give us a chance to do something for ourselves here, turn central Missouri into a paradise of commerce, improving our schools, our lives, our—"

"Your wallet," Walker said.

"Now, Miz Rains, you been offered a fair price for your land."

"Thing is, Odell"—she stood stiff and tall, her finger pointing at him—"we don't want to sell. We won't let you turn our lovely farm into a bathtub full of pig dung. So you can stop right now. It's not going to happen."

"Yes it is, Aunt Walker," Pearl stood. "The county has a legal way to claim that land, and we're in the process of doing so."

"And Cecil Harder has filed an injunction to stop you."

Cope Harder frowned and licked his lips.

Pearl smiled. "Not a problem, as you'll learn in a few days. Meanwhile, I think you should all understand that this *is* happening, and it's for the best. The land around here isn't capable of producing a lot: the brick business is gone; the first- and second-growth timber is gone, and the scrub that's left isn't worth much; the quarries all have limited value. Hungry Creek isn't going to feed us. The lake has never brought the tourists they promised. But *this* is our chance. Let's not listen to the past, let's look to the future."

Half the room, mostly men, hooted and clapped while she sat down, her face fixed with earnestness.

"Lord save us, it's Estes back from the grave," Walker said, but her lower lip was trembling despite her brave humor.

"I have something to say," Titus announced, making his way to the platform, ignoring the surprise and unease on the faces of the Heart Hog defenders. "You all know me—I'm Titus M. Bedwell, minister of the Free African Baptist Church, along with my wife, Jos, who is home taking care of our children tonight. That's what I want to talk about. See, this used to be a town where we felt safe leaving the twelve-year-old to babysit once the kids were down for the night. But that isn't so, not anymore."

People began turning to each other asking what he was referring to. "I'll tell you what's not safe now—people setting fires, killing livestock, threatening black folks again." He stopped and looked at McCall and the group near him. "We've had our troubles in the past, black and white people, but we came to an agreement so we could raise our families and work. Now we're being pushed right back to that old place—and why?"

He looked at the people seated behind him as if he were asking them the question. Odell Meachum studied his hands, the Methodist minister blushed outright, and Pearl glared at me, as if I'd somehow put Titus up to this. The two Heart Hogs men stared back, half curious, half bored, as if they were watching a made-for-TV movie and were going to turn it off as soon as this scene played itself out.

"Why is it that African-American people are being offered less money for their farms than whites? Why is it that African-American people are being harassed and driven out? Ask Heart Hogs those questions. We should all ask those questions, because they want to move in and change things for us, make a difference in our community, they say. So far the only difference I see is a return to the days of vigilantes and Sweet Billy Creed who lies up there in the Negro cemetery as a reminder to each person in Resurrection of how community hate cost a twelve-year-old child his life a few years ago, because he was black. Do you really want to bring that hate and violence back? Haven't we gotten along better without it?"

"Oh, sit down!" a man yelled. "Yeah!" another said, and the group of black people in front turned in their chairs and looked back at the two.

"I have an answer for you!" McCall wove his way through the crowd standing in the back and walked up the center aisle with a folded white paper in his hand. With a smirk he leapt onto the platform and dropped the paper in the lap of the linen-jacketed man. The room was quiet enough to hear the tiny rhythmic squeak in the motor of one of the big floor fans as the man picked up the paper and unfolded it. He read it quickly, grimaced, and waved it once at McCall, who was standing there expectantly with his arms folded across his thick chest.

"It's the deed—to the creek property you was wanting, Hungry Creek? For the drain basin?" McCall raised his voice and leaned toward the man as if he were speaking to a slightly deaf older relative.

"That's fine," the man said, and looked over at the man in new farm clothes, who promptly took the paper and reached for his wallet.

"And I'm going to pay Mr. McCall Bell double the first offer on this land to show our appreciation for his hard work and trouble. Cash on the barrelhead, like we agreed, Mr. Bell." The man counted out ten thousand dollars in one-hundred-dollar bills and placed the stack on McCall's waiting palm while the rest of us watched like poor kids at the candy window. Not a single person in that room didn't have plans for money like that, and a collective sigh went up as McCall held up the bills, fanned them, and jumped off the stage. Wild applause and hollering accompanied him back to his group of friends, who slapped his back and eyed his money.

"That's what it comes to. That poor, poor child," Walker said. "She'll starve to death without that land."

"She's moved back with her family," I said.

"Let's hope they don't get tired of her, then," Walker said, some of the fight gone out of her with this last display.

Titus looked stranded on the platform now that the mood of the crowd had shifted in the face of real cash money. The money man stood up and motioned for silence, which brought the crowd to immediate attention. "Okay, you can see what we're willing to do for this community. We put our checkbooks where our mouths are. Who else can make an offer this good?" More of the crowd clapped than had before for the company. He smiled and turned slightly toward Titus, who seemed wooden and fixed now. "And let me reassure the Reverend here that the discrepancy in the offers was based on availability and potential use of the land, not, certainly, on any intention to create racial disorder. We respect our African-American friends and want to be good neighbors here. Our corporation has a fine history of hiring and promoting African-Americans, women, and people of all ethnic and racial origins, as you'll come to see. And in that light, with all due respect, we are donating five hundred dollars to the Free African Baptist Church youth program." The crowd burst into enthusiastic clapping again, except for the front row of black people, who sat with their hands in their laps and their faces still.

"What more do you want?" someone called from the back of the room, and several other voices joined in, quickly turning the mood.

"We want to live where the air isn't fouled with the stench of pigs!" someone yelled.

"And what about the hydrogen sulfide poisoning?"

"What about the wildlife? Those drain basins don't hold that crap—it runs off into the creeks and rivers. There won't be safe drinking water between here and Arkansas come the first flood."

The new-farm-clothes man used the mike to reason louder than the audience. "We drill test wells to monitor the vertical and horizontal movement of groundwater—"

"No, that's why you're buying up the creek land, so nobody'll complain about it until the crap's so diluted we won't know it's contaminating. But the fish and birds will know—there won't be a deer left in DeWight County. You're going to ruin everything!" Claren Tebow stood and yelled.

"No!" Odell yelled back.

"Crap farms, that's what you're proposing. We'll all be driven out of business by the volume you're producing. You'll control the market. No more family farms," Levon Tebow said, and others around him murmured agreement you could finally hear in the lull.

Tul Vestal stood and said, "I only got them five sows, but it helps pay the bills. What's my future here?"

The farm-clothes man's face brightened. "Why, you can be a subcontractor. We take all the worry out of the job too. Buy top stock for you. Our feed mill offers up to two hundred and fifty different ration formulations by computer. We keep track of your schedules for weaning, nurseries, finishing, and rebreeding. Why, you can get two to three breedings a year under our program! We can guarantee to add six to eight pigs per sow per year—as opposed to optimum of sixteen to seventeen, you'll get twenty-four. And the babies don't scour, don't have that seven-day fall-back time after weaning. They're in the nursery for six weeks, then on to finishing for ninety days. Go to market at two hundred and forty-five pounds, the kind of consistent, high-quality, affordable product the markets want."

Tul lifted his cap and pushed his greasy hair back. "Sounds all right. Problem is, ya see, I like workin' for myself. No offense."

Farm Clothes shrugged and sat down.

"That's it?" someone shouted, and the crowd standing back by McCall started yelling and shoving at each other.

Titus shook his head and left the platform. Not bothering to take his seat, he leaned down and said something to the people sitting closest to the aisle, who passed the words along the line until the entire group stood at the same time and marched toward the back door. The antagonistic voices grew shriller, and the people on the stage stood and began their own exit to the little door on our side of the room.

Who knows what would've happened next if Monroe Sharpe, the deputy, hadn't stuck his head in the door and yelled, "Volunteer firemen, down at the Rains Hotel, fast!"

People started jamming the aisles as if it were the courthouse on fire, so the volunteers had to leap and fall over the chairs to get out.

"Able!" Walker yelled over the noise, and I pointed to the side door.

There wasn't any big towers of flames or crashing roofs, and the lobby was open and empty when we ran in. The fire was out by the time the volunteers arrived breathless and hot in their yellow firefighting outfits a few minutes later. I felt a little sorry for them, except I knew some of them were the rednecks who'd disrupted the meeting. Able and another man, who happened to be passing by, had used the fire extinguishers and the blanket off the bed in the backroom where it'd started in the wastebasket. The room was a little smoky, and there were scorch marks up the wall, which the firemen took turns putting their palms against to make sure the fire hadn't snuck deeper in.

"Helluva deal," one said.

"How'd it start?" someone asked.

"You take up smoking, Able?" Monroe asked, wiping his watering eyes.

"No sir," Able said, and glanced at Walker and me to keep our mouths shut about the other fires.

"Spontaneous combustion?" someone said.

"Runs in the family," I said.

It took an hour to clear the people and firemen out because nobody wanted to leave without the drama they had been promised. I saw Titus across the street watching and talking to Walker, but he disappeared before I could go out and say something about McCall and Lukey.

Able and Walker decided to close up and go to bed early. The Solomon family had gone to Springfield for more research, and they were the only guests not in for the night, so Able locked the door and sent me home, though I tried to convince them to let me stay and stand guard. Monroe said he was going to keep checking the hotel for the next few nights. I have a gun too, I almost announced, but remembered what a bad idea that was. I hadn't eaten all day, but I wasn't hungry, just lightheaded, off-balance enough to feel pissed at Dayrell for missing everything as I drove home.

"What're you doing here?" I opened the fridge to see if some miracle had occurred and the longnecks had left spawn, but it was empty as Dayrell walked in the back door.

"Here." He pulled a can from the partial six-pack hanging from a plastic ring on his little finger. Very cool. He was barechested, with his white tee shirt tucked into the waist of his jeans. Grabbing the beer and taking the initial slug off it was a way to settle my body. Maybe drunk I wouldn't care so much about the way his eyes were glowing green at me as he pushed his hair back behind his ear and took a beer for himself.

"How come you're in such a good mood?" There was a possessive tone in his voice.

"Not."

"You like the floor?" He waved the beer over the clean planks that had an almost-new yellow to them. "Sanded the whole thing. I'll seal it tomorrow."

"Missed a spot over there." I pointed my foot toward a knotty place in the board he couldn't help. I was feeling very contrary after seeing McCall get that money for Lukey's land.

He lifted the can to take a swallow without taking his eyes off me. I was the one who gave in and looked away, superstitious that maybe he really could see into my soul, see the big For Sale sign in the window.

"You act like you been rode hard and put up wet, Moline. What happened at the meeting tonight?"

I slammed the beer can down on the counter. I didn't want to tell him about his brother. He'd hear it soon enough. "Nothing. Same ole same ole. I'm just in a mood. You were in a pissant mood after the barn burned, remember? Had to go and check on McCall's alibi. Another fire tonight at the hotel, but it was nothing. McCall and all the usual suspects were in the meeting. Where were you? I'm doing my part for the town, but you don't seem to care."

"I care plenty, Moline."

"Yeah, well, I'm not jumping to your whistle. I'm not one of your damn dogs."

He stared at me, shook his head, and grinned, not exactly nice. His eyes got this weird gray going dark as tornadoes. His hands relaxed and the beer fell to the floor with a thump and slosh, spilling on the fresh floor. He pulled his tee out of his waistband and used it to wipe the sweat off his face, rub his hands and chest, then he threw it at me.

Yanking it off my face, I wanted to tear it to bits, but tees don't tear that easy when they're new, and the smell of him made my fingers not try very hard. Couldn't trust anything around this damn man.

"Come on—you want a fight?" he taunted, his arms spread, his mouth grinning. "You're right—my dogs are a lot more loyal. When they've done something wrong, they lick me all over to apologize, too. You could learn a thing or two from those dogs, Moline." He danced like a boxer, jabbing and poking with his open palms, never really connecting, just making fun of me.

"I don't have a damn thing to apologize for—and I'd as soon lick a cottonmouth as you, Dayrell Bell," I waded in, avoiding the foot he'd stuck out to trip me, closing my eyes and windmilling with my fists, hoping to hit something solid and surprised when I did and he grunted and grabbed me in a hard embrace with my arms pinned to my sides so I couldn't get loose.

"That's enough. You got me," he said hoarsely. I looked up to see a smear of blood on his lip and was instantly embarrassed, ashamed and angry. Why'd he let me do that to him?

"I'm sorry." I said it stiffly enough that he could tell I wasn't, though I was. Oh, my fucking, fucking pride. A part of me wanted to drop to my knees, but I couldn't, I just couldn't. Instead I wet his tee shirt under the tap and tried to dab at his mouth.

"Just leave it."

"But you're bleeding."

"You wanted it, so here it is—enjoy—" He spread his arms and leaned to pick up the beer. Unsnapping another can, he took the big male slug that drained half, then finished it and dropped the can. The silver cross blinked on his bare chest, which had only the dim shadows of bruises left on it as he leaned against the wall, spreading his arms out lazily as if he were being crucified. The yellow stone on the thong sat like a lump at his throat.

"You started it," I said.

"Have it your way, Moline. Whatever."

"I'm sorry, I really am. Here, let me. . . ." I stepped closer, took his face in my hands, and kissed his mouth gently, ringing his lips with my tongue so the salty metal blood got grainy with beer and spit. He put his arms around me tight again, holding me so hard I could barely breathe.

"You're just full of devilment, Moline. You need those devils squeezed out of you, that's all, squeezed and screwed out of you. Come here." His voice dropped and he put a hand on my butt and pulled me up against his hardness, pressing us together there until I could feel myself give. "Where's that devil hiding, now where is she?" He pulled the front of my shirt out and looked in at my breasts. "She in here? Let me feel." He stuck his fingers down my bra and my body let go another notch as he touched my nipple. He pulled my body up closer and whispered, "Oh, she's a bad girl, this devil—she works so hard causing trouble." He leaned over and began to nibble at my breasts through the cloth, making wet spots right where my nipples were trying to push through. I freed my hand and worked it between us, rubbing.

It was like going under water, the sinking inside, all the resistance going away, the weight overhead insistent as a hand pushing me down, down, my mouth open as I slid down on my good knee with the sore one stretched out behind me and unzipped his jeans. He held my head, tangling his fingers in my curls, finding my lips, my mouth, my tongue with his fingers, sliding them in and out until he was out and I tasted it for the first time, the little clear sweet drop at the tip. I panicked a moment as he began to push it in, but relaxed again to take it. It tasted so good, like sugar syrup, I wanted it all.

"Oh my God, Moline," he gasped, and slid down the wall to sprawl on the floor with his legs around me and his eyes closed. He pulled me off balance into his lap, wrapping his arms around me and kissing my head all over until I stopped him.

"That the devil you're looking for?" I asked.

He shook his head, smiling sleepily, and dropped his hand across my shoulder so his fingers touched my breast. When I shivered, he unbuttoned my shirt and pulled my breast out of the bra. It felt so much wilder with my clothes on, like it wasn't supposed to happen but did anyway. I pushed his hand between my legs and he quickly figured out the way to do it. This time it was me groaning to the end, as dark and dirty as the backseat of an old Chevy, lost.

18

DARK PLATE OF SKY

To dream of muddy water means trouble, to dream of snakes presages a battle with one's enemy, to dream of money means that the dreamer will be poorer than ever before. A dream of white horses is unlucky and may mean sickness or death in the family. A dream of death is good luck if the dream comes at night and usually signifies a wedding, but to fall asleep in the daytime and dream of death is unfortunate.

— OZARK MAGIC AND FOLKLORE

DAYRELL LEFT AT DAYBREAK with a series of sweet little kisses that kept me dreaming awake until Walker called and said she had something she wanted me to do today, and would I please hurry.

What it entailed was going around asking people to sign a petition calling for a vote on Heart Hogs. She'd Xeroxed a fact sheet on factory hog farms and piled a thousand on the front seat of my truck. "Call me if you need more," she said as she slammed the door. She was in a military mood today, issuing orders that couldn't be questioned, and dressed in khaki walking shorts and shirt and white high-top sneakers. She must've mugged some high school kid, I decided as I drove south and east to start my canvassing.

At the first place I stopped, Phyllis Bawdry's little white one-story house set in a carefully fenced yard full of flowers, I discovered something about myself. First, I had to take the tour of the backyard garden and comment on the cucumbers trained to the trellis with the pink clematis, which indeed was unusual, and the ornamental purple basil setting off the border of carrots and alyssum. "Never thought of that," I told the tiny woman, whose fading hair was orange with gray like heavy salt.

Next, she led me into the kitchen and insisted I have a glass of ice tea while she read the petition and the flyer. Her dead husband, Aubrey, had taught her that much, God rest his soul. "You look tired, dear—set here a while and enjoy your tea," she advised. By the time I'd left the tiny room guarded by four wrought-iron knickknack shelves inserted into each of the corners to hold her collection of china cats and dogs, I knew I had finally grown the kind of face that made people offer me comfort and stories.

At the Pillars' farm, I had to help collect eggs while we talked, and they already had anti–Heart Hog signs lining the ditch in front of their place.

Frances Spooner had to have another cancer operation, but she was eighty-three and had already come through two others that took her breasts and one kidney. She knew she'd come through this one just fine if they didn't try to baby her too much. She made me taste some of her fresh whipped cream on a waffle she'd baked for her husband and the hired man, who naturally were nowhere to be found when the food was ready, and she was way too old to be marching through those fields after them. She was a little deaf—could I hear the tractor? I listened hard at the back screen door, but couldn't make it out for the traffic on the highway out front. Well, she'd had that problem too, so maybe she wasn't so deaf after all.

By noon I had only five signatures, but I could draw the family trees of most of that part of the county, and give you pretty complete medical and marital histories too. Two more Bedwell relations turned up, according to Lenore Gleeson, but I'd have to get to them later, since they were way on the other side of Uncle Able's. It was definitely my face that invited confession, I decided in the truck on the way through Raymond and around the back road over to the farm. That and the general goodheartedness of these folks who were living their small lives on small parcels of land down here. These weren't like the big midwestern farms of Iowa and Minnesota or the ranches of western Nebraska and the Dakotas.

But we didn't see ourselves as quite like the states around us. We were Missourians. Not quite southern enough, not quite midwestern, and no one ever mistook us for easterners or westerners either. In school our teachers told us we were the gateway, the origin of the West: Lewis and Clark set out from here, the Pony Express began here, the wagon trains launched from here. At one time we were such an important state, there was talk of moving the federal capital here. Even after it had passed us by, we never lost that sense of being at the beginning of something important. But that was before the War ended everything that had begun here. Now no one wanted to claim Missouri—not the midwesterners, not the southerners. That left Missouri its own place. When I told people up north I was from Missouri, a blank look scrolled across their faces before they got polite and said, "Oh, uh-huh."

There was plenty of activity at the Rains farm when I drove up. Somebody was on the roof letting the broken slate tiles slide down and crash onto the pile below with a high sound like shattering china platters. Parking behind the trucks lining one side of the driveway, I tried to see who it was on the roof. Too short for Dayrell and too wiry for McCall, whose trucks I'd spotted. There was no sign of Uncle Able, but that didn't surprise me. Unlike Walker, he wasn't into the supervising mode. In fact, I half expected to see him on the ladder or the roof when I circled the house to the far side, where the brick was slowly rising like a tide of red mud against the bare gray wood.

Stripped to the waist and smeared with whitish streaks, Dayrell and McCall alternated slapping bricks down in beds of mortar while they argued. Every time one of them made a point, the other one barely missed his fingers with the next brick. Excess mortar dripped down in knots on the ground.

"Watch it." McCall threw a brick at their feet and Dayrell jumped back.

"Well, slow the hell down." Dayrell picked up the brick and brushed off the clots of mortar.

"Quit being such a goddamn girl," McCall said, and slathered mortar on the waiting space.

"You're clogging the weep holes dropping mortar inside the wall like that—now cut it out." Dayrell slammed the brick so hard it cracked in two and he had to throw it over his shoulder in disgust.

"Who gives a shit?"

"I give a shit. We promised Able we'd do a good job. Water gets

234

trapped in there with the weep holes clogged, whole interior wall's gonna mildew and rot."

"Since when are you such a perfectionist? The old man'll be dead by the time that shows up." McCall's hip and shoulder bumped his brother's and they started shoving at each other. When they tipped the wheelbarrow of mortar on the ground, they stopped and stepped back, both of them loudly swearing.

"Here, what's going on down there?" a voice called from the roof.

"Nothing, Daddy," McCall yelled, and gave him the finger.

"Sweet," Dayrell said, and began shoveling what he could of the mortar back into the wheelbarrow.

"Look, I shouldn't even be here today. I had other things planned until you stepped in with your big mouth this morning."

"Just forget the wall—I don't want you screwing it up because you're feeling like a pissant." Dayrell waved his trowel at him.

"Have it your way." McCall backed off and sat down in the shade of the apple trees old enough to twist and lean toward the house as if for help. "Wouldn't've happened if you'd minded your own goddamn business to start with."

"Soon's I heard you'd sold the land, I knew you were going to run off with the money."

"Like I said, mind your own goddamn business." McCall yawned, stretched, and spotted me. "Here's the other piece of tail—I mean business—you have to mind, Dayrell."

Dayrell looked up and nodded at me. "She didn't tell me."

"I bet. That's why she raced outta there last night. Maybe you should all move into that falling-down hotel together. Long's he doesn't marry you both, he can have as many women as he likes, right, bro? There's laws against bigamy." McCall's laugh made me shiver.

"McCall, you get off your behind and start working or you're never gitting out of here," Hale Bell called from the roof.

"Yes, Daddy." McCall made a face at the ground and got up.

"Dayrell, stop arguing with your brother. We got to git this work done before it starts in raining again. One of you should get on this roof job with me, you can't git along any better'n that."

"It's all right, sir," Dayrell called, and placed the next brick more carefully in its mortar.

"Yes, sir, no sir," McCall mocked. Picking up his trowel, he slathered some mortar on and slapped down a brick with a slight angle. When Dayrell moved to straighten it, McCall did it himself. "Can't let anything be, can you? I had Lukey all settled down and you go and get things riled again. What, are you sleeping with her again?" McCall glanced at me and smiled.

Dayrell looked over and shook his head. "She caught me on the way out here. She was looking for you, shithead. I didn't tell her you were at Pearl's. Apparently she was under some misconceived notion you were going to divide the money equally so she'd have something to live on." Dayrell worked with a steady rhythm, though the knuckles on his hand holding the trowel were white with tension.

"Woman's crazy." McCall glanced at me. "Ask Moline. Lukey dragged her over to Pearl's the other day, where I was fighting a hangover and one of those headaches I get, just to sign the deed over right then and there. Can't tell you how it made my head hurt. Couldn't see or hear for shit. You know how sick I get." McCall puckered his lips in self-pity.

"McCall, that's not what—" I said.

"Just stay out of this. You don't know the half of it, Moline." McCall hefted the brick in his hand.

"I know what I heard and saw."

Dayrell kept working, but glanced at each of us with a question mark on his face. I hadn't mentioned any of it to him, and now he knew I'd been holding out on him.

McCall caught the expression on his brother's face and jumped in. "You only know what she told you, and I'm telling you now I wasn't responsible. Go on—what did I say? I can't even tell you. Ask Dayrell—he knows what I'm like with that head thing. I'd agree to a trip to the god-damn moon when I'm out like that."

"You cried about missing your kids."

Dayrell didn't look at either one of us, but his shoulder muscles were bunched as he kept building the wall.

McCall sneered at me and stepped back from the house to glance at the roof in case his father caught him slacking off again. "They're my kids, and I'll do what I want with them and that money. I earned it."

Dayrell looked at me, but I couldn't read the expression in his eyes.

"What about the other thing you said—about the Tyrell girl's accident?" I knew it wasn't smart, but I wanted to shake that rotten cockiness.

McCall had pushed me back before Dayrell had a chance to pull him off. "You lying bitch!"

"What's this all about, McCall?" Standing behind his brother, Dayrell kept his arms locked around him so he couldn't move.

"Let go, you dumb fuck!" McCall struggled and tried to trip him but couldn't.

"Tell me!" Taller by far, Dayrell easily lifted McCall a foot off the ground and slammed him down again.

"Get Moline to tell you—I don't know what she's talking about." McCall quit struggling.

Dayrell released him and stepped back, pushing behind his ear a lock of hair that had come loose from the ponytail. Looking at me, he raised his eyebrows.

I shrugged and glanced at McCall, who was staring at me with this terrible, hate-filled expression in his eyes. He truly scared me, and I wanted to tell Dayrell to look at him, see for himself, but I knew the expression would be gone when he did.

Dayrell swung his attention to his brother. "Well?"

"She's making it up, can't you see that? It's nothing. Forget it. White-trash slut like Marjean Tyrell . . . It was an accident, Dayrell, wasn't nobody's fault." McCall reached out to touch his arm, but he shrank away.

"It was my fault. The girl *died*, can't you understand that? Doesn't matter what she was."

McCall grimaced. "Get over it, for chrissakes. You did your time. Get on with your goddamn life, Dayrell. Quit skunking around in my business and my women and move on."

Dayrell folded his arms and kicked at the grass. "I'll be paying for it the rest of my life."

"You're a goddamned idiot then, and I have no, absolutely *no* sympathy for you. No wonder Lukey fucked you—you're two of a kind, goddamn bargain-basement Christians. Couple of martyrs. You're so fucking pathetic. Saint Lukey and Saint Dayrell." He paused and glanced at me and spit into the space between us and looked back at his brother. "Judas

Priest, I was gonna give her something, but not now, not after you dragged the whole family into it this morning. Nope. She ain't getting a dime."

"Fuck you, McCall. She'll get part of the money—Daddy'll make sure of that, you cocksucker. Or I can just kick you to death and take it."

McCall looked at him and grinned meanly. "You know what you are, Dayrell? You're like a chicken-killing dog, can't keep away from it. You got the stink of the jailhouse in your nose and don't wanna give it up. You like that, don't you—thinking of yourself as the big, bad, murdering S.O.B.? Probably feel like maybe you wanna go back there, huh? Get a yearning for that hard dick up your—"

Dayrell jumped him and they were rolling around on the ground grunting and cursing when Hale Bell reappeared and started hollering from the edge of the roof and Uncle Able came around the corner carrying a hose crimped to stop the water.

"Here, you two!" Able yelled as he turned the water loose on them. It took the fight out, soon as they realized they were having trouble breathing with the water pouring in their faces.

"McCall, you get up on this roof right now!" Hale ordered. "Dayrell, you finish the wall by sundown or I'll know why."

Trudging to their work, neither one said a word. Uncle Able winked at me and beckoned. Glad to get away, I followed him back around the house.

"Your aunt called to see if you'd shown up yet. She's gotten three calls from folks you spoke to this morning on that petition dealie, and they kept her on the phone for forty-five minutes saying what a fine young woman you turned into. Your aunt figures you aren't moving fast enough if you have time to make such a good impression. I told her you had to help me 'cause my back was starting to pinch again, and that shut her down some. She said soon's we're done, you should take yourself out there again and collect some more signatures." He laid down the hose next to the tangle of weeds and grass he was digging. "Did the best I could to get you off the firing line, Moline."

I patted his back, shocked by the bones I could feel through the layers of underwear, shirt, and overalls. "Thanks, I know you did. It really is hard to get away from those ladies once they get ahold of you. I drank so much ice tea and listened to so much gossip, I thought I'd died and gone to Methodist heaven."

238

Uncle Able chuckled and spread his arms over the digging. "See, here's where the vegetable garden always goes. Haven't had much luck getting to it past few years, but figured I'd try some hot-weather plants, see if they have any luck. Carrots, potatoes, radishes. Have to wait on the lettuces till the cool sets in again."

"What do you want me to do?" I hated to ask, because I knew it'd be something terrible.

He glanced at me out of the corner of his eye, and I could see his lips parting in one of his silent little laughs. "Now, you could go get yourself a change of clothes in the house."

I groaned and looked at the roof, where the sun was making McCall's burning back glisten hot red. His father was standing with one leg on either side of the peak, pointing at one of the tiles. "They have to replace a lot of that roof?"

"Not so much. Hale give me a good, fair price too." He picked up his hoe and plunged it into the earth, pulling up a clump which had dark, rich-looking streaks in the red and was dripping with thick, long earthworms. "My secret ingredients. Now git."

On the way out again, I snuck around to the far side to where Dayrell was laying brick with surprising speed, stopping only to wipe the sweat running into his eyes. I unknotted the old handkerchief of Able's I'd grabbed out of an upstairs dresser to pull my hair off my face. "Here"—I walked over and handed it to him—"roll it and tie it around for a headband to keep the sweat from dripping down."

He tied it on, said "Thanks" without looking at me, and went back to work.

"I was going to tell you—"

He didn't stop work. "When?"

"We were having such a good time I didn't want to spoil it with your brother."

"When, Moline? When were you going to tell me he'd taken the land and the money?"

"He's not my responsibility. I was—"

"Last night you knew he'd sold the land, you knew he'd promised Lukey the money, and you didn't say a single word about it to me, someone who could've done something maybe?"

"I sort of—I didn't want to cause trouble, Dayrell. Besides, you always

239

stand up for him—always act like he's a kid making kid mistakes, like what he did that night to me—you never—" I stopped, because he stopped and looked at me steadily like I was a poisonous snake he had to decide whether to kill or not with the brick in his hand.

"I never what? You got drunk, let my brother come in and drank some more. If he's so dangerous, what the hell did you think you were doing?"

"There—you always stand up for him, try to get him out of trouble. Like the barn-burning thing. He's getting worse, you know."

Dayrell set the brick down and ran his hand over his bare chest, leaving gray swirls on the dark red-brown skin. "All right, okay. All the more reason to tell me things when they happen. How the hell am I supposed to get the money now? Last night I could've gone out and found him while he had the cash on him, but not now. Not even telling Mom and Dad helped. Hale thinks we have too much time on our hands, so he comes out to supervise the job and half kills himself on that roof, and Mom goes to church to talk to the preacher again about one of her sons. But no one can get him to say what he's done with the money. You same as lied to me, Moline." He shook his head and made that sound of disgust in his throat and picked up his brick and trowel again. He didn't realize how close he was coming to a much worse case of that.

"Moline?" Uncle Able's voice wrapped around the corner on the little breeze blowing hotly through the yard, carrying with it the smell of the tiny fists of green apple on the trees. Dayrell ignored me as I left. We hadn't said we'd be honest with each other, but isn't that what it means when you love each other? But I'd started with a lie, a betrayal, same as his brother's. I stopped before going around the house and looked across the yard at Dayrell, working now with a hard, angry rhythm. He'd be worn out long before the wall was done. The wind rustled the trees louder, and looking up, I saw Hale Bell perched on the edge of the roof looking down at me and I hurried away.

"It's a real simple job. You get yourself one of those buckets down at the henhouse, or better yet, the wheelbarrow in the tool shed, and you go out to the corral there, especially by those long feeding troughs, and you pick up every cow pie you find. The wet ones you'll need a shovel, of course, but there's plenty of dry ones too. Lots of 'em. You run out, you go to the pasture there. Don't have to go far to find a whole bunch. And don't bring any horse apples. They're too hot for the soil." Uncle Able chopped at the dirt some more, breaking the big pieces into smaller ones, and stooping to separate the weeds and grass and throw them into a pile.

"I should be doing that, you'll hurt your back again."

"Soon's you get done, you can take over here," he said, and brought the hoe down hard again, using both hands and his upper body so he ended half bent over.

Knowing Walker would kill me if he threw his back out again while I was supposed to be helping him, I hurried to work. I sure wasn't climbing any ladder to success here, that's what I was thinking as I picked up the patties of dried cow dung. Maybe Dayrell needed some time, that was all. He'd get over it, he'd see things my way once he calmed down, I tried to reassure myself; but the Widows wagged their heads and hooted with their mouths open like identical round dark coins.

As I bent down, my knee kept feeling like it was going to split open in all directions, like a cantaloupe left too long in the melon patch, and I had to concentrate to keep the sun's hot hand from pushing too hard on the back of my head. If I fainted this time, nobody'd come and save me and I'd probably vomit and die aspirating. Lucky I had my wheelbarrow full by the time I realized that truth, and could wheel us both back, wobbly and uncertain, to where Uncle Able was now resting in the shade of his oak tree.

"Idle hands are the devil's playthings, Moline." He smiled as I staggered down into the grass next to him.

"So what's your point?" I gasped, and he laughed long and hard.

The rain began around five, and I stood there and let it wash some of the manure and mud off me, watching it drain in yellow rivulets into the dark, worm-infested soil at my feet. Able's magic lay around me in neat rows staked with white twine and sticks. My knee ached in a blunt new way I basically ignored, thinking that the mud packs would draw the infection. Seemed to me that was a hill remedy, but the details were fuzzy, like a lot of things at the moment. Except the rain, which stood out in big individual drops that clung like jelly to the leaves and stalks and trees.

I didn't see Dayrell and McCall leave, but their trucks were gone by the time I'd rinsed in the basement and changed. Stopping at the Hardee's out by the Wal-Mart for a chicken sandwich, I thought I saw McCall's yellow truck heading down the highway toward Raymond and Lukey's. I took one bite and threw the rest of the sandwich onto the side of the road for the birds. The french fries followed. My stomach was in no mood, and I put that down to smelling cow shit all afternoon.

I felt too lonely to want to go right home, so I circled around northeast of town where the land got poorer, dropping into the deep ravines and rising to the small hilltops of the black community. When I was growing up, these streets weren't paved, and that was how you knew where you were. At first there weren't house numbers here, either, and mail delivery was sporadic. When something did come for a family, Liston Mays usually knew where the family lived, or would post a note on the bulletin board at the grocery store where black families shopped to let the person know they could come and pick up their mail. All that changed when Titus's sister Cecelia was going to go east to college, and everyone got in an uproar because the letter of acceptance sat for two weeks in the post office because Liston Mays did not feel like taking it and forgot to post the note. He was getting too old for such nonsense, was what he said when the black preachers met with the town council and finally the federal post office officials and got him retired and regular mail service established in their neighborhood, which then got numbers for all the houses.

I wondered if Cecelia Bedwell ever came back here. So far Titus and I were the only Bedwells who had ever returned alive. Iberia and Mister had moved to Tulsa to live out their days pretending they were used to the real brick of their house, the built-in appliances, and the thirty-inch TV. It didn't last very long, though. They hardly got a chance to drive around the block in their new Cadillac before fate took their lives for one more ride over to the Baptist Medical Center. I tried to imagine the disappointment on their faces in the ambulance, and later in intensive care, side by side as they'd been all their lives, their eyes staring at the white-as-snow ceiling while the black internist pronounced them dead from eating five-year-old stewed tomatoes Iberia could not bring herself to abandon to Estes's fruit cellar in the move from Resurrection. Trying to know what to feel about their deaths took its toll those first few months, until I finally settled on something I thought we could all agree upon—not far from what I was learning to feel about Duncan, but a moon away from how I felt about Paris.

I stopped at the corner across the street from Titus Bedwell's house, squatting possessively in the center of the lot with its backside tumbling down the tree-filled slope behind it. On the edge of the hill, the old out-house tilted like a drunk on one leg beside the neat stack of winter wood. The seventies black Ford sedan gleamed hugely in the gravel driveway. I saw Titus standing in the thin spill of yellow light from the side windows, staring into the thicket of woods that dropped, then rose again, on the opposite hill. In a moment I saw it: a buck with at least four points nosing his way up the hill, stopping here and there to nuzzle and grab a bite of something. He was in no particular hurry, wasn't using any particular cau-tion. If he saw the man, he gave no indication, as if he weren't going to concern himself with such mundane things.

I slowly pressed the gas and noticed Titus looking my way as I turned the corner. In my rearview mirror, I saw a yellow square of brighter light open onto his body, and his wife appeared at his side. I hadn't thought about Titus married with a family of his own all those years I was gone. In my mind, he was always just there, the friend I left staring at me through the window of the bus, his arms folded so he wouldn't wave and get into further trouble.

Tomorrow I'd call my friend Titus, see what we could do for Lukey. That was how I got myself heading back down the street toward my house. With night settled on the town, people came back alive, and as I neared home, there were kids horsing around under streetlights, and par-ents strolling their babies, and older kids on bicycles swerving in front of my truck, and business at the Dairy Daddy standing in lines, impatiently tapping its toes, and the parade of hot kid cars circling the square in sharp squealing turns, and girls' laughter floating across the evening on the green tint of the hills that flowed down upon the town after dark and held it in a breathy embrace until morning.

I was thinking maybe things weren't so bad, even with my knee so swollen stiff I couldn't bend my leg much as I hobbled up the front steps to my house. Tomorrow I'd track Dayrell down and try to explain. Then I stopped. The front door was wide open, even though I remembered shut-ting it earlier. As I came into the dark room, that disturbance of the air struck me like a blow to the chest and I panicked. Someone was here. Groping on the wall for the switch, I needed a moment to realize that that was at my old house. I started to back out the door, but stopped and listened. No, I'd been wrong; someone *had* been here, but they were gone now.

I clicked on the floor lamp by Mister's recliner and looked around the living room. At first I thought it was still wrecked from the other night, but then I saw the brown-black word smeared on the wall behind the sofa: CUNT, with the bullet hole in the middle of the C for emphasis. Leaning closer, I realized that what I thought were smears were the other, smaller words above it—"Dead Nigger"—with an arrow pointing toward the bullet hole.

My breath whooshed out like I'd been punched in the stomach, and I had to sit down in the chair opposite the wall to get it back. McCall—did he have time? Was he here just moments ago? The words were painted with a finger or a stick. I looked around the room, then I got up and examined the wall again. It stank like something familiar. Roofing tar. I smiled, at least it wasn't shit.

The kitchen was a little torn up, with more tar spilled on the clean wood floor, but nothing Dayrell wouldn't know how to take care of. My refrigerator door stood open, but that wasn't much of a loss, since it was empty except for one of Dayrell's beers from last night. It must have been frustrating for McCall trying to tear up what was already a wreck, I thought as I walked back towards my bedroom.

But he'd been here too. It looked like dirt on the bed; then I saw the lid with the prancing horses on the floor. Paris. Where was the box? I searched frantically; it was gone. There was a smudge of her on the floor, which I carefully stepped around and then raced down the hall to the back door. The silver bottom of the box glinted in the clump of weeds by the side of the chicken coop. It was dark enough now that the ash was invisible in the grass, but dropping to my hands and knees despite the protest of the infected one, I found a white shard of bone.

He'd cast her in a wide arc, like a person sowing grass seed would, and that's how I found the three other bits of bone, like shattered china in the dark. When I couldn't stand the pain in my knee anymore, I stood and cradled the last pieces of my sister and carried her back to the house. Inside, I realized what the smudges of black on my hands and legs were and started to smile, and smiled even bigger when I found myself trying to wash the bone off as if it were a treasure I'd unearthed. Wetting the tee shirt Dayrell had left, I scrubbed at my arms and legs, wondering if I should let the shirt dry and burn it to recover part of my sister. I'd never be able to explain any of this to anyone, I giggled. I should've been scared, but I wasn't. Seemed like a kid's tamper tantrum more than anything else. But just in case he felt like coming back for more, I shoved the dresser and chair against my bedroom door for protection. I tried to move the old iron bed, but it was too heavy, so I got in it instead, and closed my eyes to the dull strobe of the bones sitting on the windowsill in the moonlight blinking through the clouds. Send McCall a thank-you note, the Widows advised, with humor tickling their lips for the first time. Go to sleep, I told them, get some rest, you work too hard for being dead.

19

FORGIVING KNIVES

It is customary to depict a rock sequence in a vertical column, with the older rocks underneath the younger ones. "The Law of Superposition" states simply that in a normal succession, it is logical to assume that the lower layer was there when the upper was deposited over it. However, in areas where there has been extreme disturbance, entire rock sequences may have been overturned, revising normal age relationships, so the process of determining the relative ages of rocks is not quite as simple as it might seem.

— MISSOURI GEOLOGY

✳

"MOLINE?" The voice followed by scratching on the screen startled me awake. I pulled the covers up quickly until I recognized the voice, then I got up and unhooked the screen. While Dayrell climbed in, I crawled back in bed and closed my eyes.

His breath warmed my cheek, then he blew softly on my closed lids. "You awake?"

"I am now," I murmured, not wanting to open my eyes yet.

"Hungry?" He rustled some paper, and the deep, rich smell of barbecue filled the air over my face. I opened my eyes to the rib dripping sauce on my nose.

"Sorry." He laughed.

"I bet—give me that." I opened my mouth and he stuck the whole end of the rib in and I tore off the meat, but realized I couldn't swallow without sitting up.

He shook the grease-splotched grocery bag. "Able decided we'd done enough work, handed me a twenty and said to take you to dinner. I tried to give it back, but he has his ideas. So, here it is." He smiled, and I noticed how it made the scars on his chin and throat stand out a little more.

When I reached out and touched his chin, he pulled back an inch and left my fingertips hanging there. He piled the covers at the foot of the bed and spread paper plates, napkins, plastic silverware, and flat, square paper cartons in the middle between us.

"Got you some ice tea." He handed me a tall Styrofoam container, and I groaned inwardly at the idea of more.

We ate quickly and hungrily, finishing all the food and using the crusts of white bread to sop up the sauce. Then we leaned back and picked the meat from our teeth with the toothpicks he'd stuck in his shirt pocket as an afterthought. First there was this comfortable, full-stomach silence, but eventually that turned into another kind of distance, and I suggested he light some candles which I'd found in the kitchen the day after I arrived in town. They were for emergencies, and I figured this might become one if we didn't get down to some serious talking.

Dayrell sat and seemed to let his body settle in more at the end of the bed. He looked at me, and when I nodded, he lifted his cowboy boots and placed them pointing to the corner by the wall. He had one of those faces whose planes became both more prominent and softer in the candlelight, making him more handsome and stranger than before. His eyes took the shadows personally and hid so there wasn't anything to read.

"This lying thing . . ." I began.

"Never mind." He waved me off.

"No, really, let me explain."

He shook his head. "No. Let me ask you some things, and you just tell me the truth, the whole truth, okay?"

I nodded. I was going to tell him the truth about the accident too, as soon as he'd let me. At least I meant to.

He looked out the window next to the bed toward Pearl's house, which glowed yellow-white in the lights from the windows and street. The aluminum rungs of the ladder he'd left in the grass next to the house glinted like rows of narrow mirrors.

"Remember when we first went out there to the cave?" he asked in a soft voice.

"You picked the lock. We had to find that dry shelf for the quilt."

He looked back at me. "You asked me to bring some whiskey to make it easier. I wondered about that."

"I was scared. I never drank before that, but in books people . . ."

"I knew you were pure. It touched me—I would've done anything to keep from hurting you."

"I never wanted to before, but I knew you were the one. Even when it hurt and I froze up and couldn't relax enough and you had to push in so hard to make it happen."

"You never cried out . . ."

"I didn't want to scare you, I was afraid you'd stop."

"You loved me then, didn't you?" His voice a whisper.

"I love you now, too." There was a long silence, like that time in between the setting of sun and the final dark curtain coming down, when the world seems to inhale and hold its breath so long you think your eardrums and heart will burst, then it all starts up again, like a dim chorus arriving from some faraway place.

"What about your husband?" he said after a while.

"It wasn't the same. He was a good person. It was simple and good being married to him too. He was a college baseball player when we met, but he was the kind of ball player who always forgave the intentional hit to his body. Some nights I wanted him to roll over on me, take me with gnashing teeth, but he never did. It was like living with Mrs. Halloran, my Sunday school teacher, who only liked the happy stories of the New Testament and made us sing 'Jesus Loves Me' at the close of every class."

He stroked his arm, up and down, and I wished he'd do that to me. "You ever think about me in all those years?"

I tried to find his eyes in the shadows and stared at the dark holes where they should be. "I tried to forget you, but you always came back, especially in my sleep, I thought it was like a scar or handicap I had to learn to live with. I never imagined we'd . . ."

"Were you ever sorry you'd been with me?"

"Only at first, when the wreck happened and I ran away. After that, no—not really."

"Was your husband good to you?"

"He was okay. I guess I decided I was lucky to have you for the little time I did. Nobody stays lucky a whole life. Figured I'd worn my luck out early, and for that I was very sad. But I tried to make the best of it, my life with Duncan and my son, and I think I did. The best I could, that is, I mean."

"I know."

We sat there for a while longer, and I kept wondering about the way he was acting. What did he want? I had a life—should I be ashamed of that now? There wasn't anything I could do about it.

"What about today?" I finally asked.

"I'll figure a way to get Lukey the money. McCall goes through these things. I can usually make him pony up in the long run. I get tired of it, though. Sometimes—"

I put my hand on his leg just above his boot, but he didn't respond, and then I couldn't move it for fear he'd take it wrong. I was torn between wanting to ask him if he still loved me and knowing I should tell him about the accident, but every time I started, my mouth clogged with this tumble of words that made no sense. So I just sat there.

"Do you smell something?" he leaned forward and whispered.

I took a deep breath; there, riding on the edges, was smoke. "Oh God—"

There was a sound of crackling paper from the back of the house, the kitchen, followed by a thump and a whoosh. Dayrell sprang out of bed, shoved the chair and dresser away from the door, and ran down the hall. I struggled around the furniture and followed him into what was now a growing cloud of black smoke swirling up out of the middle of the kitchen floor.

I coughed and yelled as loudly as I could, "Dayrell!"

"Get out of there!" he called from outside.

But my house was on fire, so I ran back down the hall for the bed covers. The flames were starting to crawl out along the floor, following the trail of spilled solvent toward the stove by the time I got back. I threw the covers on the fire and used the broom that had been leaning in the corner to drag them along toward the main source. The flames tried to seep out from under the blankets, but I chased them down and the heavy wool and quilts held, although the smoke grew denser and blacker as some of the cloth underneath caught. Tears streamed from my eyes and my throat burned, but I could still make out enough detail of the room that I could fill a plastic pitcher with water and throw it on the center of the fire over and over until I was convinced it was out. By then my breath was so short I thought my heart would explode, and clutching the broom as if it could save my life, I stumbled out the door into the backyard.

At first I could only tell that there were three figures out there, swaying back and forth, yelling and grunting. I wiped my eyes on my sleeves and slowly Dayrell and McCall and Pearl emerged from the watery haze. It looked like they were in some kind of prayer circle with their arms around each other until I got closer and saw that they were struggling together, with Pearl grabbing Dayrell by the hair and Dayrell holding McCall in a head lock, pounding his face.

I ran over and began hitting Pearl on the butt as hard as I could with the broom, which quickly took her attention off Dayrell. She spun and lunged at me, but I managed to put the broom up to hold her off and she ran into the bristles with her stomach and fell down. "Stop—the baby!" Pearl and McCall gasped out at the same time, and Dayrell let go of his brother's head.

McCall straightened, checked that Pearl was all right on the ground, and came for me, but not before Dayrell reached into his boot for his knife, yelled, and slashed at the passing back. McCall stopped and tried to grab at the cut that had split his shirt across his shoulders so it hung in pieces from his arms and collar. He grabbed the front and tore it off and faced Dayrell, swearing.

"Go near her again, I'll cut you hard!" Dayrell crouched and panted, his eyes wild, the knife held at an angle with the blade out.

McCall started in, but Pearl yelled, "Stop it—don't hurt him, Dayrell! I started the fire. It was me."

Both men hesitated; then Dayrell dropped his arm and McCall turned toward Pearl and tried to reach around to touch the cut that was bleeding down his back.

"It was me, man," McCall panted. "I burned the barn, set the hotel fires. You hadn't been there, she would've gone up in this one for sure. You know it was me, Dayrell—you know I could do it. Don't believe Pearl, she's just—"

"You bastard!" I rushed at him and swung, catching him across the chest and chin and knocking him down with the broom handle. Dayrell grabbed me and held me back or I would've beat his head into the ground beside Pearl, who was sitting there stunned.

It took him a minute, but when he got himself up, he laughed. "You dumb cunt. Come back here, get Dayrell all riled up again, try to stop Pearl and me from making some real money for the first time, you don't know shit! Hell, I missed tonight, but I'll get the job done. You stay around here, I'll finish you, Moline Bedwell! You better turn and run—go on, get out of here, this is your last chance, or I'll see you out in that cemetery with that dumb-ass sister of yours."

He jumped me and I went down and Dayrell was on him with the knife at his throat just above my face, and I thought he was going to do it, kill his brother, and I yelled, "Stop, no, don't—you'll go back to prison!"

And Dayrell snarled "Who cares?" and flicked the knife against McCall's throat before he let up. McCall rolled off me and lay there, his hand on his throat as if he were bleeding to death, disbelief in his face.

"Fuck you, Dayrell!" he yelled when he saw the blood on his fingertips and realized he'd been nicked. "What if I go to the sheriff? He'd believe me, just like the last time."

Dayrell's head tilted and he squinted his eyes. "What?"

McCall's expression flicked from doubt back to anger. "It was so goddamned easy—you were too dead-ass drunk in the backseat to know you were being set up. They asked who was driving and there you were, passed out on the bank by the tracks, right where I'd pulled you to. Couldn't get both of you out—had to make a choice before the car fell off the embankment into that ditch full of water. The train was still trying to stop."

Dayrell licked his lips and frowned. "You *what?*"

"When they asked, it came out real natural. I didn't even hesitate, Dayrell. I sent you away for seven years, and the only thing I've wondered about all this time is whether I pulled you out to take the blame or to save your sorry ass. I s'pose it doesn't matter now, does it?" McCall stood up carefully, as if his head might flop off from the scratch on his neck.

Holding the bloody knife out, Dayrell started for him, but stopped and shook his head. "No."

"Yes, goddamn it."

"I couldn't ever remember," Dayrell's arms dropped to his sides, and the knife slipped to the grass.

"Nothing to remember—dead-ass drunk."

Dayrell's face got too still, as if waiting for a blow he knew would finish him as he watched his brother. McCall reached over his shoulder and touched the long cut across his back. "Son of a bitch hurts." He glanced at Pearl, who was staring at him. "Come on," he said.

"You didn't . . ." Pearl looked at him and scooted back as he started to walk toward her. "You didn't do that. You didn't send your brother to prison on purpose. Tell me you didn't do that, McCall—tell me!" Her teeth were sharp little points in the dark of her yelling mouth, and he stopped short.

"You too? What is it about him—he fuck so good, Pearl? He do things I don't do? You like them martyrs? You know that's not right—now come here—" He reached down for her and she struck at his hands.

"Keep your filthy hands off me! Don't you ever come near me! You're an animal—you killed that girl, you tried to kill Moline, now you're threatening your own brother—you're crazy, McCall—you should be locked up like an animal, on the end of a chain," she hissed. When he grabbed her wrist and yanked her up, she scratched at his face and twisted loose. "Get away from me!" She turned and ran into the house.

McCall rubbed his bloody hand on his face and turned back toward Dayrell and me. "You happy, Dayrell? Moline knew too—ask her. She ran because she knew the truth. She was with us that night."

He grinned at me, and Dayrell's face grew rigid. I had to look away from those eyes that included me in with McCall now.

"When she left us at the cemetery just before the wreck, you were passed out in back. She knew you weren't driving. I had to half kill her in Calvin's Cave before she'd run away. Had to stop her from talking. But she came back." McCall reached his hand out toward Dayrell's shoulder, and Dayrell knocked it away. "I suffered too, while you were in jail. The guilt—"

"You're a dead man." Dayrell bent to pick up the knife, his face twisted with ugliness. "Come near me, speak to me, I'll stick you good and deep in the belly, McCall. I'll make it hurt so bad, you'll wish you *were* dead." He turned and walked back toward my house. I stood there for a moment, looking at the sagging, bloody body in front of me, and then followed Dayrell.

"What were you trying to do out there?" He grabbed my shoulder and pulled me roughly through the back door.

I was off balance, but knew I shouldn't lean against him, so I let myself stumble back against the kitchen table. "I was trying to help you."

His mouth twisted, "I don't *need* your help. None of this would've happened if . . . Fuck it, never mind." He kicked the soggy, charred blankets out of the way and looked at the hole burned in the floor. "Look at this goddamn floor! Days of work—stupid, useless—goddamned nothing turns out right!" He slammed the heel of his boot into the edge of the hole and broke off more board.

"Dayrell—" I touched his arm and he jerked away. "I wanted to tell you . . . but I was only a kid. Mister beat the crap out of me for saying I was with you that night and wanted to testify. I thought you'd tell your lawyer you were with me and they'd make me come forward, but you never did. Then McCall tried to drown me in Calvin's Cave—I couldn't help it. I was sixteen years old, I had to run. I'm sorry . . . please . . ."

"Just leave me the hell alone! Always after me—you're driving me crazy! You're like this goddamned dog I had once, kept running off when we went hunting—finally I got in the truck and drove off. Looked in the rearview mirror, sure enough, there she was, running behind, yipping and crying, tongue hanging out. Drove home ten miles with her behind me, next day I gave that bitch away. McCall's right—things weren't half bad till you showed up. Least I had a brother. Now I got nothing—and I have to go out there and try to find Lukey before he can take it out on her again." He pushed past me out the back door.

My face stung like he'd hit me. When I looked out the window over the sink, McCall was standing on the cement back steps next door, his arms hanging at his sides, his head bowed as he waited. Pearl's shadow was on the other side of the door for a moment; the lights went off and I followed her progress through the main floor by the lights going off room by room, until she was on the stairs, then upstairs, and finally the house was dark. I turned off my own lights and waited, watching him as he pounded on the door long and hard enough to finally break the glass with his fist and dark blood smoothed his hand and dripped down to the step as he put his other hand in the hole and tried to unlock the door from the inside. When that didn't work, he yelled and kicked the solid oak door, but it stood. After a while he limped away to his truck out front and drove off.

I didn't know what to do then, where to go. So after I checked the burned hole in the floor and poured some more water on my ruined blankets, I went back to bed and lay there shivering and waiting.

· · ·

"You have to come with me," Lukey said, bumping the dresser as she tried tiptoeing into the room.

"Why's that?"

She stared at me oddly and folded and unfolded her arms, as if she might have to use her hands for an emergency. "You have to help. I can't do it alone. Come on. Have to take your truck."

"What's going on?"

"I can't—it's—it's just important. You have to trust me, Moline. I had to hitchhike all the way in here. Come on, I can't stay away very long." She shook her hands at her sides and her voice caught like it might tear loose from the thing it was nailed on. "Please hurry, Moline!"

"Okay. Grab my purse—it's there on the floor at the end of the bed. Just hard for me to bend this damn knee." Standing up made the room shift downhill, and I tilted backwards to keep from falling into it. It was so cold, I hauled the blanket off my parents' bed and wrapped it around my shoulders as we went through the house, ignoring Lukey's expression, which wasn't all that great now that I could see her up close.

"What the hell did he do to you?"

"Nothing," she said, ducking down in the seat. "Hurry up, here comes Pearl. Just get out of here."

I started the engine, but Pearl appeared in front of the headlights as I tried to swing away from the curb. I felt the blanket being pulled off my shoulders and leaned forward so Lukey could cover herself. As Pearl stepped around the front end, I rolled down my window. She stopped a couple of feet away, hugging her arms around herself and tilting on her tiptoes like a girl waiting to be asked for a dance.

"Moline?" There was this look on her face as if Estes had pulled the plug on all the power and she was only a small-town girl who didn't have the nerve to cross the Mississippi River into Illinois, who ended up loving the worst man in town.

When I nodded instead of answering, she took a deep breath, bit her lower lip, and looked over at her house, then mine, as if to collect some reassurance from their emptiness. "I'm sorry."

"It's okay, Pearl. We don't have to talk right now."

I started raising the window and stepping on the gas, but she called out. "No, this is the time, please."

When I braked, Lukey whispered, "Just get out of here, Moline. This is really, really important. Please go." It was her hand pushing on my swollen knee that made me stomp the gas.

"Have you seen—" Pearl stepped to the middle of the street, her face drawn and suddenly old, making me want to reach back and snatch her up with us, carry her out to the dark woods, the lake, where nobody could touch any of us again.

We took a back road out of town that was almost a single lane. And while Lukey began explaining, the rain started a steady straight downpour like someone had a real specific grudge against this part of the country and my truck in particular.

"I was back at my cabin, picking up the last of my stuff when McCall shows up and starts in about Dayrell and you. Only he's got one of his head things, and I don't have his pills. He can't find them, and he goes crazy. Starts smashing stuff, saying he has to kill all of you—Dayrell, you, Pearl for some reason. Then Dayrell comes bursting in and they're fighting and McCall grabs his rifle and Dayrell takes off and McCall goes after him. I need your help, Moline, before they hurt each other more. He's out of his head." She stopped, shaded her eyes against oncoming headlights, and leaned forward to follow the truck's shape past us.

"Did he hurt you?" I took my eyes off the road long enough to see the tear streaks on her face. Her thin arms were bracing against the dashboard as if gravity could fail her and she'd find herself tumbling sideways off the blacktop into the dark, waiting arms of the trees, maybe even the lake somewhere out there lapping thirstily at the earth. The windshield wipers were slapping as hard as they could to sweep the rain away, but that was a useless kind of thing, like putting your hand in the lake and trying to wave a place clear.

"I twisted my ankle running down the hill to the highway when my brother's truck stalled out."

"The Hungry flooding the road where we're going?" I caught the motion of her shaking head out of the corner of my eye. The headlights hardly dented the dark gray wall of water in front of us, and I was driving by Braille more than anything else, hoping the big tires had the will to find the road as it curved under us.

"Oh, turn here—right here, see the road—better use the four wheel."

We bounced onto a path into a dense stand of trees, going up a rise, then down, rear end sliding in the mud, first one direction, then the other, so it felt like an odd dance. The rain was filtered in the woods, but what got through splatted so heavily on the truck it sounded like we were under attack.

"Where would he go?" My stomach was jumping along with my knee now, and the lightheadedness was making it harder to steer around the saplings in the path.

She put her hand over her mouth as if something she shouldn't say was about to escape. She leaned back against the door. "Just a little further, road goes downhill, so watch it." Her voice was rough as if her throat hurt, and her hands rested open-palmed in her lap. Ready to meet her fate, the small shivering body said. I pulled the blanket off the floor and put it around her legs and chest. She didn't move and it slid down again from its own weight.

The tree limbs reached out and trailed along the sides of the truck as if we were going to end up in a place we finally couldn't get through and just disappear entirely. The Ozark woods. Anything could happen out here on a night like this. The rain came over us again in a big hissing sweep you could feel before you saw it, as if we were just ahead of a tidal wave, a flooding of the world. It must have felt like this to the animals and houses and even the dead the day they dammed the Osage River and the water started backing up to form the lake, as if there were finally no escape, no way out but the water. How many exhausted bones lined the bottom of that lake? Resting there in watery betrayal, not a grain of earth left to soothe their eternal waiting souls: a dead land pocked with water, soaked to the core, the dead heart, the cold hollow in a pocket of despair, the voice of the dead ringing back on itself in the stone cask, the dead alone. Was this the voice my great grandfather John Wesley Waller found and fought; was this the one Lukey felt beating her to the ground; was this God, this stone, this will, this violence?

"We're almost there now—don't stop here. Moline? Moline, are you okay? You're shaking. What's the matter with you? Just a ways now, just a little ways. See, up over this little hill, and down, and we can park there in that little clearing. We have to stop and walk from here. He's dug all these holes in the trail, but I know where they are." Lukey was already out of her seat.

I grabbed the gun out of my purse. "Wait—"

20

NIGHT'S EMPTY BUCKET

. . . The instrument which caused a wound is still a part of the situation and must be somehow included in the treatment given the wound itself. Thus when a mountain man cuts himself accidentally, he hastens to thrust the offending knife or ax deep into the soil, believing that this will stop excessive bleeding and make the wound heal faster.

—OZARK MAGIC AND FOLKLORE

✳

SHE WAS WALKING FAST, so I concentrated on the pattern of weaving feet as we went up the hill. I didn't want to end up at the bottom of one of McCall's tiger pits full of snakes. When we were kids and the boys went snake hunting along the Osage and the Hungry, the others tried to avoid the rattlers, copperheads, and cottonmouths. Not McCall. He'd never bother with a rat or corn snake. Had to be something he could fight and feel satisfaction from as he swung it by its tail like a thick lariat over his head, faster and faster, until he snapped his wrist and cracked the loop like a whip, watching as the snake's open-fanged jaw and furious eyes went sailing off the body into the underbrush. When he cut the rattles off, they'd still be twitching angrily, the long body quivering with spasms. That's how he'd known what to do at Lukey's church that time.

Dear Pearl and I would sit at a distance watching to see if it was like people said, a snake never died till sundown. The only problem was, we always got bored or had to go home too soon to ever really find out, so we'd bombard the shivering body with rocks, unconvinced it couldn't come after us, and kept its terror in our heads for dreams at night.

McCall was as powerful and frightening as the snakes he killed. That much I realized as I climbed the hillside covered with wet slippery weeds and mud. I was glad for the weight of the gun I'd shoved in my waistband. The only reason I was along on this ride was to protect Lukey and Dayrell, and I intended to do just that. Stumbling the last step onto the ridge, I discovered how sore my muscles were, but it didn't matter. That's what I told my body. "You've been so damn protected all these years. Time you got a few scars—"

"Shhh, Moline—we're trying to sneak up on him." Lukey touched my arm and peered at my face. "You okay?" She looked pretty crazy herself, muddy and lumpy, I should've asked her the same thing. "He's got one place above ground and one below, so just follow me. And watch your step."

How the hell could I do that with the dark sky blackening up again and fat raindrops starting to hit me in the face? She was squatting low and running hunched over like we were under fire. I couldn't quite do the same because nothing bent right anymore, and the gun was digging hard into my stomach. "Go ahead," I whispered. "Try and shoot me." Lukey waved her hand for me to keep it down. I tried to keep track of the dirty white canvas shoes ahead of me, which wasn't easy since they were getting darker and darker with mud.

"Okay, here's his underground storage hole. Be easier if we had a light, but I don't want to draw attention in case they're out looking for the pot tonight. Darn, I'm not thinking right. . . ." She stood there shaking her hands at her sides when the lightning hit and illuminated the clearing on the ridge surrounded by woods sloping down on either side. That was when I saw we weren't alone.

"Lukey!" I grabbed her arm and pointed at the huge man running toward us waving a rifle like a club over his head. "Jesus—run!" I yelled, and tried to pull the gun out of my pants, but the barrel got caught in the material and I couldn't get it loose. It felt like the ground was shaking as he thundered toward us and I couldn't move.

"McCall!" she cried, and he swung at her. She ducked just in time, and we both tried backing away, but we were slipping and sliding in the mud and wet and it was just lucky he was clumsy, too, like he had the drunk staggers. My gun finally came loose, but I didn't have time to aim it before it slipped out of my wet fingers into the mud.

"It's me, sweetie, it's Lukey. 'Member the cabin you rebuilt? It's just down the hill there, and we should go back and sleep now, don't you think? Aren't you tired, McCall? I sure am sleepy myself, and we need to put the kids to bed. They shouldn't be alone, not with all this thunder and lightning—you know how the kids wake up scaredy cat when there's storming out like this. Now you put that rifle down and come on with your mama." She held her hand out like he'd give her the gun and he stood still, then sort of let his arms collapse and it thudded to the ground. He grew smaller, confused and sad, his white shirt smeared with wet and dirt, his hair flattened straight against his skull. His eyes didn't focus right either, they seemed to roll just a tiny bit.

"Lukey?" His voice was a harsh rasp, like it was unfamiliar with words out loud.

"That's right, baby, it's Lukey." She stepped toward him just in time to catch him as he stumbled forward into her arms. I ran to grab him from collapsing on Lukey. He looked at me and grabbed the gun again, wrestling to separate our tangle of arms and legs on the muddy ground.

"You bitch!" he panted, wrenching his arms free and crawling away from us. "Ruined me!" He pumped the action and stood up, backing up to get a better target.

I looked around for my .38, but it had disappeared in the mud. "Lukey." I tried to keep my voice low and calm, but it came out too loud. She was half-crouched between us suddenly, wild-eyed, her arms spread as if she were defending the middle ground. "Get outta the way, Lukey, he'll shoot you too!" I cried, but she froze.

"Dayrell," she whispered, and I turned to see the tall figure running toward us with his arm outstretched.

"Stop, McCall—don't shoot!" he yelled, and was almost near enough to tackle his brother when the gun went off.

McCall dropped the rifle and reached for his brother, who stood shaking his head as if the words had run too far ahead of the action, and the separation had undone us all. "Don't—"

McCall picked up the gun again, turned, and ran toward the woods.

"Dayrell—my God!" I pulled him down just as his knees were starting to buckle, but he fought me.

"Where is it?" Lukey asked.

I found the hole in his arm. "Here." I held up my hand and she shone the flashlight on my fingers just as the rain washed them clean, carrying away the pink stream. "We have to stop the bleeding. Here—help me take his shirt off so we can use that." I couldn't quite get my breath, my fingers were too thick and clumsy, and a chant in my head kept saying, Don't die, don't die.

"I'm so sorry, Day—he didn't mean it—oh, please," she kept apologizing as she ripped his shirt into strips, while I kept him steady on his knees though his head was lolling like he might be passing out. I slapped him lightly to make him focus, and he looked at me as if we were saying goodbye. Lukey and I checked the hole, which went clean through, and found the second one, where the same bullet had gone into his side, glanced off a rib and back out. "Dayrell, please, be okay, don't—Dayrell?" I whispered. "Talk to me, honey, don't pass out, come on."

"Okay, 'sokay. Sorry . . ." He started to drop off and I shook him. "Don't . . ." He tried to lift his wounded arm and cried out and wobbled. "Don't tell," he said with his teeth gritted. Then he looked at me. "Moline . . . no sheriff, no hospital, no doctor." He closed his eyes and started to pass out and I shook him awake. "Watch out . . . gun."

I looked up and saw the figure in the shadows of the woods just as the lightning struck. I tried to see if it was McCall, but I was afraid to call out even if it wasn't. Whoever it was might be as nuts as McCall, shoot us all. Nothing made sense.

"Lukey," I whispered, and touched her arm as she finished tying the bandage around Dayrell's chest to stop the bleeding. "There's somebody out there. I think they've got a gun."

Lukey pulled Dayrell down on top of us and we had to struggle to roll his dead weight off and get him in a position where he wouldn't injure himself more. His bare skin was covered with goose bumps and I kissed his collarbone and brushed his wet hair back from his face. He smiled and started to say something, but I put my lips on his until I felt him relax.

"You okay?" I asked Lukey.

"I'm okay. Can you see if he's gone?" she said quietly.

I looked as hard as I could the next time the lightning hit, and the man was gone. I didn't see an after-silhouette. "I don't see a thing. Just hope he hasn't circled around. Think it's McCall again?"

"I don't know."

I tried to find the gun in the mud, hoping I could pull the trigger if he came closer.

"It could be one of those guys McCall sells to. They're all crazy, and he was supposed to make a delivery today. His last one, he said." She stood up and pulled Dayrell into a sitting position. "We have to get him down the hill. He'll be okay once we clean him up, the bleeding's not too bad."

"But where's McCall gone? Think he's hiding? Jesus, Lukey, we could be clay pigeons up here."

Lukey made Dayrell lie back down and picked up her flashlight again. "Come on, let's go check the other hideout. It'll just take a minute, then we'll move Dayrell to the cabin and clean him up." She pointed the flashlight at the ground and I had to scramble awkwardly to my feet to follow her quick steps.

We checked the hole McCall had dug out and put a small wooden ladder in. It was filling up with water, and a couple of field rats we didn't want to argue with were swimming around desperately. No McCall. We hurried to the shed disguised in the dense wild grape vines at the edge of the field. "This is where he keeps his shovels." The rough plank door was soaked and swollen enough to resist us like someone holding on to the latch on the other side. Sweeping the little room with her light, Lukey stopped on the corner where there was still a pallet of rags and what was left of a sleeping bag the mice had found and used, pulling out pale puffs of stuffing.

"That's new—the bag used to be on the porch for the dogs. He's been here, but where is he now?" For the first time, Lukey's voice had an edge of despair. "He's wandering out in these woods, not knowing his name or where he is—he'll be scared witless, poor baby."

"He might hurt somebody else too."

The light dropped to the dirt floor, then slowly rose again, searching the walls and the pallet bed as if to make sure he wasn't here, just not quite visible. "What are we gonna do? How're—" She gulped back the sob that was rising beneath her voice, and before she could speak again, a big clap of thunder rattled the shed like cannon fire. We both jumped.

"Let's get out of here, first of all. Get Dayrell to a doctor and notify the authorities." I started to leave, but Lukey stepped in front of the door.

"We can't do that, Moline. Dayrell already told you. They'll put

McCall in jail, they'll put me in jail, they'll take the kids. Mama's right, God's testing me, but He wouldn't let any real harm come to us. He's not that way. Not to punish me, He wouldn't.'"

The lightning struck close again, shattering the dark room with jagged spears of light through the cracks in the walls where the planks didn't quite meet and the little window covered with old plastic bread wrappers, the red and black printed logos still visible. Her face was tear-streaked and scared. She wanted to believe so damn bad, I didn't have the heart to tell her the truth. God punished everyone. Being innocent had nothing to do with it. He was just another pissed-off old man when He didn't get His way.

"What should we do then, let him hurt somebody else? Drag himself all over these woods? Let him trip over some bullshit he's rigged up to protect his drugs? He shot his own brother, Lukey, stop trying to protect him, he's a piece of shit, he always was. He'd kill anything that got in his way. Look what he did to you and Dayrell, what he tried to do to me—it might be his own kids next time, who knows?"

"He would not! He'd never do that—he loves his kids—" Her voice broke and the anger she was trying to get up against me fell away. She was scared I was right. I was scared too.

We stood there letting the storm batter the shack, shaking us, pounding the very ground beneath our feet, as if some ancient god were rising up finally to take its wrath out on us, something unleashed in the dark flood full of old curses, old voices. What were those bitter cries that tore at me trying to keep me from escaping? What did they want but life? That was all anything wanted—life, living, dark and light alike. It occurred to me now, beaten and bruised by the waters of this disaster, that I would never see my son again. That in some way he had stopped being present and real. Like Duncan, he was dead. Like Paris, he had a place in my history. I once had a sister, I once had a husband, I once had a son.

"All right," I sighed when the thunder rolled further east. "We'll take Dayrell to your cabin and see what we can do for him there."

"What about McCall?" Lukey searched the room frantically with her eyes, as if she'd overlooked something.

"I'll get help and come back. We can't do this alone in the dark. I can ask Titus."

The storm was letting up as we half dragged, half carried Dayrell down to the truck and drove back to the cabin.

Once we got him inside, I sat beside him on the sofa and felt his forehead. "He's cool—color's coming back. Think I should stop at his parents and tell them?"

Lukey looked frightened and shook her head. "Dayrell never tells them if he can help it."

"They have a right to know."

"Please don't. In the old days we never—"

I stared at the frown lines between the thick black eyebrows on Dayrell's face. The skin across the bridge of his nose stretched tight as if it were being pulled from either side. In the kerosene lamp light, his lips were cracked and sore, and a dark shadow of whiskers covered his sunburned jaw. I picked up the big battered hand with the wide knuckles, rubbed the thick calluses on his palm, and laid it on his chest. He opened his eyes and looked at me as if he didn't recognize me and closed them again.

Lukey lit the kindling in the fireplace and turned back toward us. "Better get him out of those wet things." She reached for his wet boots, stopped and looked at them. "Isn't the first time, guess you know that." She leaned over and tugged at the foot resting on the floor.

"Is the girl his?"

The boot gave and she eased it off his foot and stripped the wet, holey sock. His toes looked so helpless and white in the half light of the room. She stared at them a moment before taking them in her hands and rubbing them pink. "You got to understand . . ." She glanced at me and went to work on the other boot. "He didn't have nowhere to go when he got out of that prison. McCall said we should let him stay here till he got himself set up more. I was scared at first—convict and murderer. But he wasn't that way at all. He was so sweet, only got rough when he went drinking for days at a time. Taking drugs. I didn't much care for either one of those men they got like that. In between times, it was Dayrell was the thoughtful one. It's always been McCall who needed me more, though. That's what it came down to in the end."

I knew then that she didn't know which man had fathered her child. She'd chosen, and in her mind that was the same as it being so. Lukey stood and reached over to undo Dayrell's belt and unzip his pants and try to pull them down while I helped lift his hips, and he groaned and thrashed out with his good arm, catching me on the side of the head, which stung pretty good.

"Here you, Dayrell, stop that." Lukey batted at his arm and pulled it down and he opened his eyes and looked at her and smiled like a little boy. It made me about as jealous as could be, and I yanked his jeans down hard and she pulled the legs from the other end. Lukey treated his nakedness matter-of-factly, spreading a quilt over his lower body, then holding him up while I unwrapped his arm and chest.

"Two women . . . Lord," he mumbled, and I felt like slapping him until I saw the dark pucker of the bullet hole in his arm.

"Clean him up good as new," Lukey announced. "Spread that towel under him and let him lay down while I mix a poultice and get some clean rags." She stood and looked at me. "You better get going."

"You don't need my help?"

"This is nothing. Should've seen some of the things those two done to themselves in the bad ole days. Didn't even break that rib, I'd guess. His lucky night." She tried to smile, but it turned into a grimace. She was so tiny and thin standing there like a bedraggled child, it made me want to stay and protect her.

"Remember, don't let McCall in—don't trust him. God knows what he'd do if he saw the two of you together like this." I could sure vouch for that. "I'll be back as soon as I can. Try to bring some medicine or something."

"That's okay, I got what my granny gave me." She pulled the quilt up and pushed the hair off his forehead in a way that showed he was better off in her hands than mine.

21

AT LAST I LIE DOWN

Copperheads often rely on their camouflage pattern when resting in dead leaves, and will usually remain motionless when encountered. Young copperheads use their yellowish tail as a lure to attract small frogs or lizards.

—THE AMPHIBIANS AND REPTILES OF MISSOURI

✳

"HE JUST GOT TO SLEEP, Moline—he's been up for two nights trying to keep people from seeing a Heart Hog conspiracy every time they turn around. But I'll wake him if it's important." Jos was wrapped in a thin terry-cloth robe which was probably once mint green but had faded almost gray. Her hair was dented on one side, showing that she'd been asleep, too.

"Please, it's urgent." I pitched my voice lower and slower to keep the adrenaline from driving her away. I remembered how dirty and blood-splattered my clothes were and tried to brush some of the mud and wrinkles away while she watched.

Without opening the screen door, she turned and disappeared into the dark house.

I didn't know what time it was, but it wasn't important anymore. The moon was skirting in and out of the thick clouds bumping restlessly across the sky. The rain had stopped, but I could feel more coming on the damp palm of wind passing across the yard. There was the click and trickle of water dripping everywhere. When I'd stepped off the walk in the dark on the way to the house, the ground was so spongy, I sank in and pulled clumps of dirt out with my sneakers. I'd left my footprints all the way up the steps onto the clean floorboards of the porch. Tomorrow, Jos would be washing them off with bitterness on her breath.

"Come on, come on." I jiggled from one foot to another, unable to stop the image of McCall with his rifle coming after me.

"What's going on?" Titus opened the screen and stepped tiredly onto the porch, standing close enough that we could talk without raising the neighbors or kids. He had pulled on some dark trousers and a black tee shirt.

"McCall's gone crazy—shot Dayrell in the hills by Lukey's place after she dragged me out there looking for him. He tried to burn my house down, but Lukey and Dayrell won't let me tell the sheriff. We have to find him before he hurts someone else."

Titus rubbed the side of his face and squinted at me. "Jail'd be the best place for that piece of trash."

"I know, but please, he's sick, and I'm scared of what he'll do to Lukey if he shows up at the cabin. He confessed to Dayrell tonight—he was the one driving the car that hit the train. Told on me too. It's such a goddamn mess."

He sighed. "Okay, all right. Let me change clothes. I'll be right back." When he returned, he was carrying a shotgun I looked at but didn't question.

After that we picked up three other men close by. Junior Trot lived in a one-room shack almost covered with wisteria vines. He was a small, wiry man with cinnamon toast skin sprinkled with black dots like burnt sugar, who joked a lot getting in but turned and laid his rifle carefully in back and covered it with a black plastic rain slicker he'd brought along.

"Bill Dootrum's right around the corner," Titus directed, and we pulled in front of a neatly trimmed one-story with fresh paint and a new front porch spanning the width. A tall, thin man stood watching us for a moment before he walked precisely down the stairs toward us. "Shop teacher at the high school," Junior said. Bill had a habit of clearing his throat every few minutes, even though he wasn't very talkative.

"Lloyed's the last. He lives a couple of blocks on down," Titus said.

I recognized Lloyed from high school, and we smiled at each other as he eased his bulk into the little room left. He was a plumber, like the other men in his family, and clearly uncomfortable with the shotgun he kept shifting across his big ham thighs as the other men objected to the barrel being pointed at them.

Downtown all the bars were closed, and the hotel was dark except for the lobby light. David Solomon's dark green Land Rover was parked in front of the hotel along with five other cars. The bank clock at the corner said 3:00, then blinked 99°, the same temperature it had reported day and night for two weeks, as if nothing ever changed here.

"So it's McCall Bell we're after?" Lloyed finally asked as we headed over the little bridge where the creek spilled across the blacktop so we had to slow down and splash through. I wanted him to kill the son of a bitch, but I couldn't very well say that.

"He's got this head thing. Tried to shoot his brother," I said.

"Better get the sheriff after that honky," Bill muttered.

"Can't do that," I said.

"Have to keep it in the family," Titus explained with a sideways glance at me, and dropped his voice. "Nothing's going to change. I got no use for those hillbillies. Look what happened last time you were here. You got beat up six ways from Sunday."

"Look, Dayrell and Lukey made me promise, you have to swear not to tell the sheriff. You'll see why once we're up there."

"I can't promise anything, not now. I'm going out there to try to help that little girl. She's a Christian, and both of you are in way over your heads with that evil shit. Shoulda taken care of him years ago," he said so low I barely heard him.

"He's dangerous, Titus, don't get into a shooting thing with him." I knew Jos would never forgive me for getting Titus hurt.

There was a long silence. Finally, he said, "Just hurry up, Moline. It'll be day before you know it, and people are not going to like seeing us driving around like this."

The morning light made everything soft and lavender and pink before it crisped up with dark crayon borders. My body was so used to the dark, though, I couldn't quite focus enough, and kept running into things and stumbling because the distances were wrong and nothing wanted to stay firm underneath my feet. My hands were useless. I started using them to break the falls, and the pine needles and twigs poked into my already sore palms. My clothes were drying stiff and muddy on my skin, which felt like it was shrinking. It was getting so tight, I scratched at my arms and neck hoping to let out some of the water. Long red streaks appeared, but I couldn't feel it, so I knew they weren't deep enough. You had to feel things to get any measure of release, I told myself.

"What's wrong with you?" Titus stopped and waited for me, grabbing my arm too hard as I fell again. The whites of his eyes were pink with tiredness.

"Nothing. I don't know. Tired." I shook him loose and plunged into the middle of some sumac that didn't give as much as it looked like it should.

"You're burning up. Skin's hot as a stove." He pried the sumac apart and pulled me out.

"It's not contagious," I panted, and tried to hurry on.

"That's not what I'm worried about, wait—" Titus stopped and turned his head slowly as we all tried to listen. In the distance there was the sound of dogs barking. When that stopped, the crows cawing across the oaks high above us was the only sound. After that, there was the scolding of blue jays, and the bent twigs of buckeye behind us gave off a foul odor that made me dizzy. Titus signaled us on.

"He's got Dayrell's dogs," I said.

Right at the edge of the clearing for Lukey's cabin, we saw a piliated woodpecker as big as a pet store parrot sitting on a low branch, watching the sun rise behind us. Maybe he'd say something, he had that look. I wanted to ask him what'd been going on, where McCall was, but he ignored us as we straggled by him.

Suddenly the insects woke up too, and while the small black flies circled our heads in an angry knot, the mosquitoes netted our arms and shirts like gauze. Junior Trot broke a branch off a pagoda dogwood and handed it to me. He took another small branch and held it over his head like a torn umbrella to draw the insects. Lloyed shifted his gun from hand to hand every few yards, and Bill kept clearing his throat and pointing out how bright it was getting.

Lukey answered the door, scrubbed clean of dirt but looking exhausted. Her hands were as cut and bruised as mine. She opened her mouth, looked behind me, then shut her mouth and nodded at Titus and the men.

"He here?" I asked. She shook her head. "He didn't show up at all?" She shook her head again, glancing out the door as if she expected to see McCall burst through the woods into the clearing after us. "How's Dayrell?"

I tried to look behind her, but the cabin was still dark.

"He left. I was sleeping. He musta woke up, got himself dressed, and took off." She spread her hands as if to say, See, he's not here.

"He okay?" Titus asked.

Lukey shrugged. "Seemed okay last night after I got the wounds dressed, made him drink some heal-all and ginseng tea. Sat up and talked for a while. Like I told Moline, I seen him worse off and he come back fine. He's not dying or nothing. Scratch, really." She wouldn't meet my gaze, and I realized that that was how it was going to be. They'd decided on their version of the story.

"Uh-huh," Titus said. "He armed too?"

Lukey looked around and back. "Musta took my little .22."

I shivered at the image of Dayrell and McCall shooting each other.

"Perfect," Titus sighed. "Moline, you better get yourself some water with that fever while you get a chance. We got a time ahead of us and can't be stopping to take care of you. In fact, maybe you best be staying here with Lukey, sick as you are."

"No way." I followed Lukey's thin, slumping back to the kitchen area. She put a big black tin coffee pot on the wood stove and wiped her forehead with her wrist. Her body looked thinner than ever in McCall's white shirt. She had the old cutoff shorts on underneath. Didn't she ever eat? Had I ever seen her eat anything? I was thinking in clear chunks like blocks of ice cut out and hauled up to sit alone in the dark sawdust of the icehouse all summer long. Nothing connected beyond itself. I felt my brain trying to force the next memory, but it didn't move.

"Don't let 'em hurt him, Moline," she said.

"I already told Titus to be careful."

She nodded and spooned coffee carefully into the top of the pot, which was already beginning to gurgle. The stove was so hot it was scorching my stomach and legs standing in front of it, cooking my insides while shivers ran up and down my backside.

She paused and stared at the coffee pot rattling to a boil. "I'd start at the shed and work my way out in a pie wedge, one piece after another.

He's close to home. He'll be scared and hungry. That's the way he gets."
Her shoulders jerked with a sob she swallowed.

"We better go," Titus said through the screen door.

"I should go with you." She looked out the side window where the sunrise had made things true and safe again. "But I can't leave in case he
comes back on his own. I don't know—he's never gotten through a spell
like this without his pills."

"It's all right, Lukey, we'll find him." I hurried out the door, forgetting
the glass of water.

We followed the rise of the hill up to the ridge, hearing dogs in the distance every once in a while, but mostly trying to keep quiet to listen.
When Bill and Junior saw the pot plants, they looked at each other and
kept walking. Not their trouble, their bodies seemed to say. I showed
them the shed and we began to spread out from there. I tried to remember
I was still wearing sneakers and it was snake country as I stumbled around.
In a few minutes I'd lost sight of the men, but instinct told me if I kept
walking downhill, eventually I'd come to a road or a body of water I could
follow to people. Once in a while, I sang quietly to alert the snakes that
they did not have surprise as an excuse for biting me. The woods smelled
denser and deeper this morning, as if everything had swollen up just to
bursting with water and all I had to do was brush against a trunk or vine
and I'd be drowned. The leaves were still dripping, and for a change it
didn't look like rain. I looked for a small tree or bush with leaves big
enough to hold some water I could drink, but the basswoods were too tall
and I had to settle for trying to wring something off some baby sassafras
leaves.

Then it seemed the sun was getting hot so fast, it was a big hand
pushing too hard on the top of my head, and I kept feeling shorter and
shorter and that made my legs stumpy and clumsy. I kept having to
remind myself to look up because my eyes found the ground and I wanted
to lie down in the leaves and grass, in the little white clusters of sweet
cicely that were starting to appear on the slopes. I passed some deerberry
bushes, and horse nettle and dogbane in open places, but I couldn't stop, I
had to put my arms out to hold things steady because they kept shifting
while I was trying to find level footing around me.

I heard a voice calling hello, but it was just a cracked whisper in my
head. Then I was on my good knee, my other leg stretched out behind me,

and I figured crawling might help, except the grass in the meadow I came to was netted with long silver strands like a thousand horses had run through at dawn and blown their saliva across the grass glistening in the sunlight and I surely hated to pull myself through that web and make a hole in the world. That's why I couldn't cross it and sat down to catch something, not my breath, I could breathe, it was something not right in my ears, I decided.

I rolled over on my side, my face next to a stalky flannel-leaf mullein. A small brown spider was working hard to keep me from making a mess of her life, and I could understand that. Every time I breathed in, her web bounced one way, every time I breathed out it blew the other way. It was dotted with drops of water, and I wanted to point out, You need to be invisible to survive.

It was the sound of the dogs barking furiously that brought me upright again, followed by gunshots, close enough to ricochet around the meadow like they were following the walls of a room. I stumbled up into a half-gaited run, dragging my bad leg, toward the sounds. Just at the lip of the clearing, where it dropped downhill into the woods again, there was an outcropping of rock. The dogs were bouncing up and down, running toward something and growling, then backing off and howling. A man stood with his gun held ready. As I slowed down, I felt something at my foot, heard a rustle and a whisk like a bird taking off, and kept going, but my foot slowed, tangled in a vine. I stopped and looked. A copperhead had sunk its fangs into the thick rubber heel of my shoe.

"Oh my God—oh God—oh God!" I screamed, and tried to outrun the tail flipping in the air, the coils trying to come at me, the little slits of vertical pupils fixed furiously. "Help me!" I ran at him, not even stopping when the face blurred so badly I couldn't see who it was wearing that stupid grin on his face. He pushed me back with one hand, trying to swing the gun around. "Hurry—oh God, don't hurt me!"

I fell down, and the meadow and rocks kept tilting like I was falling into a cave. I started to hold a hand up to say Stop, don't, but I couldn't— all I could hear was the high buzzing of rattlers living in the rocks, right underneath me, ready to strike, ready to hit me over and over, ready to slide out and sun themselves on my body, paralyzed, joining the buzzing at my foot, getting louder, and I opened my mouth to beg for something and the light was blocked again and it took me a moment to sort out that the dark shadow over me was his careless, ruptured self, McCall, grinning, holding something up, the gun, the gun he was going to use. I tried to shrink back, ask the rocks and grass to open their arms and hide me, but no, there was something I was missing. He reached down, pulling at my shoe, then rose again, something draped across his arms, jaws wide and angry with a drop of poison caught on the point of a too-white tooth, the wedge of viper head slowly coming down to me . . . I closed my eyes and whispered, "Please don't—please don't hurt me."

A face bending too close its hot poison breath. "Moline, I had to take the snake off you—Moline?" Dayrell's hand hurt my skin. "Moline, you're burning up. Listen, don't move, I have to get help."

The shadow brought the sun back squinting like a knife prying open my eyes.

"Help, we're over here. I found her. Help!" He fired big booming bursts against my head. "Help!" The bone shattered again. Each one cracked and splintered from the others. Joints unlocking. Nothing stayed attached.

"Son-of-a-bitchin' McCall was at my place sleeping it off. I kicked his ass out of there. Was on my way to tell Lukey when I ran into Titus, who said you were lost—"

"Stop," I said, but Dayrell didn't stop until the dogs dragged somebody in from outside the room, and voices started talking in foreign words. I've been gone too long, I tried to explain, I don't know this language anymore. "Let me go."

"No, here, we have to get out of these rocks, there's snakes all over the place." He used his good arm around my waist to pull me up the hill a ways. "There, now." He let me down and settled beside me.

My head cleared as long as I didn't move, I discovered. "Feel funny—so hot and cold all the time." A wave of chills shook me hard like I was leaning against the cold white enamel of a freezer.

"Well, don't go to sleep on me. I can't lift you with one arm."

"Your arm . . ."

"It's sore, but it's okay. Side pulls a little, but no problem. Dumb fuck couldn't hit a lake with a rock. When he gets straight again, I'm going to beat the living crap out of him. Takes seven years of my life and shoots me. I'd like to kill him, bring him back, and kill him again. Maybe he'd see how it feels then."

"Tried to kill me. At Calvin's Cave . . . almost drowned me." My head was thick and slow, but it had the basics down. I kept my eyes closed against the bright grass and flowers whose dancing made my stomach flip over and over like a car tumbling down a hill.

"Christ almighty," he said loud enough to send pain ringing my head like a dented bell. My skin got clammy and broke out with sweat.

"I'm sorry, Dayrell. . . ."

"Here they come." He pulled back and let me drop onto the ground while he stood up and waved at Titus and the others.

By the time they got me down the hill, through the woods, and out to my truck and settled in one of the rooms at the hotel, I was coming and going pretty much all the time, only waking up for the big moments like the doctor discovering my badly infected knee. Staph. And Dayrell avoiding Aunt Walker like a dog caught with the Sunday roast in its mouth. They gave me painkillers, but it was nothing football players don't walk off the field with every Sunday, that idiot Bradford said.

Dayrell slipped in and sat on the edge of the bed. Then he picked up Lukey's stone on the brown shoestring at my throat and gave it a rub. "You sure were lucky today. That was a huge humping copperhead got stuck in the heel of your shoe. Had to throw your shoes away, but it'll make a nice belt."

I groaned and turned away from him, pretty certain I was going to vomit. Then I tried to apologize again, but he just shrugged and left. By night, I was out of it with fever and stopped being able to keep track of anything. That's when they came back for me, helpless to their words and visions in this other world.

"Get up and stop misbehaving," Paris says, filling the air blue with cigarettes. I can't stop coughing. Her eyes are as big and hard as china doorknobs.

"Who cares if I was naked? I wanted to get a tan instead of being stuck all day with these kids while you try to figure out ways to get rich quick and buy yourself out of the shame of living here like white trash next to good upstanding—" Mister's slap makes Iberia drop the pan of pork chops, the hot grease splattering all of us like shotgun pellets. It's my fault, she thinks

I told, that's what her eyes say as she hands me the butter to put on my burns. "Mama, Mama," I call as she disappears out the front door and down the walk, "it wasn't me." But the wrong stays in her back, and I know she'll never love me again.

"You're an evil girl," Estes announces and forces my hands into prayer. "I doubt even God has any time for the likes of you."

"My knees hurt," I cry.

"Good. Now stay there until you're sorry and God forgives you." Estes pats Pearl's head while they watch me.

"I'm sorry, I'm already sorry. Please—"

"God will give you a sign when He's ready to forgive you. Now don't make things worse for yourself or you'll end up in a place a lot worse than this, my friend." She taps the hairbrush against her palm, from the carved ivory set Iberia was given as a girl, that Estes wouldn't let her have when she married into Bedwell's white-trash hillbilly family, and Horras gave her the house next door, which he had formerly rented.

"There's no sign," I plead. "He won't speak to me."

"Then you go on home and don't come back here again," Estes orders. My knees hurt so bad I can barely walk. "Your heart is a dark coal, Moline, and He can see it. Mark my words." She slams the front door so hard the etched glass W shivers and threatens to fall on me if I don't hurry off the porch and away from the house.

Finally, at dawn, the fever broke, and I was lying in the soaked sheets when John Wesley Waller returned to his tale:

This morning the flames of sun water the walls of my house. The horse outside looks singed and tired by the night's ride.

Do you have to go to the river? my wife asks. Can't you miss one Sunday morning? One? The children . . .

We are so far beyond that question, I don't answer. My wife knows better, although she doesn't know why. She'll never know that. God is a mystery horse she doesn't learn to ride. She never falls in the river, the hand never pushes her, the bush never breaks out of her back, taking the bones with it, she's never bent, broken, used by anything but my hard legs when they would ride her, pushing deep into her cave, God crying like birds in my head, while I fight my way into the dark, raising her hips high on my thighs, the place I meet my devils, the desert is dark and moist, it grabs and pulls me so hard and long, I can't hold myself back, letting go, my heart purges the poison and weeps into light again.

I used to wonder if it was only women who cry afterwards, or if all over the world, men are weeping secret tears, knowing they've been to the desert again, knowing they can't win their way out. Sorrow rides a long stick between my legs, and on the road it rubs in its cloth-and-leather cradle, calling like a child left out in the dark, Help, please. It is this— the wanting and having—that spurs the horse to the next county, to the farm where a woman lies waiting for blessing, a child for baptism, and somewhere a church with people waiting all morning until I arrive or another like me, and the disappointing sighs when I do not arrive, and they climb tiredly to their Sunday feet and shuffle out again into the gray noon light.

What is it like in that little room all morning, the hush, the sniffle, the drowsing prayers in dusty lingering gloom, cool, so cool the air, even in August, it never warms there, not to the temperature of the world. They wait, watching for Christ to climb down from his cross, the only man to conquer his own desires, although it took crucifixion to do it.

So I in the cloudy, rainy morning green and heavy with wet and desires of so many, many kinds, ride toward them, plunge into the river, the bank actually falling away at the last minute to topple us, and I know right away, this is the last river and the last ride. The horse swims strongly at first, but I know, his eyes glint with angry vision, Now you'll see at last, his harsh breath says, now—and the flood tosses us like a broken tree trunk, lovers in this last fatal embrace, once you put your foot in the stirrup, you go for the ride.

Do you want to get on this horse? That's what I have to ask you, Moline—do you really want to step up?

22

YOKE OF VISION

Clay minerals originate, in general, from the weathering of previously existing silicate rocks and have therefore been called, on occasions, "rotted rocks." . . . Clays, particularly fire clays, should be thought of instead as purified or refined rocks. The original silicate rocks and minerals, which were rich in constituents melting at low temperatures, have been soaked, leached, and washed by chemically active ground water and rain water until many of the undesirable elements have been carried away, leaving a refined material which we use and know as fire clay.

— THE COMMON ROCKS AND MINERALS OF MISSOURI

✳

"MOLINE?" Pearl's pale gray and white striped shirtwaist dress looked flustered, like it'd been asked to do more than it was supposed to. The row of buttons down the front had scattered in disarray so her slip showed halfway to her crotch, and the belt that was usually cinched tight was lolling with its tongue out. There was a suspicious amount of wrinkles, as if she'd slept in the dress, and in fact she smelled musty, beddy and damp. She looked like she needed somebody on her side. I wanted to make her sit down and tell me about it, to cry so she could find the comforting arms she needed, because after all, who did Pearl have, besides crazy McCall?

"How are you?" Pearl folded her arms across her chest as if she needed to hold herself together.

"Getting better. Sit down."

She brushed my look of pity aside with a wave of her hand and stopped at the foot of my bed. "I need your help, Moline." She gripped the end rail as if she could squeeze obedience out of it too.

"Doing what?" I tried to sit up more so we were on an even field, but my knee tugged and I winced.

Pearl twisted her hands around the chipped white paint of the iron rod, then let go and stepped back, waving them in the air to make her point. "You don't understand. McCall's supposed to be working on the Heart Hog deal with me. I can't do it all alone. I didn't mean for anything bad to happen to you or Dayrell or—" She bowed her head and covered her eyes with her hand as if she'd lose something letting me see her cry.

"Oh, Pearl," I reached an arm out, but she shook her head.

My knee gave a little throb and some more gunk slid down the tube they'd stuck in. I tried not to look, but every once in a while it caught my attention, and I'd worried for the past week that the bloody yellow stuff in the clear tubing might be the cartilage, marrow, and nerves too.

I shifted my leg and the hundred-year-old springs squealed and I pretended to adjust the plastic tubing. I felt sorry for Pearl, I truly did. We'd grown up close as sisters until she took the Waller view of things.

She wrinkled her nose, took a deep breath, and started pacing back and forth across the room. "Everything was fine until you showed up again. Now everything's as crazy as it used to be."

"That's not true. Walker and Able weren't fine."

She stopped and stared out the large windows with the thick, wavy glass melting down into the rotting wood frames. I kept wanting them open, but people kept closing them, as if the natural air of Resurrection were bad for me, and the portable air conditioner coughing out mold and old cigarette breath was better.

"You've seen the farm. They're just too old, Moline. I was doing the best I could—not only for me, but for them and the whole town."

As she was talking, I realized how she was letting herself go. Her hair had salt gray in the blond, and her thin body, which looked fine in a nightgown under a full moon, was getting papery dry. There was so little left of the fires burning inside Pearl, and that old thing was happening to her face too, despite the pregnancy. Exhaustion had drawn her face so the nose jutted, the gray of her eyes faded in a nest of tiny wrinkles, lips thinned like two pencil lines drawn in obedient Methodist pink. Not the Pearl I'd taken to spy on men in their underwear on summer nights, nor the one I read the Song of Solomon and Revelation to on those lazy afternoons in July and August, when it was too hot to do more than lift the tissuey pages of the Bible and feel the tingle between our legs as the words grew loving and violent and dark. I had wanted to be taken then, to be taken and overpowered. I had wanted to do the things that got you there. So I had taught Pearl how to put her hand down between her legs and press her fingers in to get that feeling. I had tried to make her as much like me as possible, so I wouldn't have to do the wild stuff alone, but it hadn't worked. Not then at least. Now she was way beyond me.

". . . And I haven't had time to think about business, worrying about him this past week. You know there's a vote coming up soon, and Walker's managed to get people organized behind my back. It's not going to work, of course. She'd do better to go out to that farm and start packing. Personally, I think they'd have been lucky if the fire had spread to the house too. It's nothing but an old wreck anyway. They can barely keep this place afloat as it is." Her voice dropped as she paused by the window and fiddled with the knobs on the air conditioner, clicking them slowly in a circle so the overhead light blinked and faded and brightened as she changed the charge.

"I'm sorry, I was only trying to help."

She examined me closely for a minute to see if I was being sarcastic, then coughed and dug around in her dress pocket and pulled out a pack of cigarettes. The air already stank, but I didn't say anything.

She lit up and took a deep drag, which she let out gradually, as if a part of the feelings of frustration and worry were being carried away with the smoke and she wanted to watch. She looked at the cigarette in her hand and shook her head. "I know I should quit."

"The baby would probably appreciate it."

"I suppose Walker knows now, and Able too? The whole town then . . ." She took a quick puff and went to the window, heaved it open, and tossed the still-lit cigarette out and waved her hands as if the smoke would follow.

"I didn't tell her, but she knows. She knows everything. I don't know about Able. He doesn't seem to care much about gossip." I was feeling real sorry for her then and wanted to help.

"He's worse, acting so innocent all the time. You know he has a telescope on the roof? He knows most things before they even happen." We stared at each other and burst out laughing.

"Remember that time with the Skelley gas driver your mom was seeing?" I said.

"I remember him in his underwear that night. Lord, if Estes had ever found out . . ." We laughed some more and I waved at the pressed back straight chair for her and we sat there and talked about all the crazy things we'd done as kids. Neither of us asked the real question, though: What had happened to us?

After a while, it felt safe enough to come back to something that'd been bothering me. "What was McCall doing to help you, Pearl? The fires?"

Pearl got up and went to the window, and I thought she was going to light up again, but she just stood there, gazing down at the street.

"Pearl?" She started running the brittle old shade up and down the window, the wood slat at the bottom tearing away a little bit more with each pull. Finally she tried shrugging, but could only raise one shoulder.

"People might've died. Walker and Able haven't made it public because they're afraid of losing their insurance, but he set other fires at the hotel. Did you know?"

She shook her head. "He knew it was important to me . . . gave him a chance to start over with the money too. He just went too far." I waited as her face went through a series of odd expressions.

"Have you heard from him since that night?"

She shrugged. "He's called a couple of times and come by late, but I—I can't forget what he's done. I knew he was wild, on the edge, but I thought he just needed more structure, more stability was all. I thought I could make a difference because he loved me." Her voice dropped to a whisper. "I'm sorry, Moline."

"I'm sorry too, Pearl."

Pearl started pacing again, then stopped and stared at me. Focusing on the wallpaper behind her so it appeared that I was staring her down, I figured I could last as long as she could. I knew this paper, I'd been staring at it for days: its faded pastels with gray and lavender were the only colors still holding their own in the repeated fleurs-de-lis and ladies' and gentlemen's ball clothes. It was probably the ugliest damn wall covering in the hotel. Walker must've put me here to get me out of bed quicker. Between that and the Culver's root tea she made me drink yesterday, I was about to take the next Trailways out of here.

If Dayrell were here, he'd stop Walker from making me drink all those terrible teas with peculiar, bitter flavors; he'd protect Pearl from McCall and stop her from the kind of forgiveness that might get her hurt or killed. But most of all, he'd be here with me, and that was all I really wanted, I'd decided. It was a small thing I asked for, but it seemed possible, since it was the one and only thing I promised I'd ever ask for as long as I lived. I was afraid he couldn't get over what I'd done to him, though.

Pearl drew a deep breath like she was about to say something, then turned and started fiddling with the air conditioning again until the room felt like it'd dropped another ten degrees. Maybe she was hoping we'd freeze to death and solve everyone's problems. I pulled the flannel blanket up under my chin and waited in the silence Pearl was so much better at than me.

Looking at her, I could see how Pearl's shirtwaist dress might as well have had the price tag hanging off its little plastic loop, the one that said: I'm cheap, the seams are raw, the material's going to fade every time you wash me, I won't last, I won't hold off time and wear, I'll announce myself every place you go, anyone can afford me. For once she was dressed like she shopped in town.

I felt sorry for Dear Pearl again, for being pregnant at her age, for loving a man like McCall, for all the other concerns that had worn her thin and old. I started to get up and go to her, forgetting about the tube and drain, which jerked out of the bag at the side of the bed and drained liquid on the bed and floor.

"Moline, stop—what're you doing? Get back in bed!" Pearl ran over and tried to push my shoulders back down. "Walker? Aunt Walker?" Pearl yelled toward the door while she held me down in bed and tried to stand on her tiptoes on the wet floor.

"Just settle down, the both of you." Walker lumbered into the room. "Now get back in that bed, Moline Bedwell, and don't you dare get out until I say so. Made a nice mess for me to clean up, didn't you?" She inspected the floor and turned to Pearl. "You go on and shoo now—go tend your business issuing injunctions right and left to innocent people and relatives and quit disturbing your cousin. She'll never get better she keeps yanking that knee around." She flapped her apron at Pearl, who stood her ground briefly before grimacing at me and mouthing goodbye. I waved as she left.

It wasn't what Walker thought, but I didn't want to go through everything that had occurred in here a few moments before.

"On the way up to see you, she served me an injunction to stop harassing Heart Hogs. Said it was nothing personal. Can you believe the gall of that girl? Estes must feel like she's going over Niagara Falls in a barrel right now. No Waller ever stooped to this behavior. Here, take a look at this. . . ." She pulled the folded papers out of her apron and threw them on my lap. "I say it again, that girl missed her calling. Should've gone to law school. I've half a mind to hand her the money and tell her to git now before she's too old. Then maybe I could hire her to work on my behalf instead of against me."

All my life I'd taken responsibility in my dreams, so when the bed weighed down next to me in the middle of the night and the springs cried out, I didn't turn away or holler, I waited. I was not running away anymore, my body said in its dream.

"Sweet Moline," he whispered, hands moving slowly on my face, my shoulders. He took my hand and put it down there on me, then on him where he was naked. I didn't open my eyes, because in dreams like this you waited.

He was pulling off my nightgown. The cotton rasped on my chin, my nose, and smelled of bleach and salty sweat, his or mine, I couldn't tell. He was on top of me, and when he lifted my hips, I helped and the entry was so slow, so very slow it was just like the dream. I wanted to please him, no, I wanted to please myself, the way I did in dreams. I reached down and touched the wetness of him and me, letting go, moaning the sweet music of dreaming the bedsprings made.

In the morning, Walker came in and picked the nightgown off the floor and held it up with her eyebrows raised in a question. I shrugged and reached for it, glad I never opened my eyes. It was Dayrell, even if it was a dream, I knew it was him. The scars on his chin and stomach were ridges I could still feel on my fingertips as I looked at my hands.

"Moline Bedwell, what are you thinking about? You have the naughtiest look on your face. I wish I had a camera." She checked the tubing and bag, pulling the covers around with sharp jerks. "Seems to me you're about ready to get up and walk on that thing. Doctor should be up in a minute. You're lucky I came on ahead, or you'd be naked as a jaybird when he charged through that door. Now put that thing on, and we'll get you dressed and downstairs as soon as he leaves. Then maybe Birdeene Cadmus can interview you for the town gossips like she's been trying to do for days."

She picked up the dented tin wastebasket with the picture of a ship on a stormy sea painted in dark colors that had only grown darker over time, and dumped the dirty Kleenex and straws into it. "Look at this old thing. Antique now. Missed my chance to get rid of it and all its friends in the other rooms—now it's too late. That's the way of things, though—you wait too long, you're stuck with things you thought you'd never tolerate another day. This whole place is like that. I hate living so long the junk got valuable." She yanked down the covers and shook them out, then tossed them one at a time over me, so they landed square. "Haven't lost my touch." She tucked them in and attacked the pillows, fluffing and jerking them around so they sat upright and full behind me. It was good to see her strong again.

Going to the door to let the doctor in when he knocked, she paused to inspect me. "You tell him we need you up and around now, Moline. The farm and the night desk haven't been the same in days."

The doctor removed the tubing and rebandaged my knee with a lot of instructions I ignored. He'd gone from being slap-on-the-back, you'll-be-up-in-no-time to being strictly business. "You're all right, Moline. You get along good with folks here." He forced his thick old fingers with the bulging arthritic joints to wrap the gauze and tape in perfect stripes as if he were putting the grip on a baseball bat or hockey stick.

He stopped when the adhesive tape gave out at the end of the roll, and patted the leg lightly. His pale pink scalp glistened with sweat through the few remaining stubby white hairs he wore cropped military-style from the Second World War. "There, that's as good as they could do anywhere. You know it was only a touch of heat stroke the other day. That's what it was, damn it—I've lived here my whole life, seventy-one years, and I know heat stroke when I see it." He stood up, snapping his bag shut. "You know it was heat stroke, Moline. You should tell that aunt of yours the truth."

I watched his back, puffed up with hurt, disappear through the door, which he pulled shut with a sharp thump that rattled the picture of the black man leading a mule down a road toward his distant barn standing like a red stamp in the distance. The dust the two were raising fogged their legs so they appeared to be gradually descending into the earth. The green fields and trees hung with dust-laden leaves wore that tired August expression, like they'd just about had enough of things and it was time to move along. Poor Dr. Bradford. The thing that surprised me was how he took for granted that local approval meant anything to me, which of course it did. In fact, I was secretly a little proud that I could get along here.

"Well, let's get going now." Walker burst back in with some clean clothes and a pair of shoes I didn't recognize. She held them up: Wal-Mart canvas shoes like Lukey wore. "Ugly, but cheap. Saw Doc Bradford running like a hen from a hatchet. He tell you I yelled at him? Silly old man, should've retired years ago. Couldn't diagnose a broken chair leg if he was holding both pieces. You about done? I got some crutches outside in the hallway. Just a second—don't move. . . ."

Despite her unhelping hands flagging in front of me and my clumsiness, we managed to walk down the hall and start on the stairs, which seemed to take me five minutes a riser until I got the hang of the crutches.

"That deputy—can't think of his name for the life of me—is waiting downstairs in the kitchen to ask you some questions." Walker wasn't trying to hurry me any. She'd got a grip on the banister so she could catch me if the crutches went astray, or maybe in case I accidentally tripped her.

"Dear Pearl spotted his car and ran back over as fast as she could. She's still trying to save that McCall Bell, who should've been drowned in the stock tank at birth instead of being made king of the world by the women in this town. Nothing good comes of spoiling a child that's already willful. He could lead the devil astray. Look what happened to your sister—"

I stumbled on the last step and almost went down but for her arm and hip bracing me against the wall. "What do you mean?"

"Never mind about your sister," Walker said in a low voice, then greeted the deputy without calling him by name.

It was Monroe Sharpe, and I was glad to get the chance to settle into the chair and prop my bad leg up. He seemed okay before, although he looked nervous now with Pearl standing over by the stove glaring at him like an alarm clock about to go off.

"Howdy, Miz Bedwell." He lifted the hat in his hand and only peeked quickly at my bandaged knee.

"Deputy," I said.

Pearl shifted her weight and raised her eyebrows at me as a signal to get on with it. Walker went to the refrigerator and started hauling net bags of lemons out. "Lemonade," she announced, and spilled them on the table we were sitting at before going to the grease-specked pegboard next to the stove where the cooking utensils hung. She pulled down the lemon squeezer with the double handles and brought it over and dropped it in front of Monroe Sharpe. "Needs a man's touch."

After she'd tied an old apron around his neck so his uniform wouldn't get spattered, she gave him a paring knife and a pitcher for the juice. You could tell he was confused by how quickly and easily he'd been rotated out of the position of authority. Maybe there was something to getting old.

Then Dayrell slipped in the back door and stood behind Pearl. He was wearing a loose long-sleeved shirt that hid the gunshot wounds. He looked like he'd lost weight too, and there was a gaunt strain in his face. I felt better seeing him despite the ache in my knee and his frown. But when I saw his hand go to Pearl's shoulder and how she leaned back against him, I had to look away.

When he'd accumulated enough lemon halves to start squeezing, Monroe cleared his throat, popped one in the machine, and clamped the handles together. "Reverend Titus is pretty vague on what happened out there the other night, said I should consult with you. We get concerned when people get shot and then don't want to go to the hospital. What do you think?" He looked at me as juice flowed into the pitcher.

"I guess there was an accident, and nobody was too concerned."

"Your knee an accident too?"

"It got infected."

He carefully positioned another lemon in the metal circle and brought the top down gently; then his knuckles went white as he clamped the two parts together. "What were you doing out in those hills at that hour of night, in the middle of the worse rain we've had in twenty years?"

I looked at Pearl and Dayrell, who shook their heads slightly. "Went to visit my cousin Lukey, help her pack her cabin."

Walker clucked and brought a big yellow plastic bowl over and began tossing the used lemon halves into it.

"So you don't think there's any connection between all the events the Reverend's worried about—the fires, Heart Hogs, and now this? You seem to be showing up just about every time something happens, have you noticed that? But it's all coincidence, I guess."

"She's still pretty woozy, Monroe." Pearl took half a step toward us. The deputy stopped squeezing the lemon. Pushing his chair away from the table so he could see her better, he said, "Maybe you could talk about that night, then. It kind of worries me that Copeland Harder Jr. shows up to make statements for Moline and Lukey and Dayrell here, before we even got to any of you."

Pearl tossed her head and looked down at him. "He's an idiot. We're not responsible for *anything* he does."

"I'll grant you that, but you're all involved in this Hog affair, and that worries me too. Especially when McCall Bell—"

"He doesn't have anything in the world to do with this." Pearl blushed and her eyes hardened.

"Look, I was there," I said. "It was an accident. Dayrell was hunting and we ran into him and were horsing around and he slipped in the mud and fell and the gun went off. Pure and simple." I stared right at the mole below Monroe's left eye and didn't let myself blink, though my hands in my lap were trembling pretty good.

Monroe turned to Dayrell. "That right? Shot yourself? Night hunting in the rain? S'pose you had your dogs out too. Catch a good scent in a downpour. Bullet had quite a life of its own too, I s'pose. In and out of the arm, into the side. Good shooting for a man falling down. Must've been carrying the gun backwards, facing yourself, wouldn't you say?" He smiled and put another lemon in the squeezer. "Glad to have that cleared up. Now maybe you all can tell me where Judge Crater's buried, and what happened to Jimmy Hoffa. You all are wasting your talents here in Resurrection."

Dayrell's face didn't even twitch. At least I was doing something right, protecting that rotten McCall for these two, although for the life of me I couldn't see why Dayrell would care.

"She told you the truth," Pearl said. "What more do you want?"

"Someone's going to end up getting hurt real bad, maybe even killed, with this kind of business, Miz Waller. This isn't no game. I know someone's setting fires. I know someone shot Dayrell. Too much going on for coincidence. No, don't even think I believe anything you people have told me. It better not be Heart Hogs, that's all I can say. And it better not be anything you all are mixed up with. If it is, you better start running now, because the sheriff won't have it." He pulled the apron off and folded it neatly into a square he laid on the table beside the half-finished mound of lemons. Standing, he tipped his head at Walker. "Miz Rains, I'd surely appreciate a glass of this here lemonade when it gets hot later this afternoon."

"You stop by any time it pleases you, Monroe. Next time, I'll try to have some sense knocked into these youngsters. Thank you kindly for the use of your good strong hands too."

"Ladies, Dayrell, hope that arm heals up quick." He nodded and left.

"That darn Cope," Pearl muttered, and stalked out the door. Dayrell leaned against the frame, cradling his hurt arm with the good one.

"Sure you all don't have something to tell me?" Walker sat in the deputy's chair and picked up the squeezer and with a quick pump finished the lemon, popped it out, and pushed another in. She made the juice flow out in thick, steady streams, working quickly and efficiently through the rest of the pile, before she laid it down and looked at me again, then over at Dayrell. "Well?"

"Not that I can think of." I had to keep myself from flinching at those gray eyes.

"You better start thinking harder then, missy. It won't help matters to keep protecting McCall. And don't believe I don't see how you and Pearl are suddenly friends again."

"You wanted me to have some sympathy for her, Walker."

Her shoulders stiffened. "Not right this minute, Moline. Now go on, take that leg for a good long walk while I clean up around here. And you, Mr. Dayrell, make yourself scarce until you can come up with something resembling the truth."

I wanted to touch her, tell her I was sorry, but I stood and hopped toward the lobby instead, knowing it might be a big mistake to let the moment go. So many things went undone in this life, it made you want to throw your hands in the air and give up. Dayrell nodded at me and slipped down the street and around the corner before I could speak. Maybe he'd come visit me tonight again, the thought of which cheered me considerably.

It felt good to finally push my way out the front door and hobble-hop down the sidewalk just as Sugar Stimson came clicky-clacking along on his cherry brown walking horse, passing me with the tip of his straw fedora. The horse's head bobbed up and down to the rhythm of its legs, keeping time for itself, with the long mustard-colored tail sweeping from side to side, lightly dusting an imaginary table. Bits of gravel and sand popped up and pinged the hubcaps and curbs in a tinny music that joined the crunch of car tires passing, the distant yelling of two little boys running ahead of their mother toward the Dixie Donut Shop, the putt-putt of a full sized John Deere tractor coming toward me, and the clang-clang-clang of the mechanics fixing a tire at the Conoco down the street.

As if my ear were a camera, I could distinguish and see every sound—even the twerping of the three sparrows hopping and fluttering around a bread crust in the dandelions and crab grass poking through the crack of the sidewalk ahead. The creams and browns and tans of the birds glowed as if they were freshly painted on, new to this world. The beaks made sharp decisions and the feet and legs as thin as threads were as strong as they needed to be. There was something wonderfully sufficient in their noisy business.

Some of the old red brick buildings of downtown were darkened with age, I noticed for the first time, as if living burned time up and the soot rubbed itself onto everything that stood still. The white wood trims were faded and chipped, but there was an honor here, like ancient trees weathering history. These buildings had seen the first settlers in the early 1800s, the fights, the raids of the War, the battles, the losses, and they'd seen the rebuildings, the coming back over and over. One history layered over another, like the faded turquoise aluminum fronts tacked on the first floors of buildings in the early fifties, then ripped off again in the early nineties when restoration hit. Beneath it all, the buildings stood witness, the brick and stone and wood enduring, like the families themselves, the old ones lingering in the cemetery, the new ones moving in and seeing it all for the first time.

Time might be our enemy, but it didn't stop us from trying to escape, and in that escape we did become glorious, like the late morning sun and Sugar Stimson's journey through town, which was earlier than usual, another sign maybe. I couldn't tell. I saw everything as filled with possibility, potential, and mystery this morning. I didn't know why, but not even the ache of the crutches pushing hard enough into my armpits to make them sore discouraged me. My knee hurt, but it was the best it'd felt in two weeks. My head was clear, really so clear I wondered what I'd been wearing for eyes.

I stopped to give my arms a rest. It felt almost good that the ache in my arms was going to build new muscles. I'd be so strong I could keep up with Dayrell. I leaned against the newly sandblasted brick of the old five-and-dime. The front windows were covered with newspaper, and on the outside of the plate glass someone had scrawled in big, clumsy white letters: THE REBEL COFFEE HOUSE COMING SOON!

On the street in front of me cars pushed harder, faster, and I noticed they were the older models, busted up like old prizefighters, barroom brawlers with headlights torn out of sockets, trunk lids ripped off, gone, only a dark hole like a gaping wound or doom following them around, beaten, rusted doors that didn't quite close on the people inside as battered as their cars. I used to drive one of those. Then when I married Duncan and got a clean, careful life, I'd looked down on them, avoided them on the freeway as if they were going to dirty me, carry me back. Now I realized that I'd just gotten money lucky for a while in my marriage. I understood why they were the ones speeding, taking chances, in a hurry to get out of this bad luck and on to something better. They didn't want to spend any longer than they had to getting there in those uncomfortable vehicles, and I could understand that—their troubles, their efforts against misfortune. There had to be mercy, there had to be something ahead for them, because without that, none of us would ever be able to imagine life.

Looking around at Resurrection, I couldn't say for certain that there was anything like what the Methodists and Baptists and Catholics imagined waiting for us out there. I had to believe something, though. I didn't die in that cave years ago when I should have, I didn't die of the copperhead when I might have, and I didn't die of the infection when I could have. Something saved me, and even though I couldn't say for sure what, it felt more than accidental, it felt different than anything I could name or see. Maybe the only proof we got was that there was such a thing as hope to begin with. Otherwise, the world was just too damn mean and ugly to be worth staying around for. I knew I'd been in hell for years, numb to love, and I couldn't say it wasn't of my own making. I just knew that getting out of it made this place, this poorly equipped, half-ass little town in the middle of the Ozarks, as good as any place I could ever hope for. A sort of paradise. I could bear anything at this moment, just as long as I got to stand here and feel the grace of good light cleaning my skin so living sounds and smells came pouring in, and I could touch the brick behind me with my fingertips, following its rough hieroglyphs just for pleasure, and think about Dayrell, my love, someplace south of Resurrection.

After a while, I hobbled on around the square surrounding the huge four-story courthouse whose doors opened on four sides. Bedwells, Wallers, LeFays, Bells, and Rainses in one shape or another for the past one hundred and fifty years had been passing through those big white wooden doors, arguing and suing, marrying and divorcing, registering and voting and dying. I was part of that. I belonged here, as surely as Paris and Iberia and Mister, who tried to move on only to end up back here again. They were wrong, we'd all been wrong. You couldn't outrun your history, you couldn't just abandon your past. It was all there someplace, waiting for the future, waiting for you.

23

CURTAIN OF FLESH

On no account must the mourners leave the cemetery until the last clod of earth is thrown into the grave—to do so evidences a lack of respect for the dead and is likely to bring death and destruction upon the family circle.

—OZARK MAGIC AND FOLKLORE

"THAT ROOF MUST BE LEAKING worse than ever with this downpour! You seen either of those men you and your cousin are keeping off the dole these days? I left a message at Hale's over an hour ago." Walker shook the water out of her hair and threw off her clear plastic raincoat. She'd been out trying to track Able down at the Dixie Donuts. I didn't tell her it'd been almost a week since I'd heard or seen anybody but people in and out of the hotel. I went to sleep every night waiting for Dayrell to make a midnight visitation, and woke up every morning telling myself he just needed more time, but I was beginning to get discouraged.

"I told that old fool to leave bad enough alone. Now he's laid up again and the ceiling's falling in upstairs. Best I can do is lay canvas and plastic over everything and hope the weight of the water doesn't take the floor down another level. Oh, wait . . ." She trotted toward the little museum they'd turned the back parlor and dining room into and I followed her.

The door to the old walk-in safe from the bank Horras Waller owned before the Depression took it stood open to the old utility room that was now the storeroom for the historical society's records. When Walker pulled the string for the bare bulb dangling overhead, I saw the problem. Water was streaming down the mottling wallpaper and puddling on the floor despite the drain in the middle of the cement. From the stains blotching the peeling paper and the sickly yellow eruptions of plaster on the ceiling, it was clear that this room wasn't previously unacquainted with water. Some of the books and papers on the metal racks were already dotted with gray specks of mold, while others curled and warped from a cycle of damping and drying. The water level on the floor was rising as we stood there.

"Here—grab these." Walker began to load me up. A sheaf of papers sent a musty haze into our faces, making me sneeze. "Go get a box or basket or something. Hurry!"

I staggered with my armful to the far corner of the parlor, next to a wall that seemed relatively unstained, and dumped it as carefully as I could. Walker was hollering from the storeroom again, and I ran back to the front lobby to see if there was a box I could use in the office. Two young men in their thirties—one very fair, one darker-complected—were standing with their bags slung on the floor around them, waiting to check in, apparently.

"I can't help you now—we got a flood in the back room." There was a box in the closet and a green plastic garbage bag half full of trash stuffed behind the counter. I dumped the trash on the floor and scrounged around for more bags.

"Moline? *Moline*, where the Sam Hill are you?" Walker's voice ratcheted around the corners and down the hallway at us. "Moline! I'm gonna need an ark! Get back here—it's spilling into the room!"

"Just a minute—just wait a minute, okay?" I glanced at the men as I hurried past. Thunder clapped and shook the hotel hard enough to make the windowpanes rattle and the antique crystal in the display cases click on their glass shelves.

Walker had hauled more documents out, and it didn't take long for us to finish up. The water was licking at the bottom shelf a couple of inches off the floor as I loaded the last box. On top was the book of cemetery records from the town's beginning to 1980. Together we closed the door to the safe and shut down the flood.

"What happens when we open it again?" I asked as Walker sat in a wingback to take off her tennis shoes and socks.

"I have not a clue." She wrung the socks out on the worn oriental carpet, and rubbed her feet dry alongside the wet spots. "Too much water. Sewer system must've been put in about the time of Moses. Resurrection my foot. We'll be lucky that room isn't full of water moccasins we open that door again. But with any real luck, it'll drain when the rain stops."

"Please?" The dark haired young man stood in the doorway, his body stiff and useless looking.

"Yes?" She eyed him curiously.

"We'd like a room?" He stepped back as if to lure us into following him.

"All right." She stood. "Have to do it in my bare feet, though, flood's soaked my shoes."

The thunder was so loud for a few moments it seemed as if some giant were stomping across town, landing each huge foot on another building or tree, collapsing them under its weight in great sonic booms, approaching closer and closer, then passing over us in some divine accident of rescue. When it was done, the wind shifted and whipped the rain in new directions for a while. Little threads of water began rivuleting under the front doors when we got to the lobby. The two men peered anxiously out the front windows.

David Solomon, followed by his wife and daughter, pushed through the front door, spackling us with water as they shook their arms and stamped their feet. "Wet." David grinned.

His daughter, Kandera, danced up and down, begging, "Please, please let me go play in the rain?"

Her mother frowned as lightning broke the twilight of the lobby. "No. When it stops, maybe. There'll be nice big puddles and you can wear your red rubber boots. After your nap, that is."

Kandera frowned, then clapped her hands and danced up the stairs ahead of her parents, whose steps were dragging.

I checked the men in, noting they were brothers with the same last name, Greg and Tony Handel, though they seemed exactly the same age and looked nothing alike. They argued like an old married couple as they hefted their bags up the stairs too.

"What do you think about those two?" I asked. "They wanted the king-size bed."

Walker shrugged and pointed to the water coming in under the door. "Moline, go get some rags and a mop and check the other doors and windows, will you?" Then she started processing the charges.

"Think they're . . . ?" I asked as we lined the windowsills with towels and rags to catch the water, which had found new and impossible ways to enter.

"Whatever they are, they're a lot safer here with us than on those flooded roads." She stood up and stretched, rubbing the small of her back. "Now watch, it's going to quit raining about the time we get the leaks plugged." The thunder rolled over again, shaking the building one last time, then seemed to walk off to the east, taking the downpour with it.

The phone rang and Walker answered. While she was talking, I opened the front doors to let the rain-cooled air pull out some of the hotel's mustiness. I walked outside onto the porch, closed my eyes, and took a deep breath, trying to sort out the strands of hot wet blacktop from the rotting sweet flowers beaten to the ground. I spread my arms and stretched to let the air catch my skin too and something bumped into me. I opened my eyes just as McCall took me in his arms and dipped me dramatically to the floor of the porch.

"Cut it out!" I shoved at his chest and he almost dropped me.

He staggered, righted me, and let go. "Ow, Moline—you hit my new tattoo." He spread his unbuttoned shirt and touched the edges lightly with his fingertips. Pearl's name had disappeared into an ornate figure with teeth and flames, a demented, drunken dragon in red and black ink against a black heart, although it all looked a little scraggly and uninspired at the moment. "It's scabbing up pretty good, can't risk tearing it now."

I could smell the deep stale-sweet odor of old liquor underneath the fresh bite on his breath. His eyes were red-trimmed and bloodshot and that little bit unfocused that said he was in the middle of some hard drinking. Stubble covered his jaw, and white spit had crusted in the corners of his slack lips. The strands of his hair stuck together like odd fingers pointing in all directions from his head.

"Stay the hell away from me, McCall," I said, trying not to stare as he braced himself against the porch support.

"No harm done." McCall looked at his tattoo again. "How you doing?"

"I'm calling the sheriff."

McCall laughed and rocked on the heels of his cowboy boots, rubbing his round stomach.

"McCall, get the fuck away from me."

He raised his eyebrows in pretend shock and tried to button his shirt. "Still mad, huh?" He managed to get two buttons in holes they didn't match with, so the shirt hung lopsided.

"You've got to be kidding."

McCall laughed. "Fuck me, huh? Of course fuck me. You always wanted to, but you were too damn chicken."

"Cut it out, McCall, or I'm calling Monroe Sharpe."

"That pussy? He won't do anything. Besides, I got something to say to you, Moline."

"What's that?"

"I'm not scared anymore. I don't give a flying fuck. Truth is, I could've stopped the car that night—didn't want to. Doesn't change what *you* did, though, does it?" He laughed and stumbled down the porch stairs into the street, where he spread his arms and staggered in a circle, yelling "Free!" His belt was flapping and his jeans were slipping down his butt.

After two circles he fell to his hands and knees at the curb and took a moment before he got up. When he did, he wasn't laughing anymore. Titus's black Ford drove up behind him, honked its horn, and pulled in diagonally to park. Lukey jumped out and ran to McCall's side.

At first he tried to push her off, but then he put his arm around her and pressed her close to his body, looking possessively over her bent head at me and glaring. "Where you been, baby girl? Where's the kids? I been looking all over for you."

I wanted to ask if he'd really thought he'd find her in the bars, but Titus got out of the car and walked slowly around to stand just out of range and stare at the couple. When McCall noticed him, he hugged her tighter and glanced from Titus to me. "You were hiding her from me, weren't you?"

"Let her go, McCall. You already took everything she had." Titus stepped up, ready to pull her away, but McCall tightened his grip until his fingers seemed to meet at the bone of her narrow upper arm.

"Okay—here, let her decide." McCall dropped his hands and stepped away. Lukey looked at each of us, beseeching us for something. Understanding? Help? She'd lost even more weight, so her shorts and tee shirt hung shapelessly on her and her pale skin was turning translucent blue-white. Her hair lay flat and dull against her head, but her eyes were shiny with pain and fear and something else.

"He'll hurt himself," she said. "He needs me." She turned her back on Titus and me and put her arms around McCall's neck. They looked like any other couple in love, murmuring into each other's ears. She put an arm around his back and headed toward his new yellow truck parked two doors down.

"See y'all later," McCall called, and for a brief moment, as he helped her up to the passenger's seat, they looked like they really did belong together.

"He's in no shape to drive," I said. I thought about repeating it, but then I didn't, I just let it go, the way Titus did, and McCall backed out and drove past us, making a show of going extra slow and braking extravagantly at the corner. The last thing I saw was Lukey's white face staring out the window at me with her mouth open as if she were about to say something more. Then they were gone in a trail of pale exhaust.

"Oh, you found him. No time now. We have to go to the cemetery. Come on." Walker closed the hotel door behind her and started toward my truck, only stopping when she realized we were still standing there.

"Well, come on. We don't have all day. There's more rain on the way—the roof will have to wait. We got a mess at the cemetery. Darn creek is flooding. Already took a couple of markers and dumped them in the road. Lee Pettimore says dead folks rising regular as Judgment Day out there. Moline, we'll stop and grab the shovels at Pearl's. Titus, you follow us in case we need help loading anything." She looked at Titus's shoes. "I don't s'pose you had sense enough to bring anything else for those feet. See if Pearl has a pair of rubber boots for you."

"Miz Rains, I'm not here because of the flood." Titus shifted his feet and looked at the scuffed gray boards of the porch.

"Of course you are. Let's go." She marched us off.

There was already a line of trucks and cars along the roads around and through the cemetery. Walker had made me fill two old jugs with tap water for drinking and I hauled those while she brought a big tarp crusted with bird droppings she'd found in the chicken shed behind my house. It didn't seem to bother her to clutch it against her, and the chalky residues left white streaks down the legs of her green khaki chinos.

"Moline, I didn't want to upset you, but I think there's a problem in the Waller block, closest to the creek. They think Estes has disappeared. Horras is in that concrete vault, so he's not going anywhere, of course, even though his grave's under water as we speak." She shifted the tarp, pulling up an end that'd gotten loose and was in danger of tripping her up as she stomped along in her old rubber Wellingtons. "Ground's saturated with all this rain we've been having. Nowhere for it to go anymore. Be lucky if the sandbags hold. You could be saying howdy to that creek from your porch in another day or two." She turned around and yelled at Titus to hurry up. Titus caught up and promised to call for more help from his black parishioners and left us.

The creek was a rush of water spilling onto the legs of men and women who kept having to back up and drag their shovels and sandbags with them. The first line of defense was already just a tan hump the water hit and leapt over. Once outside the banks, the water churned in every direction, without a flow that could be directed or controlled. Gravestones posed only a momentary problem as the water shouldered them, pulling the ground beneath and pushing from above so that first they wobbled and finally they toppled, disappearing beneath the brown-orange flood. Every few minutes a new surge of water arrived. The only safety that the dead had seemed to be on the hills—the one behind us where the old dead watched and the one across the creek where the Negro cemetery looked down on the disaster.

Lee Pettimore drove up the gravel-and-crushed-rock road on his riding lawn mower, a damp cigarette hanging limply from his mouth, his gray rain poncho flapping around him like a big unsettled bird. He stopped and drew hard on the cigarette before putting it in his pocket when nothing came out. "Miz Walker, Moline. Sorry about Miz Estes. Rather it be my own mother than that woman, who took such great pride in this place." He paused, cleared his throat and spit discreetly on the other side of the lawnmower, and reached under his poncho and pulled out a pack of cigarettes.

"I hate to say it, but I think we're in trouble with Iberia and Mister Bedwell too. Them being fresh and all. Hardly had time to settle in—takes a few years, you know. Those headstones popped right out of the ground, 'bout as fast as toadstools after a good rain. Don't expect them graves to sit still much longer than that. Worse flood I can recall, thirty-some years. Shoulda known not to put them people so close to water. Miz Estes, though, she insisted we could control that itty-bitty creek—dig a deeper bed, that's what she said. Channel it. But you know, that's the one time I disagreed with her. You can see the water's just gonna run faster if you dig the bed deeper. That's what it done today. Now look." He lit another cigarette and let out a deep breath of smoke, spreading his heavy arm to the whole scene.

"My sister could be very stubborn—especially when she didn't know what she was talking about. Now what do you want us to do?" Walker shifted the tarp impatiently. Lee Pettimore took another deep drag off his cigarette and let the smoke out slowly, sizing up the two of us. "Best you can do, Miz Walker, is take your niece Pearl and calm her down some. She's more getting in the way than helping. Trying to wade in to find her grandmother. Already had to be rescued twice when a new slop of water took her legs out from under her. Personally, I think Miz Estes will turn up downstream. I don't think she'll go much farther than that place outside of town where the creek takes a good curve by Twitchell's. Least I hope not, or we might have to go to New Orleans to haul her back."

"Where's my niece now?" Walker squinted at the scene on the water's edge, where the light seemed to be failing, as if all the swirling brown were sucking it away in a tan mist.

"I believe Miz Birdeene put her in a car to get something hot in her." He glanced sideways at Dayrell, who was coming across the road toward us. When he arrived, Lee said, "We're trying to round up a bunch of rope, chains, old tires so we can rig a net of some sort across the culvert under the blacktop, keep the coffins from getting away on us."

"You want to use my dogs to find loose coffins or . . . ?" Dayrell asked.

"If they got good noses and don't mind getting their feet wet, I s'pose it might help. Better get a move on too, heard there's another storm coming by dark."

"I can bring them in. What else needs doing?" Dayrell lifted his cap and resettled it on, not looking at me.

"You might could go to Wal-Mart and get some more rope and chain. Tell 'em we'll settle up later—they all got relations here too, remind 'em if they give you any trouble." He puffed the last bit out of his cigarette, smashed the little bit of butt on his heel, and put it in the cuff of his pants.

Walker shifted her load again and looked at the rest of us. "Let's get started then. Dayrell Bell, you go with Moline and see if you can find McCall along the way. Maybe the sight of his worthless face will calm

Pearl down enough to get her thinking organized, so we can figure out who's staying put and who's taking to the road. Darned if I can keep track of this family. My fascination is not with the dead as a rule."

"Haven't seen you in a while." I was trying too hard to get him to smile.

He just sucked his lower lip in and held it with his front teeth, the way a kid would do when I glanced over. There were dark circles under his eyes and his hair looked greasy, like it hadn't been washed in days. His knuckles were raw on his right hand which gripped the chin-high handle by the window on the door.

"Quit it," he said finally.

"What?"

"I said, quit staring at me." His face darkened.

Rounding the curve a little ways from the intersection with Highway 11, where the Wal-Mart shopping plaza was, we were stopped by the flashing lights of police, ambulance, and fire trucks. The cars were creeping by slowly, sinking half into the shoulder while they took their look and edged around the deputy, Monroe Sharpe, directing traffic.

He glanced in the truck and waved at me. "Pull over—wait—okay, just go on ahead and pull over. Do it. Just pull over."

Dayrell heaved a big sigh. "Great, just what we need now."

"I wasn't speeding or anything," I muttered, pulling off onto the cement apron of the old independent gas station and climbing slowly out, with Dayrell reluctantly following. The police were scrambling up the hill and pushing people back as we got closer. A truck had crashed down the embankment, rolled over several times, and was lying on its side in the field like a large felled animal with its gut bursting flame, but from our angle it was impossible to tell what the make or model was. The fire truck stood useless on the shoulder, with hoses that didn't reach quite far enough, and several firemen stood below in a half moon with their foam spray cans in their arms and a Jaws of Life at their feet as they watched black smoke puffing into the damp air and the figure of a man circling and pulling at something. This was the moment I was to see and remember later as a mistake I made in watching, but I couldn't have stopped myself. I know that now.

When the explosion came, the flames billowed high into the air in a perfect red and orange swirling ball. As the smoke drifted to where I was standing, the smell of burning rubber was thick enough to rub itself on my skin and clothes like a melting eraser. There was this odd silence too, but I thought I heard something coming from the flames, something like a voice, but that must have been wrong, it was only the small pop of glass shattering outward in slow motion and sprinkling like snow into the smoke. Then I heard the sound again and started down the bank, far enough away that the police weren't watching. No one was. We were all staring at the fire popping and bursting as if someone kept throwing more fuel onto it. Suddenly there was a clearing, and the fire went down, and the firemen moved in and sprayed foam until the whole rig was crusted in dripping tan cream. That was when the form of a person appeared, the black burnt arms lifted up, frozen in supplication.

There was another voice, and I looked up and around. The police were waving at someone else, a man with a camera who was getting too close to the fire and taking pictures. And as if his presence had disturbed the scene profoundly, all the sounds that had been absent reappeared and began to char the air: the police radios, the firemen yelling, the crunch of metal cracking, and finally, a voice, wailing its ancient and wounding grief.

Monroe Sharpe had come closer and was trying to pull the man taking pictures away, yelling at him, grabbing at his arm, but the man kept skirting around him, intent, snapping the camera over and over as the smell of plastic and fabric and hide and something too sweet and meaty blew over us like infection. The man was too strong for the narrow deputy. I looked up toward the road, where another deputy and two firemen looking pissed were coming down the bank. Further down the road stood a bright red sports car with the door hanging open.

I watched the firemen push the photographer around, glad for it, glad when they tried to rip his camera away, glad when they yanked him up the hill, the deputies climbing tiredly after him. When they turned him loose, though, he walked away, then cut between the fire trucks and wove his way back down the bank, crouching low in the tall weeds, his camera held carefully above the wet. I didn't want to look at the fire again. I didn't want to breathe the air and let the smell into me.

When I looked up behind me on the road, there was a little knot of people watching, and in a black blanket, a woman standing separate, already isolated by loss. That was when I realized that grief had an icy breath we had to bundle ourselves against, and I wanted to bring my own blankets to her, whoever she was.

"Seen enough?" Dayrell came up behind me.

I got up. Turning, I saw Monroe Sharpe coming toward us, and I reached out for Dayrell without even knowing why yet.

"Dayrell, I'm sorry. . . ." Monroe stopped a few feet away, hat in his hand, trying not to look at us or the smoldering mess beyond us in the field. "The truck skidded out and rolled when he braked, and his wife was trapped in there. They tried to get her out, and they couldn't pull him away before it blew. I'm sorry. . . ." He stopped and looked down and up again. "It's your brother, McCall, and Lukey."

Dayrell looked up at the roadside and started shaking his head slowly, then looked at the smoking remains of the truck, because now we both knew. "McCall! Lukey?" he yelled, and started for the wreck, until Monroe Sharpe caught up and grabbed him from behind. He kept calling their names, though, as if that would stop it, as if McCall would pop up suddenly, laughing at the new way he'd found to play a cruel joke on his brother. And Lukey would wave and smile shyly again.

"Oh man, come on, no—McCall, come on—Lukey, no don't . . ."

"Lukey?" I whispered.

I didn't want to hurry to his side. I knew what lay ahead of us, but it still didn't take me but a second to go to him, put my arms around him, and feel his tears soak my neck and slide down inside the back of my shirt.

"I'm sorry . . . I'm so sorry," I whispered, unable to say a prayer or whatever it was you needed to do in the face of something so awful it took on TV disaster dimensions. Impossible. We let them disappear. What was Dayrell feeling now? What terrible, terrible thing was gripping his heart, like molten black plastic melting off the dashboard, a final fist of hurt, searing, permanent, squeezing the red out of his heart? He was the one I felt sorry for, the one who'd cursed his brother. But then I remembered McCall too, frantically trying to save Lukey, and felt sorry for him for the first time, because in the end he hadn't abandoned her after all.

"Lukey . . . oh, Lukey," I whispered, and began to cry silently.

"Come on, Dayrell—your mother's here, Hale's on his way." Monroe took Dayrell's arm and began leading him toward the crowd on the road. "You take your mother home now, Dayrell—she needs to go home, she doesn't need to see this. You go on, we'll take care of them now, it'll be all right. Your people need you, Dayrell, you hear—you take your mama home and get the house ready. People'll be coming soon to pay their respects. It's up to you to take care of things now." Monroe was taking him through the ditch and up the little hill, into the arms of his mother, and then Hale joined the circle of sorrow, which closed its arms to the rest of us. After a couple of minutes, people began to move away, heads hanging, with only an occasional sideways glance at the remains, as if they were ashamed that they had intruded on so private an occasion as a man and a woman's death.

I didn't know what to do then. We'd let her go, we'd let him go, we'd stood there and watched them drive away without a real goodbye.

As Dayrell went with his family to his mother's car, I felt him move away from me as if all those words and ways of love we'd had before were cardboard, the ordinary gray back of a school tablet, so flimsy, so easy to tear in two. "Goodbye," I whispered, knowing neither Bell brother could hear me now, knowing Lukey's family had yet to know their loss. Then I remembered the children too.

I pushed the cart like an underwater lawn mower down the Wal-Mart aisles, thinking, what did they need, what? Nothing applied. Not CDs, computer software, makeup, toys, pillows, crane-neck desk lamps, batteries, rugs, candy, Scotch tape. I found myself barely able to stay awake by the time I was loaded and in the checkout line. My eyes kept flattening and my knees wanted to buckle. I could hear the click and hum of the cash register, the thump of items dropped in white plastic bags with handles for easier carrying, the bang of shopping carts pushed against each other, nothing was going away, nothing was diminished by this diminishing.

Outside was too bright, though the sun was barely a glimmer behind new dark, heavy clouds that were massing in. Where was Dayrell? I looked down the highway to where the two trucks were just pulling the smoldering vehicle up the bank. Poor Pearl, did she know yet? I thought of Lukey's children again, but they seemed so out of reach. I was barely a Bedwell anymore; no one knew me anymore. Even Dayrell had his own people to go back to in the end.

I dropped off the rope and chain, ignored Walker's waving me down to the flood, and drove home. It didn't matter if she was mad or hurt, I couldn't do anything for anyone. I was still shivering from the hot killing flames when I climbed into bed, pulling the thin sheet over me, then getting up again to pull a quilt from my parents' bed. I didn't care if the whole cemetery ended up in the side yard. They were dead. They already knew what was in store for them.

John Wesley Waller tears sunlight's moist net and knocks twice on heaven's cupboard before reaching in my naked chest for the living heart he can hold perfectly in his hand. A healthy beat of red, red, red, he signs it with the burning cross, charring the outside layers with the stench of hot metal.

"These are the wounds of Jesus," he says, holding up the judgment finger an inch too short, the other nails as yellow, long, and sharp as the curved talons of an eagle. He's so close, I can see the scar denting his nose in half, the upper lip split like a crow's tongue made to talk, the livid rope under his chin as if God has tried to cut his throat.

"Where's the Christ of love?" I cry. "The Forgiving Jesus?"

"Oh," he smiles, "you've always exaggerated your own importance. He's got better things to do than think about you."

"Sin—what about sin?"

He shoves the heart back and closes the cupboard. It aches with its new scars. "Honestly? It's a mystery to me. Sin is an accident of nature. There's so little permanent and real. Forgive yourself. Forgive time. Time is a gift. Stop fighting it."

He holds up his palm with the blackbird living in its dark cell and places it over my ear. The power of milk pours into me, a white liquid of letters, more than I'll ever need, the words move with my blood, the blue doors open, and every feeling is a surprise visit from a long-lost relative. Everyone is alive, sad and happy, angry and just. I look up and see a man striding toward me, long legs that never hesitate to touch the earth, and in his right hand, a Bible, and in his left, the reins of the broken winded, fleabitten gray horse who will carry him to the river in a few minutes. And I know John Wesley Waller's gone for good this time.

24

REVELATION

*. . . When a very good and saintly person is dying, the feathers of the
pillow form themselves into a crown, a kind of symbol of the golden crown
which the dying person is soon to wear in Heaven. (also known as feather
crowns and angel wreaths)*

—OZARK MAGIC AND FOLKLORE

✳

I TRIED KNOCKING ON PEARL'S DOOR three days running before I
found it unlocked and got up the nerve to go in. She was there all right, in
a nest of nasty-smelling sheets, used tissues, and half-eaten fruit rotting on
plates beside some empty corn chip bags. But there wasn't a cigarette in
sight.

"What do you want?" she asked, and flung a leg over the back of the
black satin and velvet Victorian sofa. She was wearing his dirty gray sweat
pants, you could tell by how big they were, and his flannel shirt despite
the temperature in the dank, closed up house.

"Can I get you anything?" I didn't have the heart to hand her the bou-
quet of day lilies and daisies I'd cut from around the house.

She stared at me a few minutes before she looked away, caught her
lower lip with her teeth, and shook her head no.

"Pearl, the baby needs you to get up. This isn't going to help it any."

She covered her face with her hands for a moment, then dropped them. "He died thinking I hated him, you know." She was so matter-of-fact, it was scary.

"He went back to her and now they're both dead. Isn't that ironic? It could've been me, then I wouldn't be so all alone. . . ." Her shoulders and chest convulsed with a low moaning sob and she began to cry and shake her head.

I went over and put an arm around her and stroked her head, murmuring, "No, no, you have the baby. You're not alone. Your family's here, Pearl. We won't let anything more happen, I promise." I kissed her hair and hugged her as I should've done with Lukey. When she'd calmed down again, she curled into a ball, pulled the corner of a sheet up, and put it in her mouth and started to suck with her eyes closed.

"I'll come back later with some food. Try to get up, Pearl, take a bath. The vote on Heart Hogs is tonight, you coming?" I thought the idea of combat might get her charged, but she hiccuped and lifted her fingers at me and curled tighter. "Take care," I whispered, and tiptoed out of there, being careful not to let the front door rattle as I pulled it to.

Birdeene said Pearl had come to McCall's funeral with Copeland Harder Jr., but wouldn't speak to anyone. I hadn't been able to bring myself to go, not when I'd cursed him so many times, and Birdeene came in and told us how shameful it was for Dayrell to let his family down again, disappearing and not bothering to show up. Lukey's family had taken her away to the hills before I could find out anything. McCreavey looked embarrassed because there wasn't much left of her to send along when I went over to the funeral home and asked. I felt terrible, missing my friend, wishing I'd had more time with her.

And it'd been over a week since Dayrell had taken off too, and I was beginning to worry about him, and about us. How was I going to find him?

"Moline?" The big black Ford pulled to the curb beside me and Jos leaned across the front seat to talk out the window at me. "Get in."

Copeland Harder Jr. was on his way over to the cafe for lunch with some old man in overalls and a worn-out red plain flannel shirt who looked an awful lot like Uncle Able. I turned and squinted, wondering if Walker knew he was on the loose with Cope. What if after all the trouble they sold the hotel and farm to the hog people and I had to find a new job? I sure couldn't go back to Minnesota. Homeless and jobless. Where I started out years ago. I hadn't made it very far after all, and I was glad Mister and Iberia weren't around to rub my nose in it.

"So . . ." Jos turned to me as we waited for traffic at the four-way stop by the courthouse. "How long you staying?" There was an edge to her voice that made me cautious, even though she wore a half smile and her long fingers tapped the steering wheel lightly to an imaginary tune she kept picking up in the back of her throat like another conversation she was having.

"I don't know. Why?" We watched as a Mennonite buggy took its slow turn, the horse walking lazily, the family under the black roof staring straight ahead except for the little girl in back, who was trying to see everything at once without turning her head directly away from her mother in front of her.

"Just wondering. Your aunt seems to be keeping you pretty busy." Jos followed the family's progress with her eyes, leaning forward when they threatened to disappear from view around the corner.

"She can get on your nerves, can't she?" I laughed.

Jos smiled. "Titus's sister is a lot like her."

"How's she doing?"

"She's a lawyer now. Anyway, your aunt's at our place planning tonight's meeting." She eased the car forward, continuing to look both ways through the intersection. When we made it safely across, she glanced at me and laughed. "Kids make me cautious."

"How's the vote look?"

"We might actually win, but I'm not sure what that means exactly. Pearl and the others are right about us needing more jobs and cash flow to keep the town alive."

I let my eyes follow two teenage girls walking toward the center of town. They were still at that stage where they needed to clutch their purses in front of them to hide their chests, their thin shoulders and backs hunched against the weight of the future their bodies were trying to push them up into. They both had pimples scattered like freckles across their cheeks and the I-couldn't-care-less hairdos whose chaos was sprayed stiffly in place. Even though it was going to be ninety again today, they were wearing men's tee shirts with loose flannel shirts thrown on top, baggy jeans with holes in the knees, and black combat boots, as if they'd gone

AWOL from a hip army camp. The new puritans, covering all their flesh. I felt sorry for them having to work so hard at being something in this heat and wondered suddenly about my son. I hoped he wasn't too hot or cold at this moment. I hoped he wasn't ashamed of himself. I hoped he knew he did all right leaving and staying away. I hoped he knew I loved him. The feeling seemed obvious and simple for the first time, as if I'd never thought or believed it before. My eyes started to fill and my throat got that thick raw lump so I couldn't swallow.

"You okay?" Jos drove slowly around the courthouse, past the Pinkneys' restored house and the three-story stone Orphans' Home turned Gospel Music Center.

"Actually, it's been hard coming back here. Things I left behind . . . well, coming here, I thought they'd all get resolved, and I could start a new life or something. Isn't quite working out that way."

"I know what you mean." She turned the corner and pulled up to the cemetery gates. "Seems like we drag our histories with us wherever we go, like a bunch of old clothes we can't bear to part with. You and Titus, for example. And maybe when we try to start over again, we're really just adding a new item to the old wardrobe."

She put her hand on my arm. "Moline, don't forget about the Lord. Whatever that means for you, don't forget about the Spirit. Don't forget about love. . . ." She leaned over and gave me an awkward hug and I found myself pressing her thick black hair with my lips, tasting the smell of lemon and honey from her shampoo. I didn't exactly know what she was forgiving me for in that instant, but I understood it.

We separated and laughed and she said, "Let's drive down and see if that creek's behaving itself."

The tombstones were lopsided and stained with mud, but the creek had returned to its ordinary strip of ankle-deep water. On the hills beyond, the Negro cemetery looked calmly down on the scene as Lee Pettimore on his lawn mower chugged into view, followed by three workmen with shovels and rakes—one white, two black—who stopped and leaned on their implements while Lee gave them instructions. In another week, all evidence of that afternoon would be erased, and I felt sad for that.

Jos let me out in front of my house, which was still such a wreck I didn't bother going inside before walking uptown. The Dairy Daddy was jammed with the lunch crowd. Two little kids reminded me of Lukey's, and I felt sadder worrying what they were feeling. That last haunting image of Lukey about to say something as the truck pulled away seemed to float just in front of me, making it seem like I could grab her back, stuff her in the safety of the hotel, not let her near that truck and McCall. I hadn't listened carefully enough, hadn't seen how fragile her life really was, and now . . . The tears started and I wiped at them all the way back to the hotel, where Walker was waiting for my report on Pearl. I hadn't realized how many would be undone by McCall when I pushed and pressed and fought against him.

Last night my son had come back in my dreams. We were all together and happy. We were all laughing and horsing around down at the spot by the Hungry where I used to go as a kid with our family and later with Titus and Dayrell. Tyler was seven, the happy age when his front teeth were missing and his brown hair got gold streaks from the sun, and I was teaching him how to catch crawdaddies which made him gasp with wonder. Paris had come and brought presents for everyone, because it turned out she'd just been away traveling. Her death was a mistake, after all. Iberia and Mister had foolish grins on their faces, like dogs so darn happy to see you they lift their lips and click their teeth, crouch down and beat your legs with their wagging tails.

Then Lukey had shown up in a hippie bus, trailing bright scarves and long, long golden hair. I love you, I love you, I kept telling her, and then I had felt something behind me and turned and there was Duncan as tall and handsome as he was that first time I saw him in his baseball uniform after the College World Series game they'd won, walking into the Bronco Burger in North Omaha with his buddies.

He was the most lovely man I'd ever seen, bathed in white and gold, his uniform so clean and pure it looked like he'd never worn it before. My heart got big in my chest, pushing against my lungs so I could barely breathe. Here he was, here was the man I was going to marry, here was the man I'd love. And I started sobbing, choking with the worst pain and sadness I'd ever felt, because it was true, I loved him, I *had* loved Duncan. I had never admitted it, though. I always felt like I had to hold something back, something little and hard that kept making me feel like I was lying when I said "I love you" back to him. All those years I had lied to myself thinking I was lying to him. "I loved you," I sobbed. His face got so kind and understanding I could barely stand it, and he put his arms around me, kissing my tears and hugging me. "I know, Moline—I always knew. I loved you too."

I had woken up with a start and immediately tried to go back to say something more. I touched my face, but it was dry. My chest had felt torn and empty, though, like I'd been crying as hard as I dreamed I was. My body felt like it'd been there, with those people I couldn't stand to leave now, couldn't stand to think I'd lost all of them, and could only hope they forgave me. Taking responsibility wasn't enough. Finally, it depended on other people too, the good part of them that said, Okay, you've suffered enough, come back to us, come back and be a part of our family, you're forgiven. I forgave everybody, but it seemed that no one forgave me. Not until last night. All morning I felt the soreness of sorrow in my chest and the longing for Dayrell, who couldn't not love me, no matter what he said.

"Come on now. We have work to do. I need help making dinner before the vote tonight." She was dressed in her white high-top sneakers which glowed fluorescent in the shadows of the room and white Bermuda shorts that made her long, bony legs look like old tree limbs stripped of bark. She had on an old sleeveless white blouse and her hair clumped damply on her forehead.

"We should eat out," I muttered, following her into the kitchen.

"You just sit here and snap these beans. Lost the peas in the heat when Able was laid up. Now he's bound and determined to get back on that ladder. At his age. I said, Fine, you just do that, but first we're going to Copeland Harder's and get our wills straightened out—with your luck, you'll fall on me this time and kill us both, and I don't want a bunch of haggling like happened after Horras's funeral." She lit the burner, slammed the big black cast iron skillet on, and poured a dollop of congealed bacon grease from the can sitting over the stove. She tipped the skillet and watched the grease skid across the bottom.

"What're you making?" I picked up the empty yellow china bowl and put it in my lap and tipped the paper bag of beans over on the table.

"Pork chops, pan gravy, and rice. Just what the doctor ordered for the whole lot of you. Put some spine in the men and some sense in the women. And you'd better get to snapping faster'n that or we'll be having the beans for dessert. Should cook a day in bacon or fat back, but don't have time. Have to serve them Yankee style and hope everyone's too busy to notice. . . ."

"How that house of yours coming along?" It seemed like she was wearing this sly expression when she looked over her shoulder at me after she dragged the pink chops through the flour and tested the grease.

"It's not. Saw a snake in there the other day."

"What do you mean?" She dropped the chops in the splattering grease and stepped back from the popping.

"Rat snake looking for mice, I guess. Came up in the hole in my kitchen floor. Honest." I snapped beans in earnest for a minute.

"I don't know, Moline." She picked up the edge of the first chop to check for brownness. "I suppose it could be. Always said there was something wrong with that house. And Iberia claimed she saw an awful lot of snakes there when you were a youngster. I put it down to overactive glands. Estes was a terror on the snakes she found, even as a child. She could've cleared all of DeWight County if Daddy'd let her."

The kitchen was filling up with that burned grease smell as she turned the chops. I snapped faster, trying to keep the rhythm so I didn't end up reversing where I put the ends and the bodies. "Heat's getting to the beans too," I said, when I noticed how big and yellow some were getting and how they wanted to pop out when the ends were too soft to snap.

"Maybe the heat'll dry things out. We sure could use that. Had enough rain to last the summer. Too bad it had to come in one bunch like it did. The corn's shot to hell out there at the farm. Got it in too late and the rain swamped it. Hay didn't get baled in time, either. Able can't keep running both places, and I'm too damn tired. Time I started enjoying my golden years, with or without that old fool keeps insisting he can patch the roof. Least I made him call Hale Bell to go up there and help him this time. I was thinking, Moline, since you got no place to live now, with all your remodeling, maybe you should go out there for the rest of the summer and keep things going." She wiped her hands on the skirt of the flour-sack bib apron she was wearing.

I stared at the beans and they didn't say a word, so I looked out the window, where the heat had laid a mirror on everything so it shimmered back at you. "I don't know what to say, Walker. I'm, well, I really appreciate the offer, I do. It's just that . . . I don't have any money, there wasn't anything left after Duncan's illness and funeral, and I sort of need the job here to survive."

"We'll work something out. If you're careful, you can make it pay, too. Hire yourself some cheap help. Couldn't do much more damage than Able's been doing over the years. Why don't you run on out there tomorrow and see what you think? You could do a lot worse. Your cousin has. Imagine taking on motherhood at forty-one. Too bad McCall wasn't a bull instead of a man—we could have made some real money off that kind of potency." She wiped her hands again and pulled a net bag of apples from the shelf beside the sink. "Pie," she explained.

"What's going to happen to Pearl?"

"She'll be fine. She has her house, and don't let her working fool you. She's got something from Estes and her mother still. Pearl's as tight-fisted as an old nesting hen. She's got the first and last penny her fingers ever touched." Standing at the counter, she began to unravel an apple in one continuous peel that made me want to play with it like we did as kids.

A farm of my own until fall or winter. I couldn't make sense of it—too big, too unreal.

"What about Heart Hogs? Aren't you afraid of losing the farm?"

"Well, to tell you the truth, the winds are shifting a little, it seems. Titus and I filed our own injunction against the company three days ago, and Pearl has yet to respond. Unless she said something this morning when you went to see her." She stopped and stared at me.

I shook my head. "I don't think she gives a darn about pigs at this point, Walker. She's really, really sad. I'm worried. I was thinking maybe you could go down there and talk to her, get her back on her feet."

"Before the vote? Now what kind of sense would that make unless she wanted to come in with us?"

"I mean it, Walker. I'm worried about her, and the baby. She's not eating right, she's just crying, locked in that closed-up house all day. You have to do something. She'll listen to you—she's used to the older generation telling her what to do."

"I swore I'd never step foot in that house again after the way my sister treated Able when we got married, and I've stayed true to my word for fifty-some years. No point in breaking a record like that now, especially for a girl who's trying to steal everything I have in the world."

We worked in silence for a while, letting the dull snap of the beans and the hiss of the knife peeling apples speak our minds.

"Still—" I finally said.

She slammed the knife and apple down. "All right! My lord, girl, don't you ever give a person any peace?"

"Tonight?"

"First thing in the morning, I promise. Now leave me be or I won't have supper ready in time to go to the meeting and vote." She dropped another peel into the growing pile and cored the apple.

"One more thing . . ."

"What now?"

"Do you know where Lukey's family lives? I didn't get a chance to say goodbye, and I'm worried about the kids."

"I know. It's a terrible thing." Walker stopped peeling and bent her head. "That poor child. Such a good, good heart. I was beginning to love her like my own. Guess her folks are heartsick too. Took her on home to the hills. I'll find out from someone at the meeting tonight where her mother lives. And those two youngsters . . . If McCall weren't dead, I'd kill him myself."

"Wish we could've done something more for her, don't you?"

"That'll be my regret to my dying day, Moline. I should've interfered— they'd both be alive. I think about that, and there's no mistaking, it's my burden. Taught me a lesson." She let her face get old and work its way down her body, collapsing something inside her as it went along. This was what tired us: not work, not love, but the holding up of all the burdens we created and carried, bent double, until gradually we collapsed back into the earth, glad to have it over and done with, glad for the forgiveness the cool, moist darkness promised.

"That wasn't anything you could control. She loved him too much to let him go, no matter what he did."

Her voice got quiet, and with her head bowed over the sink, I could barely hear her words. "We can't be for sure."

"No, she loved him too much."

"And he never loved anyone enough. Isn't it all such a mystery?"

I finished the beans and brushed the dirt off my lap.

"Never seen such a summer, not in a long, long time. But they always say the chickens come home to roost." Walker finished slicing the last apple and reached for the flour bin to make the pie dough.

"It really was him, McCall, who set the fires, you know." I looked down at the bowlful of beans and over at the table where the last scrawny pieces lay shriveling in the crumbles of dirt on the side of the bag.

"I heard that from Titus and Monroe Sharpe. Figures. Poor Dayrell, having to spend his life with a brother like that." She mixed the dough with her hands, made a damp-looking ball, and dropped it in the middle of a puddle of flour on the waist-high wooden table in the center of the room. She pushed the rolling pin into the middle of the dough and rocked back and forth until the lump flattened, and she began to roll it out carefully.

"Thought you didn't like him."

"Now where'd you get an idea like that, Moline? And here I was considering whether you should start managing the hotel here if you won't work the farm. Can't have it taken over by a bunch of strangers who won't know a thing about keeping people's teeth on edge in this town. They'll come in and try to dress it up and restrict it so the outsiders don't have a place to sleep. There's a history to this place, and someone needs to keep it alive in all its quirky, ornery glory. You're friendly and you don't mind getting your hands dirty and taking on the town conscience. Best of all, you've been out there in the world and come back. You have something to show these people."

"I don't know, Walker. Give me some time to think. You aren't ready to retire, no matter what you say. I can keep helping out here, but I don't think I'm ready to take over, not yet. Maybe I can be the matriarch in training or something."

Smiling, she draped the dough over the pie plate and pinched the edges, cut the excess off, then set it aside and began the process again. "I can understand that, Moline. And I'll give you a piece of advice while I'm at it. Spend the next few years learning about plumbing, wiring, and carpentry. Wished I had done that—would've saved me from Able's poor excuse of a job many times."

"Let's hope Titus has done his job." Walker marched ahead of me through the door to the auditorium promptly at ten to eight. The entire front five rows were already filled with black people wearing serious expressions as they talked quietly among themselves. Standing in front with Jos, Titus nodded at us with a satisfied look on his face as we sat down on the edge of the sixth row next to the ancient black farm woman and her husband I'd seen that first day at the rally. She and Walker nodded to each other, their thin lips in identical straight lines.

The rest of the room filled quickly, but when I turned to look for Pearl, I was surprised to see that over half the faces were black. The redneck men who had disturbed the last meeting were nowhere to be found—probably because McCall wasn't around. The Heart Hog corporate men were absent too, leaving Odell Meachum to walk to the front of the room alone, then back again, looking for a chair. No suit tonight, I noticed. Copeland Harder Jr. came in and quickly sat in the back row next to Odell, keeping his sunglasses on and not speaking to anyone.

I watched Titus greeting people, getting them places to sit, and thought back over the early years we'd spent together as friends. I remembered this time in junior high school when Titus and I were out in the woods on the natural stone bridge. I'd broken a small branch off a willow where Anderson's pasture met the woods and we had to step over the sagging remains of the rusty hog wire two feet high. I'd peeled the bark in long green strips and was whipping the yellow white stick at Titus.

"Watch it!" he'd yelled when I flicked his arm hard enough to leave a dark welt.

"Back to work!" I laughed.

He looked at me and grabbed the stick and flung it off the bridge. "Don't say that, Moline."

I was feeling that distance rushing across my face, rumbling in my skull. "Why not? We used to own you, Mister said."

He jumped up. "Don't!" He was standing behind me, and I could feel the heat of his legs on either side of my body. What was he going to do?

"You were our slaves. We owned—hey! Jesus Fucking Christ, Titus!"

Grabbing my purse, he threw it off the bridge, and it quickly disappeared in a deep thicket of spring underbrush.

"What's the big goddamned deal, Titus?" But I knew what it was and kept my eyes from looking directly at him as I stood and carefully edged around him, unsure for a moment whether he was going to toss me after the purse or not. It was Paris's little red leather bag with the gold stamp clasp, but that wasn't why my eyes were tearing up. It was the sudden shame of what I'd said, half-prideful, imitating my father the day he'd shown me a copy of the church vestry records listing all the first Bedwell's property, including three slaves, right after the wagon and right before the span of mules, following which was a listing of all the other livestock. I'd never seen evidence before, or heard the peculiar pride in Mister's voice, the way he ignored what it meant as he tapped a thick, freckled finger on the page. "This is the proof," he'd said to my question about black and white Bedwells having the same name. The white family members' names were all listed. Our ancestor, his wife, and their twelve children, living and dead, were all listed by name. Not the slaves, though:

1 Male	$850
1 Female	480
1 Child	40
2 Mules	80

Their dollar worth was noted instead of names, because you had to tithe from the value of your property. Mister had kept rubbing the page with his fingertips, brushing imaginary dirt off with his palm, smoothing it with the edge of his hand.

I had felt an empty place open and yawn like a hungry mouth inside me. A child worth less than a span of mules. Maybe valued less to cheat the Lord, maybe too small to be worth more.

"When they were freed, they took their masters' white names—stole them really, didn't have full names before." Mister had tapped the black ink scrawls as if he could force them back to that burned-down house and make them do the real work of saving it instead of marching off with the first abolitionists who ever bothered to stop at the Bedwells' run-down, sorry-ass farm, and free those three people. Whether they were related as a family or not, the document failed to mention. Whether the child was strong enough to work or not, it never said. They had made it as far as Resurrection and stopped, too tired to go on, and managed to find a friendly family to shelter them. That's all he knew. White Bedwells followed after the war.

After I told Titus the story, I apologized. "I'm sorry. I didn't think . . ."

"It's all right."

"No it's not."

"You had to test it. White people have to do that some time or another. They use the words, "nigger" and the like, or do like you just did. Have to come up to that line, give it a shove. See what will happen. What we'll do—what you'll do. Just the nature of your people, Moline." I'd never forgotten my shame, or the fact that no matter how much I wanted to believe otherwise, a part of me was still my father's daughter, and would have to be watched every day the rest of my life.

A few minutes after the meeting was scheduled to start, some of the white farmers and their wives I'd spoken to were still hurrying in to claim the last chairs, sunburned and tired from the work they'd just left. Nobody talked much, as if this were a grim job ahead of them. Finally, the mayor and the city council filed in and filled the stage, but they didn't smile or campaign.

"It's hot and I know you all are tired," Ross Que, the mayor, began. He was a very tall, solid man with a shy streak, who looked over our heads and closed his eyes when he spoke. "So let's just get to it. We've had our discussion. Both sides have had their say. Even the lawyers have had a chance at it. This meeting's been posted for almost a month now, so this vote here tonight makes the decision on Heart Hogs. The council and I have final say, of course, but we want this vote to clearly reflect the community's desires on this issue."

Sheriff Holken and Monroe Sharpe stood up to help count the show of hands and the vote commenced. Being an outsider, I was unsure whether I could vote, but Walker stuck an elbow in my ribs and my arm shot up.

"You're a taxpayer," she muttered.

Just looking around, it was clear we'd packed the room with two-thirds of the hands waving in the air. "A hundred and thirty-five against," Monroe said.

Odell was slumped in his chair, arms folded across his chest, face pale and sweaty. Cope looked down at the floor as if he'd lost something there. Some of the white farmers looked disgusted as they voted for Heart Hogs. Now they'd have to go back to struggling to make ends meet.

"Thirty-nine for," the sheriff said.

Nobody clapped or booed, but the blinking fluorescent light up front decided to finally quit, and a corner of the room went gray.

"That about does it," Ross Que said, and the council members behind him nodded. They weren't going to rock any boats.

By the time we stood up, Cope and Odell had already slipped out.

"We'll reconvene in the basement of the Free African Baptist Church," Titus announced in a loud voice. I knew "we" didn't include me. Passing Walker, me, and Able, who'd come in unnoticed to vote, Titus looked in our direction and nodded slightly. Things would never be the same with us, I guess. Like Jos said, we were each other's old clothes, hung way back in the closet, waiting to rot into rags.

The next morning I got up early to the banging of someone on the hotel roof overhead. I threw on some clothes and quickly climbed up to find Able seated behind his telescope, scanning the town on the far side of the roof, just out of earshot of the roofer. The sound of the banging made me shade my eyes and look up at the eaves that rose over the flat part where I was standing. Hale Bell had one knee braced on the roof with the other leg extended behind him, like a runner about to start a sprint. He was pounding shingles.

"Hey, Mr. Bell—hello, stop!" I called, and climbed the short ladder to talk to him.

He stood up, bracing lopsided on the slope. "Miz Bedwell." He hefted the hammer in his hand.

"Uncle Able's got you working here too?"

He frowned and tucked his chin to look down at me. I couldn't see a trace of either son in him, except maybe the small, alert eyes that reminded me of McCall. "Your aunt and I hashed this whole thing out yesterday on the phone. Now don't tell me I got to go around that same bush with you too."

"What bush is that?"

He heaved a sigh like talking to me was a worse chore than roofing in hundred-degree heat. His chest and back were burned bright pink, which made the gray hairs stand out like frosted grass. "Like I told Walker, we had our share of misfortune of late, so this here job is gonna be late. I can't say more than that."

"Where's Dayrell?"

316

He squatted down, using the hammer to keep his balance against the roof. "Now listen, Moline, don't go asking around about him. Sheriff is looking to blame somebody for all the trouble lately, and my boy is the closest candidate now that his brother's—" He looked at the roof, sniffed, and wiped his nose between his thumb and forefinger. "I don't know where Dayrell is. I hope he's so far south of here he's eating crawdaddies and listening to Dixieland jazz."

"He wouldn't just—"

"Moline, please. I got McCall's kids and ex-wives stacked to the ceiling to take care of. I got a business to run on my own now, at my age—so please, don't say anything, just let it go, okay? Let my boy be, he's not very straight in the head right now, and—and I can't lose another one, you see?"

"I just want to help, Mr. Bell. . . ." I could feel the darkness trying to come down on me again. Dayrell in trouble, needing me.

"My boys—well, my boys just weren't ever very lucky." He looked across at the hotel roof in the direction of Pearl's house, and I wondered if he knew about the baby on the way. "And if a person ain't lucky, they don't have much luck in love either, you see. I know, I can tell you the difference. I been lucky all my life up till now. Best not set your hopes on Dayrell, he's—well, he's run out of what little luck he ever had, I'm afraid." He stood and shaded his eyes and looked at me. "I best be getting back to work now."

"Mr. Bell?"

He was back in his running-roofing position and turned to look at me. "Yeah?"

"Don't you know where he is?"

"Couldn't say. Haven't seen him since his brother—" His hand shaking, he set a nail and started pounding again.

I climbed down and walked over to where Able sat at his telescope, the little stone Lukey had given me for luck bumping like a thumb at my throat keeping track of my blood. I'd forgotten about our stones. Maybe Dayrell's was working for him; maybe his father was lying.

"Best leave Hale alone, Moline. A man of sorrows. Will be for a good while. He's not the only one. You don't find Dayrell at home, you go out to the farm. Saw a campfire down by the creek in that big pasture those horses claim. Can't think who else it might be. Tell him I said to get that bricking done now we got some nice weather." He shook his head. "There goes Cope and his little red-haired secretary."

"Thanks, Uncle Able." I kissed his cheek.

"Come here," he said. "Take a look at this fella opening that cellular phone place."

"I have to go. Keep track of things while I'm gone, okay?"

He grinned and waved without taking his eye from the telescope.

25

SOUTH OF RESURRECTION

The innoxious little green tree snake is believed to carry a deadly poison. It is called the snake doctor, and is supposed to cure all other kinds of snakes when they are sick or injured. I once found a large timber rattler which had been badly wounded, apparently by deer or goats. An old hunter who was present said "Look out for the doctor!" and began to search the bushes nearby. Sure enough, in a few minutes he found one of these little green snakes in a blackberry bush.

— OZARK MAGIC AND FOLKLORE

"WHY DIDN'T THEY TELL ME, damn it?" I was looking at the pile of black ash and rubble that used to be Dayrell's trailer and shack. The trunk of the tree the dogs used to be tied to was black all the way up to where the limbs branched out, and the needles were scorched on that whole side. He'd burned everything he owned—all those stars on the ceiling, all those dreams in the dark sky gone. No wonder he wasn't here. He hadn't been, had he? Someone would've said something instead of . . . No, Dayrell was alive, Able had said so, and I could feel it.

I drove carefully around the site twice, watching for the shards of broken glass that had exploded into the surrounding weeds when the fire got hot enough. I didn't know what I was looking for, a clue maybe, a something, but all I could see was a tiger swallowtail butterfly floating over the dark glistening ruin as if it were a black flower streaked with sweet yellow pollen. Some dragonflies with fluorescent blue bodies and cellophane-transparent wings staggered by and locked onto each other as I sat there listening to Hungry Creek gurgling on the other side of the matted-down brush. Where would he go? How far, how far would I have to drive to find him? But Able had pointed me to the farm, he'd know if anyone did. I headed my truck down Dayrell's driveway, but had to brake hard as the two dogs ran out of the underbrush into the road and stood facing me, tongues hanging, tails drooping, and rough coats full of burrs and dirt. I put them in back, figuring they needed to find Dayrell as much as I did now.

I parked near the old, unlicensed brown pickup Able kept for farm use, and let loose the dogs, who promptly took off into the fields. There was no sign of Dayrell up by the house and barns. I hurried down to the corral, where the horses were standing by the water tank keeping the cows away and slapping flies. Harry Truman had his lips resting an inch into the water pretending he was drinking while he slept, using Jimmy Carter's big body as shade. Jimmy eyed me when I came through the gate, but didn't do more than flick an ear back and up. "It's okay, you're all right," I told him, and snapped the rope on his halter.

I hadn't brought the saddle or bridle from the cow barn, only grabbed a rope hanging on the fence, I was in such a hurry to find him. I finally managed to climb backwards up the steps of the ladder leaning against the barn and convince Jimmy he could come right under me so I could drop on his back. I kicked off my shoes and let my bare feet dangle against his warm sides. On my way through I pulled the gate leading out to the pasture shut so Harry wouldn't follow and hassle us.

The hay was down, having been cut and then ruined by too much rain; it lay in long tan rows smothering the new green trying to replace it. The grasshoppers kept up a steady whirring and sawing, jumping just ahead of us all the way across the wide field into the woods.

When I got to the creek, I saw the tent and some of his stuff beside the campfire, but no Dayrell. My stomach got balloon light with worry. I'd have to wait, but didn't dare get off Jimmy without some way to get back on in case Dayrell didn't come back till dark. I couldn't let Jimmy Carter graze for fear he'd pull me off, so I put the rope under my butt, brought it over my thigh, and took two wraps around my hand, then lay back with my head on his rump so we could close our eyes together in the shade of the trees by the little creek. There were all kinds of sparrows twittering in the branches overhead, a woodpecker thumping on a tree trunk, water shushing along the gravel creek bottom, and insects rattling in the weeds. . . .

I must've been dozing because the next thing I knew, there was a big noise and something pulling me over Jimmy's rump, only the rope wrapped around my hand was pulling Jimmy back too and then up and up and I was flying toward the ground and Jimmy was snorting and dancing around my upside-down body, trying not to step on me.

"Whoa, whoa! Hold still—Jesus Christ, hold still!" Dayrell said, and I tried to look through the tangle of legs and bodies to see him. Jimmy steadied and looked around at me like I was some kind of new idiot, while I managed to loosen the rope, which had wrenched my wrist good. Dayrell appeared at my head, bending down to the deep grass where I was lying.

"Don't let him go—I can't walk back in my bare feet," I said. He nodded and tied the horse to the trunk of a medium-sized hackberry tree.

"You okay?" He sat down beside me. He looked terrible, worn out, hollow eyed and cheeked, like he'd lost too much weight too fast. He hadn't shaved in days, and his hair was tangled with bits of dirt and twigs. "You're lucky nothing happened—what the hell were you thinking?"

I reached out to pull a dried leaf from his hair and he flinched and grabbed my wrist. "What's wrong with you?" I snapped as I pulled it away.

"Don't want anyone touching me." He laid back in the thick green and put his arm over his eyes, his fingers too loose and lifeless. His whole body looked like a sofa somebody'd pulled the stuffing out of.

"I went to your place, what happened?"

"Burned it. Burned everything. Burned the truck. Time to let go of it all—burned it. Decided I'm leaving—can't stay here."

I had to think. If I said the wrong thing I could drive him off. "I found the dogs—"

"Turned 'em loose. Don't want 'em—don't want anything."

"Not even me?"

"It's no good, Moline."

"No, shhh, that's not true, Dayrell. It wasn't your fault what happened. I love you, I want to help. Please, can't you forgive me?"

"Oh, Moline, don't you understand at all? I forgave you a long time ago. It wasn't anything you had to do with. You had to run. That's not the point."

I had to do it, touch him, and at first it was just my hand covering his, then my lips pressed against his fingers, searching for the current of blood I knew I could find and follow up the inside of his arm with the tip of my tongue, to the place under his arm, the wet, dark nest that smelled like all the things he was full of—worry and sorrow and work—and I kissed there, and went to his neck, to the place where the vein got thick and blue, pressing out against the tan skin like a long bruised stem, up under his chin, to his ear, letting the tip of my tongue enter the whorls of rigid flesh, until his breath quickened and he growled something deep in his throat and pulled my mouth to his.

It wasn't like any kissing we'd done before. It was harsh, filled with his anger and hurt, and everything went too far and too hard. He slammed me down into the grass, holding my hands over my head, biting my neck, and I fought back, biting his shoulder until I tasted the metallic salt like a bloody penny and we contended against each other trying not to break apart while we pushed so deeply into the grass I could hear the tiny tick and buzz of insects at the roots when he stopped, not waiting or caring where I was as he rolled off me just far enough away that we weren't touching.

I opened my eyes and saw that his little silver cross was gone and it made me mad. "Is this what you wanted?" I straddled him with my knees bent on his shoulders and arms, holding him still before he could do any-thing. I stuck my fingertip in the bubble of blood and smeared it on his cheek. "Is this it, Dayrell—does it feel good? Bleed and wash away your sins?" His eyes had this crazy darkness in them, darker than I'd ever seen, like the gold lights had gone out for good. "Stop it," I said, and went to slap him and he slipped his hand out and grabbed my wrist, digging his fingernails into the thin underside so it pinched. Then his dogs galloped across the creek and stopped next to us, panting hungrily, flinging saliva on our faces as they shook and licked.

"Let me up, Moline! Get out of here, Winifred, Bob—git, go—go on!" he yelled, but the dogs ignored him, backing up only a foot and dropping to their bellies.

"Are you mad? Good and mad now? Not feeling sorry for yourself any-more?" I rolled off him.

He stood without a word, looking down at me like I was something left in a ruined field after a flood. His eyes were muddy with it, and I guessed mine might be too. He reached down and held out his hand, and when I took it he jerked me to my feet. I wanted him to hug me then, just to stop it from running away from us, but he didn't. The dogs thumped their tails wildly and whimpered, but he refused to look their way. He untied the horse, boosted me up, and swung up behind me, ignoring Jimmy's inquiring look at the extra weight and jamming his heels in his sides instead. The dogs leapt up without invitation and stood beside us, watching us anxiously. Jimmy took off at a fast trot that broke into a canter and a dead gallop as soon as we cleared the woods, the dogs barking wildly as they raced beside us. With Dayrell's weight pressing me forward, all I could do was clamp my legs and hang on to the mane whipping my face with little stinging blows.

At the corral, he slid off, opened the gate into the barnyard, pulled me off, and half carried, half threw me in the shade while he went back and chased the horses and cows out into the field. Jimmy needed to be walked out, but I wasn't going to argue at that point. He'd probably be okay with Harry nudging him along back down to the woods. The dogs waited with me, moaning softly and panting from their run.

Dayrell came back and stood over me, blocking the sun, his face a dark stain in the middle of all that light. "Get this straight, Moline: Leave me alone! Hear? Go away. You left before, you know how to do that—now get out of here. See what just happened—that's it, that's the way it is now! So run—git! Go on!" He waved his arms and the dogs flattened into the grass. I knew I should get up and leave—there was a terrible shame inside me at his treating me this way—but I sat there, waiting him out.

"No. I'm not going, not this time. No way—no." I stood up. "I'm not running from you anymore!"

He started forward with his fists clenched at his sides and I thought, Now he's going to beat me up, but he didn't, he stepped back, glared at the house, then the barn, and stepped back again. The dogs jumped up, wagging their tails.

"No, don't, Dayrell—don't!" But he was in Able's old brown truck, backing around in a cloud of dust, before I climbed in my truck with the dogs and got the engine started, and he was sliding past me and out the driveway before I turned around, with the two dogs scrambling for footing on the backseat.

Following him down the dirt road was easy with the dust leaving this big plumy trail, but the blacktop was harder. He was pressing seventy and eighty around the curves, and I could see the truck wobble and lean, threatening to go out of control. I kept praying there wouldn't be anybody in his way, because I didn't know how he'd avoid smashing them. I prayed for a cop too, but that might make matters worse—what if he resisted arrest, tried running, tried. . . ? The dogs whined and cried, digging their nails into the soft gray leather seat.

He ran the red light at the intersection with 23 into town, but nobody got hurt. I stopped and waited while three other cars turned to follow the road he was on. "Stay out of his way, stay out of his way," I chanted until the light flicked green and I stomped on it, leaving a long trail of burning rubber and flying gravel. He didn't slow down through Raymond or Laurie, but I did, I couldn't afford to get stopped and lose him. It looked like he was going to the lake. Christ, I didn't want to think about what that meant—Bagnell Dam.

I lost him before we got to Sunrise Beach, and I didn't know whether he'd turned off or gone on to Camdenton, but I had a feeling he was somewhere near, so I kept driving on through all the way to Osage Beach, going up and down the strip, past the huge outlet center, the water slides, the restaurants, the hillbilly-theme miniature golf course, and motels perched like small, colorful scabs on the bone of hills overlooking the lake.

"Come on, Dayrell, come on—I know you're here, tell me where you are, come on." I rolled down the windows and the dogs stuck their heads out and sniffed at the air and whined some more. Finally I had to stop for gas and the bathroom and decided to go back to Camdenton. I didn't see Able's truck up there, and drove behind and around the McDonald's, Hardee's, Ozark Gifts, the little strip with JP's Custom Boots on the corner, but no Dayrell. I drove back to Osage Beach and on around to the cutoff for the dam, crossing it on the narrow road, trying not to look down for fear the truck would follow me over, for fear I'd see him dropping down and down with the millions of gallons it took to make the 215,000 kilowatts of power they bragged about, for fear I'd see him becoming part of that conversion of water winding in and out of Missouri hills and caves, to come up to this one place, give over its secret life, and plunge away, lost forever.

I couldn't face that, so I drove back to Osage Beach's strip and decided to check all the bars. The third place was down a dirt road on the edge of a cove. The bar was actually part of a restaurant stuck onto the side of a bait-and-boat rental shop run by the owners of a little resort that was old enough to be having trouble competing with the big chains and newer places that were being built in the current boom. The little forties cottages staggering up the hill were newly painted a pink fleshy tone and on each small concrete apron that served as a porch sat a metal lawn chair with the tulip-shaped back and seat painted the same tone. Although I didn't see the brown truck, I parked and left the dogs in my truck with the windows partly down, ignoring their worried noses smearing the glass as I walked across the dirt parking lot.

Dayrell was sitting at a table in the far corner, the only dark spot between two walls of windows. There were several men in various kinds of dirt-and-grease-splotched work clothes and gimme caps perched on the backs of their heads sitting at the bar, drinking beer and smoking cigarettes one after another. Not a vacation crowd.

"Draft and a glass of water," I said to the bartender, who produced a red plastic basket of popcorn along with the drinks. I paid and had trouble trying to pick up the glasses and the basket at the same time, until one of the men slid off his stool, took the glass of beer, and followed me over to the table. I thanked him and sat down. He touched the bill of his hat and looked at Dayrell curiously because he did look like hell with the dried blood on his cheek, his tangled hair, and his face wearing a kind of wife-beater expression that said I must be crazy coming over to bother him again.

"I told you to leave me alone," he muttered through gritted teeth, and looked away out at the rainbowed water lapping at the dock, nudging an empty cigarette pack and a plastic cup against the dark wood.

I drank some beer, which was cold enough to sting the roof of my mouth. "Well, I'm not going to do that, Dayrell. Might as well get used to it, I'm here to stay."

"You can't save anything here, Moline. 'When I see the blood, I shall pass over thee,'" he said, quoting one of the old-time hymns, but wouldn't look at me.

"Yeah, well, 'Everybody I met seemed to be a rank stranger'—so what?" I said, but he ignored me.

We sat there for a while, the bartender fetching Dayrell's tequila shots and beer backs, and me switching to ice tea so I could drive when the time came, and watching the sea gulls and sparrows and ducks coming and going about their business, regardless of how dirty the water was in that little cove. Further out on the lake, the speedboats and jet skis criss-crossed each other in a steady drone like big city traffic. The sun shone and glittered the lake and the sky hung blue and innocent as all get out. The only dark place in the world at that moment was sitting right beside me, and I had to figure some way to bring him back before he got lost to me for good.

The men at the bar had been watching us for some time, eyeing my grass-stained clothes and bare feet the bartender had ignored, noticing the swollen bite mark on Dayrell's shoulder when his shirt pulled at the neck. They weren't bad men, they just had some time on their hands and the kind of curiosity that arrives after a while in an afternoon of drinking. One of them got up and put some quarters in the jukebox, playing some old Freddy Fender songs, "Wasted Days and Wasted Nights" and "Before the Next Teardrop Falls," things like that, followed by Dale Watson's "Liars Hall of Fame" and "Cheatin' Heart Attack." I could tell that after a few more songs and another pitcher, we were going to have some action, those men, Dayrell, and me.

When I got up to go to the bathroom, the man who'd helped me origi-nally was being egged on by his buddies to ask me if I needed help in there too. They noted that I must be a real rough ride too from the looks of Dayrell's neck, and something about what else that mouth of mine could do, which I hoped Dayrell didn't hear. By the time I got back, Dayrell was pushing his chair out and standing unsteadily. Two of the men had slipped off their stools and were putting their cigarettes out in the ash-trays. I tried to move in between, but I wasn't agile enough, and Dayrell walked around me to the waiting men.

"Say that again," Dayrell slurred.

"You're drunk, man—go sleep it off," the bartender urged, his hands under the bar.

"Dayrell, come on." I touched his arm and he jerked away, catching me with his elbow and throwing me off balance into the waiting arms of one of the men, who was standing behind us. I shrugged him off. "Dayrell . . ."

"Come on, Day-rell, push me around instead of the woman." The shorter of the two men shoved his face closer and Dayrell swung at it with his forearm, clipping the guy on the chin because he didn't expect any speed out of a drunk. The other guy caught Dayrell in the stomach with one blow, and the side of the head with the other, sending him crashing into the tables next to the window.

The bartender slammed a two-by-four on the top of the bar with such a bang, the action stopped. "Get the hell out of here!" he ordered Dayrell and me. The men didn't move as I pulled him up and led him out to the parking lot, staggering with the unsteady weight of his body.

"Fucking shit! Coulda killed that fucker—"

"Shut up, Dayrell, just shut up." I started the truck, turned on the air with the windows open, waiting for it to cool down. The dogs took turns wetting Dayrell's neck and hair down with their tongues until he shoved them off.

"Where's Able's truck?" I asked.

"Quit on me, like everything else—died," he mumbled.

"You mean you drove it into the ground," I said. "Now listen, I'm getting a little tired of this self-pity crap. I know you feel bad about your brother. I know it's awful painful to lose him, but you cannot go on blaming yourself. He got drunk and died. You couldn't save him. And Lukey, well, she didn't want to be without him. You want to feel bad, feel bad about her."

He stopped rolling his head back and forth against the headrest as if he were fighting something and seemed to sober some. "I did it before."

I shut the windows with the power switch. "Did what?"

"Saved his ass when he killed that girl. Went to prison for him." He squeezed his eyes tight and tears rolled down his cheeks.

"You took the blame and he let you? You're nuts. That saved him? Weren't you listening to him? It ruined his life. Lukey's too."

He nodded and gulped and made fists and hit his thighs, but the tears came out anyway. "Felt like I deserved what I got—prison. I hated the way my mom looked when she visited me in the hospital. And Hale. They were counting on me for something. They just didn't realize I'd already done it."

"It's none of it your fault, Dayrell—you did the best you could. We all did." The dogs got real still as he started choking and crying, and I held him, which was about all we could do for each other in the long run, I figured, give the comfort grief needed.

When he quieted down, I asked him again if he really could forgive me. He stared at me with those red, pain-filled eyes and said, "What else could you do?" And I felt that weight of responsibility that comes with forgiveness.

"No more running away," I said.

"No more running," he said.

26

MULBERRIES

. . . One of the state's most distinguished sons, Reinhold Niebuhr . . . recommended a skeptical approach to all things mortal. History, he said, taught the limits of man's nature and, consequently, the importance of foreseeing only modest results from human effort. . . . He preached that while men ought of necessity to strive toward improvement, they should approach their work not with the expectation of certain progress and perfection, but with anticipations of error and folly.

— MISSOURI: A HISTORY

✳

THE MULBERRIES HAD BEEN RIPENING every day in the trees down by the charred remains of the hog barn, and when I got up I decided to take a paper bag and collect as many as I could to make a pie for the Fourth, which was the next day. When I'd called Walker and told her I'd take care of the farm like she'd wanted me to, she sounded relieved to have that worry off her shoulders.

"I have my hands full getting the hotel ready for the people who come home once a year for the big Fourth of July celebration," she said.

"Anything I can do besides running this end of things?" I asked.

"Pull some carrots and spinach from the big canning garden out by the cow barn and see if there are any more beans and bring them with you the Fourth. I'm having the whole clan to dinner after the parade."

I shuddered to think who that included. "How's Pearl?" I asked.

"Don't worry—I finally got her out of that house this morning. Threatened to bring the Reverend Bedwells, both of them, to visit her. She's back at work. And I just saw her a minute ago coming out of the House of Pawn door. Wonder what that's about. . . ."

"Well, anyway . . ." I said, glad Walker had a new problem to occupy her.

"You can bring Dayrell too, if you've a mind," she'd said. But I didn't want to put him under any more stress, so I kept quiet about the invitation.

The ripest berries were on the branches above me, and I was in such a good mood, it seemed easy enough to slip my sneakers off, standing in the crushed berries, letting their liquid ooze up and around my toes, turning them purple, and step up onto the lowest branch of the tree. As kids, Pearl and I always made our forts in the mulberries because they were short and easy to climb, and we could eat sitting a few feet above the ground on our little wooden platforms we'd nailed up in trees opposite each other. Those had long since come down, I noticed, but the trees were still easy to climb, even with my slightly stiff knee.

I was busy picking and eating, doing more eating than picking, actually, when I looked out and saw Dayrell walking in my direction, with the dogs weaving around him from one good smell to the next hidden in the weeds and grasses. Dayrell just got up from sleeping, as he had been on and off for four days. Every day he looked and acted a little more alive, like Lazarus moving slowly out of death, struggling to be free again. We'd gotten in the habit of eating lunch and lying down for a nap, and it had a simple domesticity that I liked. Nothing was in much of a hurry to get done, I figured, so why not enjoy the loose wrap of his arms in the fan-rippled air of the big master bedroom looking out over the back of the farm while the cottonwood leaves outside the window glittered like green glass in the afternoon wind and I kept waiting to hear them tinkling?

The dark expression on his face was almost gone now, and he was eating again, and his stride had some of its old grace. He spotted my shoes and came to stand just below my position in the low fork of the two thick branches. I chose a fat juicy berry, mushed it, and plopped it right on his forehead as he looked up.

"Moline!" he laughed, wiping the juice away.

"Dayrell!" I threw another one, aiming for his face again. This one splashed on his cheek. He laughed and wiped again, noticing that the stain was staying on his hands.

"You do that again and—"

I plunged my hand into the paper bag, grabbed a handful, squeezing them enough that they were nice and pulpy, and dropped them on his upturned face. He didn't bother wiping this time. He quickly grabbed a branch and hoisted himself up to where I was, and before I had a chance to move, he took a handful of berries and rubbed them on my cheeks.

"Okay," I laughed, and took another bunch and smeared his face some more, plus his neck. He took my palm and licked it, sucking the berry pulp from between my fingers in long slow swipes.

Our hands met in the bag and we took turns smearing our hands and our arms to the elbows. Holding them out for comparison, we laughed at the deep violet-red skin glistening and dripping in the sun-spotted shade. Then he tried to press me back against the trunk and kiss me, but his wet hands slipped and he grabbed at me as we fell out of the tree.

The grass was high and deep enough to cushion us, and the fact that we were so relaxed made it easy not to resist the earth that came too rapidly up to get us. Besides, we couldn't tell if we were covered with bruises or mulberry stains.

"Are we still alive?" Dayrell asked when we stopped laughing to catch our breaths.

"So far so good."

"We're going to end up killing ourselves at this, Moline." He flopped his arm on my stomach.

"Probably."

It wasn't long until something bit our backsides hard enough to make us get up, brush at the wasps clustering on the fallen fruit, pick up the empty sack, and go to the stock tank. We would've gone to the creek, but Jimmy Carter took one look at us in the corral where he'd been dozing and trotted off through the open gate and down the pasture into the woods with Harry right behind him kicking his heels at us.

We hosed each other off, playing with the water for a while, then started back for the house to get dried off to do chores. "That takes care of the mulberry pie I was making for Walker's dinner tomorrow," I said in the kitchen, where we were toweling off.

"What dinner?" He asked and I remembered I wasn't going to say anything.

"Oh you know—Fourth of July. Walker's having a family deal." I couldn't look him in the eyes, so I stooped and pretended I was sorting our clothes for the bleaching I had to do.

"Weren't you going to tell me about it, Moline?" He bent and put his hands on mine so I had a choice, study them or look at his face. When I didn't answer, he put his thumb under my chin and raised it. "Moline?"

"Well, I didn't think it'd be a good idea, you see. . . ." None of my reasons sounded so good with his eyes that tawny yellow I liked so much.

"Are you ashamed of me?" His face got very still, so there was nothing I could read, nothing I could play off of to use as an answer.

I wanted to look away. "No, of course not. I just don't want people giving you shit, Dayrell. I wanted *us* to have some time without all their damn attitude getting in the way."

He nodded once and smiled without parting his lips. "You don't trust me." He shook his head, keeping his eyes fixed on mine. I must've looked so pained, he laughed and kissed the top of my head. "Stop worrying so much—really, everything'll be fine."

"You sure?"

"Positive. Now go fix some food while I do chores." He stood and pulled on some jeans he'd left on the kitchen chair from morning chores.

"Yeah, right. Dayrell?"

"Yeah?"

"What's going to happen to us?"

He looked down at me, smiling with the sides of his lips curving up. "I don't know. Maybe try to stay together?"

"How? I mean, I don't know. . . ."

"Well, I'd better get to work before you have us divorced then, shouldn't I?" He tousled my hair and grabbed one of Able's flannel shirts hanging on the hook by the back door on his way out.

The next morning Dayrell was awake before me for the first time, and when I came downstairs he'd made morning tea and a big breakfast I didn't have much stomach for, but ate anyway because he'd fixed it. I'd washed our clothes and gotten some of the mulberry stains out, but not all. Dayrell had saved his clothes from the fire and we'd gotten them from the tent by the creek, and he looked nice in an almost-new pair of jeans and a gray western shirt with pearl buttons I practiced ripping apart for that sexy popping sound. He had on these real nice gray leather boots with a single red ace of spades cut into the sides, too.

The phone rang once before we left, but the man asking for Dayrell wasn't a voice I recognized, which was weird since I didn't think anyone knew where he was. He stared at the yellow oak woodwork saying, "Yes . . . No . . . Okay . . . Yeah . . . Okay . . . See you soon," and hung up. Seeing my expression, he said, "Don't worry," and that worried me. He'd told me Lukey's kids were at her brother's down in the hills, and I wondered if that was him on the phone.

Before leaving the house, we kissed some, and I felt this tugging sadness at seeing our good days come to an end. I was reaching for the back screen door when he stopped me and said, "Close your eyes and hold out your hand." I did, and when I opened them again, there was the stone from around his neck in my palm.

"Dayrell . . ."

"Just so you know," he said, and looked away shyly.

"Then you take mine." I pulled the string over my head and put it over his, and he put his on me.

"Feels different," I said.

"Feels good," he said, and we kissed some more. Lukey'd been right after all, and I felt another little rush of missing her, my so-quickly-gone friend.

We were in my truck driving to town for the parade at one when he asked if he could borrow the truck and meet me later.

"What for?"

"Have to run an errand." He put his hand on my thigh and looked over quickly. "You mind me driving your—"

"No, of course not. I just wondered where you were going."

"Have to check on Able's truck. Left it in Camdenton with a blown head gasket. Man said he'll buy it for salvage, have to talk to him and then call Able to finalize. Figured you didn't want to come along."

"Yeah, okay. Thought we were going to watch the parade together, though."

He smiled and squeezed my thigh hard, digging the fingers in between the layers of muscle and fat so I yelped. "I'll find you, Miz Worrier."

"Stop calling me names."

"Stop questioning everything I do then." His tone was light, but his expression was serious.

"Okay, okay—let me off at the hotel and I'll watch from the porch with Walker."

He pulled up in front of the hotel and stopped.

I opened the door and put one foot on the running board. "Dayrell?"

"Yes, darlin'?" he said with mock tiredness.

"Don't forget to leave the windows cracked for Bob and Win?" I looked in the very back, where the dogs were standing and wagging their tails with approval.

"Kindly get yourself out of the door. I raised these dogs by myself, and so far there haven't been a lot of complaints."

"They just don't want to hurt your feelings."

He shook his head and drove off, the dogs balancing awkwardly on the carpet, their legs spread and heads down.

As we were watching the parade going by, big clouds building to the west and south started their march across the sky toward the sun, almost as if folks and the weather were in a kind of contest of wills. I started thinking about Dayrell south of here—maybe already in the storm, driving on slick blacktop, somebody coming around a curve—and got scared all over again, so I was barely listening to the music when the band started up with its tinny brass and big booming drums. But I couldn't help getting into the rhythm with the senior majorettes from our high school throwing their batons way up and catching them most of the time, while the junior girls in their big-girl makeup and sequins, twirling their miniature batons, smiled, their eyes filled with longing for what lay ahead of them each time the full-sized silver sticks shot up into the air, spun slowly, paused, then came feathering down into the waiting hands.

Dressed in red with blue trim, the band was made up of black and white, boys and girls, big and small, from junior high on, and really they weren't too bad. Inching along, they played some dance tunes with disco beats, and a Garth Brooks song, "Friends in Low Places," I wasn't sure Garth would recognize, but it put everyone lined along the street in a fine mood singing along. Then a brand-new red Chrysler LeBaron convertible pulled around the corner and took its place ahead of the band. There was a very, very old black woman with white hair haloing her dark head riding in the backseat next to a younger man it took me a moment to recognize as Titus.

"That's Granny Cairo Bedwell, his great-great-grandmother, oldest person in the county, not counting me and Able," Walker said from the chair next to me. "Must be a hundred and six at least. Been here since Noah. Her mother was a slave. She knows the whole Bedwell history, if a person could get her to talk. Hasn't said boo in ten, fifteen years now. And that's Cecil Harder driving."

A big, square white Continental convertible, one of those last models before they trimmed the size down, driven by Copeland Harder Jr. rode up on the LeBaron's bumper. Perched on top of the backseat were Ross Que, the mayor, and a young blonde in a white prom dress with a silver ribbon across her chest proclaiming her Miss Resurrection.

"Those two brothers do this every Fourth of July—compete for position in the parade. Keeps 'em young." Walker said. The crowd along the curbs began clapping and shouting as the cars bumped along. The band changed its song to "Rocky" and a drum and bugle corps dressed in snappy black and gold ran up to the front of the cars and began performing precision moves to the dirgelike beating.

"Hope they get this thing done with while I still have some hearing left," Walker said, and lifted the glass of ice tea she'd brought with her. "You have a fight with a mulberry tree, Moline?" she asked, and nodded toward my hands, which were still lavender to the wrists.

"Not exactly."

The bands suddenly took a break at the same moment, and my words hung too loud in the air and the people around us laughed. Around the corner came Sugar Stimson sitting in a silver-mounted black western saddle holding silver-laced reins to a silver-studded bridle on his black stallion. The crowd oohed and clapped and the horse's legs snapped harder, the hooves coated with silver glitter splashing in the light. Flecks of foam from the bit flew out across the crowd and the kids pressed through their parents' legs to get closer to the horse and to stay protected both. Sugar was dressed in a sequined black and white fringed western outfit with a white hat dusted in sparkle that shone like snow on his head. I thought of Jimmy Carter and laughed at what his expression would be if I dared get him up like that.

"That's his breeding stallion—quite a beauty, isn't he?" Walker shaded her eyes, following the flashing horse to the head of the parade, where he half reared, and we could hear his bellowing breath all the way back on the porch. A troop of Girl Scouts and Brownies followed Sugar Stimson. After that, a group of businessmen in clown outfits leading a donkey and a goat marched by.

"I haven't seen those hog people in the parade," I said.

"No, they're long gone. Lost the vote, saw the handwriting on the wall. Haven't heard a peep out of your cousin about it, either."

There was some more juggling and a group dressed like old-time guerrillas from Quantrill and Bloody Bill Anderson's Raiders on horseback came prancing up, carrying the state, Confederate, and American flags to cover all their bases. With the backs of their wildly embroidered shirts proclaiming their sponsor, Rebel Motors, they laughed and waved to the crowd. Following them were uneven rows of men and a few women, young and old, dressed in various uniforms all the way from the American Revolution to the war in Vietnam and Desert Storm. None of those soldiers were smiling.

Three street rods, fifties Chevys with chopped tops, leg pipes, duel exhausts, rolled and pleated interiors, and twenty coats of lacquer, rumbled by with cardboards in the windows saying: SHOW ME HOT ROD CLUB. The drivers were paunchy old versions of the greased-back-hair boys with cigarette packs rolled in the sleeves of the tee shirts. What remained after they'd lost the danger in their faces was the love of their machines that showed in their shy, proud smiles.

The Free African Baptist Church with Jos and a mess of kids, followed by several stern-looking women in dark blue and black dresses and little church hats with black veils came along and waved at us. Walker waved to the women she'd introduced me to at the town meeting. The kids were handing out penny suckers with "Sweet Jesus" printed on the cellophane, one of which I took but couldn't quite bring myself to eat.

"See that woman walking next to Jos?" Walker asked, pointing with her glass.

"Yeah? About the same age?"

"That's the one. Rosalee Willson Bedwell. Found her when I read that cemetery book. Whole bunch of Bedwells gone unclaimed for years. Figured it was time to start rounding up the troops, since the Wallers and

Rainses have about run out of themselves. You'll meet her at supper. You're coming, right?"

"Of course."

"I s'pose Dayrell Bell will be back in time too." She sipped her drink and glanced at me out of the corners of her eyes.

I shrugged.

"Can't count on food waiting around."

"He'll be here."

"Just so he knows."

"Don't you want to watch the parade, Walker?"

"Being in love sure makes some people cranky as a dry cow in spring."

We both laughed.

Some churches and businesses had made floats using colored tissue depicting historic scenes or promoting progress. The volunteer firemen rode by on their two fire trucks, followed by their old retired truck, driven by Delbert, Virgil, and Orville Okum, brothers I went to school with who now ran the 4-Way Gas Station, Grocery Store, and Bait Shop at the County Road 6 intersection on the way to Elwood. I'd have to stop in and say hi, I decided as they rode by looking like every one of us looked now, a little older, a little let down into the shape of their lives.

Bob's Friendly Service Station sponsored the baseball team with uniforms that had so many stickers on them, they looked like race car drivers. The mixed couples bowling team came by with balloons they were pretending were bowling balls with the finger holes Magic Markered on. They carried a banner advertising something called Glow in the Dark Bowling. There was a whole sports section after that: five golf carts full of golfers, tennis teams from high school, the Hungry Creek Saddle Club, and a group of men pushing lawn mowers, which they put through little drills we all laughed at. There was more music from a jazz-blues sextet that rode on the back of a flatbed, five black guys and a white guy, seriously cool as they played with their eyes closed, pretending they were some place else than the straw-strewn truck. They were pretty good and probably did deserve to be some place else, but like the rest of us here in Resurrection, this was where they'd got to.

I kept thinking Dayrell would be along any minute as the parade went around the square for the second time, with a worn-out-looking green Travel-All bringing up the tail end so it was impossible to tell whether it was really in the parade or not. I turned to point this out to Walker when I noticed that the dark clouds were already squatting down, taking the wind with them, making the music dull and flat. More and more people in the crowd turned their eyes up and muttered about the coming storm. A few started to leave, having to push their way out. Another big old white Continental came along with a huge red tin rooster mounted on the front grill and placards in the windshield and back window proclaiming: NATIONAL POULTRY MUSEUM. "That's Jack Bluetell's car from the House of Pawn, biggest item he ever took in," someone behind me said.

I looked at the sky again, and tried to imagine the Moorish points of the Royal Theater catching those clouds and holding them off of us, giving Dayrell time to make it back here before the storm. When the first thunder rolled, I jumped, and Walker said, "Moline, you need a drink. Come on, the rain's starting." Sure enough, the big drops were coming straight down. Then the tornado sirens went off, and people started hollering and running. I didn't want to leave in case he came, but Walker held the door open for me.

Walker poured bourbon in both our glasses and topped them with ice tea. It tasted terrible, but I took a couple of swallows to calm down. He was fine, he was just fine, I kept repeating.

"Shouldn't we go to the basement or something?" I asked, looking at the weird greenish light outside while the sirens blared warning.

"What's the matter with you, Moline? It's just a little storm. I never go—those sirens are set way too sensitive. Seems like every time a child sneezes, they go off like it's judgment day. Besides, I want to see the disaster's going to take me with it." Walker smacked her lips over her tea.

In the kitchen, she went directly to the refrigerator and pulled out four chickens on an old black cookie tray. "I have a meal to cook, and I need some help. You up to it?"

We got the chickens ready to fry, putting the giblets in a little paper bag of flour—she'd cook them separately since they were her favorite pieces. "You might want to change those clothes, Moline. This is a big family dinner—wouldn't want folks remembering you that way, would you?" She looked me up and down in my jeans and tee shirt. "When'd you change your rock thingie?"

I shrugged and put it up to my lips, hoping I could taste him.

"Uh-huh. You have a dress, don't you?"

338

"I'll go change," I called over my shoulder as I went to take the elevator to the second floor.

Looking out over the square from my window in case he drove up, I watched the horses being loaded in stock trailers, the floats with their tissue flowers draining color in long ribbons onto the wet pavement being parked until after the storm, and up the block Copeland Harder Jr. struggling with the convertible top that seemed to be stuck, soaking both Miss Resurrection and the mayor, while his brother sat behind him in the dry LeBaron hoking his horn.

27

THERE WILL BE STARS

In November, 1934, the Associated Press carried a long story about "The Ghost of Paris"—a specter which has been seen at intervals in Paris, Missouri, for more than seventy years. The "Ghost of Paris" was a woman, tall, dressed in black, carrying some sort of wand or cane in her hand. She appeared every year about the middle of October and was seen now and then about the town until spring. The story identified this ghost as the jilted sweetheart of a Confederate soldier; on her deathbed she swore to haunt her faithless lover and the whole town forever.

—OZARK MAGIC AND FOLKLORE

✳

I PUT ON THE ONE DRESS I OWNED, red with a tiny printed short full skirt that made my knees stick out. I didn't have any panty hose either. While I was watching for Dayrell, McCreavey's hearse drove slowly by and turned toward the funeral home. He always drove more carefully with the dead. It bothered me that you could die on a holiday, that there wasn't anything that said, No, wait, you don't have to go, it's Christmas, it's your birthday, it's the Fourth of July. The rain was washing the sparrow nests from the gutters and in between the big silver letters of the bank sign; I was feeling so darn sorry for them, I almost didn't see my red truck pull up and park just below. I threw up the sash and called out when the door opened—"Dayrell!"—and motioned him upstairs. He waved and leaned back in to bring out a box.

He was safe, he'd made it, he'd come back. "Thank you," I whispered, unsure whether there really was anyone listening, but comforted by saying it anyway.

"I bet you thought I wasn't coming back," he said, hugging me.

I smiled. "Maybe."

He kissed me and smacked his lips. "Taking to drink now?"

"Walker made me."

"Uh-huh, that's what they always say. Anyway, don't you want to hear what I've been doing?" He stepped back and let me see that not only was he wet, he was muddy too.

"What happened?"

"Here, sit down on the bed—no, don't do that, we'll never make it to dinner, sit here on the chair and I'll sit on the windowsill like this."

"Don't fall—"

"Can't help worrying, can you? Okay, I went down to Camdenton, did what I had to do, was on my way back, and stopped at Lukey's younger brother's to see her kids. I'd met her brother before, but of course we didn't have much to say to each other. He was looking pretty wiped out, and I asked how the kids were doing and he and his wife got real quiet. Said they didn't know how they'd keep 'em. He'd lost his job at the sawmill, and she was getting cut back in her hours at the basket shop in Sunrise Beach, and they already had their five youngsters to feed, and their mama's so laid up with lumbago she can hardly get around as it is. So you know what I did?"

I shook my head, afraid of what I was about to hear.

He nodded. "Told them not to worry—maybe we could take those kids for a little while. What do you think?"

When I didn't answer right away, he cupped my hand in his, his fingers making a rough, dry rasping on my skin as he rubbed. They were hands that told me not to worry, he could take care of me, he wasn't afraid to work, to do what he had to. He might not be the best carpenter around, he might make mistakes and have to jerry-rig things to keep them going, but he was willing to try. He wouldn't lay down and die on me.

"Now don't get mad. I apologize for not talking to you first. It seemed so natural, and I figured you'd already raised one so you knew what you were doing." He tilted his head and stared at me.

"Yeah, but look what happened."

"Listen, maybe your son was a real independent kind of person. How is that your fault? Besides, these kids are different. *We're* different—you and me. And we're here in Resurrection, not some big city. They'll be fine. We'll all be fine. We can get married and—"

"No, I'm not sure I can do that. I can be with you, but I can't do that other thing again."

He dropped my hands and stared at me, searching my face for the joke or the doubt that could be used to convince me. "You're serious."

"It's not that I don't care. I just don't want to be married again. I'm no good at it. It doesn't work."

I could see that I'd said the wrong thing, because he smiled as if he'd found what he'd been waiting for. "Of course it does. Look at my parents, look at Walker and Able, look at—"

"My parents, my marriage, your marriage, Lukey and McCall—"

He picked up my hands again and held them trapped in his. "It's too soon, that's all. You don't trust me yet. I don't blame you, after everything between us, but see, it'll all be different now. The most important thing is the kids, Moline. They're Lukey's and my brother's, they're your cousins. I know you loved her as much as I did. And they miss her so much—they're alone and scared down there. They don't know what's going to happen next. I had to promise them, Moline, I couldn't not. Can't we just try for a little while?" He squeezed my hands so hard the bones of the knuckles cracked.

"Dayrell, we haven't even lived together yet and suddenly I'm the mother to two kids? I don't know. . . ."

"Tell you what, I'll give you back that .38 you like toting around so much, and if things get too bad, you can put a bullet in me and ride on outta here, okay? Just don't be a chicken, Moline."

I shook my head and rubbed my thumb over a hand stained darker than mine. What if it meant not having those hands on me ever again? The Widows appeared in my head, like a row of tall, narrow white marble grave markers, neat and uniform and very still. Outside, the rain fell in a steady hushing against the red Resurrection brick of the hotel, and a sparrow hopped on the windowsill with a piece of straw in its beak, staring out across the street at the bank.

"Well?"

I stared at the little red-brown stone caught in the hollow of his throat and thought about the day Lukey had given it to me, how I'd felt the warmth of her body in the cheap brown cotton lace when she'd put it on me, how I'd believed in her luck and grown to love this simple woman, my cousin, and how I was going to miss her for as long as I lived, going to miss her for everything we'd done together, and for everything we hadn't had a chance at yet. She'd been so willing to share her luck, to give it away to me, and I'd hoarded mine, afraid of losing it for years. I swallowed and Dayrell's yellow stone pressed back gently, reminding me that she was the only one who saw it from the beginning, what there was between Dayrell and me. She was the only one who never stopped believing in us, never stopped believing in all of us as human beings, including McCall, who at the last minute didn't leave her to be alone in that truck. Lukey would never have hesitated if they were my children, or anyone else's. She'd loved too well and too completely to exclude anyone. That was why she died. "We can try it for a couple of weeks, I guess."

We talked a bit about the kids and the fact that we weren't going to get married. At least not right away, he kept insisting, and I finally agreed to that wording to stop the debate. But it didn't mean I'd changed my mind. Dayrell was going to find out about Bedwell and Waller stubbornness.

"Okay, well, so then, after seeing the kids, who by the way are here—I dropped them off at the Dairy Daddy for ice cream and they're supposed to be walking over with their cones. They've got that umbrella of yours I found on the floor in back. You don't mind, do you?"

"You brought them now? Without talking to me first?"

He set his jaw. "They could use a good meal too."

"Oh, and you'll take them back afterwards?"

He looked out the window. "I'm sorry. Just got carried away, I guess. Figured you'd see it the same as me."

"Great. Now what am I supposed to do? Act like the wicked step-mother in some damn fairy tale you've made up for them?"

"I told you I'm sorry. You want me to take them back now?"

He was hopelessly impulsive, and I didn't feel like spending my life putting on the brakes. What chance did I have? "Okay. All right. Next time, though, just call or something."

"No problem." He patted my hand.

I shook my head. What difference would it make anyway?

"So then I decided it was time to stop and face my parents—try to explain about missing the funeral and ask them to keep the dogs while we eat." He stopped and looked out the window, then back down at our hands. He kissed my fingers and touched the stone around my neck, then his, and put a finger to his lips, then mine.

"So then what happened?"

He looked surprised. "Well, then I came right straight here, of course, like I said I would."

"You were gone for hours," I exaggerated on purpose.

"I was? Seemed awful short—stop here, stop there. Oh, and I'm going to have to run a hose over your truck. All that mud from the dogs—it'll wash right offa those leather seats, I bet. And soon's it's dry, I'll brush out the carpets."

"Dayrell! Oh, never mind. Let's go see if Walker needs any help. It must be going on four o'clock."

"Maybe we could scare up some clean clothes for me first—I always seem to need them these days. You look awful nice in that dress, by the way." He stood and let me pop the pearl buttons on the shirt again. I pulled him down and pressed my lips against the blurred red of the scarred heart tattoo.

"Just one thing . . ."

"Yeah?" He straightened, hooking his thumbs in the waistband of his jeans and cocking his leg in a way he knew was sexy.

"Whose heart is that?"

"This?" He blushed and laughed. "Yours, who else? I couldn't get a good angle on it in my cell, and the ink from the ballpoint ran out. Wanted blue, but red was all I could get. Maybe I should get it fixed at the new place." He rubbed it.

"Maybe I should get one that says 'Dayrell'?"

"On your behind?"

"No, my forehead."

He took the shirt off and threw it at me and I went to see if I could scrounge any more clothes from Able, who seemed to have undertaken the job of feeding and housing and clothing us in his old age.

We could hear the clatter of dishes and talking voices all the way to the front desk. "Sounds like the whole town's here," I said as we walked down the hallway into the dining room off the cafe.

"They're here!" the three boys folding white paper napkins at the long line of red and white checkered cloth covered tables pushed end to end across the room hollered toward the kitchen. One of the boys was Lukey's and the other two were Titus and Jos's. Two of the smallest of their kids were on the floor in the corner, stuffing straws into metal holders, then pulling them back out to explosions of delighted laughter. Their oldest boy sat stiffly between Titus and Granny Cairo at the farthest table. He looked fiercely proud of the attention he was receiving.

Dear Pearl was standing over by the windows looking out with her hands stuffed in the side pockets of a baggy yellow housedress while Walker, sitting in an old captain's chair, leaned forward talking earnestly to her. Pearl looked like she was in the principal's office. Poor Pearl.

Maybe the Estes training would finally pay off, but not in a way she ever imagined. I kept hoping that if Estes and Iberia and Mister and Paris could see us, they were smarter now, wised up about things, wanting us to forgive them, as they'd learned to forgive us, because if that wasn't the job of the afterlife, then I sure didn't think I could ever really care much about it and I'd just have to stick with the here-and-now, trying to get along the best I could with people, trying to help them and maybe even learn to accept a little help myself. Because really, that was about the best we could do, whether God cared about us or not. Otherwise, we might as well spend our lives in the bitter bed of John Wesley Waller.

Jos came through the double swinging doors to the kitchen carrying a heaping platter of fried chicken, followed by the new Bedwell woman Walker had pointed out with a bowl of mashed potatoes so big it took a hand on each side of the tureen to hoist it waist high. Walker got up and went into the kitchen. A crash followed, and Walker's yelling pushed out behind Jos lugging a long crystal relish tray I recognized from Estes's house.

"She's just a little disorganized," Jos advised the room, and set the tray down hard enough to bounce the radishes and carrot sticks and make Pearl wince. "Sit down, Moline." Jos pulled out a chair in the middle of the line of tables and patted the back.

"Be better to put us on the end, near the kids," Dayrell said, and took my upper arm in his hand as if I'd gone blind and stupid too. "She can sit here and I'll be here and the kids across from us." He pushed me down in the corner chair and pulled another out for himself. Jos started to say something, then just looked at the two of us, smiled, and went back into the kitchen before I had a chance to introduce the two of them. Then I decided they probably had a pretty good idea about each other by now anyway.

"Walker can sit here at the head of the table," he said, and sat down next to me. "I'm starving—hope they hurry." He reached for a chicken leg, but Walker came up behind him and slapped his hand.

"Now you'll wait your turn like the rest of them, Mr. Bell, and don't be giving me any of your sass." She plunked down a basket of biscuits at each end of the table and stepped back for Jos and the new woman with bowls of gravy, green beans, fried corn, and leaf lettuce scalded with hot bacon and vinegar and onions. They came back with plates of butter and salt and pepper.

Walker looked up and down the tables and said, "All right now, you folks get yourself in here. Leave room for those girls I have making that ice cream. Should be about done. Pearl, you go and see about Able. Rosalee, you sit there and save her place." Walker and Jos went back to the kitchen, and I wondered what could be left to bring out when Walker returned with a plate of liver and onions she set down at our end.

Pearl came back and announced that Able was not coming to eat yet, he had to finish the roof repair before the next rain. Walker pointed Titus to the chair at the end opposite her, and he placed Granny Cairo there and with a sulky expression sat down next to her. The rest, including the girls from the kitchen, filled in between the two. Lukey's kids sat across from us with brave confused little smiles on their faces.

"Could have told that old fool there's rain predicted for a week, but let him alone, that's what I've done for years. Have the best marriage in town that way." Walker raised her eyebrows and winked at me and reached over to tap Dayrell on the back of his hand resting on the table. "Don't think I'm not watching you, Mr. Bell. Well, if the Reverends Jos and Titus don't mind, I'm going to say a prayer I've been composing all day and let us get down to eating before things get cold."

She bowed her head but didn't get more than "Dear Lord" out before Copeland Harder Jr. came straggling in. He was wearing two sports jackets and carrying a hanger with three shirts flung on it in one hand and an extra pair of shoes in the other.

"I'm—oh, I'm sorry—nobody at the desk—I need—" He held up his hands so we could see.

"Put those things over there by the window, Copeland, and pull up a chair. We're having our dinner and you probably haven't eaten from the looks of things." Walker gestured toward the extra chairs that lined the wall.

When he was seated, she started again, the kids trying hard to keep still. "Dear Lord, we thank you—" A huge crash occurred overhead, followed by silence that had half the adults out of their chairs, then cursing and thumping. Walker didn't move. She shook her head and eyed her liver and onions.

Finally she said, "Sit down. He's walking, he's fine. Serves him right, whatever happened—he should be here with his family eating dinner. One more time: Dear Lord, thank you for all this bounty and for the family you have brought together after too many years of strife and misunderstanding. Bedwell, Waller, LeFay, Rains, and Bell—they're only names, Lord, and they don't mean much in the long run.

"And thank you for the child that Poor Pearl is about to bring into the world. And thank you for Granny Cairo and Rosalee Bedwell gracing us with their presence.

"And thank you for clearing up the mess we all made of things lately, and for helping those in charge to realize that we're just a bunch of hillbillies acting up with some good innocent people caught in the middle of it. I know you've never expected anything more or less out of Resurrection.

"And bless Hale Bell and his family that have to struggle on without their son now, and bless all these people at this table who keep getting lost and found all over again. And especially give our love to little Lukey and bless these fine children of hers.

"And Lord, we ask that you continue to bless Titus and Jos and their children and all the good they do. And help Titus to get over that sulkiness which is not becoming on a man his age. I knew his mother and his grandmother, Lord, and his great-great-granny at this very table, and they would want me to say these things to him, I'm sure."

She paused and peeked one eye open at me and smiled. "And Lord, thank you for bringing Moline home to us too, and for finally making her stop moping around town, it was getting quite wearisome, Lord, and I want to applaud you for having the good sense to bring Dayrell Bell into the roofing line of work so Moline can have someone to fight with and Uncle Able Rains can finally get off that ladder. Amen."

Everyone laughed and clapped and grabbed for food just as Uncle Able in tattered overalls came in, holding his left wrist bound with narrow slats of wood and silver duct tape. "I heard my name in vain again, Walker?"

"What did you break this time?" She sighed and pushed back from the table, but he waved her down and sat in the chair Dayrell had gotten for him.

"You just cut up my liver, woman. We'll get this wrapped later. I can't stand to see good liver go to waste." He looked at me with sharp brown eyes and said, "You giving up that room upstairs?" Walker snorted and handed him a plate of food.

Dayrell stopped chewing and suddenly the table was quiet, down to the last child, as if I were about to announce the second coming. "I don't know. Can't stay at my place. I thought—" The silence was embarrassing, and I looked at all the familiar faces to see if I could trust anyone to help me out. They were holding their breath, it seemed, curious and anxious for what was next, and I didn't want to give an answer that would disappoint or hurt or anger them, because I did care, I did, this was my family. There was a little wash of hopelessness at such responsibility, such love that weighed and held us in its cradling concern, and sometimes wouldn't let us go.

A hand covered mine, and Dayrell said, "She's going to be with me."

"Those youngsters yours too?" Able pointed his fork toward Lukey's kids, and Dayrell nodded.

"S'pose you'll take 'em on out to that farm then, set up house there. Moline's already been working pretty hard cleaning the place up, haven't you, little sister?" His eyes crinkled and he laughed when I shook my head and grimaced. "I'll come out periodically and make sure she's got the heavy work under control, Dayrell, so you can take it easy from now on."

"You be good to this little girl, Mr. Bell, or I'll take you out back and give you a thrashing," Aunt Walker said. "Should've done that when you first showed up in the girls' gym class that day in sixth grade. Saved us all a bunch of trouble. You were just as girl crazy as Miss Moline was boy crazy."

I looked down because I was scared and everything was real quiet, and then people started eating and talking and laughing again like we'd just announced the sunset or the temperature. When I looked along the table, only Titus was still watching me. Catching my eye, he frowned and I shrugged. Pearl shook her head, as if to say, I knew it all the time.

Jos glanced up from her plate and laughed at the kids seated around her, who were struggling with honey-dripping biscuits and fried chicken, trying to stuff as much in their mouths at once as they could. I wished I had been her with my son. I'd been too nervous, too anxious that something would fail and break away and tear everything else with it. But maybe now I had another chance. This time, I promised, I'd be more like Jos and Lukey, more—

Dayrell moved his chair as close to mine as he could get, so we were shoulder to shoulder, then he reached around my back and tried to spoon some of the mashed potatoes in my mouth. "You need to eat, woman, you're getting peaked." The spoon clicked against my teeth and when I opened to protest, he shoved the food in. He was right, they tasted great. Not even a hint of liver. The kids across from us were giggling with their full mouths open. I smiled back.

"Now don't you go spoiling her, Dayrell, you'll have your hands full," Able said, and winked at me. "I can tell you from experience."

Walker sliced his biscuit in two and slid a slab of butter inside. "Don't you listen to a word he says." She held it up to Able's mouth. "Moline deserves to be spoiled every day for the rest of her life, and I'm going to be watching to make sure you do, Mr. Bell. Now you need to feed her some of this liver and onions, get her blood up again. Go ahead, don't listen to her. You know, she's pretty smart, but sometimes she gets notions. That's what we used to call them when she was young, notions. Some days she gets to acting like a tourist, and we sure got enough of those rolling through here like marbles on a downhill grade. But she's home to stay now and we can finally put some sense in her head." She held up the plate of liver, to the horror of the children on both sides of the table, who dropped their eyes and shrank. "Who else wants some?"

With Dayrell's thigh warm against mine, I felt safe. And maybe that was all we were afforded in this life, a few moments here and there, and we should hang on to them as long as possible, and after that their memory, because it helps us through the rest of the time when it seems like we're in hell, and who knows, maybe we really are.

". . . It wasn't anything." Cope's whining voice floated toward me from the other end of the table. "I told her that. It just happened that yesterday afternoon the air conditioner piddled out in the office and we had to get this work done so I suggested we go to the new motel out 11 past the Wal-Mart to finish and—I just don't see how she heard so darn fast. I mean, can't anything stay buried in this town?" Cope stuffed a big chunk of chicken breast in his mouth out of misery.

"Not even in the cemetery." Walker looked down the table at Pearl picking at her food. I hated to see that, another child coming into the world with misery to meet it.

"They get Estes back in the ground, Pearl?" Walker asked, and she nodded. Walker sighed and put her napkin on the table. "Now, Able, I'm going to call Dr. Bradford and you're going to walk yourself over to his house for an X ray and cast, like always."

When she'd gone, Able chuckled. "You know, she can't go with me." He leaned back and took a small ivory toothpick from a little round wood case in his shirt pocket and picked at a front tooth. "Upsets her too much to see me hurt. Gets her hysterical. After the first couple of times, I told her, No more. Now she stays home and I try not to show how much a thing hurts till I'm well out of the way. That's been our agreement for fifty, sixty years. She's too tenderhearted. Loves me as hard as a person can love, and I wouldn't trade a minute of it, not a single minute. Even days she's cranky as an old dog."

He eyed us and put the toothpick away. "You young people decide on a wedding day, let me know. I got a ballroom on the top floor hasn't been used in thirty years, not since the Chamber of Commerce boys pulled out over that black couple I rented a room to. 'Bout ready to hear some music again, I think, 'bout time." He stood and waved his free hand at the tables and left as Walker began to call his name from the front desk.

I peeked at Dayrell out of the corner of my eye, and he was smiling. We'd just see about all that, I vowed.

Walker returned, wiping her eye with the corner of the apron she'd left on. "Damn old fool always getting himself hurt. Anyone for ice cream? Everyone clean their plates now, and then you youngsters can clear, and Pearl, you need to eat everything on that plate, and a big bowl of dessert for that baby, you expect it to be worth a thing. Titus and Jos have some of the best-behaved children I've ever seen. They get as much dessert as their little stomachs will hold for being so good at their Aunt Walker's dinner table. You kids, too." She patted Lukey's kids on their backs and they sat up extra straight and got serious about finishing their dinners.

I closed my eyes and leaned my tired head against Dayrell's shoulder, just soft and strong enough to hold me. I had kids to worry about again, trouble out there waiting for me, but it was taking its time. The worst it could do was kill me, and I figured I could always do better than that.

"Now Moline, you're as bad as Pearl. You need to eat and quit worrying about Dayrell and those youngsters. They're fine. I'm personally going to see about them from now on, you can count on that. How's Granny Cairo doing, Titus?" We all turned to look at the ancient woman, who could neither hear nor see anymore but seemed to peer out of that locked room as if she understood every single one of us. We waved and she waved back, with the full plate of untouched food in front of her.

I was grateful for the chance to let myself be lulled by the faith in Walker's voice commanding and cajoling our lives into an order only her old eyes could see well enough because she wasn't afraid to open her arms and welcome us all. "And Titus M. Bedwell, you can say all you want to about how the civil rights movement has failed in this town, but you have never once asked me over to your house for supper."

"Consider yourself invited, then. 'Specially if you do the cooking," he said, and actually laughed, the way he used to when we were kids.

After we cleared the table, we sat and talked until the last of the sun was falling in violet and rose sheets on the windows of the trucks and cars parked outside. And we let the children go play hide-and-seek in the empty, unrented rooms overhead, not wanting to turn the lights on yet, because at least for now, everything was comfortable and right, and there was every possibility that we would stay safe for another day.

Finally, Dayrell moved his shoulder and I lifted my head. "I have to go do something—be right back," he whispered.

"Not again," I said, but he smiled and got up.

Copeland Harder Jr. was looking miserably down the table, as if he'd fallen from grace and couldn't climb back out. "You get the top up on that car?" I asked. He nodded.

"I ought to be mad at you, Cope Junior, putting us to all that trouble with those hog people," Aunt Walker said.

"Your cousin forgot to file the right petition anyway," he said without looking at Pearl. "We lost against your injunction."

"You should give Pearl a break, Cope—she's had a lot on her mind lately," I said and she gave me a weary thanks with her eyes.

"Just a matter of time before these big ag businesses crop up all over the state. Prime use for this kind of land," he said. "Might as well face it."

"If I ever find out who set McCall to starting those fires and bothering my animals, I'll give them a good spanking, I'll tell you that." Walker looked down the table at Pearl, who suddenly found her empty glass noteworthy. It wasn't Pearl's fault, I wanted to say.

"Moline?" Dayrell stood beside me holding something behind his back. "Close your eyes and don't peek."

As soon as I felt my shoe coming off, I opened my eyes. They were the most beautiful boots I'd ever seen, dark blue on the bottom and violet on top, sun, moon, and stars circling the tops, sun rising for day and moon rising for night.

"What is this, Cinderella goes hillbilly?" I laughed as he struggled to put the boots on until I stopped him and used the boot hooks myself. Then he helped me stand up and everyone admired them and we walked out into the lobby to see how they fit. "Perfect," I pronounced.

"Joe Patrickus at JP's Custom Boots in Camdenton made them from a drawing I did of your foot when you were sleeping, plus an outline of your boots. We were hoping they were right."

"Thank you." I hugged him and started to pull away again, but he stopped me.

"I put everything you'd need on those boots. Maybe you'll stay now."

"Maybe." I pushed the hair behind his ear and smoothed it down.

It's coming the end of August now, and Dayrell's ripping off a lot of the rotten boards under the slate tiles that have to be replaced on the roof and thinking of starting the whole project over. He's covering the north side of the roof with enormous sheets of blue plastic I remember from Pearl's, and I can only hope that he'll work hard and keep his mind on his job now that I'm here with these kids waiting for him to come down off that ladder. He's only half done with the brick work too, and I keep having to shoo the kids away from the stacks for fear they'll get hurt. When I tell Walker about the repairs, she just shakes her head, sips her bourbon-laced tea, and says, "what else is life about, Moline, but the comings and the goings?" Then she asks after the kids because she's taken on the job of making them Christians, her kind, she says. I figure they'll be the most interesting people in DeWight County when they grow up.

352

My sister, Paris—well, part of her is still in the yard between the Waller and Bedwell houses, and part of her is on the windowsill in the bedroom here at the farm where I can keep an eye on her. Someday, I'll take the last shards of bone to the flower garden and put her beneath the rarest, most beautiful rosebush I can find, but not yet. I'm still not ready to let her go.

And it's true that every once in a while, I see a ghostly figure that looks an awful lot like McCall drifting sadly around the farm at night, pausing in the char of the pig barn and floating along the sagging chicken-wire gate to the backyard, like he's real lonesome, and the dogs set up something terrible, but I don't mind. I hope he finds some comfort in our company those nights, and that someday he'll be able to join Lukey and the others that have gone before him and finally get some peace.

I guess sometimes it's us the living that hold the dead back, and sometimes the dead can't bear to be without us.

Some nights after the kids are in bed, I dress up in my new boots and one of his pearl-button shirts and Dayrell chases me down into the little orchard where the last of the mulberries smell rotten sweet and the apples are coming on ripe, and we lay in the deep grass out by the hayfield surrounded by crickets and all kinds of creaking, chirping things which go quiet until we lie still for a few minutes and watch the sky and then they start up again.

Sometimes we catch the fireflies drifting like tiny drunken boats in the dark and take turns opening our cupped hands against each other's chests to see the light blink green-yellow against the skin like a miniature star while Dayrell tells me about heavenly things like celestial pull and new comets that fill my dreams with new stories. He says that there will always be stars, as long as someone is here to watch them. "The universe is so huge, you can't imagine it, Moline," he adds with a little catch of regret in his voice.

I guess in a better world, he would be up there too, an astronaut. And me, I can't imagine where I'd be except here, close to the good Ozark earth, listening to the way the night fills itself up so full of smells and sounds it has to rush out across the land and spill itself into morning.